Ava the Destroyer Series - Book 2

By

CATHERINE M. CLARK

Wylde Publishing

 ISBN. 9781919227634

Content Warning

This novel explores dark themes and intense situations. It contains:

- Graphic violence and blood.
- Detailed, visceral fight scenes and supernatural combat.

CHAPTER 1

IN THE SPACE BETWEEN HEARTBEATS

The world is narrowing.

It isn't a sudden snap, like a twig breaking underfoot. It's a slow, agonising dissolution, a fraying at the edges of my consciousness that feels less like dying and more like being unmade. One moment, there is the chaos of the battlefield—the sharp *phut-phut* of gunfire, the guttural snarls of things that should not exist in a civilised world. The next, there is only this. the crushing weight of Rose's arms and the terrifying, rhythmic thud of her heart against my ear.

Every breath I attempt feels like swallowing shards of jagged glass. My lungs are no longer organs meant for life; they are bruised, weeping bellows struggling to pull oxygen through a throat constricted by blood and terror. Each shallow gasp scrapes against my splintered ribs, sending white-hot lightning bolts of agony dancing across my nervous system.

Gods, I think, the thought sluggish and heavy as lead. *If this is how it ends, I'm going to be so incredibly pissed off.*

I can feel the heat of my own life spilling out, soaking through my tactical gear, mixing with the damp, cloying scent of churned earth and spent gunpowder. It's a thick, metallic warmth that makes me feel heavy—impossibly, lethally heavy.

"Ava? Ava, look at me. Stay with me, damn it!"

Rose's voice. It's a jagged thing, stripped of its usual playful, seductive edge. The woman who usually navigates the world with the predatory grace of a queen is gone, replaced by something raw and desperate. I try to focus on her, but my vision is a kaleidoscope of grey static and pulsing crimson.

I force my eyelids up. It feels like lifting heavy iron shutters.

There she is. My beautiful, terrifying Rose. Her blonde hair, usually a shimmering silk curtain, is matted with grit and dark drying blood. Those emerald eyes—the eyes that have looked at me with such maddening, flirtatious heat just nights ago—are wide, frantic, and drowning in a sea of terror.

Don't look at me like that, I want to tell her. *You're going to make me want to stay even more, and I'm really trying to let go here.*

"I'm... here..." The words are nothing. A wet, pathetic rattle in my throat. I can taste the copper, thick and cloying, pooling in the back of my mouth. It feels like I'm drowning on dry land.

A sudden, piercing scream tears through the air, slicing through the haze of my fading senses. It isn't a combat shout. It's high-pitched, primal, and laden with a soul-deep horror that makes the hair on my arms stand up despite the creeping chill in my limbs.

I wrench my head to the side, an action that sends a fresh wave of nausea rolling through my gut. Through the blur of tears and blood, I see her.

Reya.

The girl is no longer standing; she is being consumed. She is at the centre of a violent, swirling vortex of orange and yellow flames. But this isn't the controlled magic we've seen before. There is no elegant purple hue or the terrifying shadow-black of hellfire. This is primal. This is hungry. It's the kind of fire that eats everything it touches, licking hungrily at her clothes, blistering her skin with a sickening hiss.

What in the actual hell? My mind tries to process the impossibility. *Is she spontaneously combusting? Is there a chapter in the Paranormal Survival Guide for 'When Your Teammate Becomes a Human Torch'? Because I missed that memo.*

The fire licks at her face, twisting her features into a mask of pure, unadulterated agony. Her mouth is open in a silent, soundless scream, the air around her shimmering with intense, localised heat.

"Rose," I rasp, the effort making my vision go black for a terrifying second.

"Don't talk! Just breathe, Ava. Please, just keep breathing!" Rose's hands are on me, her touch frantic yet trying to be gentle, as if I might shatter if she holds me too tightly.

I can feel the vibration of her voice through my very bones. And beneath that, something else. A shift in the air. The scent of Rose—usually a heady, intoxicating blend of rolling storms and wildflowers with a hint of sweet vanilla—is changing. It's sharpening, turning into something darker, more metallic. The scent of a predator preparing to kill.

"Rose, she didn't... do this..." I struggle, my fingers twitching uselessly against the gravel. "She tried... to help."

I remember her shoving that bleeding wrist toward me. It had been chaotic, desperate. *Thanks for the impromptu blood transfusion, Reya. Very subtle.*

The world tilts on its axis. The sound of the battle and the heavy thud of large paws pounding the ground begins to recede, replaced by a dull, underwater hum. I feel like I'm sinking into a deep, dark ocean, and the surface is getting further and further away.

Then, the fire vanishes.

It doesn't fade; it simply *snaps* out of existence with a sound like a vacuum sucking in air. In the sudden, ringing silence where Reya stood, something else emerges. A shadow. A creature of sleek, terrifying darkness that blurs against the backdrop of the battlefield.

"Did Reya just shift?" I hear Freya's voice. It sounds miles away, trembling with an incredulity that mirrors my own. "Is that... a hellhound?"

"She shifted," another voice whispers—Maya, perhaps, her tone thick with a grief that hasn't even fully settled yet. "I guess we now know what she got from Beastie."

A shifter? The thought is so absurd it almost makes me laugh, if my lungs weren't currently being occupied by my own blood. *Of course. Why wouldn't she be a shape-shifter? Because being a witch wasn't complicated enough.*

Suddenly, the world explodes into motion again. A heavy vehicle screeches to a halt nearby, tyres spitting gravel like buckshot. The rhythmic, muffled *phut-phut-phut* of suppressed weapons echoes through the clearing.

"Over here! I need help! We need to get Ava to the Doc! RIGHT NOW!"

Rose's roar is primal. It isn't the voice of a woman; it is the voice of a beast, a command that vibrates through my very skull, making my teeth ache.

Darkness begins to press in from the periphery, thick and heavy as velvet. I feel myself being lifted, the movement jarring my broken body, but Rose's grip is an anchor. She holds me with a ferocity that tells me she isn't just holding a comrade; she is clutching her entire world.

"Get Ava and Rose to the safe house immediately," Luca's voice cuts through the chaos. It is steady, commanding, the absolute authority of an Alpha. "The rest of you, clear the perimeter. Move!"

I am hoisted onto a rigid stretcher. The sensation of being airborne is disorienting, a nauseating sway that makes me want to retch. I hear the sounds of the skirmish passing by—the guttural howl of a shifter cut short, the heavy thud of something massive hitting the dirt, the frantic shouting of men in tactical gear.

Then, the sudden, jarring transition to the interior of a van.

The air is cooler here, smelling of sterile metal and old upholstery. The floor beneath the stretcher vibrates with the roar of the engine. Rose is there, pressed tight against my side. She hasn't let go of my hand. Her grip is so intense I wonder if she's actually crushing my bones, but her thumb is moving in slow, rhythmic circles over my knuckles.

Stay, her touch pleads. *Don't you dare leave me.*

The engine revs, the tyres spinning against the gravel before we catch traction and tear away from the carnage. Rose leans down, her lips brushing my ear. Her breath is hot, frantic, smelling of salt and iron.

"Ava, listen to me," she whispers, her voice cracking like thin ice over a deep, dark lake. "We are going to save you. I won't let you go."

She pauses, and I feel the tremor in her entire frame.

"But if we can't... if we can't get you back to one hundred percent..." She swallows hard, a jagged, broken sound. "Do you want me to bite you? On the full moon. I can turn you. It will fix everything. The injuries, the scars... it will make you whole again."

My heart stutters. *That's a heavy conversation for a week night, Rose.*

Most people discuss marriage or moving in together before they suggest turning you into a supernatural predator. But this is Rose. She isn't asking to share a life; she's asking to share a soul, even if it means changing the very essence of what I am.

"Ava? Answer me. Please," she pleads. Her voice drops to a shattered whisper that tears at my heart more than the wolf tore at my chest. "I will not do it without your permission. But gods... I really, really want to."

The pain in my chest flares—a living, breathing monster with jagged claws, ripping me apart from the inside out. But there is a secondary pain, one that isn't physical. It's her.

Through our bond, I can feel it. Her anguish is a tidal wave, crashing against the shores of my fading consciousness. It's a raw, bleeding thing—a terror so profound it threatens to drown us both. She isn't just afraid of losing me; she is experiencing the death of her own soul in real-time.

I have to answer her, I think desperately. *I can't leave her in this darkness.*

I attempt to move. I try to command my limbs, to force a nod, a shake, anything. But my body is a traitor. My fingers are numb, my toes are dead weight, and my tongue feels like a massive, useless stone in my mouth.

No, I scream internally. *No, Rose. I won't make you break your code. I won't let you carry the guilt of turning me just to keep me breathing. I love you too much to be your selfish mistake.*

With a monumental, soul-draining effort, I manage to twitch my head—a microscopic movement, a mere suggestion of a shake.

No.

The word echoes in the void of my mind. *I'd rather die human than live as a monster because you couldn't let me go.*

A sob breaks from Rose—a sound so guttural and devastated that it feels like she's being physically torn in half. She collapses against my chest, her hot tears soaking through my ruined clothes, searing my skin like acid. Her heart beats a frantic, broken rhythm against mine, a desperate bird battering itself against the bars of a cage.

The drive is a blur of sensory overload and encroaching nothingness. Sirens wail in the distance, a discordant symphony to our private tragedy. My pulse slows, each beat becoming a lazy, distant drum echoing in a vast canyon.

I'm still here, I realise with a flicker of grim amusement. *Stubbornness is a hell of a drug.*

Then, something shifts. Deep within the marrow of my bones, a faint, golden warmth begins to bloom. It's subtle at first, like the first lick of sunlight hitting frostbitten earth. It spreads through my veins, chasing away the icy numbness.

The memory surfaces then—vivid and visceral. Reya's blood. The taste of it. copper pennies and crackling, wild magic. She had whispered something about her blood having healing properties.

Well, shit, I think, a hysterical edge creeping into my thoughts. *I guess that 'juice box' wasn't just for show. Remind me to thank her later... or kill her. Whichever comes first.*

The van slams to a halt with a violence that jars my very soul. The rear doors fly open, and the world descends into chaos once more.

"Quick! Get her to the Doc!"

"He's ready, Marshal!"

I am jolted as the stretcher is pushed through narrow corridors. The sounds change—the muffled roar of the engine replaced by the rhythmic, terrifying *beep... beep... beep* of medical monitors. Each beep feels like a countdown.

"What are her vitals? Do we have an assessment of the internal damage?" A sharp, professional voice cuts through the fog. Doctor Stevens.

"She was mauled," Rose's voice responds. It is cold. It is lethal. It sounds like the edge of a razor. "And one of the witches... something happened to her."

"Can we question the witch for specifics?" the doctor asks.

There is a pause, and in that silence, I feel the sheer, murderous intent radiating from Rose.

"No," she snarls. The venom in her voice is so potent I can almost taste it. "If she's still alive, I'll finish what the wolf started."

Easy, killer, I think, though my strength is failing. *Save some of that rage for the bad guys. Two hundred years of you brooding over a murder is a sentence I'm not sure I want to serve.*

The pain returns, sharper now as they begin to work on me. I feel the cold bite of electrodes against my skin. I hear the rhythmic *snip-snip* of surgical scissors cutting through my clothes—the fabric giving way like broken promises. A sharp sting pierces my arm—an IV, perhaps? Or something stronger.

A heavy, sweet drowsiness begins to pull at me. It's a velvet curtain, descending slowly, invitingly.

I really hope they're drugging me, I think, the darkness swirling around my mind. *Because if this is just... natural... then I am in serious trouble.*

As the light fades into the black tide, my final thought isn't of the pain, or the war, or the impossible magic. It is of her. My Rose.

Her smile that lights up the darkest rooms. Her scent of storms and vanilla and wildflowers. Her infuriating, beautiful, soul-shattering existence.

I'm coming back for you, I vow to the darkness. *Even if I have to haunt you for eternity just to make sure you don't forget.*

CHAPTER 2

ECHOES IN THE BLOOD

I am drifting in a sea of static and excruciating, unrelenting pain.

It isn't the warm, weightless void I first fell into during the attack—that had felt like sinking into honeyed oblivion, a merciful descent into a soft, velvet nothingness where the world couldn't reach me. This is something far more sinister. This is a cold, churning ocean of grey sludge, thick as tar and smelling faintly of ozone, burnt copper, and old despair.

Disconnected sounds—the distant, muffled shouting of men, the frantic, rhythmic *beep-beep-beep* of a monitor—aggressively break against the fragile shore of my consciousness. They are like stones thrown into a pool, creating ripples that I can feel but cannot grasp, before being violently sucked under by a relentless, punishing undertow that drags me deeper into the dark.

My body feels like a foreign country I no longer hold a passport for. I am an occupant in a broken, bleeding vessel, adrift on a tide that pulls me further from the shore of humanity with every useless, thready pulse. The phantom sensation of my own blood—salty, hot, and metallic—stings wounds I can't even see, making me feel as though I am being dissolved from the inside out.

Is this it? the thought drifts through my mind, unmoored and ghostly. *Is this the great transition? Because if so, the decor is terrible.*

Then—the beep.

Rhythmic. Relentless. Cruel.

It is a sinus rhythm hammering like a coffin nail into my skull, steady as a tombstone's inscription. It is the absolute only constant in this void, a clinical metronome counting down the seconds I can't name toward an end I am not yet ready to accept. The *not-knowing*? That is the true killer. It is a pure, icy terror that coils in my gut like a live wire, sparking every time my heart stutters in its struggle to stay upright.

A groan tears from my throat—raw, alien, and shocking in my own ears. This pain isn't clean or surgical; it's a symphony of destruction. My ribs feel like splinters of bone grinding against my lungs, and my spine... gods, my spine feels as though it has been pulverised into gravel. Every micro-movement sends shards of white-hot agony flashing behind my eyes, blinding me even in the dark. Nerves scream in a silent, neuropathic chorus, threatening to shred my very essence.

I try to twitch a finger. Nothing. My limbs are lead weights submerged in wet concrete, unresponsive and heavy.

Am I paralysed? Am I already a ghost, doomed to wander this world as a passenger with no body of my own?

The thought hits like a spike of pure, unadulterated panic. For the first time since I was a child cowering in a dark cupboard, gripping my knees while the shadows of monsters took everything from me, I have zero control. It floods my veins, freezing me from the inside out—a toxic venom that paralyses not just muscle, but hope itself.

"You have to hold on! Ava, look at me!"

Rose's voice shatters the fog like a stone thrown through glass. It's sharp, desperate, and threaded with a terror so profound it makes my heart ache more than my shattered chest.

Suddenly, memories explode behind my eyelids—sharp, deadly, and impossibly vivid. I see Nathaniel's ash spiralling into a bruised twilight sky, a final, silent goodbye. I see Reya, a human torch against the darkness, her screams swallowed by flames. I feel the terrifying glint of lupine fangs in the moonlight and that chest-deep roar of pain that vibrates in my very molars as the memory resurfaces, a memory I hoped to never relive.

I was halfway through ending the life of one of the bastard wolves when I suddenly felt a presence behind me. But it was too late. Pain ripped across my back as teeth sank in—deep, brutal, precise. Once. Twice. More. White-hot spikes punched through muscle and dragged me off balance. The wolf snarled as I tried to stay upright, the cost was dropping my sword, and that was when the wolf slammed into me from behind. Its jaws are locking around my waist and wrenching me clear off the ground. The shaking came next—violent, careless, like I was nothing more than a toy to play with. My head snaps back and forth, my breath shattered, the memory washes over my mind, hard and fast. *Not like this, don't let me die like this.* Then Reya came to my rescue, killing the wolf. Reya cradled me in her arms as she decided to feed me her blood after Beastie sank his teeth into her wrist.

Rose, her beautiful face, a devastating mask of fury and fear, appears and rips Reya away from me, and she then takes over the role of cradling my bleeding form. In the chaos of death, her warmth had been my only sun, a blazing light shoving back the encroaching ice age of my impending demise. She is my anchor. My only tether to the shore of the living.

"...we cannot stop the massive haemorrhaging," a voice says, sounding distant and strained, like it's coming through a long, metallic tunnel. "The necrotic tissue around the primary bite radius won't coagulate. It's as if the blood is refusing to recognise the injury."

It's Doctor Stevens. His tone is raw, the sound of a professional confronting an invisible, invincible enemy. my failing biology.

"Stage four hypovolemic shock," he continues, his words stumbling over each other in a frantic attempt to keep pace with my declining vitals. "We've pushed prothrombin complex concentrate, but her blood is... it's fighting us. It's actively resisting the clotting process."

A low, incredibly dangerous growl rumbles through the air. It isn't a sound made by a human throat; it's a vibration that travels through the bed frame and settles deep in my bones. Rose. Even through this narcotic haze, I can feel her mounting anger—a simmering, lethal heat born of fierce, protective fury. It wraps around my consciousness like a shield forged in hellfire.

Then—warmth.

It isn't the warmth of a blanket or a hand. It is a slow, golden river seeping outward from my throat, threading through shredded veins like liquid sunlight. It is alien and persistent, a quiet, insistent hum pushing back against the medical cold.

I wonder if it's Reya's blood.

It is still inside me. It is fighting. I can taste copper pennies on my tongue and smell atmospheric ozone in my nostrils, sharp and electric. It feels ancient and wild—like storm-light trapped in amber thrumming in my veins. It feels profoundly wrong, yet it is the absolute only thing keeping the flatline at bay. It is a whisper in the dark, an insistent, magical pulse saying. *Not yet. Not while I still breathe.*

I sink back into the grey fog, clinging to that golden lifeline as if it were the only solid thing in a shifting universe. As I drift, a memory surfaces—not of war, but of peace.

A Pittsburgh motel room. The rain was drumming a frantic rhythm against the thin walls, isolating us from the rest of the world. Rose's soft lips had been pressing urgently against mine, her hands tangling in my hair. There was no Captain Bekke there. No soldier. No survivor. Just Ava. The sheer, electrical shock of feeling something so real, so perfectly right—the sensation of being truly seen, not as a weapon or a leader, but as a woman. It was the feeling of home, fragile and fleeting, a tiny, brilliant spark of light I claw at with everything I have left, refusing to let it gutter out.

"...her immune system is fighting back with cellular resilience that defies every single medical textbook I've ever read!"

Doctor Stevens' voice is closer now, rising in pitch, bordering on bewilderment. "The foreign substance in her bloodstream... the pathology lab we sent her blood to, cannot identify the compound. It isn't causing a cytokine storm or haemolytic anaemia. It is somehow completely integrated at a deep cellular level—integrated, not invading. I'm seeing localised hyper-accelerated mitosis. Spontaneous tissue synthesis. It's medically impossible. It's like watching stone grow flesh in real-time."

A warm hand slides into mine—calloused, trembling, and vibrantly alive. Rose. Her presence is a brand against my cold skin, a constant reminder that I am still tethered to something beautiful.

"She is a fighter," she whispers, her voice thick and choked, raw as if she's been screaming for hours. "She will not give up. She won't leave me."

The transition from one state of being to another is seamless and cruel. One moment I am lost in the golden hum of Reya's magic, and the next, I am hyper-aware of the physical reality of my captivity.

I am aware of the scratchy, irritating weave of the blanket abrading skin that feels raw from sweat and salt. I feel the heavy, air-conditioned chill blowing across my face, carrying the faint, clinical tang of antiseptic mixed with the scent of Rose's shampoo—lavender and something sharp, like crushed green stems.

I know she has barely left my side. Somewhere in the fog of my semi-consciousness, I can feel the hard plastic of her chair scrape against the metal bed rail, and the heat of her body, a blazing furnace pressed flush against my side, fighting the stark medical chill with sheer, stubborn presence.

I surface to hushed, heavy voices. Luca and Rose. They think I am under. Sedated. Deep in the mercy of the drugs.

They are wrong.

"...we cannot just sit here, Rose. We have to formulate a tactical plan," Luca says. His voice is a low, strained rumble of pure Alpha authority, but it's threaded with an exhaustion that speaks of sleepless nights and heavy decisions. "Sam is handling the operational cleanup and liaising with the backup team, but we need to know exactly what happened to Reya. We cannot move forward without understanding the threat level."

"I do not care what happened to her!"

Rose's voice is pure, dripping venom—a low, terrifying hiss that makes the fine hairs on my arms lift like startled birds. I feel a massive wave of her fury radiate through our bond, searing and sharp. "She did this! Look at Ava! She is barely holding onto life! Whatever that witch did to her is making her organs shut down. Every time the doctor tries to stabilise her, her vitals crash!"

She spits the last word like it's poison in her mouth.

"Rose, Pickle told the sisters Reya was trying to help," Luca counters, his voice a calm anchor in her storm. "We have to carefully consider the possibility that—"

"Consider what, Luca? That a black witch wielding daemon fire is actually on our side?" Her laugh is brittle, broken, devoid of any humour. "She probably pushed a lethal neurotoxin into Ava! For all we know, it's a parasitic curse—slowly killing her from the inside while we just sit here and watch her die! Look at her!"

Ice lances through my chest, a shard of dread more piercing than any physical wound. *Poison?* Is this warmth—this golden, wonderful life—actually a slow-acting toxin? I search my senses. It doesn't feel like poison. It feels like life. A quiet, brutal biological battle is being waged inside my veins right now, cell against cell, and I genuinely do not know which side is winning. Is it healing me... or hollowing me out to make room for something else?

The bitter argument fades as I sink once more into the heavy, inviting darkness, the question a splinter under my skin.

The next time I breach the surface of consciousness, it is to the soothing, rhythmic pressure of a cool, damp washcloth against my burning forehead. I know it's Rose without needing to open my eyes.

"You have to wake up, Ava." Her whisper is a frayed thread, desperate and thin.

The EKG monitor is slower now—*thoom... thoom... thoom*—like a heart finally learning how to beat again after a long, traumatic pause. Her voice is a raw, completely broken thing, scraped clean of all her usual bravado and pretence.

"You have to wake up because I desperately need to tell you how sorry I am," she continues, and I can hear the hitch in her breath. "For being an idiot. For letting fear turn me into someone you don't recognise. I am so incredibly scared, Ava. The agonising thought of losing you makes my panther want to literally tear the entire world apart—starting with whoever hurt you, and ending with whoever dared to make you doubt my love."

She breaks off, a sob catching in her throat. I feel a single, hot tear splash violently onto my cheek—salt and sorrow and something much fiercer. a promise.

"I need you to wake up right now so I can kiss you again," she pleads, her voice dropping to a desperate, breathless hush. "Because I really, really want to. Just once more. Please, Ava. Do not leave me in the dark. I just found you. It is not fair."

Her words are a hook buried deep in my soul, a sharp, insistent pull yanking me from the icy brink of the void. I fight toward her voice with everything I have left, viciously clawing my way through thick, suffocating layers of somatic pain and the heavy, narcotic weight of the IV drip. Each inch gained feels like dragging myself through miles of shattered glass.

With a monumental, agonizing effort that steals my breath and turns the world white, I finally manage to pull my consciousness from the depths. My eyelids feel as if they have been sealed with molten lead, but I stubbornly force them open.

The sterile room is a blurry, unfocused mess—shapes and smears of grey and white against the harsh, diffused light of the monitors. But her face... her face is the absolute first thing I see, razor-sharp through the haze. Her incredible green eyes are heavily red-rimmed and swollen from weeping, yet they are filled with a desperate, glowing light that perfectly mirrors the tiny, stubborn spark of life finally flickering inside my own chest. Like two stars colliding in a dead galaxy.

"Rose!" My voice is a dry, pathetic, cracking whisper—barely more than air scraping over ravaged tissue.

Her exhausted face instantly crumples. A sound escapes her throat—half a shattered sob, half a hysterical, relieved laugh. "Ava. Oh, gods, Ava. You are actually back."

The wonder in her voice is a physical blow. She leans down immediately, her soft lips meeting mine in a kiss that tastes of salt and the devastating relief of survival. It lacks the blazing, electrical fire of our usual kisses—the storm-and-sunshine spark that usually sets my blood on fire—but it is packed with so much raw, unadulterated emotion that it steals what little breath I have left regardless.

When she finally pulls back, I see the truth of her struggle. The bone-deep exhaustion etched into her features, the bruised, half-moon shadows dragging down the skin under her eyes, her lips chapped from worry. She looks as if she has been fighting this brutal medical battle right alongside me, pouring every ounce of her strength into keeping me tethered to this world.

"How long?" I rasp, the dry words brutally scraping against my throat.

"Almost two entire days," she murmurs, her thumb rubbing incredibly gently over my pale cheek. The touch is so light it's almost not there, yet it anchors me to the bed. "You have been drifting in and out. The doctor... he really does not know what to think. He just keeps calling you his literal medical impossibility." She manages a watery, fragile smile. "You're my impossibility, I know that for sure."

I absorb that, another impossible fact in a world overflowing with them. I can acutely feel the thick plastic of a central venous catheter taped to my inner elbow and the heavy, restrictive cervical collar locked tight around my neck. The edges bite into my jawline. I am weak. I am so profoundly, disgustingly weak that I feel like a newborn creature—limbs useless, head too heavy to lift. But I am actively breathing.

The heavy door creaks open with a protesting groan. My hyper-vigilant instincts, honed in a thousand kill zones, instantly sense the arrival of Luca and Sam. They freeze in the doorway, silhouettes against the harsh hallway light. Their expressions are grim, worn thin as old parchment. Sam looks like he hasn't slept in a week; Luca's usual, overwhelming Alpha confidence is completely overshadowed by a deep, weary sadness that sits in his shoulders like lead.

"What is it?" Rose asks sharply. Her panther instincts snap to attention, her muscles coiling even as she stays curled over me.

Luca's eyes meet mine—dark pools reflecting the ceiling lights, swimming with something I cannot quite name. Pity? Regret? The weight of command? He opens his mouth to speak, but it is Sam who finally breaks the suffocating silence. His voice is flat, devoid of emotion—too flat, like a wire pulled too tight.

"We just got off a secure line with Agent Moore," Sam says, his exhausted gaze fixed on a spot above my bed. "He pulled some strings for us. The local Sheriff finally took his call."

My stomach violently clenches, a fist of ice closing around my heart.

"Reya Harper has been officially arrested," Sam continues. The words land like concrete blocks in a still pond. "She has been formally charged with the brutal murder of Deputy Jacob Davids and two other local men, along with felony arson. Sheriff Bradshaw stated he found her at the primary scene, completely naked and covered in the victims' blood."

The entire world aggressively tilts on its axis. Again.

Arrested? For finally killing that absolute monster? The thing that had violated her? That had tortured her?

A blinding anger is sudden and fierce, so righteous it momentarily eclipses my physical pain. It is a white-hot, explosive surge of injustice that burns clean through the narcotic fog. Reya saved my life. She poured her own magic into me to keep me from the dark. And now she is being treated like a common criminal?

I remember the devastated, haunted look on Reya's face when Rose and Sera brought her home—her eyes were hollowed pits of trauma. I have seen that look far too many times in my line of work. It is the shattered look of a survivor who has been hunted by their own trauma of being raped. She went after him. She destroyed him. And now she is being thrown into a cage for it?

My broken body, which only moments ago was a useless sack of meat, is suddenly flooded with a new, urgent energy. It isn't physical strength; it is pure, unadulterated willpower.

With an agonising effort that feels like trying to deadlift a military transport vehicle, I fight the gravity of my own injuries. My vertebrae grind, and the world dissolves into nauseating grey as my blood pressure plummets, but I push. I swing my heavy legs over the side of the bed. Stars explode behind my eyes.

Rose makes a sharp, startled sound of pure panic, her hands flying out to secure my swaying frame before I can pitch sideways. Her grip is iron.

"No," I croak. It's a desperate, guttural command.

Luca takes a cautious step forward, his hands raised placatingly. "Ava, you need to lie back down immediately. You are not stable. You could tear your sutures. You could—"

I try to shake my head, but the cervical collar locks me in place. I can only glare at them—at Luca's authority, at Sam's worry, and at Rose's terror.

"We help those who cannot help themselves," I say, my voice a frayed thread of lethal conviction. "And right now? There is no one more in need than Reya. Go. Get her out. You have to."

The words are not a request; they are an oath.

As my anger builds, a sudden, overwhelming thirst floods my mouth. It isn't dryness; it is desiccation. My mouth feels like scorched desert sand. It is a deep, clawing biological need that no saline drip can touch. It is the thirst of injustice.

"Water," I croak.

Rose returns seconds later with a cup, holding it to my cracked lips with infinite care. I drink greedily, each swallow a small rebellion against the dark. But the liquid does nothing to quench the unnatural, bone-deep thirst that settles in my marrow.

The door swings open again. Doctor Stevens strides in, his usual professionalism replaced by purposeful urgency. He stops dead when he sees me sitting upright.

"Agent Bekke!" he gasps. "Welcome back to the land of the living. But it is far too soon to be mobilising! You have multiple fractures along your lumbar spine—compound in places. Moving like this risks paralysis. Death."

"Well," I say, my voice dark with a sarcasm that feels like home, "that would certainly explain the pain! Feels like I got kicked by a mule wearing steel-toed boots."

Rose and Luca assist me back down, their movements synchronised and careful. The doctor rushes to my bedside, checking my telemetry and shining a penlight into my eyes.

"Remarkable," he mutters, shaking his head. "The osteogenesis and rapid cellular regeneration in your deep tissue are proceeding at a biological rate that is... well, it is simply not human. And your hepatic system? It seems to completely metabolise any synthetic analgesics we try to push through your line in record time. We need to run a full MRI and draw another venous blood sample—now—to track the progression of this substance in your system."

"No." My voice is sharp, lethal as a snapped tendon. "I do not give my consent for any more blood draws. And I am not being moved to a hospital. Period."

My gaze locks onto his. Let him see the resolve. I will not let them treat me like a specimen once they find out what is really running through my system, which will likely also prompt them to make Reya disappear so they can study her.

"Agent Bekke, I need to know what is happening internally," Stevens pleads. "You are reacting like a paranormal entity..."

"I literally do not care," I cut him off with the finality of a judge's gavel.

Rose looks at me, her eyes burning with fierce, unconditional pride. Then, a thought strikes her. She turns to the doctor, her voice dropping to a conspiratorial whisper. "Could... could our prime bond be having a biological effect on her? We are deeply linked."

"What exactly is this bond?" Stevens asks, his scepticism plain.

"We share a prime mate bond," Rose says, her voice steady and unwavering. "It is an ancient form of magic that binds two people together irrevocably. It is not superstition, Doctor. It is law. As real as gravity."

The doctor rubs his chin, considering. "Perhaps... but I would still like that blood sample."

"No!" I say again, pouring every ounce of my soul into the refusal.

I look around the room—at the machines, at the men, and at the woman who is my entire world. My stare is a silent vow. *Test me, and you will regret it.*

As the darkness begins to pull at me once more, I feel the golden hum of Reya's blood advance. It pushes back against the void like a shield forged in starlight and spite. As my vision tunnels, I watch the warmth expand, holding the dark at bay as I suddenly fall back into the void.

CHAPTER 3

The Predators Awakening

The oppressive, chemical-induced fog that aggressively claimed my consciousness finally begins to recede—not with a sudden gasp of air, but like the tide slowly, reluctantly pulling back from a blood-stained shore.

It is a slow, agonising reclamation of self. For what feels like an eternity, I have been nothing more than a passenger in a vessel of meat and bone, drifting through a grey, featureless void where time has no meaning and light is a distant, forgotten myth. Now, the edges of my existence are fraying back into reality, but the transition is not a mercy; it is a violent intrusion. Each millimetre of awareness gained feels like dragging my soul through wet concrete, heavy and resisting every movement as if the universe itself is trying to pull me back into the dark.

I am not healed. I am not even close. But I am *present*.

The leaden weight in my limbs has lessened from an immovable anchor to a stubborn, pulsing ache, and my breath—though still shallow—draws deeper without that iron-band constriction that had been strangling my very life force. Yet, this minor victory is instantly punctuated by the arrival of a new, more localised torment.

Agonising flashes of acute pain shoot rapidly up my damaged spinal column. These are not random, dull throbs; they are precise, lightning-like jabs that originate at the base of my spine and race upward like white-hot needles being driven into my nervous system. Each strike makes my vision go blindingly white at the edges for a split second, a strobe light of pure agony that threatens to plunge me back into the unconsciousness I so desperately fought to escape.

Gods, it feels as though my nerves are being re-strung on a harp made of barbed wire.

Muffled, distorted sounds of the living world begin to filter into my sluggish mind, sounding as if they are being broadcast from underwater. I hear the distant, low hum of the HVAC system, a mechanical drone that feels intrusive in the silence. There is the soft, rhythmic *tick-tick-tick* of a wall clock, marking the passage of time I cannot reclaim. And then, there is the heartbeat of the room. the rhythmic, clinical *beep-beep-beep* of the monitor beside my bed.

Voices drift like ghosts through the grey mist still clinging to the corners of my awareness.

Rose's voice is there first. It is heavily laced with a frantic, jagged worry that I can feel even without seeing her—it is tight at the edges, vibrating with a tension so high it sounds like a rope about to snap under a heavy load. Then comes Luca's voice, a low, structural rumble that acts as a stabiliser to Rose's chaos; he sounds steady, assessing, his mind clearly already calculating the tactical next steps in a war that never sleeps. And finally, there is the older, clinically detached tone of Doctor Stevens. His voice is threaded with a professional bafflement, a sense of scientific confusion that makes my skin prickle.

I have absolutely no idea how long it took my brain to successfully fight its way back to the surface from the moment I first heard sounds from the room around me. It genuinely feels as though several agonising years have passed in the dark, each minute an epic struggle against the crushing gravity of the void. I am not just fighting the catastrophic damage to my physical body, which currently feels as if it has been repeatedly run over by an armoured personnel carrier and then left to bake in the sun while scavengers pick at the wreckage—I am fighting a war against the very substances meant to sustain me.

The heavy, synthetic sedatives cling to my thoughts like suffocating cobwebs. They slow my reflexes, dull my edges, and make the world feel muffled, unreal, and dangerously distant. I am a warrior trying to fight through a layer of thick, viscous oil.

My eyelids feel as if they have been injected with molten lead—thick, unresponsive, fighting every millimetre of lift. When I finally manage to pry them open, my dilated pupils violently protest the sharp, sterile, blinding white light of the safe house ceiling. A fresh bolt of pain lances behind my eyes, a sharp, electrical spike that forces me to squeeze them shut again.

I wait, breathing through the afterimages, waiting for the world to stop spinning. My very first conscious thought is not an assessment of my extensive physical injuries or a check of my vitals. It is a cold, hard, lethal spike of pure, unadulterated rage.

Reya.

The thought isn't abstract; it's a physical sensation, a clenched fist in my gut and a burning, corrosive pressure behind my sternum. She is trapped in a cold, iron cell by that monster of a sheriff. The injustice of it feels like a personal insult, a violation of the very laws of cause and effect that I have lived my life by.

I cautiously turn my head, a movement so slow and deliberate that I am practically counting the seconds between each micro-adjustment to avoid triggering another wave of spinal fire.

Rose is right here.

She is slumped awkwardly in an uncomfortable plastic chair beside my bed, her beautiful head pillowed on her crossed arms, lost in a deep, heavy sleep. Even in repose, she looks battle-worn. Heavy, bruised dark circles smudge the pale skin beneath her closed eyes—like thumbprints of exhaustion pressed into porcelain. She looks utterly, bone-deep exhausted, the kind of weariness that seeps into the marrow and refuses to leave with sleep.

A pang of something tender and painful twists in my chest. I wish she had managed to get some decent, restorative rest. The nightmares must have been vicious; I can almost see them dancing behind her eyelids. I understand her stubbornness—I am just as bad—but seeing her look so hollowed out makes me feel a profound sense of failure.

Shifters need more than sleep, I think, a trace of my internal sarcasm flickering to life. *They need movement, sunlight, and the ability to run until their lungs burn. Seeing her like this... it's wrong.*

A low, involuntary groan escapes my dry lips as I attempt to lean toward her. It is a pathetic, weak sound, but it is enough to break her slumber.

Her head snaps up. Those incredible green eyes, initially blurry and unfocused with the fog of sleep, instantly lock onto my face. A massive, physical wave of relief visibly washes over her features—her shoulders drop a fraction, the tension in her jaw eases, and a shuddering breath escapes her lips as if she has been holding it for hours.

"Ava."

She is on her feet in an instant, hovering over me with a frantic, desperate energy. Her warm hand finds mine, serving as a familiar, anchoring weight—calloused, trembling, and undeniably real. "You are back. Oh, gods, you are actually back. I was so incredibly worried." Her voice is rough, scraped raw by fear and the sheer exhaustion of her vigil.

"How long?" I rasp. My parched throat feels as if it has been heavily coated in crushed glass and sandpaper; each syllable is a struggle against abrasive tissue.

She looks physically pained as she delivers the answer. "Another day and a half," she finally admits, her voice thick with unshed emotion. She reaches out, running her soft thumb incredibly gently over the curve of my pale cheek. The touch is so light it's barely there, yet it grounds me like a lifeline in a storm. "You desperately needed the rest. You tried to get out of bed earlier... you nearly caused permanent damage to your spine."

Something in her careful tone—the way her voice drops, the

subtle hesitation—sets my assassin instincts on high alert. It isn't just concern. It's guilt. She is hiding something from me.

I narrow my eyes, studying the telltale flush creeping up her neck. "It is incredibly strange how I could feel my brain having to actively fight off a heavy narcotic haze as I came around," I say, keeping my voice deceptively calm despite the ache in my throat. "Like I was being held under by force."

She winces, the flush deepening into a crimson stain. "Okay, fine. The doctor heavily sedated you. After you woke up the first time and literally tried to launch your broken body out of bed, he was terrified you would cause permanent paralysis. He firmly stated your body required uninterrupted, chemically induced downtime to properly fuse the bones."

Her confession hangs in the air between us—thick, heavy, and smelling of betrayal.

He drugged me.

The thought makes my hands clench into tight, white-knuckled fists, my nails biting half-moons into my palms. The righteous anger is instant and razor-sharp. It isn't the hot, blind fury of a battlefield; this is cold, focused, and deadly precise. I am a soldier, and being rendered helpless by one of our own is an unforgivable breach of protocol.

"He had absolutely no right to do that," I snap, the words tearing from my throat like shrapnel.

A bizarre, unnatural sensation washes over my system as my anger mounts. It isn't just thirst; again, it is a deep, agonising desiccation that makes my throat feel as if it is drying up into dust. My mouth tastes of copper and parched earth.

"He had every right, Ava," Rose counters gently, though her tone remains unyielding—steel wrapped in velvet. Her grip on my hand tightens with unshakeable resolve. "You have shattered vertebrae in your lower back. How would you have felt if you had caused permanent, irreversible damage to your spinal cord? He still isn't sure if you even have nerve damage." Her eyes search mine, pleading for me to understand the logic of her protection. "He is still completely baffled by your chart, anyway. He keeps demanding more blood samples for pathology."

"No!" The word is a command, lethal and final.

I need to stay conscious. I cannot allow myself to be rendered helpless again. More importantly, I must ensure that the doctor continues to believe it is the prime mate bond accelerating my regeneration, and not the magical essence of Reya's blood knitting my flesh back together. If they discover the truth? They won't treat me; they will dissect me. They will turn Reya's gift into a laboratory specimen.

"No more diagnostic tests. No more blood samples. Ever," I declare.

Rose gives me a look that makes my heart ache—fierce, proud, and loving all at once. "Don't worry, honey. I firmly told him he would have to go through my dead panther to get to your veins. He wisely decided to back off."

A tiny ghost of a genuine smile touches my lips. *My girl. Always my girl.*

"How are you actually feeling?" Rose asks, her green eyes intensely studying my face, searching for the cracks in my facade.

"I am completely fine," I grit out, the blatant lie tasting like bitter ash on my tongue. In reality, my body feels like a shattered porcelain vessel haphazardly glued back together with sheer willpower and prayer.

"No, you are not," she retorts softly, her thumb stroking my cheek in a slow, rhythmic motion. "You completely passed out. You scared the absolute hell out of us. Just... let whatever Reya did keep working. I am still incredibly furious with her, but I won't try to rip her throat out. Do you remember what she actually did? What specific spell was it?"

I force my expression to remain neutral. *I honestly do not remember,* I lie smoothly. I pray that the overwhelming cocktail of pain receptors firing in my brain will mask the subtle chemical shift of a lie from Rose's enhanced senses. Pain is a great liar's ally; it provides the perfect cover for any tremor of deceit.

The heavy door swings open with a decisive, commanding push. It isn't the soft entrance of Doctor Stevens; it is Luca.

"She is finally awake," Luca states, his dark gaze locking onto mine. There is no pity in his eyes—only a shared, violently simmering fury.

"She is. She seems significantly better," Rose says, offering a rare, genuine smile.

"She does," Luca agrees, stepping fully into the room with predator-smooth economy. "Sam asked me to rendezvous here. He discovered something massive and wants to share the intel immediately. He'll be pleased to see you conscious, Ava."

Speak of the devil. Sam walks into the sterile room, his jaw set in a grim, stone-cold line. He looks like he hasn't slept in a week; his usual sharpness is replaced by a hollowed-out exhaustion. His eyes are burning with a terrifying, feverish intensity.

"Hey, sleepyhead," Sam says, though his voice is tight and strained. "I am so incredibly glad you are finally awake. We really missed you." I'm surprised to hear it, as it wasn't that long ago that we weren't getting on well, as he didn't like my way of doing things, who knew almost dying would break down all the barriers.

"I would say the feeling is mutual, but I have been medically comatose for three and a half days," I rasp. "What exactly did you find?"

Sam nods sharply and steps forward, holding a secure agency tablet as if it were a heavy slab of damning evidence. He flicks the screen awake, the blue-white glow painting his face in stark relief.

"While you were recovering, I have been digging into the digital archives," he begins, his professional voice flat and controlled. "I contacted Agent Moore. I had him pull some serious international intelligence from across the pond."

My stomach violently clenches. *Here it comes.*

"Deputy Jacob Davids..." Sam pauses heavily, taking a deep

breath. I see the slight tremor in his hand as he grips the tablet. He is rattled. "He is absolutely not Jacob Davids!"

The room narrows down to the image on the screen. On the left, the handsome, disarmingly charming deputy with the sunlight in his hair. On the right, a man with darker hair and a distinctly crueller, sharper set to his jawline. The underlying bone structure is identical, but the eyes are different—they possess an absolute, dead-eyed coldness that is unmistakable.

"His actual name is Jason Lorcan."

The name hangs in the air like poison.

Instantly, the temperature in the room seems to drop. It isn't the HVAC; it is the freezing hostility radiating from Rose. She has gone entirely rigid, a low, guttural snarl vibrating up from her chest. Luca lets out a string of harsh curses in a foreign language, his face twisting into a mask of predatory rage.

"The Lorcan pack!" Rose hisses, her hands clenching into white-knuckled fists. I see her fingernails briefly lengthen into obsidian claws before she forces them back.

"Who are the Lorcan's?" I ask, my mind already cross-referencing old intel files.

"Absolute butchers," Luca spits. "A pack of wolf shifters so fanatically obsessed with pure-blood lineage that they were cast out by the shifter councils centuries ago. They view magic users as either threats to be eliminated or..." His gaze darkens. "...as breeding stock."

Bile rises in my throat. *Breeding stock.* It perfectly outlines the horrifying motivation behind the attack on Reya's mother. This was never a random act of violence; it was a coordinated, methodical hunt.

"We had a run-in with them as children," Rose adds, her voice vibrating with a lethal snarl. "They were trying to kidnap a child from a witch my mother was close to. They wanted to use her to forcefully breed magic back into their bloodline. The girl was only six."

"John Lorcan is currently dead," Sam interjects, his voice flat as a mortician's table. "The intelligence Moore secured states John and his wife were found murdered in England. They were found with an unidentified female corpse. Authorities discovered a bathtub entirely filled with blood and water upstairs in the primary bathroom. When forensics tested the DNA, it perfectly matched their supposed daughter. However, they simultaneously discovered she was not actually biologically related to John and his wife at all. After investigating, they discovered the daughter had been stolen from a human family who were subsequently slaughtered. She is technically classified as missing but presumed dead."

Presumed. The word rings like a bell.

"Does that mean you might have located her?" I ask, my pulse hammering.

Sam looks uncomfortable. "I did not find her. She found us."

"What do you mean?" Luca demands.

"Not all of us," Sam says, glancing between Rose and me. "Just you, Ava, Rose, and Reya have visually engaged with this specific girl."

My blood runs colder than the room's chill. There is only one possibility. "Devika."

The woman commanding the demon attack.

"Seriously? She was the exact girl the Lorcan's kidnapped," Luca says, his voice dark and deadly. "And now we have to go up against her and her legion of hell spawn."

"There's more," Sam continues, looking even more terrified. "Forensic evidence from the UK crime scene suggests Devika might have murdered the unidentified woman found in that house. Furthermore, she was physically present when a young boy named Tom Cummings went missing. And... has anyone checked the news about the ghost town in England where every resident vanished?"

"No," we answer in grim unison.

"That is exactly where Devika lived," Sam says. "It is also where the UK faction of the Lorcan pack operates, commanded by their Alpha, Sean Lorcan."

"Are you serious?" Rose asks, her voice vibrating with panic.

"What else is there?"

"As you know, Jacob is directly linked to the mobilisation in Chicago," Sam explains. "The wolves in Luna Falls are merely a fraction of the full pack. This operation is nowhere near over. With what is happening in England and over here in Chicago, the Lorcan pack is a massive threat to us. Before long, we might not be able to go anywhere without encountering them again, that is, if they aren't already on their way to Luna Falls to get revenge."

"Un-fucking-believable," Rose spits. She looks at me, her eyes filled with a deep worry. She thinks my fragile human body won't survive another assault.

"Anyway," Sam says, turning back to the immediate issue. "The real Jacob Davids was reported missing from Tennessee ten years ago. His vehicle was found abandoned. It is crystal clear that Jason infiltrated Luna Falls for one reason."

"To get to Reya," I finish.

The pieces slam together with sickening precision. The assassination of the mother, the isolation of the sisters—it was all a long, psychological game played by a man with a handsome face and a hollow soul. He didn't just stumble upon them; he orchestrated every detail to ensure they were vulnerable when he finally struck.

The anger that settles in my gut is not hot or chaotic. It is the cold, patient, methodical fury of an apex predator. The Destroyer inside me—the part of my soul forged in the fire of my parents' murder—stirs to life. I feel it as a low, resonant hum in my bones, a readiness coiled in my spine like a spring.

Let her come.

I look directly at Luca, then at Rose, and finally at Sam. When I speak, my voice is terrifyingly steady. It is the cold tone of a captain with a new, crystal-clear objective.

"Get me a secure line to Agent Moore. Now."

CHAPTER 4

Shadows & Shifters

The silence in this room isn't just quiet. It is a loaded weapon, heavy and suffocating, pressing against my chest until every breath feels like I am inhaling molten lead. The air is thick, charged with the electric aftershock of Sam's revelation, vibrating with a frequency that makes my teeth ache.

The name Lorcan hangs in the space between us, a single drop of poison that has sucked every ounce of oxygen from the room. My lungs burn, protesting the shallow, ragged breaths I am forced to take. Each inhale is a struggle, a battle against the crushing atmospheric pressure of our shared shock.

Across the room, Luca is no longer just a man. He is a statue carved from granite and pure, unadulterated fury. He stands perfectly still, but it is the stillness of a predator seconds before the kill. His hands are clenched into fists so tight that the tendons in his forearms strain against his tanned skin like taut wires, pulsing with a rhythmic, violent energy. I can see the vein in his temple throbbing, a ticking clock counting down to an explosion.

Beside me, Rose is a different kind of storm. She isn't still; she vibrates. It is a low-frequency tremor, a violence she is barely keeping under wraps. A guttural growl ripples deep in her chest, a sound so primal it sends a cold shiver racing down my spine and makes the fine hairs on my arms stand on end. I catch the flicker of her movement in the periphery of my vision, noting how her nails lengthen into sharp, lethal obsidian claws for a split second before she forces them back with a visible effort of will. Her knuckles are stark, ghostly white where she grips the edge of my mattress, the fabric groaning under the pressure.

Even Sam, ever the professional G-man, looks like he has aged a decade in ten minutes. His posture stiff, but his eyes are wide, flickering between Luca and Rose with a touch of genuine alarm. The weight of this new, uglier truth seems to be physically crushing his shoulders, bowing him under the gravity of what Lorcan represents.

And then there is me.

The pain in my back is nothing more than a distant, dull echo now, pushed into the background by a surge of adrenaline. The shattered vertebrae, the lacerated flesh, the subcutaneous hematomas blooming in deep purples and sickly yellows across my skin, the way my nerves scream every time I shift an inch, it is all just background noise. A cold, clinical focus begins to crystallise in my veins, pushing back the haze of exhaustion and forcing the lingering weakness into a dark corner of my mind. It is a familiar sensation, a mental armour I haven't allowed myself to embrace in a long time.

The Destroyer is awake.

And she is absolutely pissed.

"Get me that line to Moore," I repeat as I swing my heavy legs over the side of the bed. This time, there is no dizziness. No hesitation. My sudden movement seems to have gone unnoticed by everyone, as they are still reeling from the news.

My voice isn't loud, but it cuts through the suffocating tension like a serrated blade through silk. It is flat, devoid of the vulnerability that has plagued me since I woke up in this bed.

Sam startles, fumbling for his phone as if the device has suddenly become coated in grease. His fingers slip, and he nearly drops the phone before regaining his grip. "Ava, are you sure? You are in no condition to be stressed. Your vitals are still stabilising, your blood pressure is erratic, and you need absolute rest. I can speak to him for you, relay the information, and get back to you with his directive."

I level a look at him, my eyes narrowing with enough heat to melt steel. I don't move a muscle, but the intensity of my gaze is a physical force. He actually flinches, the words dying on his lips as he realises that "resting" is the last thing on my agenda.

Doubt me one more time, Sam. I dare you. See if I can find a way to throw this IV pole at your head.

He swallows hard, his Adam's apple bobbing in a nervous rhythm, before he finally punches in the number and puts it on speaker. The call connects, and Agent Moore's voice fills the room, sounding tinny and frustratingly distant through the phone's speaker.

"Any news on Bekke, Sam?" Moore asks. His tone is measured, that classic CIA blend of professional concern and strategic detachment.

"She wants to speak to you," Sam replies, his voice regaining its professional clip, though he still keeps a cautious distance from me.

I snatch the phone from him, my movements jerky but determined. "Sir, I need your help."

"Bekke? Sam told me you were holding on. I am relieved to hear your voice, truly. How are you feeling? Do we need to adjust your medication or bring in a specialist for the neurological assessment? The report on your spinal trauma was concerning, to say the least."

"Peachy," I clip out.

I am in absolutely zero mood for medical pleasantries or a lecture on my recovery. Every word of concern feels like a polite way of reminding me that I am currently broken. "Sir, I need your help."

There is a brief pause on the other end. Moore knows that tone. He knows when I have stopped being a patient and have returned to being a soldier. "What do you need?"

"Help getting Reya Harper out of prison. We need her if we are going to make it out of this alive."

A tense silence stretches over the line, heavy enough to feel. Beside me, I feel Rose shift. The discomfort radiating from her is a palpable wave of agitation that hits me through our bond, a sharp, jagged energy that tastes like copper and ozone. She doesn't say anything, but her presence is an objection in itself.

"While you were recovering, I took the initiative to ask the others to compile detailed reports regarding the recent events," Moore says, his voice steady but edged with an unmistakable uncertainty. He hesitates, then continues, "However, Rose has expressed some valid concerns about Reya. She is worried that the girl might ultimately betray us, or worse, lead the enemy straight to our doorstep."

My jaw tightens so hard it aches, a sharp click echoing in my skull.

You have got to be kidding me.

"After reviewing the feedback from the others and having a conversation with Freya," Moore continues, "I have concluded that Reya has, thus far, shown a genuine willingness to assist. I am prepared to take a calculated risk on her."

My eyes dart to Rose. I shoot her a look so piercing I expect it to leave physical marks on her skin. She won't meet my eyes. Instead, she drops her gaze to the floor, her posture radiating an unmistakable sense of shame and stubbornness.

Un-freaking-believable.

I cannot believe she actually did it. She took her unfounded, irrational hatred for Reya and whispered it straight into Moore's ear while I was unconscious and unable to defend my position. Luca should have stopped her. But then again, I know Luca. He feels exactly the same way. A surge of raw, white-hot anger flares in my gut, fuelling a frustration so deep it makes my vision swim for a second.

"Thank you, sir," I manage to say, though every word feels like it is being dragged over broken glass.

"I will keep you updated as soon as I have more information," Moore assures me. "In the meantime, if you happen to cross paths with the Sheriff, I suggest maintaining the narrative that we requested Reya to infiltrate Jacob's circle. It appears the F.B.I. has been investigating these Lorcan's for quite some time, though they lost the trail when it came to Jason. Additionally, it would be beneficial if you could track down Dhara, the one who warned Reya and her sisters. If you can obtain a statement regarding her community's intention to attack them, it could lend the necessary credence to getting Reya released."

My head drops, a heavy, defeated sigh escaping my lips. Great. Just perfect.

Dhara is the last person I want to deal with, but she is part of the pack, even if she was not directly involved in the assault. And Reya... god, Reya would have a total meltdown if she knew I was trying to use her as a pawn. But there is no time for morality plays or playing nice when we are dealing with people who treat human lives like disposable napkins. If this is what it takes to get her out of that cage, we take the chance.

"Thank you. I will see what we can do," I say, forcing a mask of gratitude over my face while apprehension tightens its grip on my chest.

"Well, make sure you are fully healed before you go back into the field," Moore advises, his tone shifting to something more serious, almost parental. "I would understand if you chose to head home to recuperate."

Home.

The word hits me like a physical blow to the solar plexus. It feels like a cruel joke, a word from a language I forgot how to speak long ago. I barely have a grasp on what that even means anymore. Since I turned eighteen and stepped into the machine of the military, my life has been nothing but a blur of dusty bases, temporary quarters, and sterile bunk beds. There is no home for someone like me. No porch swings, no family dinners, no place where the air doesn't smell like gun oil or antiseptic.

"That is okay, sir. I am happy to stay. I cannot wait to get back to the mission," I reply.

It is pure bravado, a hollow shell designed to mask the ache of longing for a place that does not exist. The lie tastes bitter in my mouth, but it is the only currency I have.

"Good. We need you. Speak soon."

"Bye, sir," I mutter, tossing the phone back toward Sam.

The sudden movement sends a fresh bolt of agony lancing through my spine, white-hot and screaming. It feels as if someone has driven a red-hot railroad spike through my vertebrae and twisted it slowly. I grit my teeth, refusing to give them the satisfaction of seeing me wince, though my vision blurs at the edges. I turn to Rose, my frustration finally boiling over.

"You are in so much trouble," I whisper, my voice dropping to a dangerous, low register that usually makes recruits tremble.

She reaches out, her hand brushing mine in a brief, tentative gesture of affection, her skin warm and soft. But the touch feels wrong given the betrayal. I pull away sharply, the movement jarring my ribs. "Lay off the hatred toward Reya. Please. She saved my life, Rose. Does that not count for anything?"

"She could have poisoned you! Or cursed you!" Rose snaps back.

The sudden volume makes me flinch. A low snarl bubbles up from her throat, and she clenches her fists so hard I think her skin might actually tear. The tension radiating off her is like heat coming off a pavement in July, shimmering and oppressive. "We do not actually know what she did to you, Ava. All I saw was you dying, your heart stopping, and a black witch hovering over you with that terrifying energy. How do we know she didn't just tie your soul to her for some sick purpose?"

Her words hit home, dragging up the memories of darkness and the suffocating taste of fear. I can still feel it, that desperate, primal longing for survival, the sensation of being pulled through a straw from a place of absolute void. It was Reya who reached into that abyss and dragged me back to the light. But I realise now that in Rose's eyes, the lines between saviour and monster are completely blurred. To her, a witch is a witch, regardless of whether she saves lives or ends them.

"And what choice did we have?" I retort, my voice rising despite my better judgment. "I would not have made it out without her. We are in this together, whether you like it or not."

Rose's face twists, a flicker of doubt crossing her eyes before she masks it with stubbornness. If only she would drop the prejudice. If only she could see that Reya is as terrified and lost as any of us.

"I would be dead without her," I continue, pushing myself up slightly against the pillows. My spine screams in protest, a jagged sensation that makes my breath hitch and my heart hammer against my ribs. "So maybe park the 'black witch' obsession for five minutes and focus on the fact that she fought on our side."

I pin her with a stare, then shift my gaze to Luca, dragging him into the fray. He has been watching us with those intense dark eyes, his expression unreadable but his presence commanding. "Please. We need her if we are going to have even a snowball's chance in hell of saving this world."

I take a breath, trying to steady the tremor in my hands. The adrenaline is starting to wear off, leaving behind a cold, hollow exhaustion. "How long will it take to get Reya out? And we still need to find Dhara."

Sam is the one who answers, his expression grim as he looks at his tablet. "It could take up to a week. The justice system is not exactly known for its speed, and getting a 'special' release requires several layers of signatures from people who do not like being hassled." He pauses, scrolling through data. "I already have my programs running, trying to track where Dhara went after she left the Harpers. She is good at disappearing, but everyone leaves a digital or physical footprint if you look hard enough."

"That is too long," I bite out.

A week is an eternity when you are hunting monsters and being hunted in return. There is no point in arguing about Dhara; people like her know how to vanish into the shadows of this country if they have half a mind to. I just hope she leaves a trail somewhere, some breadcrumb that leads us to her in the end.

"Until you are fully healed, we cannot really go after Devika and her demons," Sam reasons, his voice calm but firm. "You are a liability in the field right now, Ava. You can barely sit up without looking like you are about to pass out from pain. So, realistically, a week is not that bad."

I shoot him an *are you serious?* look. He ignores it with practised ease, though I see the corner of his mouth twitch.

"What we really need to worry about is Devika attacking again, or the Lorcan pack coming for revenge," Sam continues. The look on his face is not just professional concern; he is genuinely scared. He knows that against a full pack of shifted predators and demonic entities, our tactical gear and CIA protocols are little more than toys. I glance at Luca and Rose, seeing the same dread mirrored in their eyes.

A cold coil of fear settles in my gut. Even if we walked away right now, they know who we are. They have tasted our blood; they know our scents. They would hunt us to the ends of the earth. And the Harper sisters? Maya and Freya wouldn't last a week against a pack like that.

"I am debating our options," Luca says, his deep voice cutting through the mounting anxiety in the room. He speaks with an undeniable authority, the kind of tone that demands silence and attention.

"What options?" I ask.

"Right now, I am considering asking Freya if we can relocate to their property. Or at least see if she can bolster the protection on our motel rooms and this safe house."

"You cannot be serious!" Rose explodes, standing up so quickly her chair screeches against the floor. "We cannot stay at the Harpers'. I am already uncomfortable with the rest of our pack being there as it is. It feels like we are inviting the enemy into our bed. I would much prefer we stay here and have Freya reinforce the perimeter from a distance."

I know exactly why she is protesting. It is not about the safety of the pack. It is not about tactical advantage. It is Reya. The very thought of being in close proximity to the black witch makes Rose's skin crawl.

"Actually," I interject, "staying at the Harpers' is the best tactical move. The magic on that property aids in cellular regeneration and healing. Freya mentioned it, and if it is true, it would get me back into the fight much faster than these sterile walls and painkillers."

Luca looks intrigued, his Alpha brain clearly running through the logistics of the advantage. A healed Captain Bekke is a far more effective weapon than a bedridden one. Then, his expression falters. His face falls, and I know exactly why he is hesitating. It has nothing to do with the mission or the danger of the Lorcan's.

"You are worried about the bond you have with Reya," I state flatly. "The one neither of you wants to admit exists."

Rose shoots me a look that screams *you did not just go there*. Sam's eyes widen, and Luca's expression shifts into something dark and irritated. He looks as if he has been caught stealing from the treasury.

He carefully schools his features, attempting to regain his impassive mask before he speaks. "You are right," he admits, his voice dropping to a low, thoughtful rumble. "I am concerned about the proximity. Being that close to her would give our bond every opportunity to deepen, and that makes me uneasy. I was raised on the same cautionary tales as Rose, and despite my attempts to remain objective, I cannot shake the image of Reya as nothing more than a black witch." He pauses, his eyes meeting mine with a raw honesty. "However, unlike Rose, I am willing to extend a measure of trust for the time being. Elijah has a knack for uncovering truths, and I trust him to keep me informed if he learns anything significant."

"Wait. You have Elijah spying on the sisters?" I ask, my heart skipping a beat.

Of course he does. Why wouldn't the Alpha Panther have a spy in the house?

"No! Not spying," Luca clarifies quickly, though the speed of his response is suspicious. "Just... keeping his guard up. He is protecting our people. And he has already reported something concerning."

"What is it?" Rose demands, leaning forward, her predatory curiosity piqued.

"I was going to tell you, Rose, but we got sidetracked," Luca says. "The first night our pack members stayed on the property, they were all woken by Reya screaming."

"What the hell is that supposed to mean?" Rose mutters.

"When Elijah and the others woke up, they realised their animal sides had taken control in their sleep," Luca explains. "Instinct took over. They all instinctively made their way to Reya's bedroom. They just... found spots to sleep around her. Like she was the centre of a circle. A huddle."

"I told you! She cannot be trusted!" Rose cries out, her voice rising in pitch. "She is using some kind of pheromone or mind control! They are at risk, Luca!"

"Rose, cool it. She did not do anything to them," I say, trying to de-escalate the situation before Rose actually shifts and destroys the room. My mind flashes back to the look on Reya's face after what happened... what Jason did to her. Waking up to a room full of naked, shifted men? Honestly, if that were me, I would be screaming too.

Luca continues, "I am not sure what this pull is. The stories we are taught say that when we are in the presence of our god, we are naturally drawn to them. A biological imperative for protection and submission."

"She is not our god!" Rose snaps. "She shifts into a damn hellhound!"

"I never said she was. Rose, if you cannot maintain control over your emotions, perhaps you should go check in with our backup team leader."

Rose flinches, glancing at me with an apologetic look before sinking back into her chair. The fire is still there, but the Alpha's command has dampened it.

"I have also heard legends of certain types of magic that can affect shifters," Luca adds, his eyes distant, as if he is reading a book only he can see. "Magic that draws out our animal sides for protection. The old stories say some packs used to live alongside witches for that very reason. They called them Guardians."

Guardians? Like supernatural bodyguards? What the hell is Reya, if she can make an entire pack of mixed shifters want to huddle around her while they sleep? It sounds less like a curse and more like a sanctuary.

"Do you really think she might be one of them?" I ask, the idea sending a shiver down my spine. If she is a Guardian, then we haven't just found an ally, we have found the most powerful asset in this war.

"I am not sure," Luca says, and there is a profound sadness in his tone, a longing that he refuses to name. "Whatever this pull is, it is just another reason I do not want to stay there. Between the bond and this... it might be impossible for me to stay away from her."

I cannot help myself. The sarcasm bubbles up before I can stop it, a reflex born of my need to poke at Luca's stoicism. "Or maybe you could just try getting to know her. You might find you actually like her. I think she is pretty amazing."

Both Luca and Rose turn to me with identical, judgmental stares. One of shock, one of disbelief. I shrink back against the pillows, feeling like a teenager caught talking about a crush in the middle of a briefing.

"I am going to check for updates," Luca says, turning and heading out of the room. He pauses at the door, his gaze lingering on me with a mix of concern and authority. "Ava, make sure you continue to rest. Do not push yourself. And for heaven's sake, stay in bed. I told the doctor not to remove your catheter until your spinal stabilisation is complete."

"You did what?" I shout at his retreating back.

The shock is so sudden, so absolute, that I do not even feel the pain in my spine. I hurriedly reach under the thin hospital gown, my fingers brushing against a plastic tube and the crinkle of medical-grade bagging. Sure enough, there it is. A foley catheter.

His only response is a burst of laughter echoing through the hallway, followed by the muffled snorts of Rose and Sam. They are actually laughing at me.

I cross my arms over my chest, but even that small movement sends a fresh, agonising bolt of pain through my neck, ribs, and arms. I grimace, staring up at the ceiling with a look of pure hatred.

A catheter. Seriously?

I am Ava Bekke. The freaking Destroyer. I take down terrorists in the middle of war zones, I dismantle cartels from the inside out, and I hunt monsters that would make most men piss themselves. And right now, my greatest enemy is a plastic tube and a bag of my own urine. This is the absolute height of indignity. It is a professional failure of the highest order.

Oh, he will pay for this. Every single one of them will pay.

I imagine various ways to torture Luca once I can walk again. Maybe I'll find a way to knock him out and insert a catheter to limit him. *Okay, that might be going too far...* maybe he has a point about the spinal stability. But they are still paying.

CHAPTER 5

The Hunger and the Hollow

I am so bored that I can actually feel my soul starting to atrophy.

It is a slow, agonising process, like a piece of fruit left to rot in the midday sun. If I have to lie here for one more minute, staring at the sterile, pitted acoustic tile ceiling of this makeshift hospital room, I might just spontaneously combust out of sheer monotony. The air in here tastes of industrial bleach and stale ozone, a chemical cocktail that clings to the back of my throat and makes every breath feel clinical, cold, and devoid of life.

I track a single water stain on one of the tiles. It looks vaguely like the coast of Italy, or maybe just a smudge of mildew. I have spent the last hour analysing its geography. *This is what my life has become. From leading tactical strikes and hunting monsters to playing 'find the shape' with ceiling mould.*

Since I regained consciousness, which has become a recurring and increasingly annoying theme in my current existence, I have been subjected to a constant stream of visitors. Rose, of course, has practically grafted herself to my bedside. Her presence is a mixture of profound comfort and suffocating intensity. She doesn't just sit in the room. she occupies it. She smells of rain-drenched cedar and something deeply primal, a scent that speaks of ancient forests and predatory grace.

Usually, that smell grounds me, acting as an anchor when my mind starts to spiral. Right now, however, it just reminds me that I am a broken bird in a cage while she is the sleek black panther guarding the door.

Then there are Luca's pack members. They visit in rotating shifts, their well-meaning check-ins feeling less like emotional support and more like a high-security guard duty. They hover at the edges of the room, their heightened shifter senses probably picking up every spike of my frustration, every erratic thrum of my heartbeat, and every flicker of irritation that crosses my face.

I am a Captain of a specialised joint task force. I am trained in urban warfare, interrogation, and high-stakes leadership. I am not a prized poodle in a grooming salon.

I had hoped Freya and Maya might have stopped by. It was a ridiculously optimistic thought, a sliver of hope that I should have crushed the moment I woke up. Hope is a dangerous thing when you are dealing with witches who have every reason to hate your association with the government agents who put their sister in a cage. When Elijah visited yesterday, his handsome Viking face all grim and serious, he confirmed what my gut had already been screaming at me.

He had perched on the edge of the visitor's chair, looking deeply uncomfortable, as if the very air of the room was too tight for him to breathe. He smelled of old leather and cold mountain air, a scent that usually suggested stability but now felt like a funeral shroud.

"They are not interested in talking to us, Ava," he had said, his voice low and rough, sounding like stones grinding together in a riverbed. He wouldn't look me in the eye, instead staring at my bandaged arm with a look of profound pity. I hated that look more than I hated the pain. "Freya was... clear. Until Reya is out of prison, we are on our own. I am surprised they haven't asked us to leave the property, to be honest."

The news had a lovely domino effect. Luca, ever the pragmatic Alpha, decided it was too risky for us to be split between locations without the Harpers' magical backup. He doesn't like vulnerability, and right now, our team is one giant, gaping wound. So, while I have been enjoying the five-star amenities of this safe house. which is to say an IV drip that makes my vein ache with a cold, stinging pressure, a catheter that is an absolute affront to human dignity, and back pain that feels like a hot iron being pressed into my lumbar spine, Luca, Sam, and Rose have been bunking here too. The entire tactical team has essentially turned this house into a barracks. A very *cramped* barracks.

When Elijah had broached the subject of placing protective wards on the property to keep us safe from whatever was hunting us, Freya's response was apparently succinct.

"Get Reya out of prison."

And then, as a final, shimmering garnish of spite, she had added, "And then I would think about helping."

I get it. I really do. Stubbornness must be a witchy superpower, passed down through the bloodline like a genetic curse. But a small, selfish part of me wishes they had at least texted me. *Seriously? Not even a 'hope you aren't dead' emoji?* I really thought we had started to become friends. Or at least, allies who didn't want to incinerate each other on sight.

Then again, there is the issue that my phone was smashed into a thousand pieces of glass and silicon during the battle. They could have texted one of the others or passed on a message through Elijah. I guess it has really only been Reya I have been dealing with, so maybe I was expecting too much from sisters who view me as just another cog in the machine that imprisoned their kin.

It has been three days since I woke up. Three days of Doctor Stevens poking and prodding me, his face a permanent mask of utter bafflement. He is a good man, but he is a man of science, and science is currently screaming in the face of what is happening to my body.

My back, according to his daily scans, still has several cracked vertebrae and deep tissue bruising that should have me bedridden for months. The images on the monitor showed hematomas that looked like dark stormy clouds beneath my skin. But the rest of my injuries are healing at a rate he keeps calling "medically impossible." He watches the purple bruises fade to yellow in a matter of hours. He watches lacerations close without leaving jagged scars, the skin knitting itself back together with an efficiency that defies every textbook he has ever read.

He is desperate for another blood sample, a request I deny with a sweet smile that doesn't quite reach my eyes.

Yeah, Doc, let me just give you a vial of magical-hellfire-daemon-witch-whatever-the-hell-she-is blood. I am sure that won't end up with me or Reya on a dissection table in some black-site lab run by people who make the CIA look like a Sunday school.

Hard pass.

We have stuck to the story that the prime mate bond is accelerating my healing. It is a thin explanation, a flimsy piece of fabric trying to cover a gaping hole in logic, but it is all we have. I refuse to betray Reya. Not after she saved my life. I have kept that particular detail, the part where she literally poured her own blood down my throat while I was dying in the dirt, from everyone. Even Rose.

The secret sits like a lead weight in my gut, cold and heavy. It is a debt I cannot pay, a bond forged in blood and desperation. Whenever I think about it, I can almost taste the metallic tang of her power on my tongue, a ghost of a flavour that makes my heart race.

Two more days of mind-numbing boredom crawl by. The walls are starting to close in. Every time the door opens, I hope it is someone telling me I can leave, but usually, it is just Rose bringing me water or Luca giving me a nod of "Alpha authority" that tells me I am still a patient and not a soldier.

Finally, Doctor Stevens gives me the go-ahead to get out of bed for more than a trip to the bathroom. The news is so good I almost kiss him. The removal of my catheter was a moment of sheer, unadulterated bliss. It was like being released from a very specific, very invasive kind of prison. I had nearly forgotten what it felt like not to have a tube where a tube should not be.

Of course, I haven't forgotten that Luca was the one who told the Doc to leave it in longer just to keep me from trying to escape. He knew my stubbornness would drive me to walk out of here the second I could stand.

Oh, I have plans for you, Alpha. Just you wait. When I can actually walk without wobbling like a newborn giraffe, I am going to make your life a living hell.

I am actually looking forward to returning to a motel room. Any room that doesn't smell of antiseptic and my own slowly healing flesh. I love Rose, I really do, but being stuck in this room with her hovering over me twenty-four seven is starting to make me feel like a bug under a microscope. She watches me breathe. She watches me sleep. I can feel her eyes on me even when I am not looking, a physical heat that makes the hair on my arms stand up. It is an intoxicating feeling, but it is also exhausting.

For only the second time since I woke up, Rose has been prised from my side. Not willingly, of course. Luca had to pull Alpha rank, practically flashing his glowy red eyes at her in a display of dominance that probably would have terrified anyone else. All he wanted her to do was go on patrol with the backup team to ensure the perimeter was secure. You would have thought he had asked her to volunteer for ritual sacrifice.

I, for one, am grateful. I need a minute to just breathe without feeling her desire and protectiveness wrapping around me like a velvet shroud. Sam is off somewhere, still digging into Jason Lorcan's twisted history, his mind probably lost in a labyrinth of encrypted files and redacted reports. Luca is making his daily supply run to our old motel rooms to grab fresh clothes and essentials.

Doctor Stevens had cleared me for a shower, a fact that almost made me weep with joy. His only condition was that Nurse Philips had to stand guard outside the bathroom door. Just in case something goes wrong. Rose, naturally, had insisted that she should be the one to watch over me. That is when Luca had deployed the Alpha glare and sent her packing.

I am glad he did. As much as I know Rose would take full advantage of a shared shower situation. a prospect that is both thrilling and exhausting to contemplate, I just don't have the energy for it right now.

Besides, I still don't feel right. It is a subtle thing, a low-level thrum of wrongness under my skin that I can't explain. It feels like electricity humming in my veins, a vibration that doesn't belong to me. It is as if there is a second heartbeat pulsing somewhere deep in my marrow, out of sync with my own. How could I possibly explain that to anyone without sounding like I have lost my mind?

Nurse Philips breezes into the room, her expression professional but with a familiar glint of mischief in her eyes. She is a sturdy woman with a sharp wit and a way of looking at me that suggests she knows exactly how much I hate being incapacitated.

"Agent Bekke, are you ready to give this a try?"

"What have I told you? Call me Ava," I sigh, the formality grating on my last nerve. It makes me feel like I am back in a briefing room, waiting for an order that will send me into a war zone.

"Agency protocol, Agent," she says, her lips twitching. "Sticking to it is a matter of professional integrity."

"Fine, whatever," I grumble, pushing myself to sit up. The movement sends a sharp spike of pain through my lower back, and I hiss, clutching the sheets as the world tilts for a fraction of a second. "Yeah, I'm ready. It has been a while since I have felt this yucky."

"Well, you had better get your arse out of bed then," she says, her professional mask finally cracking. "We can smell you all the way on the other side of the house."

My jaw drops. I stare at her, utterly speechless. *Excuse me?*

She is trying so hard not to laugh that I can see it in the way the corner of her mouth twitches and her eyes keep darting away. A moment later, she fails, a loud snort escaping her before she doubles over, howling with laughter. The sound is jarring in the quiet room, but it is almost welcome.

I cannot help but shake my head as I swing myself off the side of the bed. My feet hit the cold linoleum, and for a second, the world spins. I test my weight, wobbling for a heartbeat before finding my balance. The weakness in my legs is frustrating, a reminder that no matter how fast I heal, I am still fragile.

I walk past her, patting her on the shoulder with a deadpan expression. "Just wait," I say, my voice flat. "I will get you back. I have started a list."

She sobers up quickly at my comment, wiping a tear from her eye as she follows me to the bathroom.

The shower is short. My body protests every movement, and a wave of dizziness hits me the longer I am on my feet. The heat of the water feels like a miracle, scrubbing away the feeling of sickness and the lingering scent of my injuries. For the first time in days, I feel human again. No longer do I feel like I am growing a new life form in my armpits.

The steam from the shower has filled the small room, turning everything into a white haze that smells of cheap soap and hot minerals, I move over to the mirror. I wipe away the condensation with the palm of my hand to see my reflection for the first time since the fight.

My hand freezes mid-swipe.

I lean closer, my breath fogging the small patch of clear glass. I look... pale. Not the sickly pale of blood loss or hypovolemic shock, but something different. Something translucent, almost luminous, like moonlight hitting polished marble.

And my eyes. They have always been a standard, boring brown, the colour of coffee and earth. But now, they are lighter. There is a gold ring around the pupil, and the iris has shifted to an ash-brown, a shimmering, metallic hue that looks alien in the mirror. My hair, slicked back and wet, looks lighter too, as if the pigment is being bleached out from the inside by some unseen force.

What the hell is happening to me?

Panic flares in my chest, a cold spike of adrenaline. This isn't just healing. This is transformation. I reach up to touch my cheek, and the skin feels different. smoother, tighter, as if it has been reinforced.

"Agent Bekke, are you okay?" Nurse Philips calls from the other side of the door. Her voice sounds distant, as if she is speaking through a wall of water.

"Agent Bekke?"

The door flies open, startling me. I stumble, my balance shot by the sudden noise and the vertigo swirling in my head. My back collides with the wall with a sickening thud, and I slide down to the floor in a heap of limbs and searing pain. The impact jars my spine, and for a moment, the world goes black at the edges, replaced by a chorus of white sparks.

Nurse Philips rushes to my side, her face etched with worry. "Sorry! You didn't respond. I thought you had passed out."

I manage to crack one eye open and glare at her from the floor. My vision is slightly blurry, but she looks genuinely concerned. "That is two places on my revenge list now, Philips. Keep it up."

She cringes, then helps me to my feet and guides me back to the bed. She is gentle, but I can feel her curiosity. She noticed the paleness. She noticed the eyes. She doesn't say anything, but the way she looks at me tells me she knows I am not the same woman who was originally brought into this room.

"I have laid out fresh PJs for you," she says, avoiding my gaze. "I will guard the door while you change."

"Thank you."

Once she is standing with her back to me, I slowly get dressed. The soft cotton of the pyjamas is a relief against my sensitised skin. It feels good to be out of that damned hospital gown, to feel like I am no longer just a patient waiting for a verdict.

"All clear," I call out.

Philips turns around. "Anything you need?"

"A beer would be nice."

"Sorry, no alcohol for now. If there is nothing else, I will let Doctor Stevens know you showered without issue."

"I am all good, thank you."

"See you later." She leaves, and the click of the door closing echoes in the silence.

I lie back against the pillows, my mind racing. Paler skin. Lighter eyes and hair. A strange vibration under my skin. *What is Reya's blood doing to me?* I can feel it shifting things deep inside, rewriting the code of my DNA. Am I becoming something else? Or am I just imagining it because I have been staring at a ceiling for five days? The thought that I might be losing my humanity is terrifying, yet there is a part of me. a dark, hidden part. that feels more alive than I ever have before.

Before I can spiral too far down that particular rabbit hole, the door bursts open again. This time it is Sam, and he looks panicked. His usual G-man neatness is gone, his tie loosened, his face pale and sweating. He is breathing hard, as if he has run a marathon.

"Luca just called," he says, his voice tight and strained. "Our motel rooms have been broken into."

My heart hammers against my ribs. I sit up abruptly, ignoring the protest of my spine. "What! Does he know who is responsible?"

"He said from the smell left behind... it was the demons."

My blood runs cold. The memory of those creatures, flashes through my mind like a nightmare on loop. "Why would the demons target us? It is the Harpers they want."

"I asked the same question," Sam says, pacing the small room, his hands shaking slightly. "He thinks they plan to take us out first, so we cannot help defend the sisters. He said it is what he would do. I think it would be something I would do as well."

"Yeah, it is a sound tactical move," I agree, my mind automatically shifting into combat mode. The boredom vanishes, replaced by a cold, sharp clarity. I begin running through threat assessments in my head, calculating exits and defensive perimeters. "Do you think they will find this place?"

"If they found our motel rooms, I am sure they will find us here," Sam says, and the look on his face tells me he is just as worried as I am. He looks at me, his eyes landing on my frail form in the pyjamas. "And you are the only one with a weapon that can deal with them, and you are still bed-bound."

"I am healing quickly," I say, though the words feel hollow. I look at my pale hands and wonder if they are even capable of holding a gun right now. "I am sure it won't be long until I am back in fighting form. Does Rose know?"

"Luca was going to notify her next, along with Elijah and our backup team commander."

"Great," I mutter, which makes Sam smirk despite the tension. "She is going to be unbearable now. She might even refuse to go on patrol again."

"You might be right," Sam says with a small smile.

"Might be right about what?"

Sam and I both jump at the sound of Rose's voice. She is standing in the doorway, still in her patrol gear, looking from Sam to me. Her green eyes are narrowed, flashing with an intensity that borders on the predatory. She looks dangerous. a weapon wrapped in human skin.

I think fast, noticing how Sam looks like a deer in headlights. "We were just talking about why the demons would come after us instead of the sisters."

"Oh, yeah," she says, walking over to the bed. Her movements are fluid, almost liquid, as she closes the distance between us. She leans down and kisses me, her lips warm and demanding. For a second, the world narrows down to just her scent and the feeling of her skin against mine. The kiss is deep, flavoured with desperation and possessiveness. It is an anchor in the storm.

"Luca and I discussed that as well," she whispers against my lips, her breath hot on my skin. "We need you back in the game, honey, but part of me is worried you will get hurt again as you are not fully healed yet."

"I will get hurt again," I say, the truth of it stark and unavoidable. I pull back slightly to look at her. "It is inevitable going up against paranormal beings when I am only human."

"Well, that doesn't help," Rose says, looking horrified. Her protective instinct is a physical force in the room, thick and heavy, almost like a blanket.

"Even in my old job, it was inevitable I would get hurt, even though I was at the top of my game," I remind her. "Pain is just data, Rose."

"Still doesn't help," she mutters. She reaches out to brush a strand of hair from my forehead, and her fingers linger. I wonder if she can tell. I wonder if she can smell the change in me, or see the gold leaching into my eyes. "Anyway, how did your shower go? Any issues?"

I debate for a split second. But Rose is a shifter. her keen senses would sniff out a lie in a heartbeat. She can hear the skip in my pulse, the hesitation in my breath.

"Went well, but I had to keep it short," I admit. "I started to get a little dizzy."

"Do I need to get the doctor? I will go get the doctor." She is already half-turned toward the door, her movements urgent and protective.

"Why? It was expected. I haven't been on my feet for long since I got hurt."

"Okay," she concedes, though she still looks unconvinced. "I might still ask the Doc when he does his next checks."

"The big question on my mind," I say, changing the subject to steer her away from my health, "is where do we go now? I am almost ready to leave this place."

"When Luca gets back, we will have to discuss it," Rose says. "This place is too small for all of us. We are sitting ducks in a fishbowl."

"I have actually been considering this problem," Sam pipes up, stepping back into the conversation. "While I have been conducting my research, looking for Dhara, I have also been looking into potential new locations we could move to. I am just going over possible vulnerabilities at each location, as I have a few places that might work."

"What and where are these places?" Rose demands, her voice taking on that authoritative edge she uses when she is in Beta mode.

"We can discuss it when Luca gets back," Sam replies firmly. He has grown a backbone since he first saw a shifter change form.

"Fine," is all Rose says, though she looks like she wants to shake the answer out of him.

"Has anyone spoken to Freya or Maya today?" I ask. "To see if they have been attacked?"

"Not as far as I know," Sam says.

Rose adds, "I certainly haven't."

I cannot help myself and say, "Didn't think you would," which earns me a strange, confused look from Rose.

I mean, why would she? She's barely talking to the people who aren't currently licking my wounds.

"Sam, do you mind sending Freya a message, please? Also, do you have my new phone yet?"

"I will check on them," he says. "And I will have your replacement tomorrow. I tried to repair your phone, but there was a crack in the motherboard."

"Thanks for trying."

My stomach chooses that exact moment to let out a roar worthy of Rose's panther form. It is not a normal hunger pang. It is an empty, yawning void that feels like it could swallow the entire room. I feel a sudden, sharp cramp in my abdomen, and I gasp, clutching at my stomach.

"What are we having for dinner? I am starving. And thirsty."

"Since you woke up, you have been constantly hungry and thirsty," Rose observes, her brow furrowing with concern. "Your body clearly needs the fuel for healing."

She is not wrong. It is like there is a furnace inside me, a white-hot engine burning through every calorie I consume, leaving me perpetually wanting more. The hunger is an ache in my bones, a craving that never truly disappears, no matter how much I eat.

But the thirst... the thirst is the weirdest part. It is a deep-seated, primal craving that water barely touches. No matter how many glasses I drink, there is a dryness in my throat that feels like sandpaper, an itch that can't be scratched. A longing for something thicker, something richer.

It has been getting better over the last couple of days, but as the adrenaline of the demon news fades, the thirst returns, pulsing in time with the hum under my skin.

I hope it is just part of the healing process, I think, glancing at Rose's pulse jumping in her neck, the rhythmic throb of blood beneath the surface of her skin. *Because if it isn't... I don't know what I am becoming.*

CHAPTER 6

Death Incarnate

Reya

The transport van lurches violently to a stop. The sudden deceleration sends a bone-jarring jolt through my spine, a sensation so sharp it makes my teeth rattle against one another. It is an ugly, jarring impact that leaves a lingering, metallic tang on the back of my tongue and a dull ache at the base of my skull. Around me, the metal cage vibrates with a harsh, rhythmic clatter. The sound is relentless, echoing through the cramped space like a funeral knell. It feels final. It feels heavy. It feels like the closing of a door on the life I used to know.

The back door swings open with a piercing, high-pitched shriek of protesting metal. Immediately, the dim, suffocating interior is flooded by a sudden, violent beam of daylight. The light isn't warm or welcoming. It is an assault. It hits my eyes like a physical blow, blinding and unapologetic. I instinctively flinch, my muscles recoiling in a defensive reflex that has become second nature to me, and I squeeze my eyes shut so tightly that colourful sparks dance behind my eyelids. I want to hide. I want to crawl into the darkest corner of this steel box and disappear, but there is no darkness left for me to inhabit.

Welcome to your new five-star resort, Reya, I think, my internal voice dripping with a sarcasm so thick it feels like acid. It is a desperate attempt to shield my crumbling composure with a layer of bitter wit. *All-inclusive misery. Complimentary beatdowns included with every stay. Just don't look at the guards or any other inmate the wrong way, and maybe you'll survive until Tuesday.*

As I force myself to stand, the heavy steel cuffs bite into my wrists. The cold metal is a constant, punishing reminder of my new status. Every time I shift my weight, the chains clink together, announcing my presence to the world. It is a sound that says. prisoner. Threat. Monster.

I take my first real look at this place, and the bile rises in my throat. The prison looms over me like a monolithic beast of grey concrete. It is a structure designed specifically to strip the soul from anyone unlucky enough to cross its threshold. Its windows are narrow, barred slits that stare back at me with a vacant, soulless intensity, like eyes watching a slow-motion execution. Against the washed-out, sickly sky, the building stands as a monument to despair. If the exterior is this grim, I can only imagine the carnival of filth and broken spirits festering within these walls.

My mind involuntarily drifts back to the holding cell. I can still feel the suffocating silence of that room where Sheriff Bradshaw played his little games. He had taken every opportunity to gloat as he paced past my bars, his eyes gleaming with a sadistic sort of pleasure that made my skin crawl. Each visit was a twisted reminder of my degradation, a slow, steady erosion of my dignity. An acidic knot twists in my gut, tightening until it feels like my internal organs are being wrung out like wet rags.

Maya. Freya.

I can see them so clearly in my mind's eye. I see Maya's eyes wide and shimmering with unshed tears, her hands trembling as she tries to find peace through a recipe. I see Freya, masking her terror with that sharp, biting sarcasm of hers, standing tall even when her knees are shaking. They are my heart, and right now, my heart is being held hostage by a system that doesn't care if I live or die.

Beastie is strong, but he isn't invincible. We have seen him bleed. The fear that our enemies will see my arrest as a chink in the armour, a weakness to be exploited to get to my sisters, poisons my thoughts. It seeps into my mind like an insidious toxin, turning every shadow into a threat and every silence into a countdown.

The last time Beastie and Pickle managed to sneak in to see me, I had to be the monster. I had to be the wall they could lean on.

'Forget about me,' I told them, my voice sounding hollow even to my own ears. 'Just protect each other.'

They wanted me to fight. They wanted me to use my magic, to glamour myself, to break these chains and run just like we had discussed in those frantic, whispered moments back home when we first read our mother's letter after her funeral. But I shut it down. Hard. My sisters deserve a chance at a life that doesn't involve looking over their shoulders every second of the day. The paranormal dregs of this world already hunt them; they do not need the full weight of the human justice system breathing down their necks, too.

The most agonising part of this confinement, however, isn't the guards or the cage. It is the power.

It churns just beneath my skin like a restless, starving beast, clawing to get out. Since the moment I shifted, since that terrifying instant I realised I was something more than human. something shaped like a goddamn hellhound, my control has been slipping. My emotions are no longer just feelings; they are live wires, electric and unpredictable, surging through my veins with enough voltage to kill. I can feel the raw energy simmering under the surface of my skin, desperate for release. Why now? Why after all these years did this latent, volcanic power decide to wake up just when everything was falling apart?

In the dark moments, when the silence becomes too heavy to bear, despair claws at my heart. It amplifies the shifting energy, making the ripples beneath my skin feel like they might actually tear my flesh asunder.

And then come the memories.

The recollection of Jacob's betrayal hits me with the force of a physical blow. The shadows of that room, the sickening violation that left indelible, jagged scars on my very soul, force my hands to ache with a phantom heat. It feels like hellfire is branding my skin all over again, a searing reminder of the night my world ended.

Then there is him. My father.

The image is etched into my retinas. the way his life drained away in those final seconds, the heroism in his eyes as he shielded me, and then the horror of watching his body turn to luminous, shimmering ash, floating away on a breeze that should not have existed. The memory pierces me with a sharpness so acute it feels like my insides are smouldering. It is a cocktail of fury and sorrow, a fire I can barely contain in a world that has turned its back on me.

I thought maybe, eventually, the rage would fade into something softer. Maybe I would even find room for forgiveness. But the truth is, he died because of the choices our mother made. For twenty-four years, her decisions dictated the trajectory of our lives, and they were all wrong.

She had come to Luna Falls with the intention of sorting out that dilapidated property, a final gesture to leave us something. Instead, she created a catastrophe that is fundamentally unforgivable. She was only a few miles away from him. She possessed magic. a gift that could have pierced through the veils of space and time. She could have felt him. She could have searched for him with a flick of her wrist and pulled him back from the brink of whatever darkness was swallowing him.

Instead, she chose Chicago. She chose her new life. She turned her back on Luna Falls and let him rot in that dark, lonely room, a casualty of her neglect. Now, he is just... gone. There isn't even a ghost left to scream at, no spirit to confront with all the bitterness I have carried for so long.

I can find it in me to consider forgiving him, but her? Never.

Not in a thousand lifetimes. Even if he and Cat used her as collateral damage in their grand, misguided plan to save the world, she still chose herself. The weight of their legacy is a heavy, suffocating shroud, and the scars they left behind are far from healed.

"Move it cop killer."

The words slice through my internal monologue like a serrated blade, sharp and unforgiving. A hard, sudden shove to my back propels me forward, catching me off guard. I stumble, my boots skidding on the pavement as I struggle to find my balance.

The guard's voice drips with an unmistakable contempt, a sound that has become the haunting soundtrack of my existence here. I shuffle my feet, the heavy chains around my ankles clinking together in a morbid, rhythmic cadence that echoes against the cold concrete as I am herded through the sally port and into the sterile, biting chill of the interior building.

A deep, primal fear wraps itself around my gut, heavy and unyielding. I can feel the weight of every eye in this room pressing against me. a thousand silent judgments waiting to pass. They all know. Every inmate peering through a slot, every guard on patrol, will be aware of why I am here.

I didn't kill a cop. I ended the life of a monster, a man whose darkness had seeped into the lives of too many innocent people. But the legal jargon doesn't care about nuance or morality. The paperwork doesn't account for justice. it only sees the title. *Cop killer.*

Some prisoners might see me as a symbol of resistance, perhaps even a hero for doing what was necessary. But it is the guards I truly fear. Their loyalty to their own is a thick, impenetrable brotherhood that brooks no deviation. I can practically taste the hostility in the air, an unspoken tension that makes the hair on my arms stand up. They eye me with a blend of disdain and cautious predatoriness. I swallow hard, my throat feeling like it's lined with sandpaper. I know I have to navigate this landscape with extreme care if I want to survive.

Processing is a monotonous, dehumanising nightmare of institutional grey. The atmosphere is thick with the scent of industrial antiseptic and old, stagnant air. I am led into a stark, dimly lit room where the lights flicker with a nauseating rhythm.

Then comes the search. It is relentless. They strip me of my possessions as if they are stripping me of my humanity. Every movement feels invasive, a psychological assault disguised as procedure. The cold metal of the scanning wand travels over my skin, leaving a trail of goosebumps in its wake. When they apply the chemical delousing spray, the acrid, stinging odour lingers in my nostrils like a ghost of indifference, a sterile reminder that I no longer own even my own skin.

The orange jumpsuit they hand to me is damp and carries the cloying, heavy scent of bleach. It feels like an emblem of defeat, a fabric shroud that clings to my body with a weight that drags at my very spirit. Throughout the ordeal, I am shoved, prodded, and handled as if I were nothing more than an inanimate object. a mere inconvenience in their shift. The names they hurl at me are sharp jabs, intended to humiliate, to diminish who I am until there is nothing left but a prisoner.

I keep my gaze fixed firmly on the floor. The cold tiles beneath my feet mirror the desolation inside my chest. I maintain my expression. stoic, professional, a carefully crafted mask designed to conceal the boiling rage that threatens to erupt from my marrow.

If they could see it, I think bitterly, *if they could feel the storm brewing inside me, they wouldn't be so damn casual.*

But vulnerability is a luxury I cannot afford in a place like this. So, I bury it. I twist my emotions into knots so tight and so deep that they feel as if they might snap at any moment. *Not here,* I tell myself, the command a mantra against the dark. *Not now.*

Finally, I am led down an echoing corridor where the air turns frigid, wrapping around me like a damp, heavy blanket. The sensory assault of the prison is overwhelming. the pungent, metallic tang of unwashed bodies, the sour scent of stale sweat, and an overarching aura of despair that seems to have seeped into the very concrete walls.

"Open cell four," the guard barks. Her voice is flat, devoid of any human interest, as if she is merely operating a piece of heavy machinery.

With a loud, mechanical clank followed by the grinding whirr of rusted gears, the heavy metal door slides open with a low groan, revealing the cramped quarters inside. I brace myself, my heart hammering against my ribs like a trapped bird, preparing for whatever fresh hell awaits.

When I finally lift my gaze, the cell is exactly what I expected. a dreary concrete box furnished only by a grimy toilet, a stained sink, and a set of narrow, cramped bunk beds. The atmosphere is heavy with an oppressive sense of hopelessness. It feels like a place where dreams go to die.

As I step inside, my brain struggles to process the math of the room. Two beds. Three women.

Unless someone is sleeping on the floor, the numbers don't add up.

One woman occupies a small, plastic chair in the corner. Her arms are crossed tightly over her chest, and her dark, shrewd eyes assess me with a piercing mix of curiosity and caution. She is sizing me up, calculating my threat level before I even have a chance to speak. The other two women are perched on the lower bunk; their faces display a bizarre blend of shock and something that looks suspiciously like amusement. It sends an uneasy twist through my stomach.

I turn back to the guard, Maggie, noting the way her name tag flaps in the dim light of the hallway. "Are you sure this is the right cell?" I ask, my voice betraying a hint of uncertainty.

"It's the right cell. Get in," she barks, her tone leaving absolutely no room for debate. "Su Ling will give you the rundown on how things work around here."

The woman in the corner must be Su Ling. As she rises from her chair, I am struck by an unexpected elegance that seems to defy the harshness of this environment. There is an undeniable air of control about her, a sense that she has mastered the art of self-preservation in a world that demands constant vigilance. Her movements are fluid, reminding me of a coiled spring. beautiful, yet ready to release with lethal intent. I cannot shake the feeling that there is something extraordinary hidden beneath her calm exterior.

"Sure, I can do that," Su Ling says, her eyes never leaving mine as she studies me. "What's she in for, Maggie?"

"Killed a cop," Maggie replies flatly.

The words strike me like a physical blow to the solar plexus. I see Su Ling's eyebrows shoot up in genuine alarm.

"Seriously? And you're putting her in with me?" Su Ling exclaims, her voice laced with disbelief. Behind her calm demeanour, I sense a flicker of something dangerous, something primal.

"She's with you until her court date," Maggie retorts, her eyes narrowing.

"Great," Su Ling mutters under her breath, a hint of sarcasm mingling with what looks like genuine concern. Before I can respond, another shove from Maggie sends me stumbling into the cramped cell.

This is the third cage I have been shoved into in a very short span of time. The novelty has long since worn off, replaced by an unsettling, heavy sense of foreboding. I lurch forward, my hands instinctively shooting out to catch the edge of the bunk bed. The metal frame is biting and cold beneath my palms.

As I steady myself, I hear a snicker from the two women on the mattress. They sit with their backs against the wall, their legs dangling lazily from the side of the bed, their eyes glinting with mockery at my clumsiness. I open my mouth to demand where I am supposed to sleep, but the cell door slides shut with a deafening, final clang.

Maggie is already striding away, her heavy footsteps fading into the distance of the corridor.

I turn back to face my new cellmates, a cocktail of apprehension and curiosity swirling in my chest. "Hey. I'm Reya," I say, my voice barely rising above the low, rhythmic hum of the flickering fluorescent lights overhead.

Su Ling is the first to react. Her expression turns flat as she studies me with an intensity that feels like a pickaxe digging into my skin. "Welcome," she says, her tone dripping with venomous sarcasm. "You know your time here is going to be hell, don't you?"

"Yeah," I sigh, letting the weight of the situation settle deep into my bones. My shoulders slump forward. "I'm starting to get that."

The other two women remain silent. Their gazes are locked onto me like predatory cats sizing up a piece of meat. I nod toward them, desperate for even a shred of normalcy or camaraderie. "Who are your friends?"

The question hangs in the air, thick and heavy with tension. Su Ling shoots me a look that mixes pity with genuine concern, her brow furrowing as the women on the bed exchange glances filled with disbelief.

"Please don't tell me you're crazy, too," Su Ling says, shaking her head in exasperation. "I guess it explains why you'd kill a cop."

"I'm not crazy!" I snap, my patience fraying like an old, weathered rope. "And he was a monster. I am not sorry he's dead. Now, who are they? How can four of us fit in a cell with only two beds?"

I look back at the women huddled on the bunk, waiting for an answer, but as I focus my vision, a cold dread creeps up my spine like a sheet of ice.

My stomach drops. *Oh, hell.*

The dim light from the hallway passes directly through them. Their forms shimmer at the edges, blurring into the air like a mirage in the desert heat.

Oh, gods. They aren't solid. They're... fucking ghosts.

"What the hell are you talking about?" Su Ling demands, standing abruptly just after she had decided to sit back down as if trying to put distance between us.

"She can see us," one of the ghosts whispers. Her voice is a faint, hollow rustle, like dry leaves skittering across a sidewalk in autumn.

"It does seem that way," the other ghost agrees, her tone laced with a profound, ethereal disbelief. "But that's impossible."

I stare at them, my mouth suddenly bone-dry. *Great. Just great. My new cellmates are dead. At least they probably don't snore,* I think bitterly, trying to use sarcasm to stave off the rising panic.

Su Ling throws her hands up in frustration. "There is no one else in this room! This isn't fair. I don't deserve to be locked up with a crazy bitch!"

"Language, Su Ling. I never taught you to speak to others that way," the first ghost scolds. Her voice carries a certain motherly firmness that strikes a chord of recognition in me.

Su Ling glares at me, her eyes narrowing with suspicion. "Don't get comfortable. I'm requesting a transfer as soon as possible. Also. the top bunk is mine."

"That's fine," I mutter, my eyes still captivated by the ethereal presence of the ghosts as they float, not sit, but float on the bottom bunk.

"Hey!" The mother-ghost snaps, her voice suddenly sharp enough to cut through the tension in the room. She leans toward me, her eyes burning with a protective instinct that resonates deeply within my own chest. "Hey! I'm talking to you. If you can see us, then what are you? If you hurt my daughter, I will find a way to hurt you back!"

I can't help it. The words slip out of me in a low whisper. "I have no intention of hurting your daughter."

"Good," comes the terse reply.

"Who are you talking to?" Su Ling's voice is sharp, slicing through my thoughts.

"Just talking to myself. Don't worry about it," I say, trying to sound casual, but the words feel like lead in my mouth.

"Oh, I'm worrying." The edge in her tone heightens my anxiety.

The mother then says in a soft, pleading whisper, a sound that seems to cling to the very edges of my mind. "Please, can you tell my daughter I'm here? That we're proud of her for keeping herself safe from the attacks. I worried so much when our pack was attacked; she was so young."

Pack? My thoughts race. The implication settles in my gut like a stone. Su Ling is a shifter. What kind? A wolf? My hand tightens into a fist, a visceral reaction to the ghost's plea. *She better not be a wolf.* I shake my head slightly, a silent "no" against the mother's haunting request.

I am standing there like an idiot, caught in an invisible web of uncertainty. Su Ling has the only chair, her ghostly mother and their friend are hovering on the lower bunk, while the top bunk remains claimed. Just as I consider curling up on the cold, hard floor, the entire atmosphere of the cell shifts.

Suddenly, the air turns frigid. It isn't just a chill; it is a biting, slicing frost that seeps into my skin and twists my stomach into knots. The shadows in the far corner of the room begin to deepen, twisting and unfurling like dark, oily tendrils reaching out from the concrete. My breath catches in my throat.

A figure begins to coalesce from the darkness. It is a silhouette of pure night, a void that seems to absorb the very light from the hallway. It mirrors my own form with an unsettling, terrifying precision. Then, two points of light ignite within that shadowy shape. piercing, glowing red eyes that seem to bore directly into my soul.

Tension crackles in the air, electric and heavy. I realise with a jolt of terror that this is no figment of my imagination.

For one fleeting second, I thought it might be Sera, coming to check on me. But this is different. This feels ancient. This feels hungry.

"What the hell is that?" the second ghost whispers, her voice trembling with a fear she can no longer hide.

Su Ling jumps up from her chair, her eyes wide with a terror that mirrors my own surprise. She lets out a low, guttural sound. a half-growl of pure, primal fear. "What's going on?" she demands, her voice shaking as she instinctively backs toward me.

"You can see that too?" I ask, stunned.

"Yeah, I can see it!"

"I didn't think shifters could see much of the paranormal world," I blurt out, the words tumbling from my lips before I can rein them in.

Su Ling's head jerks toward me, her eyes widening in a mix of fear and suspicion. Her posture shifts, her body instinctively drawing back as if she is bracing for an unseen threat.

From the corner of my vision, I catch a glimpse of the mother's spirit, shimmering faintly. "We are Kitsune shifters," she says, her voice echoing like a whisper carried on a winter wind. "Some members of our pack possess the gift of sight. It is why I came here. I hoped my daughter might be able to see me, to connect across this vast divide. So far... she doesn't seem to be able to."

The room feels charged, the silence heavy with unfulfilled hopes.

I answer her without thinking, my eyes locked on the red glow in the corner. "That means this shade is letting her see them."

"A shade?" Su Ling echoes, her voice barely a breath. "What's a shade?"

"A shade is a type of demon spirit," I say, my voice steady despite the way my heart is trying to kick its way out of my ribs. My eyes are fixed on that red luminescence that pierces the encroaching dark. "And I think... I think it's here for me."

As I finish speaking, the temperature in the cell plummets even further. A chilling wave sweeps through me, twisting my insides into knots. I can see the vapour of my own breath misting in front of my face, swirling like tiny ghosts in the dim light.

The shadow that had merely been dancing on the walls begins to solidify. It transforms into a three-dimensional being of writhing, liquid darkness. It steps forward silently, its creeping presence an unsettling contrast to the stillness of the cell.

Su Ling, her instincts sharp and primal, lets out a low, choked growl. She drops into a defensive crouch, her muscles coiling with lethal tension. “Stay back!” she snarls, her voice fierce. For a terrifying second, I witness a transformation. the tips of her nails elongate, sharpening into vicious claws that glint menacingly in the light.

Adrenaline floods my system, a hot, rushing tide. My heart races under the weight of everything. the ghosts, the visceral terror, and now this thing. It all crashes over me in a chaotic symphony of fear.

As the shadows thicken and begin to consume the room, my anger ignites. It isn’t just a feeling; it is a wildfire spreading through my veins. Su Ling shoots a terrified glance in my direction, her eyes wide with a fear that baffles me. Every instinct in her body urges her to retreat, and she stumbles back, struggling to escape the corner.

It makes no sense. Why is she so frightened of *me* when there is a shade standing right here, poised to attack?

I take a moment to survey our surroundings, trying to find a way to fight, and that is when the shocking truth hits me like a physical blow.

The pervasive darkness encroaching upon us isn’t just a natural occurrence. It isn’t coming from the corner.

It is emanating from *me*.

Tendrils of shadow reach out from my own form, swirling and expanding, claiming the room and blurring the very edges of reality. The atmosphere grows thick and oppressive, each breath becoming heavier as the darkness tightens its grip on the air itself. I realise with a sickening jolt that I am not just a bystander in this nightmare.

I am the source.

“Stay away from my daughter! You can’t have her!” Su Ling’s mother screams, her voice piercing through my thoughts. She positions herself between me and Su Ling, her eyes churning with frantic terror. “Su Ling, get away from her! She is death incarnate; she will take your soul!”

What are you talking about? I’m not death! My heart hammers against my ribs. While I can't ignore the unsettling darkness unspooling from my skin, I know I have no desire to hurt anyone.

But as I start to process her wild accusations, something else catches my eye. In the corner of the room, the shadow begins to shift and glide toward me. My breath hitches as I realise it isn't just one thing. More phantoms are emerging from the dim corners, each one seemingly drawn to my lightless energy. They are all heading straight for me.

CHAPTER 7

The Devouring Dark

The emotional whiplash isn't just hitting me. It is tearing me apart, limb by limb, until there is nothing left but a collection of raw nerves and jagged memories.

The last few hours have been a blur of impossible horrors, a frantic descent into a reality I never asked to inhabit. The shock of the ghosts, the cold, crushing weight of my imprisonment, the sheer, unadulterated absurdity of it all. it crashes over me in a singular, devastating wave. It's not a gentle tide. It is a tsunami of grief and confusion that threatens to pull me under into a dark, silent abyss where I might never surface again.

My vision swims. The edges of my sight begin to fray, pulsing with a rhythmic, Publishednauseating static that makes the world tilt on its axis. Every time I blink, the darkness seems to press closer against my retinas, heavy and thick like velvet soaked in oil.

Please, just let me go under, I think, a desperate, silent plea echoing through the hollow chambers of my mind. *Just five minutes of nothingness. No ghosts, no cells, no gods. Just... silence. Is that too much to ask? God, I'd kill for a bed that doesn't smell like antiseptic and failure.*

I try to steady my breathing, but it comes out in shallow, ragged hitches. My lungs feel tight, as if the very air in this cell has grown heavy, saturated with the scent of old copper and damp concrete.

The shadowy figures in the corner are not receding. They aren't fading into the periphery of my consciousness like a hallucination born of exhaustion and trauma. They are advancing. Every time I blink, they have reclaimed more territory from the dim light. The thought that this might be Sera—that she has finally tracked me down to deliver some final, soul-shattering judgment—vanishes as a new sensation takes hold.

A jolt of pure, undiluted malice hits me. It isn't just a feeling; it is a psychic assault that slams into my solar plexus, knocking the breath from my lungs.

The sensations radiate from those growing pockets of darkness. a hatred so ancient and jagged it feels as if it could cut skin, while their red eyes seem to bore into me.

Then comes the cold.

It isn't the refreshing chill of a Chicago winter or the hollow void of an empty room. This is the bone-deep, marrow-freezing chill of the grave. It's a predatory, hungry cold that doesn't just touch my skin; it sinks through my pores, past the muscle, and settles deep into my very essence. It feels like something is reaching inside me, clawing at my heart, trying to snuff out the tiny, flickering spark of life I have left.

Not Sera, I repeat to myself, the thought a frantic, rhythmic mantra behind my teeth.

The realisation that I am trapped in this cramped, wretched cage with an innocent girl, *well,* maybe not so innocent if she's in this place, slaps me across the face like a bucket of ice water. The sheer vulnerability of her presence, the way she stands there paralysed by terror, vaporises my exhaustion.

Adrenaline, sharp and electric, floods my system. It's a frantic, jagged surge that forces my heart to hammer against my ribs like a trapped bird. The world snaps into a terrifying, hyper-focused clarity. The darkness that had been encroaching on my vision recedes, replaced by a predatory sharpness.

I clench my fists, the grit of the concrete floor biting into my palms. Every muscle in my body coils, turning from leaden exhaustion to high-tension steel. Deep in my marrow, I can feel it. the fire. It's simmering, a low, volcanic heat that responds to my sudden, desperate need for survival.

The shades lunge.

There is no time for a tactical assessment. There is no room for a battle plan. There is only instinct—raw, primal, and utterly deafening.

I didn't ask for this, I think bitterly, even as my body moves with a lethal, practised grace that feels entirely foreign to the woman I thought I was yesterday. *But if the universe wants a fight, it's damn well going to get one.*

Su Ling is still frozen where she stands. She is a deer caught in the high beams of a speeding truck, her eyes wide and glassy with a terror so profound it has rendered her motionless. Beside her, the ethereal form of her mother is screaming, a frantic, silent movement of lips and desperate gestures that should be impossible to see, yet I feel the weight of her panic like a physical pressure in the air.

"Get back and stay down!" I snarl.

The words are raspy, sounding more like a command from a commanding officer than a girl trapped in a cell, but they carry the weight of absolute authority. I launch myself forward, my boots skidding slightly on the grime-slicked floor, and grab the back of Su Ling's clothes. I yank her backwards with a strength born of pure desperation, shoving her behind the meagre cover of my own body.

I am the shield. If they want her, they have to go through me first.

The shades are on me in a heartbeat. They move with an unnatural, gliding speed, their shadowy limbs stretching out like ink spilled across parchment. Their claws—if you can even call them that—reach for my throat, looking like blackened talons carved from the void itself.

I don't think; I react. I lash out with my leg, swinging my foot in a desperate, heavy arc. My foot connects squarely with something that feels like a chest, and the impact sends a shockwave up my leg that surprises me.

What the hell? I thought they were smoke!

It isn't like hitting air. It's like kicking a heavy, freezing sack of wet sand. There is a solid, sickening thud, followed by a wave of nauseating cold that shoots up my leg, making my teeth chatter and my vision blur for a split second. The shade stumbles back, its form flickering violently, like a dying candle flame caught in a draft.

With horrifying, boneless fluidity, the other shades begin to peel themselves away from the shadows. One unspools from beneath the lower bunk, a viscous movement that makes my skin crawl. Another oozes from the corner behind the toilet, a slow, creeping darkness that feels like it's swallowing the light itself.

They have no features, no faces, just humanoid silhouettes of deeper darkness. Their eyes—those hateful, blood-red lights—burn with a singular, focused malice.

My heart is hammering so hard against my ribs I can feel it in my throat. *Three... four... five.* The cell, which already felt claustrophobic, suddenly feels like it's shrinking, the walls closing in as the air grows thick and heavy, tasting of ozone and old copper.

I thrust my hands out, reaching for that well of power in the library of my mind. I reach for the fire, the heat, anything to push them back. But the balls of fire I normally see in that place in my mind are gone. Well, there is a slight flame still burning, and I can feel something is changing in that place in my mind.

I try everything. *Come on! Give me something! A spark, a flame, a damn explosion!*

Nothing.

A hollow, terrifying emptiness greets my call. My magic feels locked away, stifled by an invisible, suffocating weight. *Is it because of Su Ling? Am I holding back because I'm afraid of burning her?* The thought is a physical ache in my chest. Is my fear acting like a magical straitjacket, strangling my power before it can even reach the surface. Or maybe... maybe I'm just empty. Maybe the battle with Jacob took every last drop of juice I had left.

The shades realise my hesitation. They see the gap in my defences, and they converge.

I dodge, twisting my body with a frantic energy to avoid a sweeping strike that passes so close I feel the frost of its passage raising the hair on my arms. A few blows find their mark. A shadowy claw rakes across my forearm, and I wince as the skin breaks. It doesn't bleed like a normal cut; it feels like the cold itself is being carved into my flesh, leaving a trail of stinging, freezing fire in its wake.

I duck under another swipe, the air whistling above my head, and drive my right fist into the midsection of one of the silhouettes. The impact is jarring, sending a vibration through my bones that makes my brain feel like it's bruising against my skull. My knuckles connect with something that is both solid and ethereal, and a wave of nauseating cold shoots up my arm, turning my limb numb and useless for a terrifying second.

The shade lets out a silent scream—a psychic shriek that vibrates in my very marrow—and its form flickers violently before it stumbles back.

I can hit them. I can actually hurt them. The realisation is a small, flickering light in the dark.

Another one lunges from my flank. I pivot sharply, using the cold metal frame of the bunk bed as a brace to swing myself around. I slam my elbow into its head with everything I have. The entity dissipates slightly, turning into a cloud of dark smoke before reforming, its red eyes burning with renewed hatred. They are hard to damage. Harder to kill.

Don't make noise. The professional part of my brain screams through the fog of panic. If the guards hear us, this whole prison could be in danger. Keep it quiet.

Two more shades descend simultaneously. I drop low, rolling under their synchronised attack with a practised grace that feels entirely alien to me. I come up behind them, my fingers curling into claws of my own. I grab the back of one's head and slam it down against the metal frame of the bunk.

The impact is silent. No thud, no clatter. Just the sickening sensation of shadow meeting steel. The thing writhes in my grip, a boneless mess of darkness, and I use its momentum to shove it into its companion, sending them both stumbling into each other.

"Stop toying with them," Su Ling's mother whispers.

Her voice is a trembling thread of sound, ethereal yet heavy with an ancient dread. "You are death. Just absorb them and get it over with."

I freeze for a fraction of a second, the words ringing in my head like a funeral bell. *Death? Why does everyone keep calling me that? I'm just trying to survive the night without dying myself.*

I think back to the attack outside our house—the way I had connected to those shades and torn them apart from the inside out. I wonder if I can do it again, but the concentration required feels impossible right now. My mind is a shattered mirror of panic and pain.

But wait. If I can touch them... if they are physical enough to kick and punch... maybe I don't need a torrent of fire. Maybe I just need to hold on.

I reach out, my hand trembling with the effort of staying steady, and grab one of the shades by its shoulder. The entity lets out a shriek—not a sound, but a vibration that rattles my teeth and makes my vision swim. Its arm dissolves into smoke, but then, something impossible happens. The smoke doesn't dissipate into the air. It moves toward me. It drifts toward my skin and vanishes into my pores before my eyes can even register the movement.

An energy washes over me. It's subtle at first, like a sudden, sharp jolt of caffeine hitting an empty stomach after a sleepless night.

Then, the pain hits.

A surge of cold fire tears through the fabric of my orange jumpsuit, raking across my side like a serrated blade. I cry out, the sound dying in my throat as I stumble back, clutching my ribs. The sensation is agonising—a searing, freezing heat that makes my breath hitch in a pained gasp.

I look down, and the sight makes my heart stop. Blood, warm and sickeningly slick, is already seeping through the coarse material of the jumpsuit.

"Get off her!"

The shout rips through the cell, shattering the silence like a hammer to glass. Su Ling has finally broken free from her paralysis. Her face is no longer pale with fear; it is a mask of primal, predatory fury that I have only ever seen in mirrors during my darkest moments.

As I watch, her hands transform. They are no longer human. Her fingers have elongated, tipped with long, wicked-looking claws that are dark and sharp enough to catch the dim light. With a snarl that sounds more animal than girl, she launches herself at the shade that wounded me.

She is a whirlwind of shifter rage. She tears into the shadowy form, her claws shredding the darkness like black silk under an assault of steel. The shade lets out another one of those silent, agonising screams as it struggles to reform, but Su Ling gives it no quarter.

How? I wonder, my mind reeling through the pain in my side. *How can she see them? How can she touch them? Rose couldn't even see these things.*

The other shades realise she is a threat and begin to converge on her. I press my hand against the wound in my side, trying to stem the flow of blood, my mind racing through a thousand terrifying possibilities.

Then, it happens.

A surge of energy washes over my body, but it isn't like the last one. This is deeper. It's fuelled by the white-hot agony in my side and the mounting rage in my chest. It feels... different. It doesn't feel like my own anger. It feels like something deep within me reacting to the threat, a dormant part of me waking with a violent, volcanic roar, as it has before, and I am still clueless about what it is.

My power. It's not just fire. It's something more.

The memories rush in—Jacob's face, my father's death, the suffocating helplessness of being a child watching the world end. I don't push them away this time. I let them in. I wrap them around the pain and the fear until they become a cold, controlled inferno. I need an edge. I need to end this before I bleed out on this filthy floor.

One of the shades disengages from Su Ling, sensing that I am the more vulnerable target. It sees me as the prize. It lunges, its movements confident, its red eyes glowing with a smug, predatory light.

I don't meet its charge with a punch. I meet it with an open palm.

I focus every ounce of that icy rage, every scrap of my desperate, dying will, into a single point at the centre of my hand. I am not trying to call forth a storm. I am trying to summon a single, defiant spark.

Burn.

A tiny, almost imperceptible spark of black fire ignites on my palm at the exact microsecond of impact. It isn't a flame; it's more like a concentrated needle of darkness and heat.

The effect is devastating.

The shade shrieks—a sound that is both silent and deafening, exploding inside my skull—and then it implodes. It collapses inward, turning into a pile of fine, greasy dust that coats the floor.

The other shades recoil. I can see it in the way they drift back, their burning eyes widening in what looks suspiciously like genuine shock. They weren't expecting that, neither was I.

Su Ling capitalises on their hesitation. She spins with lethal grace, her claws becoming a blur of motion as she disembowels another shade. It shreds apart, its amber eyes flickering out like dying embers in a drafty room.

I don't give them a chance to recover. I launch myself into the fray, moving through the shadows with a newfound, frantic energy. I strike, I push, and I destroy. One by one, they fall. The last shade looks from me to Su Ling, then back again. I can feel its panic—a cold, fluttering sensation in the air.

It makes a desperate break for the wall, trying to melt back into the shadows of the corner.

"Oh no you don't," I grit out through clenched teeth.

I throw myself forward, tackling the entity around its non-existent waist. We crash to the concrete floor with a heavy impact. It is so cold—a freezing, soul-sucking chill that makes my muscles seize. It thrashes beneath me, its claws scraping against the floor inches from my face. I can't get a grip. I can't summon another spark.

But as it struggles, it starts to change. Instead of fighting me, it begins to melt. The darkness flows into me, seeping through my skin like liquid shadow. Within seconds, the shade is gone.

And with it comes another hit of energy—a dark, heavy rush that settles in my gut like lead.

I push myself up onto my feet, my breath coming in ragged, shallow gasps. For now, the fight is over.

Silence descends on the cell, thick and oppressive. The only sound is our laboured breathing. The bone-deep chill begins to recede, leaving behind nothing but a clammy, uncomfortable coldness on my skin. I look at Su Ling. Her claws are still extended, her chest heaving with exertion. We are both covered in minor cuts, sweat, and the disgusting, oily dust of the shades.

The adrenaline finally fades, and the pain in my side returns with a vengeance, more intense than before. Despite the boost of energy I just received, exhaustion hits me like a physical blow. My knees buckle, and I slump against the metal bunk, my entire body trembling uncontrollably.

What was that? Did I... did I really just absorb it? Is that thing inside me now? The thought is terrifying, but I don't have the strength to process it.

We won. But as I look at Su Ling and the dissipating wisps of darkness, a sickening realisation takes root in my mind. This cell isn't a prison meant to keep us in. It's a hunting ground.

And we are nothing but bait.

They are going to keep coming. And eventually, Su Ling is going to get caught in the crossfire. She might even die because of me. The weight of that realisation is heavier than any physical wound. *I'm the reason my sisters are in danger. I'm the reason this girl is being hunted. I am the centre of the storm.*

Before I can even attempt to form a plan, a new darkness begins to coalesce on the opposite side of the cell. A thick, oily black cloud starts to swirl and thicken. Su Ling and I scramble backwards until our backs are pressed hard against the cold metal bars of the door.

Then, I hear it. Muffled shouting from the corridor. The fight hasn't gone unnoticed. The guards will be here any second.

"What is happening now?" Su Ling asks, her voice small and trembling with pure terror.

Su Ling's mother glides closer to us. As she moves through the dim light, her ethereal presence brushes against my arm. In that fleeting contact, a jolt of energy surges through me—a fragile, golden thread that seems to bind us together.

As she touches me, her form solidifies. She is no longer just a shadow; she has weight, colour, and a presence that commands the space.

An astonished gasp escapes Su Ling's lips. "Mother... oh mother, you were right! I can see you! But how? How is this possible?"

"Your new cellmate made me stronger when she touched me," the woman replies. Her voice is a mixture of warmth and profound disbelief.

I stare at her, stunned. *Me? I'm making ghosts solid? What kind of monster am I becoming?*

We don't have time to ponder the implications. Two colossal figures emerge from the swirling black clouds looming in front of us. They are massive, their dark bodies blotting out what little light remained in the cell. Their presence is suffocating, filling the cramped space with an aura of ancient, overwhelming power. A chill runs down my spine, and my first instinct is to reach for my magic.

But when I try to summon it, there is nothing but a hollow ache. I am too drained. Too broken.

I look at the giants. Their eyes are fixed on us, filled with a twisted, sadistic enjoyment. They aren't here to guard us; they are here to savour the chaos. My heart hammers against my ribs, but as I look at Su Ling—at her terrified, wide eyes—a strange calm settles over me.

I won't let them hurt her. Not like this.

I raise my gaze to meet their malevolent stares. I find my voice, steady and laced with a sharp, jagged defiance.

"I surrender," I declare. A small, bitter smirk tugs at the corners of my mouth. If they want a villain, I'll give them one. "Take me to your leader. I'm the one who stole the hellhound, and I'm ready to face my punishment."

The silence that follows is deafening. I expect a blow, a snarl, or perhaps a laugh. Instead, they move with cruel, efficient precision. Large, dark hands seize my arms, pulling me toward the thick black cloud hovering behind them.

"NOOO!"

Su Ling's scream rips through the air, echoing in my mind as I am dragged away from her, pulled headfirst into the suffocating darkness.

CHAPTER 8

The Severed Thread

Ava

The kitchen air hangs heavily, thick enough to choke on, infused with the acrid, stinging scent of stale coffee that clings to the walls and our clothes like a physical weight. It is a smell that has become all too familiar over the last few days, mingling unpleasantly with the gnawing, hollow dread that has been my constant companion for the last week. Every breath I take feels filtered through a layer of grime and desperation.

Sam is hunched over his laptop at the small, battered dinette table. The worn wood creaks under the heavy pressure of his unease, sounding like a dying animal every time he shifts his weight. His fingers move in a frantic, blurred rhythm against the keys, each stroke laced with a desperate urgency as he meticulously scrubs through the motel's grainy, flickering CCTV footage and the surrounding perimeter. The blue glow of the screen bathes his face in an eerie, ghostly light, illuminating the deep, jagged lines etched across his forehead. Those are lines that tell stories of sleepless nights, caffeine-fuelled vigils, and an unrelenting worry that he tries to mask with professional detachment.

Around us, the dim kitchen feels claustrophobic, the walls

closing in with every tick of the clock. The flickering fluorescent bulb overhead casts erratic, twitching shadows that dance like spectres along the peeling wallpaper, making it feel as though we aren't alone in the room.

On top of the high-stakes task of ensuring the world doesn't obtain any footage of the monsters we hunt, he is still hunting for any sign of Dhara. We need her. Without her, getting Reya out of prison is a mountain we aren't equipped to climb, a vertical cliff face with no handholds and a long way down.

Luca is a looming, predatory shadow against the counter. His massive arms are crossed over a chest that looks as though it were carved from solid granite, but it's the aura he's radiating that's the real problem. He isn't just angry; he is vibrating with pure, undiluted fury. It is a physical weight in the room, a heavy, oppressive thundercloud waiting for the lightning to strike. I can almost see the static electricity crackling off his skin, smelling faintly of ozone and old forests.

The news he brought back was just the bitter cherry on top of this disaster sundae. Someone broke into our rooms while we slept. And the smell they left behind? Sulphur. The pungent, rotten-egg stench of hell itself, a scent that lingers in the nostrils long after the air has cleared.

Great. Because regular burglars were just too boring for our lives. Why settle for a stolen wallet when you can have a demonic home invasion?

I find myself squeezed between Sam and Rose at the kitchen table, a welcome change from the agonising confinement of my bed. With the chance to escape those same four monotonous, white-washed walls, I leapt at the opportunity like a starving woman. My bedroom had become a cell, a place where the silence was too loud and the memories were too vivid.

Rose's hand envelops mine, her grip acting as a solid, warm anchor in the storm. Her skin is hot, almost searing, a reminder of the predator that lives beneath the surface. She hasn't left my side since that harrowing, blood-soaked night when I was brought here, teetering on the razor's edge of death. The memory of the fight at the Harpers plays in my mind like a nightmarish, visceral fever dream. I can still hear the sickening sound of breaking bone, taste the metallic tang of copper on my tongue, and feel the sensation of my life ebbing away with every shallow, rattling breath.

Though I'm awake now, that phantom ache lingers deep in my bones. It is a constant reminder of the epic, soul-crushing battle I've just endured. I am utterly, bone-deep drained. Every muscle in my body feels as though it has been shredded and sewn back together with rusty wire. Had I not been lost in a thick, suffocating haze of fog, which they dare to call sleep, I'd be searching for the softest bed imaginable, eager to sink into its depths and sleep for an eternity.

Rose's pulse thrums against mine, a strong, rhythmic beat that echoes with an undercurrent of raw, unmasked fear. She hasn't left me all week, clinging to me as if I'm a fragile, guttering candle in a violent gust of wind, convinced that if she lets go for even a second, I'll either spontaneously combust or simply drop dead.

I love her, but god, the hovering is exhausting.

I'd almost find the gesture sweet, if it weren't for the soul-crushing exhaustion that comes from being treated like porcelain, a delicate, precious object that might shatter at the slightest touch. I am a soldier. I am a Captain. Being handled with kid gloves feels more insulting than the injuries themselves.

When we entered the kitchen earlier and settled into our seats, I caught the intense, starving look in her eyes. It was a silent, desperate plea for closeness, a desire to pull me into her lap and shield me from the world. I had beaten her to the chair, but she nonetheless dragged hers so close that our legs are almost melded together. Our heat merges in the cramped space, the friction of her denim against my pyjama bottoms creating a spark of intimacy that distracts me from the pain in my ribs.

Beneath her protective exterior, I can feel her vibrating with a low-frequency hum of anger and frustration. It isn't aimed at me, nor even at Reya. It's directed solely at the demons, those lurking, shadowy threats that seem to hover just beyond our line of sight, mocking us with their invisibility.

"We need to take care of these things," Rose says. Her voice is tight enough to snap, brimming with a desperate urgency. There is a growl hidden in the depths of her tone, the sound of a panther who has been teased for too long.

While we sit here discussing our survival, Rose's need to be physically fused to me is starting to grate on my nerves. I can feel the warmth of her thigh pressing firmly into mine, her scent, something like rain-drenched earth and wild musk, filling my lungs. It is intoxicating, but it is also suffocating. I'm wondering if being back in that bed, which was barely big enough for one person, might actually be the better option right now. At least there, I could breathe without feeling her heartbeat drumming against my own.

Luca's voice cuts through the tension like a low, menacing rumble of thunder. "And how do we do that? Unless they possess someone, we can't see them. We can't touch them."

He pauses, his gaze darting to me. The look is silent yet loaded with heavy, dark implications. It is a look that says *you are broken* without needing to utter a single word.

"Ava is the only one who can, and she's..."

I can feel the weight of his unfinished thought hanging in the air like a shroud. *Not in a position to take them on,* I complete in my mind.

Thanks for the vote of confidence, big guy. I'll be sure to add that to my list of achievements.

I know I don't possess the strength they expect from me right now. All I feel is the crippling, heavy weight of my own limitations. My body feels like a stranger to me, a clumsy vessel that refuses to obey the commands of my mind. The frustration is a bitter pill, coating my tongue in acid.

"We have to do something!" Rose snaps, her frustration finally boiling over. She shifts violently, her chair scraping against the floor with a jarring screech. "I'm done feeling like a caged animal in this house!"

I squeeze her hand, trying to inject some reassurance I don't actually feel. My fingers are cold compared to hers, and the contrast makes me feel even more fragile. She gives me a flickering, hollow smile, the kind that doesn't reach her eyes, before turning back to Luca with a predatory intensity.

"Has Elijah made any headway with the witches?" I ask.

Luca sighs, his head dipping for a moment in exhaustion. The Alpha's mask slips, revealing a man who is just as tired as I am. "No. They're still digging their heels in. Elijah is going to offer to keep their shop running until Reya gets back. He's hoping it'll buy some goodwill."

I perk up, the first spark of hope hitting my chest like a physical blow. It feels like a small light flickering on in a dark room. "That's actually a solid move. The last thing they need is to lose their business while their sister is behind bars. It gives them a reason to keep talking to us. It turns a request into a partnership."

Luca's expression sours instantly, his brow furrowing into a deep V. "I don't like it. It puts them in the line of fire."

"It's the best plan we have," I counter. My voice is firm despite my weakness, though it carries a slight rasp that betrays my damaged lungs. "If we want them on our side for whatever war is coming, and trust me, it's coming, we need to show them we aren't just here to take. They'll be safe. Reya warded that place herself specifically to keep her sisters protected. She wouldn't have left a gap in the armour."

Sam's fingers hit the 'Enter' key with a final, decisive click that sounds like a gunshot in the quiet room. He lets out a breath that sounds like a deflating balloon. "I've got the footage. It's a wash."

We all lean in, the tension spiking.

"The only camera facing our wing 'glitched' during the break-in," Sam explains, his voice flat and defeated. "No evidence of demons, but no evidence of possessed humans either. We've got nothing to track.

It's as if they just blinked into existence and then blinked out."

"Reya sent Sera to follow Devika," I remind them, my mind racing, trying to piece together the fragmented puzzle of this conflict. "Can't we just ask Freya where they're hiding?"

"Like they'd tell us," Rose mutters, her eyes dark with cynicism. She doesn't trust anyone who isn't in our immediate circle, and her distrust of the Harper sisters is a wall that seems impossible to climb.

I turn to Sam, my voice tinged with a sharp urgency. "Sam, have you had any luck locating Dhara? We need her if we're going to pull Reya out of that cage."

Sam shakes his head, his expression downcast and heavy. "Nothing so far, sorry."

His disappointment hangs in the air like a thick, suffocating fog. The silence that follows is oppressive, broken only by the hum of the refrigerator and the distant sound of traffic from the main road.

Luca interjects, redirecting our attention with a sharp shift in his posture. I can sense that he isn't as emotionally invested in Reya's situation as I am, and that realisation stings more than my bruised ribs. It feels like a cold splash of reality. To him, she is a means to an end, or perhaps a complication he'd rather avoid.

"I was hoping to find them without their help," he admits, his gaze darting away from mine and towards the floor. He looks braced, like he's preparing for an impact. His posture shifts, becoming rigid and tense, his shoulders squaring as if facing an enemy. "But... I have a different plan."

Oh great, here it comes. The moment where I'm likely to be told to sit in a corner and eat my vegetables while the grown-ups come up with a more palatable solution.

My heart sinks, a cold weight settling in my stomach.

"What plan?" Rose asks, her voice softening slightly as she looks at Luca. Even in her frustration, her loyalty to her Alpha is absolute.

Luca finally meets my gaze, his eyes full of a weary, strained light. "I think we move on. There are other towns, other threats. We've done what we can here."

I open my mouth to protest, the words already forming in my throat, but he holds up a hand, cutting me off. It is a gesture that usually works on shifters, and while I am human, the sheer force of his will is enough to make me pause.

"Ava, listen. You aren't at a hundred percent. If we head North, back to the original plan, it gives you time to heal. It gives us time to figure out how to get Reya out of legal limbo. The sisters have enough on their plate; they don't need us hovering, and quite frankly, we can't fight shadows if we're half-dead."

Rose doesn't even blink. "I agree. This whole trip was a mistake. Let the sisters handle their own demons for once."

I stare at them, my head shaking slowly in disbelief. I feel a surge of betrayal, a hot flash of anger that makes my fingertips tingle. *Are they serious? We're just going to tuck tail and run while Reya is sitting in a cell?*

Sam looks between us, his frustration mirroring mine. He doesn't like leaving a job unfinished; it goes against every grain of his CIA training. "So, am I ditching looking for a more defensible location, or should I start looking at Rockford or Milwaukee?"

"Green Bay," Luca says, his voice final and heavy. "Let's put some real distance between us and the pack in Chicago."

I'm absolutely stunned, speechless, overwhelmed by a whirlwind of passionate arguments ready to erupt. I want to scream that we are abandoning our only lead, that we are leaving Reya to rot. But just as I'm about to unleash my fury, I glance at Luca.

His face suddenly drains of all colour, leaving him ghostly, waxen pale. The usual vibrancy of his tanned skin is completely replaced by a deathly pallor, and his jaw drops slightly. His wide eyes seem to draw in every scrap of light, dilating into terrifying, bottomless pools of darkness that swallow the iris whole.

Rose feels the sudden shift in the air, the tension crackling like an approaching storm. With a sudden movement, her grip on my hand loosens as she leaps to her feet. The screech of her chair against the tile pierces through the silence like a siren.

"Luca? What's going on?" she demands, her voice layered with a frantic, sharp worry.

But he doesn't reply; he can't. A sharp, strangled gasp escapes him, and his hand clutches at his chest as if an invisible force has struck him down. He looks like he's been hit by a physical blow to the heart. A mix of panic and pure disbelief breaks from his lips, and in one shocking, swift motion, he crumples to his knees.

The tiles crack beneath the weight of his fall, the sound echoing through the room, amplifying the intense gravity of the moment as reality crashes down on us. He doesn't just fall; he collapses as if the very pillars holding him up have been demolished.

"Doctor Stevens!" I scream, my voice ricocheting off the kitchen walls. A jolt of pain shoots down my spine, a searing heat that makes me gasp, but I push it aside. The urgency is all-consuming. "We need help! Now!"

In an instant, Rose is at Luca's side, her every instinct kicking into high gear. She is no longer the flirtatious partner; she is the Beta, the protector. Sam and I stand frozen for a heartbeat, gripped by a paralysing terror as we witness the mighty Alpha fall apart before our eyes.

What do I really know about Shifters? Can they even have heart attacks? Is it possible to break a heart so immense that it actually stops beating?

"Luca, please, talk to me!" Rose's voice trembles, her composure fraying as she hovers over him, her hands shaking as she tries to find where to touch him, where to help.

Just then, Doctor Stevens bursts through the kitchen door, his brow furrowed and eyes wide with alarm. He scans the scene, confusion flickering across his features until they land on Luca's collapsed form.

"What happened?" he demands, urgency pouring from him as he rushes forward.

"He just... collapsed," Rose stammers, her voice quaking. "He grabbed his chest!"

Stevens drops to his knees beside Luca, his movements precise and clinical. "Heart condition? Is he having a myocardial infarction? I need to check for tachycardia." He moves quickly, his fingers searching for the pulse at Luca's neck, his eyes scanning for signs of cyanosis around the lips.

"Not possible!" Rose replies fiercely, her determination sparking like fire. "Not for someone like him. His heart is stronger than any human's! Luca, look at me!"

Luca's face contorts with agony, a mask of pure, unadulterated pain that sends a chill racing through my bones. He attempts to lift his head, his jaw working as if trying to summon strength from the very depths of his soul. But the only sound he manages to produce is an earth-shattering roar.

It is not a human scream. It is a primal, visceral cry, akin to a great beast in mourning, a sound that carries the weight of a thousand losses. The raw vibration reverberates through the room, creeping up my skin and making every hair on my arms stand on end. It is a sound filled with such profound despair that it feels like the world itself is breaking, as if the fabric of reality is tearing open right here in this dingy kitchen.

We all instinctively cover our ears, the sound echoing in the cramped space until, at last, it fades into a ragged, broken sob. Luca sags against the kitchen units, his eyes sunken and hollow. He looks utterly lost, as though he has just awakened in a universe where the sun has been extinguished, leaving him cloaked in a darkness he cannot navigate.

"Luca, please," Rose whispers, her voice barely rising above the erratic crackle of the wind outside. The tension hangs thick, like fog rolling in from a cold sea.

After what feels like an eternity, he finally breaks the silence, his voice a fragile, broken whisper that barely reaches us.

"It's gone."

I dart my gaze toward Sam, whose bewilderment reflects the chaos swirling in my own mind. "What's gone?" I urge, urgency creeping into my tone like a thief in the night.

Rose's eyes flicker back to Luca, a silent question darting between them with the speed of a lightning bolt. He gives a nearly imperceptible nod, a small, devastating admission that seems to age him ten years in a single second. Turning to face me, Rose's features drain of colour, as though she has glimpsed something otherworldly and terrible.

"The bond," she manages, each syllable falling from her lips like a heavy stone dropped into still water, sending ripples of dread through my soul. "It's gone."

The word hangs in the air, heavy and suffocating, a sentence of absolute despair wrapped in the weight of our intertwined fates. I feel the confusion tightening around my chest like a vice, making it hard to draw air.

"What?" I exhale, disbelief clawing at me. "You mean..."

Doctor Stevens looks confused, his brow furrowed as he looks around at us, still holding Luca's wrist to monitor a pulse that is now slowing but steady. "Is this related to the bond you and Rose share?" he questions earnestly, his clinical concern cutting through the tension.

"No!" Rose snaps, her voice suddenly sharp, filled with a venom that cuts through the atmosphere like shattered glass. Her reaction is visceral, as if he's struck a nerve buried deep within her very being. "He has a bond with someone else."

"He's bonded to the witch who saved my life," I interject, determination lacing my words as I slice through Rose's bitterness. The frustration surges within me, a tidal force. I know I need to clarify the truth. That connection, forged in moments of blood and desperation, still pulsates within me, even amidst this tidal wave of uncertainty. It is a golden thread that connects my soul to his, though right now, it feels like it's being pulled taut until it snaps.

Luca slumps further against the cool, worn cabinets, the weight of defeat draping over him like an oppressive shroud. His shoulders are tense, and his eyes are dimmed with a profound despair. Doctor Stevens stands across from us, his gaze fixated on me with that familiar blend of clinical curiosity and detached observation. To him, I'm nothing more than an intricate puzzle, a case study waiting for his sharp intellect to dissect.

A shiver runs down my spine as I muster the courage to speak. "So what does this mean?" I ask, my voice trembling slightly as my heart begins to hammer against my ribs like a frantic drum. "You mentioned that the only way to break it is to reject each other face-to-face. Unless..."

The realisation hits me with the force of a blow to my chest, taking the breath from my lungs, and the air vanishes from the room.

"Wait. Are you saying Reya is dead?"

The words hang in the air, heavy and suffocating, as the cruel possibility settles over us like a dark cloud. Silence crashes down around us, a thick, suffocating fog. No one dares to meet my gaze. The only sound is the humming of the fluorescent light, which suddenly sounds like a scream.

"She has to be," Rose declares, her voice slicing through the stillness like a blade, cold and unwavering. There is a hidden relief in her tone, a darkness that makes me recoil.

The words ignite a fire within me, forcing anger to bubble up and overflow. "As far as you know!" I retort, my voice tinged with desperation and defiance. "You've said it's been centuries since anyone's witnessed a bond! There has to be other options, a spell, a magical dampener, anything!"

"Should I call Freya?" Sam chimes in, his fingers already reaching for his phone, his face pale with the thought of delivering such news.

"No!" Luca gasps, his face paling as if all the life has been sucked from him. “Don’t!”

“Why not?” I retort, the frustration boiling in my veins, mixing with the pain in my back to create a cocktail of pure volatility.

“Because if she were dead... Elijah would have called us. He would have called *me*,” Luca insists, determination flashing back into his eyes through the heartbreak. For someone who claimed to want nothing to do with a ‘black witch,’ he now appears as though half of his very soul has been torn away. The denial in his voice is a shield, but it’s one that is cracking.

I watch his pain, and it strikes me that our fates are intricately woven together in ways I don’t yet understand. If Reya is dead, everything is unravelling. Freya and Maya will never trust us again, and our best hope for winning this war will be gone before it even begins. We will be blind, deaf, and alone against a tide of demons.

“I don’t care what any of you think!” I shout, the room tilting for a heartbeat as I fight to stay upright. A wave of dizziness washes over me, but I cling to the edge of the table. “I’m going to see Freya and Maya!”

“You aren’t going anywhere until you’re healed!” Rose barks, her intense ‘Protective Mate’ instincts kicking into high gear. She steps in front of me, blocking the exit, her green eyes flashing with a primal warning.

“Enough with the theatrics, Rose! I’m just hopping into a car, then taking a quick walk from the car to the house. It’s not like I’m training for the Olympics!” I shoot back, my eyes blazing with determination.

“Where do you think you’re going?” she demands, her voice dropping to a dangerous, low register.

“To get dressed,” I reply, turning my back and striding defiantly toward the door. Every step is an agony, a sharp pull across my shoulder blades that makes me want to hiss in pain, but I refuse to give her the satisfaction of seeing me stumble.

“Doc, you need to stop her!” I hear Rose insist behind me, her voice echoing through the hallway.

"I've worked with agents far too long," Stevens interjects, a hint of resignation and amusement in his tone. "Trying to stop an agent when their mind is made up is impossible. There are notes in her records... she has a habit of leaving against medical advice."

I find my bag and dig out leggings and a black T-shirt with a faded grey star on the front. Every movement is a lesson in pain, a sharp, pulling sensation across my back that reminds me how close I came to the end. It feels as though my skin is too tight for my muscles, as if the sutures are fighting against the swell of inflammation. I grit my teeth, pulling the shirt over my head, refusing to let out even one whimper of agony.

When Rose walks in, she finds me standing there, fully dressed and breathing through the ache. She looks like she wants to argue, her lips parted to deliver another command, but the sight of me standing on my own two feet steals her thunder. I look at her not as a patient, but as a Captain.

"Don't," I say before she can start. "I need to see them. They deserve to know what happened to Luca, and they deserve the truth."

"You can't defend yourself if something happens," she sighs, her frustration turning into a dull, heavy ache. She looks at me with such longing it almost hurts, her hand reaching out to touch my waist before she catches herself and pulls back.

"Rose, look at the big picture. We're running out of allies. The Harpers are the real deal. Their father was an Archangel. I don't care about your old pack's superstitions. If Reya were evil, her sisters wouldn't be standing by her like this."

I perch on the edge of the bed, my heart racing and energy crackling beneath my skin like static electricity. The room is thick with tension, and Rose remains silent for what feels like an eternity. Five minutes stretch out like a tightrope before she finally sinks down beside me, her fear palpable, radiating off her in waves.

"Ava, I'm terrified," she whispers, her voice trembling with raw emotion. "I almost lost you... I can't bear to lose anyone else. It's like we're trapped in a nightmare where the people we love just vanish."

I turn to her, my expression fierce and unyielding. I reach out, cupping her cheek with my hand. Her skin is burning, as always. "Have you ever heard of a soul bond twisting into betrayal?" I raise a hand to stop her before she can respond. "Do you honestly think your gods would tie your Alpha to something malevolent? If you place your faith in them, then you have to trust in this bond."

She stares at the floor, her mind racing through years of scepticism and doubt, fighting against the traditions of a pack that exiled her for who she loved. The silence stretches, heavy and suffocating, until at last she exhales a shaky breath.

"You're right," she concedes, determination rising in her voice. She looks up at me, and for a moment, the predator is gone, replaced by a woman who is simply terrified of being alone. "I can't let fear take control anymore. I trust them... and I trust you."

About time!

As we step back into the kitchen, we find Luca and Sam already standing by the door, their silhouettes framed by the dim light of the hallway. Luca's expression strikes me immediately; there is a fierce, burning determination etched across his features. It is as if the loss of the bond has ignited a fire within him, burning away his doubts and revealing a truth he had been desperately resisting.

He seems to have come to a painful realisation. Reya, the girl he once considered an adversary, isn't the monster he believed her to be. The weight of his stubbornness hangs in the air, a stark reminder that by refusing to accept her, he may have jeopardised their connection forever. He looks like a man who has finally realised he was holding the key to his own salvation and threw it away.

"Are you ready to head out?" he asks, his voice returning to its deep, authoritative rumble, though there is a new edge of vulnerability to it.

"Let's go," I say.

The dizziness persists, lurking at the edges of my vision like a dark tide, and my body feels as if it's been put through a meat grinder. Beneath the exhaustion, however, there's something else. A low, thrumming vibration, starting in the base of my spine and radiating outward, as if my nervous system has been replaced with live wires.

It is a strange, electric feeling, one that makes me feel more awake than I have in years. Something is changing within me, something that doesn't feel entirely human. And I have a feeling we're all about to find out exactly what that means.

CHAPTER 9

The Scent of Blood and Shadows

We hit the turn-off for the Harpers' property, and the road effectively becomes a dead end, a narrow strip of grey gravel that winds through the oppressive humidity of the Mississippi landscape. One of our backup team members is playing doorman, their car angled sharply to block the entrance like a high-stakes bouncer at an exclusive club. I am grateful that Luca and Sam had the foresight to set this up while I was busy dying in a safe house, though the sight of the tactical perimeter makes my stomach churn with a reminder of how volatile our lives have become.

Sheriff Bradshaw has been a relentless, power-tripping thorn in our sides. He is a man driven by a narrow, suffocating brand of justice, determined to harass the sisters until he finds a single thread he can pull to unravel them, hoping for any scrap of evidence that will bury Reya deeper in a cell. But even our team cannot hold this line forever. Eventually, the law or the monsters will find a way through, and we will be left with no one to guard the gate.

As we crawl up the gravel road, a sensation I haven't felt since I was eighteen washes over me, sudden and jarring. It is that same, raw, skin-crawling nervousness I had the day I walked into the recruitment office to sign my life away, trading my youth for a uniform and a set of orders. My body is awash with it, a prickly, electric heat that makes the hair on my arms stand up.

Why am I shaking? I've faced demons. I've been gutted and brought back from the brink. Why does this feel like I'm walking into an execution?

The house finally looms into view through the haze of heat ripples rising from the asphalt. I shift forward, sitting dead-centre in the back seat and staring through the windscreen with a fixed intensity, as if I can manifest safety through sheer willpower. I expected to see a graveyard, smoking ruins, or the blackened scars of battle that usually follow our wake. Instead, the place looks like a damn postcard. It is almost eerie how peaceful it sits under the oppressive gold of the Mississippi sun, a yellow-painted sanctuary surrounded by greenery.

It is only when I squint that the trauma appears. The landscape is littered with gnarled trees toppled over like discarded toys, their trunks split clean in two to reveal jagged, white-wood stumps that look disturbingly like broken bone. It is a silent testament to the violence that occurred here, a scar on the earth that no amount of sunlight can erase.

Sam wheels the SUV off to the side, putting a tactical buffer of space between us and the porch. Always leave yourself an out, as they teach you in the field. It takes us a beat too long to get out of the car; the air feels heavy, charged with static that makes my skin itch. We aren't surprised when a deep, guttural growl vibrates through the air, originating from somewhere deep inside the house. It is a sound that doesn't just hit your ears; it rattles your teeth and echoes in the hollow of your chest.

Then, the sky dims.

Sera comes swooping over the roofline, her massive, shadow-drenched wings beating the air with a rhythmic, heavy thud, thud, thud. She lands hard in front of the house, the impact sending a choking cloud of red Mississippi dirt swirling around her shadowed feet. The dust hangs in the air, thick and metallic. Of course, my colleagues are effectively blind to her, staring at the empty space where the air seems to ripple and distort like a mirage.

"Hello, Sera," I say quickly, my voice steady despite the adrenaline spiking in my veins. "I hope you are well."

"Is Reya's shade here?" Rose asks, her voice dropping into a low, predatory snarl. She shifts her weight, her muscles tensing as if she is ready to tear through the veil and drag something out of the darkness.

Seriously? Now is not the time for the 'big bad shifter' routine, Rose. Read the room.

I feel a sudden, sharp urge to slap her, just to bring her back down to earth. The tension is already high enough without her trying to assert dominance over a shadow.

"Yes, she is here..."

The words die in my throat as a phantom pain lances through my chest, a sharp, stabbing reminder of the void where Reya's presence should be. The realisation hits me like a blow to the solar plexus, knocking the wind from my lungs. Sera cannot feed without Reya. Without that specific, magically-charged blood, this shadow is going to wither and turn to dust. I don't have time to dwell on the fact that we are essentially delivering a death sentence to one of our few allies.

Beastie bursts through the front door, looking fierce, primal, and somehow even more massive than the last time I saw him. He races toward us, skidding to a halt next to Sera, his paws kicking up more of that suffocating red dust. I can practically feel their eyes tracing every inch of us, scanning for threats with a precision that makes my skin prickle.

They recognise us, and the tension in the air snaps like a dry twig. Beastie rushes me, burying his massive, warm head into my chest with enough force to nearly knock me over. I stumble back, gasping, but I don't pull away.

Instantly, my mind is a kaleidoscope of blood and fire.

He isn't just hugging me; he is flooding me with images, replaying the attack through his eyes in a torrent of sensory overload. Seeing it from the outside makes it feel like a miracle that I am even breathing. I see the moment he sank his teeth into Reya's hand, the spray of crimson against the grass. I see her hold that bleeding hand over my mouth, her expression a mask of desperate determination and raw love, forcing her lifeblood down my throat because I was too far gone to swallow on my own.

From Beastie's perspective, I see how I dangled over the edge of a black abyss, my soul fraying at the edges. My heartbeats were so far apart, thump... long, terrifying silence... thump, that I am not entirely sure I didn't actually cross over for a second. I remember the cold. I remember the absolute, crushing silence of the void.

When Rose pulled Reya away, I heard my heart hitch in the vision, a desperate little uptake, and then the images blur into a smear of motion. Beastie's attention was ripped away as he watched me being carried off like a corpse, limp and pale. He really thought I was dead. The vision shifts rapidly now. Reya, transforming into a hellhound, her form twisting into something nightmarish and dark before bolting around the lake in a frenzy of grief.

I can feel the guilt radiating off him in waves; he blames himself for not following her, for staying behind while she vanished into the dark. He only stayed because he knew Reya would want him to protect her sisters and Pickle, the little pixie he has grown attached to. The devotion is heartbreakingly pure.

The images cut off abruptly, leaving my head spinning and vision swimming with ghostly red spots. I crouch down, burying my hands in Beastie's thick fur, feeling the heat of his body against mine.

Then, the front door swings open. Pickle comes storming out.

And she is carrying a... knitting needle? She is wielding it like a damn broadsword, her tiny face twisted into a mask of absolute fury. Just like Sera, she beats her wings with a frantic energy, shooting toward us like a shimmering dart, leaving a trail of light behind her that looks like rippling water in the air.

"Pickle, it's us!" I call out over Beastie's back, trying to avoid being skewered by the craft supplies.

She pulls up short, her tiny features morphing from warrior

rage to pure, unadulterated shock in a heartbeat. Before I can even stand, she launches herself at me, slamming into my neck with the force of a much larger creature. Thankfully, she has the presence of mind to drop her weapon, or I would be explaining a knitting-needle-shaped hole in my eye to the agency doctors.

"Ava! I thought you were dead! How did you survive?" she cries, her voice high and trembling against my skin. Her tiny arms wrap around my neck as tightly as they can, and for a moment, I feel a lump form in my throat.

A dry, breathless chuckle escapes me. "Reya saved me," I say, the weight of that truth heavy in my lungs. "That, and a very good Doctor at our safe house."

"How did Reya do that when she doesn't have healing power?" Pickle counters, her wings fluttering with agitation against my collarbone. "Maya does, but she can only heal things with leaves and fur."

"I'm not sure, Pickle. I wasn't exactly in a condition to take notes."

"I'm just so glad you're okay," she whispers, then her voice turns sharp, vibrating with an anger that feels too big for her tiny frame. "Have you heard what that horrible sheriff has done?"

Yeah, I heard. A sharp pang of grief shoots through me, not just for Reya, but for the news we are carrying. The guilt is a cold stone in my stomach. And the fact that Sera might be fading out right behind her makes the air feel thinner.

"Yeah, I heard," I say quietly. "It's why we're here."

"Are you going to get her out? So she can come home?"

I don't have an answer. I don't want to be the one to break her heart, not when she is clinging to me with such desperate hope. I just carefully wrap a hand around her, mindful of those delicate, iridescent wings, and rest my head against the top of hers.

Freya, Maya, and Jenny come storming out next, looking ready for a brawl. Their expressions are hard, their eyes narrowed with suspicion. Elijah follows them, looking annoyingly relaxed; no doubt he picked up on his Alpha's scent, which tipped him off that we weren't a strike team coming to finish the job.

"What are you doing here?" Freya demands, her voice tight and defensive. She stands with her arms crossed, her stance mirroring Luca's.

I take charge, pushing through the lingering dizziness to stand slowly. My back protests with a sharp, pulling sensation, but I ignore it. "We have come to talk. We have news we need to share with you."

Their heads snap toward me. Just like Pickle, shock washes over their faces like a cold wave, leaving them momentarily breathless.

"You're alive," Maya gasps, sounding utterly gobsmacked. Her eyes well up with tears, and she looks as if she might collapse.

"Sure am," I reply, trying to sound a lot more put-together than I feel. *Inside, I feel like a jigsaw puzzle that's been put together wrong.* "Now, can we please come in? This is a 'sitting down' kind of conversation. Sera, you should come too; this affects you as well."

The sisters look reluctant, their eyes darting to Luca and Rose with deep-seated distrust, but they finally step aside. I wait for the protective barrier to kick in, expecting it to toss our shifters through a metaphysical window for their insolence. But they walk right through. It seems that with Reya gone, both Luca and, especially, Rose's minds don't contain violent thoughts towards Reya at this moment, which is the only reason the wards are letting them pass.

We follow them inside. The house smells of dried herbs, beeswax, and a lingering scent of ozone. The sisters start dragging kitchen chairs toward the area with the couch, creating a makeshift war room. Pickle is still glued to my shoulder, talking a mile a minute into my ear, her voice a buzzing hum of anxiety.

"Are you really all better?"

"I'm getting there, Pickle. How are you coping without her?"

I feel her tiny body slump against my neck, the fight leaving her. "I'm coping," she says, her voice small and hollow. "But it's horrible. No one should be kept in that room with the bars and no privacy. I snuck in to see her... she was so sad. She told Beastie and me to go live our lives. Beastie tried to get her to leave, but she said it would make things worse. Would it?"

"I'm afraid so," I say, the weight of the legal system feeling as heavy as any monster we have fought. "If she escaped, she'd be hunted by every police force in the country because they think she killed one of their own."

"She was just protecting us," Pickle whispers fiercely.

"I know. We have news about Reya... maybe you'll be able to help us," I say, an idea beginning to spark in the back of my mind.

"I will do anything to help my go... I'll do anything for Reya," she corrects herself quickly. I catch the slip, but I don't push. Whatever she was going to call Reya, the devotion in her eyes is unmistakable and heartbreaking.

Once we're all settled, mostly, the rest of the pack sneaks in like shadows and hovers by the back door. Beastie wedges his massive frame between Freya and Maya, providing a physical shield of warmth and fur. Sera stands like a silent, tragic statue to my left. Even though she is just a silhouette, the slump of her shoulders screams heartbreak.

"So," Freya demands, her eyes sharp and suspicious. "What is it you need to tell us?"

I can feel Luca itching to take the lead, his Alpha instincts pushing him forward, but instead, he turns to face me, giving a small, respectful nod.

"First, we should tell you what we found on Jacob," I say, indicating for Sam to take over.

Sam lays it out with clinical precision, his voice devoid of emotion as he describes the monster's real identity and the links to a pack in England. He explains the theory that they are responsible for the towns' residents vanishing, potentially turning the people into shifters. He tells them about the links to Devika, the woman leading the demons, who has been possessed by a high-level demon.

The room goes cold with a collective, simmering anger. I can feel the temperature drop, the air thickening as the Harper sisters react.

"The fuckers," Freya says, her teeth gritted so hard I am surprised they don't snap.

"Wolves have always treated humans as a means to an end. The world would be a much better place if they weren't in it," Elijah says from the back, his pack nodding in grim, sombre agreement.

"So even though we dealt with the wolves, they're still going to be a problem?" Freya asks.

"They will be," Luca says, his voice a low, authoritative rumble. "I hope the fact that we managed to defeat them causes the rest to think twice, but I doubt it. Power like that doesn't just go away."

"Well, we have no chance without Reya," Maya says, fixing us with a glare that could peel paint. She clearly blames us for her sister being behind bars, and she isn't hiding it.

We all exchange a look of pure, unadulterated dread. The silence that follows is suffocating, broken only by the ticking of a clock in the hallway.

"What is it? What has happened to Reya?" Freya and Pickle shout in unison, their voices cracking with panic. Maya and Jenny clamp their hands over their mouths, and Beastie starts to growl, a low, vibrating sound that rattles the floorboards beneath our feet.

"We don't actually know anything has happened," I say, shooting Luca a look. He looks like he would rather be back in the line of fire than explain this part.

"I presume everyone knows about the bond that Luca and Reya seem to have," I say. Then, under my breath, I can't help but add, 'For some reason, one of them is obsessed with stories they grew up on, so they won't explore it.'

Luca glares at me. Yeah, I know you heard me, Alpha. Own it.

"Yeah, we know about the bond," Freya snaps. "What about it?"

"Well... earlier today," I look at Luca again. He looks like he wants to crawl into the floorboards and vanish.

"Out with it!" Freya demands, leaning forward in her chair.

"Something happened to Luca; he felt the loss of the bond. It caused him a lot of pain," I say, the humour gone from my voice.

"It was just pain, Ava," Luca snaps, his pride wounded. "Not 'great' pain."

"If you say so, Great Alpha," I say, and I can't help a tiny snicker despite the gravity of the situation. It is a reflex, a way to keep from spiralling into the dread myself.

"So..." is all Freya says, her face turning ashen, the colour draining away.

"There are only two ways to lose a bond," I start. I notice the pack members' faces drop; they already know where this is going. The silence becomes an entity of its own, heavy and oppressive.

"Again, so... Our sister isn't interested in the bond thingy. A shifter killed our mother, so she was never going to end up with one."

Rose, as usual, cannot keep her mouth shut. "That's a bit hypocritical, considering Reya is a shifter herself now."

"We believe she got that from her bond with Beastie," Freya states firmly.

Luca does not look convinced. "Hellhounds cannot shift. I believe her form may have come from the bond, which means she would have had a different form before she bonded with it."

Beastie starts growling at the word 'it,' and the sisters shoot Luca looks that could kill. He quickly adjusts his tone.

"I think Reya might have always been a shifter," Luca clarifies quickly. "Bonding with Beastie just... changed the shape."

"If that's the case, we should be able to shift, too," Maya says, her face tightening as if she is trying to force a snout to appear through sheer willpower.

Pickle speaks up from my shoulder, her voice tiny but authoritative. "Remember when I explained about your powers? Abilities are split between siblings. Twins and triplets won't gain the same ones."

I quickly relay Pickle's words to the others, explaining the biological lottery of their magic.

"That is very true, Pickle," Luca says, nodding.

"Wait a minute, Ava," Freya says, her eyes narrowing as she glares at Luca with renewed intensity. "You explained the bond to us and how you can break one. Since our sister is in prison, she cannot exactly stand in front of Luca and break it face-to-face. You better not be trying to say what I think you're trying to say."

The air in the room shifts, becoming heavy and stagnant. I push through my own fear and say what needs to be said. "The only other way for the bond to break... is for the other person to die."

The reaction is instant. Anger floods the room like a burst dam, and then something strange happens. the house itself starts to groan. It sounds like something massive is pressing down on the roof, the wood creaking and straining as if the structure is about to buckle under an invisible weight. The windows rattle in their frames, and a vase on the table shatters without being touched.

"What is going on?" Rose demands, her hand hovering from her lap as if she is ready to shift into claws at any second.

"We don't know. Every time we talk about our sister and what has happened to her, the house makes these noises," Maya says, looking around with wide, worried eyes. The house is reflecting their grief, a physical manifestation of their collective heartbreak.

We sit in a tense, vibrating silence until the house finally settles, leaving us all shaken.

"If something happened to Reya, they would have notified us," Freya states, her jaw set in a line of pure denial. She refuses to accept it; she cannot.

"I actually have an idea for finding out what's going on," I say, cutting through the gloom before we all drown in it.

"What idea?" The room asks as one.

"We take Pickle, even Beastie, if need be, to the prison. They can infiltrate it. No one will see them, and they can find her."

"Beastie and I will do it," Pickle says immediately, flying up and gripping her knitting needle like a lance. She looks like a tiny, shimmering Valkyrie.

"Are you sure, Pickle?" Freya asks softly.

"I'm sure. No one can see me, so what are we waiting for?" She is practically vibrating with readiness.

"I will come too," Freya demands.

"I don't think that's wise. Coming to Jackson with us will put you right in the path of the demons hunting you. I'm willing to take Pickle and Beastie myself."

"Over my dead body," Rose snarls at me. "You're not fully healed. You're not going anywhere on your own."

"You cannot even see them, Rose. It's not like you can help in a stealth mission."

"Tough. Do you really think your back will cope with that drive? I've noticed how you've been walking, Ava. You're in agony."

I hesitate. She is right. My back feels like it is being held together by rusted staples and prayer. Every bump in the road here was a fresh hell, but I have to know. The uncertainty is worse than the pain.

It takes some time, but we finally persuade Freya to stay behind for her own safety. While Luca talks with his pack, I catch Sera's purple gaze and tilt my head toward the door. Rose tries to follow, but I whisper that I need a private word with the shadow. She isn't happy, hovering by the kitchen window like a hawk as I lead Sera out to the barn for privacy.

The barn is quiet, smelling of dry hay, old wood, and the warm, musk scent of horses. Three of the horses are out grazing in the field, but Reya's horse is still inside, looking absolutely miserable, its head hanging low. I go over and stroke its mane, the coarse hair familiar under my palm.

I turn to Sera. I have been dreading this conversation, but it is necessary. "Sera, Reya explained that you can only survive on her blood. If something has happened to her... I'm worried you'll perish. I was wondering if my blood might be able to help you."

Sera starts to shake her head, her form flickering like a dying candle.

"Wait," I say, holding up my hand. "I think it might work because Reya fed me her blood to save my life. I can feel it in my system. It's doing something to me. It might be enough to keep you going."

Sera cocks her head, her glowing purple eyes scanning my body like a thermal sensor, looking for the trace of that magic. She moves closer, a cold, weightless presence, and points to my left wrist. I pull up my sleeve, exposing the pale skin and the thrumming pulse beneath.

I didn't expect her to hesitate, but she does. Her eyes move from mine to my wrist and back again. Then, she gently grabs my arm. Her touch is ice-cold, but it doesn't chill my skin; it is more like a mental sensation of freezing, a numbing cold that spreads through my veins.

I watch, mesmerised and slightly horrified, as she lowers her head. I feel the sharp, pin-prick sting as her fangs pierce the skin. It is a bizarre sensation. I can feel her sucking on the wounds, and suddenly, my entire body is hit with a massive adrenaline spike. My throat goes bone-dry in seconds, a desperate, primal thirst clawing at my chest. Every cell in my body starts to hum, as if electricity is being poured into my veins instead of blood.

When she finally pulls away, I get a strange, dark impulse, a fleeting desire to know what my own blood tastes like. It is a hunger I have never known, something predatory and deep.

Sera's voice rings in my head, and it sounds exactly like Reya's, haunting and melodic.

'Thank you, Ava. I don't think the sisters realised I would die without her. We will find her safe, and I won't have to trouble you again.'

"It's okay. Does that mean it worked?"

'It does. Your blood tastes similar to hers. But there is a strange aftertaste... and a smell. You used to smell like Jenny. Now you smell different. You smell like the sisters. You smell like Beastie.'

That hits me like a freight train. I freeze, my heart hammering against my ribs. What the hell has her blood done to me? Am I changing? Am I becoming something other than human?

I rejoin the others, feeling like I am walking on air and lead at the same time. Rose grills me immediately about the blood she can clearly smell on me, her nose twitching with suspicion. I am forced to whisper a half-truth as we reach the car, telling her that I gave Sera some blood because of the 'magic' Reya used on me. I feel like a liar, but until I know why I am starting to smell like a hellhound, some secrets are better kept. Of course, Rose isn't happy about this, her eyes flashing with jealousy and concern, but I tell her I don't want to hear it.

We pile into the SUV. Beastie reduces his size, a neat trick I didn't know he possessed, fitting himself into the cabin. We head toward the prison in Jackson, the road stretching out before us like an uncertain future. Pickle is curled up in my lap, her tiny face a mask of worry and determination.

I lean back against the seat, closing my eyes, but all I can think about is that smell. The scent of shadows and fire. I can't help but wonder if we are driving straight into a wake, or if I am becoming part of the very world I was sent to hunt.

CHAPTER 10

The Shadow of a Doubt

The tyres of our heavy SUV groan, a low, guttural protest that vibrates through the chassis as we take the sharp turn into the prison grounds. I can feel the tension humming in my fingertips, a static charge that makes the fine hairs on my arms stand on end. We pull to a halt just outside the imposing perimeter of Jackson Prison, and for a moment, the world seems to hold its breath.

Then, the silence is shattered.

The atmosphere is instantly swallowed by a chaotic, bone-rattling symphony of sirens and distant, echoing shouting that bounces off the grey concrete walls. It is a wall of sound that hits me like a physical blow, triggering a flicker of memory, a flash of cordite and screaming from a lifetime ago. Something monumental is unfolding within those walls, something that has turned this high-security facility into a hive of desperation. Several patrol cars scream past us, their sirens acting like jagged blades cutting through the thick, humid Mississippi air. News vans tail them, hovering on the periphery like hungry vultures sensing a fresh kill on the horizon.

I lean forward, my chest tightening with a familiar, cold dread that settles in the pit of my stomach like lead. I have spent the better part of my life immersed in hostile environments, deploying to war zones where the air tastes of copper and burnt ozone, but the energy humming off this place is fundamentally different. It is not just human chaos. It is thick, jagged, and carries a sharp, metallic tang that mixes with a frantic, primal desperation.

Great. Because our day wasn't already a glorious dumpster fire in the making.

I sink back into my seat, my eyes scanning the perimeter. *What else could possibly go wrong? Please, universe, just give me one hour where something doesn't explode or vanish into another dimension.*

As we pull into the overcrowded car park, it looks as though all hell has officially broken loose. I haven't seen this many blue uniforms in one concentrated area for a long time. The tactical division is out in full force, creating a sea of matte black kevlar, dark visors, and assault rifles held at the ready. My pulse spikes, becoming a frantic, syncopated drumbeat against my ribs that echoes the urgency of the scene. This isn't just a standard procedure or a botched transfer. This is a state of emergency.

"Does anyone have their ID with them?" I ask. My voice is tight, commanding, the tone I use when I am leading a breach. I glance at the others from my seat in the rear, my eyes flicking from Sam to Rose. I can feel the phantom weight of my sidearm, an itch in my palms to reach for something solid, something that provides a sense of control in a situation that feels increasingly volatile. "If this has anything to do with Reya, we are going to need every bit of authority we can muster."

"You're in luck," Sam says. His voice is a steady anchor in the storm, a stark contrast to the madness outside the windows. He reaches into his tactical bag with measured movements and pulls out our leather-bound badges. The silver glints under the harsh sunlight. "I have all our badges right here. If this truly has to do with Reya, what on earth do you think she has done to warrant this level of response?"

Beside me, Rose shifts. The movement is fluid, predatory, and entirely too graceful for the confines of an SUV. Her striking green eyes flash with a preternatural heat, the pupils slitting slightly. I can feel the pheromones rolling off her in waves, a scent of musk and wild forests that tells me her panther is clawing at the surface, eager to be unleashed.

"Maybe someone tried to intimidate her, and she finally snapped," Rose states. Her voice is flat, chillingly matter-of-fact, as if she is discussing the weather rather than a potential massacre. "Maybe she shifted and killed someone."

I shake my head, my internal monologue snorting at the suggestion. *Reya? The girl who literally saved my life, gave a home to two beings that would never normally live together, while giving a home to a group of shifters who are the last type of creatures she would want to be around after what happened to their mother? Not a chance.* Reya is many things. hot-headed, impulsive, and prone to bouts of volcanic rage, but she is protective, not a mindless killer. She wouldn't slaughter innocents just because they pushed her buttons.

"I can't see her losing it like that," I respond, my voice firm despite the chaos swirling around us.

"Reya is stronger than that," Pickle pipes up from her spot on my lap. Her tiny voice is a silver bell of conviction, cutting through the tension in the cabin. "It's far more likely she was attacked by the demons."

The air in the cabin suddenly feels ten degrees colder. A localised winter settles into my bones, freezing the breath in my lungs. *Demons.* The word carries a weight that makes my skin crawl. If they have followed her here, to a place where she is literally trapped in a cage with nowhere to run and no way to defend herself...

"She has a good point," I say, relaying the pixie's insight to the others. I hadn't even let my mind drift toward that possibility yet, but once the words are spoken aloud, they hang in the air like a poisonous fog. After a moment of heavy, oppressive silence, the team nods in grim agreement. It is the only thing that explains the 'wrongness' I am feeling, the psychic static that makes my teeth ache.

I instruct Sam to pull up directly behind the line of idling patrol cars. "Pickle, Beastie, wait in the car until we know exactly what we're walking into," I command.

I see Pickle's face scrunching into a mask of pure, tiny indignation. She opens her mouth to argue, her wings fluttering with agitation. She starts to insist that she is invisible, that she can be our eyes and ears inside the facility, but I cut her off with a sharp look. I use Beastie as the ultimate trump card. The hellhound looks like an ordinary dog right now, but it would look incredibly suspicious if a stray canine started wandering into a high-security crime scene on its own without a lead. He needs his handler.

Thankfully, the logic holds. Pickle settles back with a loud, dramatic huff that vibrates through my thigh, crossing her tiny arms over her chest.

As we exit the vehicle and head toward the main cluster of officers, we clip our badges to our outfits. The silver catches the harsh Mississippi sun, blindingly bright. Sam clutches his tablet like a shield, the screen dark but loaded with the damning evidence we found on the man known as Jacob. Every step I take feels heavy, my boots crunching on the grit of the asphalt.

I immediately spot Chief Jefferson Hawk. We have met briefly before, but he looks like he has aged a decade since our last encounter. There are deep, hollow bags under his eyes and a tremor in his hands that he is trying desperately to hide. He notices our approach and manoeuvres through the crowd of officers, his expression one of strained relief.

"Agents, I'm happy to see you, though the timing is wretched," Hawk says, his voice raspy. "Have you come to help with our escaped prisoner?"

Escaped?

Why the hell would Reya escape? She refused to when she was in the sheriff's custody, so why now? What has happened? Unless it's not Reya at all. The world tilts for a moment. Sam steps forward, instinctively prepared to take charge, but I grip his arm firmly, stopping him instantly. My hold is strong—a silent command. I must control this story, and I need to do so loudly enough for every nearby officer to hear.

"We actually came to update someone we've been working with to bring down a corrupt cop," I say. I lean into the 'Destroyer' edge of my voice, making it cold, precise, and impossible to ignore. It is the voice that makes subordinates tremble and enemies hesitate. "The local sheriff in Luna Falls has taken things way too far. We just wanted to let her know the charges are a sham, and she'll be released any day now."

The moment I mention a 'corrupt cop,' a low ripple of mumbling starts among the rank and file. Heads start shaking, and I feel dozens of eyes boring into us, filled with scepticism and curiosity. *Good. Listen up. Your precious brotherhood has a cancer in it.* I am hoping this seeds enough doubt to speed up Reya's eventual processing, assuming she is even still in the building.

Chief Hawk looks as though he has just sucked on a lemon. "Are you still peddling this story that the woman arrested in Luna Falls is innocent? The evidence seemed fairly conclusive."

"We are," I say, my eyes narrowing into slits. "And we have the digital and physical proof that 'Jacob Davids' went missing ten years ago, the man who has been pretending to be him is a monster with what he and his family have been upto for years. His real name was Jason Lorcan. He belongs to a family of high-level criminals linked to a village in England where every single resident vanished without a trace. He wasn't a hero, Chief. He was a predator."

That stirs the hornet's nest. The air practically vibrates with the sudden surge of tension among the officers. I can see them exchanging glances, the seeds of doubt taking root. But Hawk's next words are what truly knock the legs out from under me.

"If what you're saying is true, I want to see that data immediately," Hawk says, stepping closer, his voice dropping to a conspiratorial whisper. "But that doesn't explain why Reya Harper has vanished from her cell. There are signs of there being a fire, but no actual damage, just lots of ash littering the cell. Her cellmate isn't talking; the girl just keeps whispering that she was asleep and the Harper girl simply... vanished."

I am lost for words. *Vanished.* The idea of a voluntary jailbreak feels absurd given Reya's temperament. A forced extraction or a kidnapping by demons feels far more likely. My heart hammers against my ribs, a frantic warning.

Sam sees me struggling and steps in, utilising the smooth, clinical tone he uses for CIA debriefings. "We'll need to talk to that cellmate immediately," Sam says. "I find it impossible to believe Reya would escape of her own free will. It's more likely she was extracted. A prisoner could have been tasked to take her out, or a guard decided to play judge and executioner because they believed she killed a cop. We're also searching for a witness who can testify that the Lorcan family was planning to kidnap Reya Harper for a forced pregnancy ring they've been linked to in England."

Hawk looks genuinely rattled now, his composure fracturing. "If even half of that is true, then I am sorry she has been treated this way. We can't ignore the fact that she's gone, though. I'm happy for you to speak to the cellmate, but I expect you to help us find her, regardless of the circumstances."

"We will," I promise, my mind already racing through tactical possibilities and exit points. "We actually have a highly trained dog in the car. Sam can walk you through the Lorcan files while the rest of us walk the perimeter to see if Beastie picks up a scent."

As I speak, my lower back gives a sharp, grinding protest. I wince internally, feeling the tug of the non-absorbable sutures where the doctor tried to repair the damage from my last fight. The sensation is like a hot wire being pulled through my fascia, and I wonder if the stitches are going to hold under the strain of a perimeter sweep.

"Agreed," Hawk says. "Start on the west side. That's the location of the cell she was placed in. By the time you return, we should be finished questioning the remaining staff."

Luca decides to stick with Sam, providing some much-needed muscle and an intimidating presence while they go over the files. Rose and I head back to the car to retrieve our hidden reinforcements.

"Pickle," I say as I lean into the SUV, my voice softening slightly. "Can Beastie make himself look like a different breed? He doesn't look official right now, not a police dog."

Pickle shrugs her tiny shoulders and places a hand on Beastie's massive, obsidian head. Moments later, she looks up and asks for a reference. I quickly find a high-resolution photo of a German Shepherd on my phone and show it to the hellhound.

The transformation is incredible and unsettling to witness. I watch as his body ripples and shifts, bones clicking and fur lengthening in a way that makes my own skin crawl with a sympathetic itch. It doesn't take long before he is a convincing, if slightly oversized, German Shepherd.

Pickle hitches a ride on the back of Beastie's neck, her tiny hands gripping his new fur as we make our way toward the western wall. The looming shadow of the prison feels like it is pressing down on us, an oppressive weight that smells of bleach and old fear.

"Why do you think she's gone?" Rose asks, her voice low. Her eyes scan the barred windows above with a predator's intensity. "Do you think the fire damage means she was attacked?"

"She might have realised she was a sitting duck in that cell," I speculate. "I'm guessing escaping would be a cakewalk for a witch of her calibre."

"With what I know about her line? It would be effortless," Rose agrees.

I look at Rose and see the conflict etched into her features. The hardness in her eyes has softened, replaced by something that looks like genuine guilt.

"I'm sorry I've been so pig-headed about her," she says, her voice thick with regret. "It's hard to change how you feel about a group of paranormals overnight, especially with the stories I was raised on. But given the situation, I need to start seeing the person, not the label."

I scan the area, checking for any prying eyes or the red light of a security camera. As soon as I am certain the coast is clear, I reach out and grab Rose, pulling her into a fierce, sudden kiss. She responds instantly, her lips crashing against mine with more force than she probably intended, almost knocking the wind out of me.

It has been a lifetime since we had a moment of actual intimacy, and the sensation is overwhelming. It is like a dam breaking, a flood of repressed desire rushing through my veins. Everything about her is amplified in this moment. She smells like a storm front rolling over a field of wildflowers. intense, electric, and intoxicating. I can feel every millimetre of her lips, every ridge and dip, the heat of her skin burning through the cool morning air like a brand. It is as if my senses have been dialled up to eleven, making the world around us fade into a blur of grey and blue.

I struggle to break the kiss, finally pulling away when I hear a distinct, tiny giggle followed by Beastie's deep, rhythmic chuffing. I feel the heat rising in my neck, a flush of embarrassment that clashes with the adrenaline. I glare down at Pickle, who is just giggling harder, her tiny wings fluttering in a blur of amusement.

When we reach the location Hawk indicated, I look up at the towering wall and spot an open window, a small gap in the fortress's armour. "Pickle, you're going in solo," I say, showing her the prison layout on my phone and pointing out the route to the cell block. "If her cell is empty, do a sweep. Call out to her. If she's hiding in the shadows, she might recognise your voice."

"I will do everything in my power to find her," Pickle says. Her expression has turned uncharacteristically solemn, the sass replaced by a fierce, unwavering loyalty.

"I know you will," I say softly.

"I know you will too, honey," Pickle adds, her eyes flitting to Rose for a split second with a mischievous glint. "You have a good heart, unlike some I could mention."

I can't help but smile as she grips her new weapon, a small, gleaming needle-sword that looks like a sliver of moonlight, and flutters up toward the window, disappearing into the dark maw of the prison.

Pickle

When I reach the ledge of the window, I stay low, my belly pressing against the cold stone. I peek over the edge to confirm that wherever this window leads is safe for me to enter. It is a sterile, boring place, devoid of any soul or colour. It is nothing like the vibrant, chaotic rooms the sisters keep in their home, which always smell of cinnamon and old books. Here, it just smells of stale coffee.

There are metal filing units that look like grey coffins and a woman hunched over a glowing computer screen, her face washed out by the blue light. I sneak in, keeping my wings to a steady, silent beat, staying well out of her peripheral vision. I have to be careful; some humans possess a trace of the Sight, and if she catches a glimpse of me, my mission is over before it begins.

I am lucky. The door to the corridor is cracked open just an inch. I slip through, entering a hallway that is blissfully empty. It looks far too clean for a place meant to hold people captive. We have prisons in the Fae realm, but they are not like this. Ours are jagged, organic places carved from obsidian and root, smelling of ancient moss and the kind of sorrow that stains your soul. This human prison just feels dead.

I flutter down the hallway, the silence of the building feeling heavy and artificial, as if the walls themselves are holding their breath. At the end of the corridor, I find the heavy iron bars I remember from the sheriff's station. Seeing Reya behind those bars before, miserable, broken, and stripped of her dignity, had torn at my heart in a way I cannot describe.

A sharp pang of guilt hits me then, a cold needle in my chest. *I should have been honest with her about her heritage.* I was just so afraid she would not handle the truth, especially after finding out her father was an Archangel or hearing about Hecate's hand in her birth. I wanted to give her time to breathe before the weight of destiny crushed her.

I slip through the bars, making sure my weapon does not clatter against the iron. I have to be careful not to touch the metal itself; iron is a poison to my kind, and it would burn my skin like a branding iron. I head for the stairs, climbing two floors until I reach the block where Reya was supposedly kept.

The air here changes instantly. It feels scorched, thick with the lingering scent of burnt ozone and something rotten. It is wrong. It is fundamentally wrong. I start to call out, my voice a tiny, hopeful whisper in the vast, echoing hallway.

"Reya? It's Pickle. Are you here? I'm here to bring you home."

I keep calling as I fly, my heart drumming against my ribs. But no one answers. The silence is oppressive, mocking me. Then, as I approach the cell numbers I was given, I hear a voice drifting from a nearby unit, a low, raspy sound.

"Do you hear that? It sounds like someone is calling for the Harper girl. Don't they know she's long gone?"

I race toward the source of the voice, flying right up to the bars of the neighbouring cell. My wings are buzzing with an urgency I cannot control. "You can hear me! Please, do you know what happened to her?"

In my haste, I am being reckless. If she can hear me, she can definitely see me, and in this enclosed space, I am incredibly vulnerable. The woman inside the cell jumps, her eyes widening in pure, unadulterated shock.

"What the fuck? What are you, some kind of fairy?"

"Do... not... call me that," I snap, my wings buzzing with sudden annoyance. "I am a Pixie, if you must know. Now, where is Reya?"

The women inside are speechless for a moment, their gazes darting to each other as if they are seeking guidance.

"Well? Help me!" I demand, hovering as close to the bars as I can. One of the women, the youngest of the group, finally beckons me inside. I hesitate for only a second before darting through the bars, slipping into the cell like a breath of wind.

The interior is a disaster area. There is ash everywhere, coating the floor and the walls like a grey snowfall. It clings to everything. There was a massive fight in here; I can smell the sulphur and the acrid tang of demonic energy. It makes my stomach churn.

"Please," I beg, my voice trembling with desperation. "I have to know what happened to my Reya."

"Who is she to you?" the woman asks, her voice cautious. "And who are you?"

"I'm Pickle. Reya gave me a home when I had nothing. She is... she is the most important person in this entire realm."

"I've heard of her kind, I think you can trust her, dear," one of the women says. She is sitting on a weird, stacked bed thing, her voice sounding hollow and distant. I cannot help but wonder if this weird bunk bed is some form of punishment, forcing them to take turns sleeping.

"Okay. I believe you. If mother says I can trust you, I will."

I look at the woman sitting on the bed, and that's when I really see them. My breath hitches. Both of them are spirits. They are translucent, shimmering with a pale, ethereal light that doesn't quite illuminate the darkness around them.

"Thank you," I say to the girl's mother. A realisation washes over me. I know I can see Sera and the shades that attacked us, but I didn't realise I could see the dead in this form. There is so much to learn about how my powers interact with this clumsy human realm.

"You can see them," the younger girl says, her eyes wide. "I couldn't until Reya did something... she cast a spell or shared her energy, and now I can finally see my mother."

I am fascinated. The magic lingers in the air, a faint golden thread that only I can perceive. "What are you? Most humans cannot see ghosts or pixies."

"I'm a kitsune. A fox shifter. My pack has always carried the gift of the Sight."

"Really? The shifters we live with are blind to me," I mutter, thinking of Elijah and Quinn, who are my favourites. The woman's posture shifts, becoming defensive and nervous.

"What shifters do you live with?" she asks.

"Panthers, leopards, and a very special one who has two forms," I list off, feeling proud of my unconventional family.

"That... that's actually incredible."

"It is. You know my name, what's yours?"

"Su Ling. And I'm not a criminal, not really. My pack got word of the attacks years ago and made me break the law to get into the system; they thought I'd be safer in juvie than out in the woods. I've been moved around ever since."

I listen to her story, and just like with Reya, my gut tells me she is a good soul, trapped in a bad situation. "So what happened? Was she attacked again?"

Su Ling's expression darkens, and she shivers despite the warmth of the room. "She was. These shadows... they were everywhere. They didn't just attack; they hunted. I tried to claw them off, but Reya fought them with a type of power I've never seen. Fire that didn't burn the walls, only the darkness."

I lean in, my heart racing. "And then?"

"Then, this black cloud, like a hole in the world, opened up right here in the centre of the cell. It was a void that sucked the light out of the room. Two massive demons stepped out. They were terrifying, hulking things with eyes like dying stars. For some reason, Reya just... she stopped fighting. She looked at us, and then at them. She said she'd go with them to keep the rest of us safe."

I gasp, my hand flying to my mouth. My weapon clinks against the floor as I drop it in shock. *She sacrificed herself.* The thought is a physical blow, leaving me reeling. Before I can ask more, heavy footsteps echo in the hall, loud and rhythmic.

A woman and two men, including a man I recognise who was talking to Ava, stop at the door. "Su Ling, time for more questions. Let's go."

I dive down and retrieve my weapon before any of them can spot me, my wings blurring as I vanish into the shadows of the frame of the bed torture device.

Before Su Ling is led away, when everyone is facing away from me. I fly up so I'm close to Su Ling's ear and whisper one last thing. "Thank you. If you ever escape this place, find us in Luna Falls. Luna Lake, the Harper property. We'll protect you."

As she walks out, she does not look back, but I see her lips move in a tiny, almost imperceptible motion. She mouths the words. *'I will, thank you.'*

CHAPTER 11

The Weight of Sight

Ava

Waiting for Pickle to return is an exquisite, agonising form of torture. I am standing on grass that looks in need of a good downpour while we are all slowly being baked alive in the unforgiving Mississippi sun. The heat does not just sit on me; it radiates off the ground in shimmering, viscous waves that distort the horizon, making the facility's concrete walls look as if they are melting into a puddle of grey sludge.

I can smell the cloying scent of hot asphalt and the metallic tang of old exhaust fumes lingering in the stagnant air. Every breath I take feels heavy, as if the oxygen has been replaced by warm wool.

Rose is beside me. She tries to soothe me, her hand sliding down to rest on my thigh. Her touch is a warm, grounding anchor, her fingers pressing firmly into the fabric of my leggings, but it isn't working. I can't focus on her. I can't even really feel the comfort she is trying to offer because my own body has become a traitor.

Beneath my skin, in the very depths of my veins, it feels as though someone has replaced my blood with a volatile mixture of battery acid and liquid fire. It pulses with a rhythmic, stinging heat that synchronises with the frantic hammering of my heart. I am vibrating with a toxic, restless energy, a manic surge that makes every nerve ending scream for release.

I feel like I could sprint ten miles through a brick wall without breaking a sweat.

It is an insane, unnatural surge of adrenaline that refuses to subside, leaving me on the precipice of some violent outburst I cannot name. I shift my weight from one foot to the other, my boots crunching on the dry grass. The sound is somehow too loud, too sharp, grating against my raw nerves.

I seriously need to start working out again, I think, as a flash of my inner warrior takes over. *Just to burn off this surge. To get my body back into some semblance of fighting shape before I go crazy with all this energy running through me.*

"She will be okay," Rose says. Her voice is smooth, like dark honey, laced with an easy confidence that I desperately wish I could steal for myself. She shifts closer, her shoulder brushing mine, the scent of her—something primal, like rain-drenched earth and wild musk—filling my senses. "It's not like anyone can actually see her in there. She's safe behind those walls, Ava."

"You don't know that," I snap back.

The words leave me too quickly, sharpened into jagged blades by the sheer volume of anxiety clawing at my throat. I feel the tension in my chest tighten into a physical knot, a hard ball of dread that refuses to unfurl. I turn to look at her, my eyes probably wide and manic. "Just because this is a human prison doesn't mean there aren't paranormals hiding within those walls. This is a hub for the desperate and the dangerous, Rose. If there is just one creature in there with the Sight, do you really think they will be friendly to a stray pixie?"

Rose pauses, her brow furrowing slightly. She looks at the imposing concrete structure of the prison, her green eyes scanning the perimeter with a predator's precision. I can see her processing my logic, the gears turning behind that beautiful, confident mask.

"I guess you're right," she concedes softly. "I just can't see a powerful paranormal being, allowing themselves to be captured and locked in a mundane concrete cell. It doesn't make sense. Why risk the indignity of a human cage when you have the power to break it?"

Her comment sparks something in me, a flicker of professional curiosity that forces my racing mind down a dark, analytical rabbit hole. I forget to breathe for a second as I stare at her.

"Are there specific prisons for paranormals?" I ask.

Rose's expression shifts. The flirtatious, playful edge vanishes, replaced by something clinical and distant. She is no longer just my partner; she is a Beta of a powerful pack, a repository of lore I am only beginning to understand.

"Not in the human sense," she explains. "There are no bars or guards with badges. I know some of the older, more traditional covens would banish criminals to a different plane of existence, tossing them into a void world where they can't hurt anyone."

She pauses, her gaze drifting toward the shimmering heat haze on the road. "But most factions that police our kind just end up destroying the threats. They believe someone possessing that level of dark power will never truly change once they go bad. Once the corruption takes root in the soul, it is permanent. It is an unfortunate truth that power corrupts absolutely."

A cold knot tightens in my stomach, a stark contrast to the fire in my veins. "I guess that makes sense," I mutter. "But what if someone is set up? What if they are framed?"

"Lethal action would never be taken without absolute, undeniable proof," she assures me, though there is a flicker of something in her eyes, perhaps a memory of a time when the "proof" wasn't enough.

"I'll have to take your word for it," I reply.

My cynical side is screaming. Having spent years in the belly of government agencies, I know that "absolute proof" is a flexible term. Justice is rarely blind. usually, it is just looking the other way while the monsters win and the innocent are erased from the record.

I am about to press her for more information when Beastie suddenly reacts. The massive dog shifts his head with a violent snap, his eyes locking onto the prison window. His ears flatten against his skull in a gesture of pure, instinctual warning. A low huff escapes his nostrils.

A split second later, Pickle materialises out of the window.

She looks absolutely wrecked. Her iridescent wings, usually humming with energy, are drooping like wilted flower petals in a storm. Her tiny shoulders are slumped, and her delicate face is a mess of tear streaks, her eyes red and swollen.

"Is she..." I start to ask, my voice trembling.

Before I can finish the sentence, Pickle launches herself at me. She slams hard into my chest with a force that knocks the breath from my lungs, though she weighs next to nothing. It is the emotional weight of her impact that hits me harder than the physical one.

I glance over at Rose to gauge her reaction. She cannot see the pixie, but she tracks the sudden, violent jerk of my body. She sees the way I instinctively cradle my hands over my heart in a protective stance, my fingers curling around the air where Pickle is clinging to me.

Rose's posture changes instantly. Her muscles tense, and her eyes sharpen. She knows something is wrong.

Then, the sound reaches me. A tiny, broken sob. It is a high-pitched, heartbreaking noise that pierces through the distant wail of sirens and the hum of the highway. Pickle is crying hysterically, her entire body shaking against my sternum. I feel a small, cold patch of moisture soaking through the fabric of my dark shirt as she weeps into me, her grief palpable, an electric current of sorrow that transfers directly into my skin.

"What's wrong?" I ask softly. My eyes are already darting around, scanning the perimeter for any immediate threats, my military training kicking in even as my heart breaks. "Pickle, talk to me."

"What's happened?" Rose demands. Her panther instincts are flaring now, her voice gaining that low, predatory growl as she picks up on the sharp spike of distress radiating from me. She steps closer, her body shielding mine, her gaze searching for an enemy she cannot see.

I just shrug helplessly at Rose, my heart sinking into my shoes. I am desperately trying to listen to the frantic, muffled words Pickle is gasping into my collarbone. Her voice is a chaotic blur of a language I don't recognise and broken English, her breath hitching in her throat. Finally, she pulls back just enough to look me in the eye, her voice a shattered whisper.

"Sh... she's gone."

The bottom drops out of my stomach. For a moment, I feel hollow, weightless, as if the gravity holding me to the earth has simply ceased to exist.

"What do you mean she's gone?" I ask, my voice sounding distant to my own ears. "Do you mean she managed to escape? Did she find a way out?"

Pickle shakes her head violently against my collarbone, her iridescent wings giving one last, pathetic flutter before falling still. "No. She was taken. She was taken after she was attacked by demons."

The word *demons* causes anger to rise within me. My voice turns to ice. The dread is no longer a knot. it is a frozen block of lead in my chest, suffocating me.

"How do you know this?" I demand. "Who took her? Where?"

"What's going on, Ava?" Rose demands, her patience evaporating. She can feel the tension reaching a breaking point, and the lack of information is making her volatile. "Tell me what is happening!"

Beastie registers the panic. He seems attuned to Pickle's emotional state, and right now she is a storm of terror. A low, terrifying growl begins to vibrate in his chest, a sound so profound it feels like a physical earthquake shaking the ground beneath our feet.

Suddenly, his illusion as a normal dog shatters.

It is a violent transformation. His form begins to warp and expand, muscles bulging with unnatural power, skin stretching and shifting as he loses control of his shape. He grows larger, more menacing, his eyes glowing with an inner, hellish light.

“Pickle says Reya has been taken after a demon attack,” I relay to Rose quickly. I force my voice to remain steady, the External Warrior taking the lead even though the Internal Human is screaming in agony.

Rose looks utterly bewildered, her head tilting. “How can she possibly know that? She’s just a pixie. How could she have seen...?”

I shrug again, drowning in a sea of frustration and confusion. I want to shake the answers out of the universe. I want to scream at the sky until it gives me a map. But I have no idea how to gently coax a traumatised pixie into giving a tactical debriefing while her entire world is falling apart.

Thankfully, Beastie’s escalating meltdown forces the issue. His growling deepens into a demonic rumble that shakes the very air in my lungs. Then, actual, literal flames begin to lick across his coarse, shifting fur. They are a deep onyx, spitting sparks into the air. The heat around us spikes instantly, making the atmosphere shimmer with sudden, oppressive intensity.

Pickle pulls away from my chest. Her tiny face is no longer just sad. it is a mask of fierce, tearful determination. She flies straight down, diving through the heat, and throws her arms around a small part of Beastie's burning neck.

She clings to him, burying her face in his fiery fur. Her sobbing intensifies for a breathless moment, a tiny creature embracing a monster of flame.

“Pickle, no!” I almost scream.

I reach out, terrified she is going to be burned alive by the hellfire. My hand is outstretched, my fingers clawing at the air, but I am way too slow. It doesn't matter. The flames have absolutely no effect on her fragile, magical skin. She is a creature of Faerie, and the fire seems to slide off her like water.

As soon as she embraces him, the physical contact acts as a grounding wire for Beastie's rage. The flames flicker once, twice, and then vanish into thin air, leaving a faint, stinging smell of ozone and sulphur in their wake. He regains his composure, his form settling back into something manageable, though his eyes remain glowing pools of misery.

After taking a shaky, shuddering breath, Pickle turns her tear-streaked face back to me. She prepares to deliver the final blow.

"The woman sharing the cell with Reya is actually a shifter," Pickle explains, her voice trembling but clear now. "She said she is a kitsune, whatever that is. Her name is Su Ling, and her kind possess the Sight. Su Ling explained that shadows attacked them in the cell... shades from hell."

I feel my breath hitch.

"They managed to fight off the shades," Pickle continues, a fresh tear rolling down her cheek. "But when two very large, terrifying demons stepped out of a black portal, Reya just... she surrendered. She didn't even fight them. She let them take her to protect the other girl. She gave herself up so Su Ling wouldn't be harmed."

Every single fibre in my body seems to double in weight. A crushing, suffocating gravity pulls me down, and for a moment, I feel as if I might simply sink into the ground and never return.

My mind immediately spirals to the darkest possible conclusion. *Reya is already dead.* Or worse, she is being tortured in some place where light cannot reach. This was a woman I had started to bond with, a woman who had literally poured her life-force into mine to save me from death. She is our only real hope of making a difference in this hidden war, and that hope may have just been extinguished.

I update Rose, keeping my voice as clinical and detached as possible to hide the fact that I am screaming internally. "We'd better get going and update the others. Maybe we have a slim window of time to do something."

Though I have no idea what.

"I don't know where she would have been taken," I admit, my voice cracking slightly. "Well, I guess I know of one place. If they dragged her down into the Underworld, I really don't have a single clue how we would ever get her back."

When we return to where Luca and Sam are waiting by our vehicle, the tension is palpable. It is thick enough to touch, like a heavy curtain draped over the parking lot. Both men look incredibly worried. It is an expression I am not used to seeing on Luca's usually stoic, commanding face. He looks less like an Alpha and more like a man who has just seen a ghost.

As we approach, Luca wastes zero time with pleasantries. His dark eyes are burning with a need for answers, his posture rigid.

I update them quickly, acting as a translator for Pickle's devastating reconnaissance. As I speak, Sam and Luca exchange a dark, heavy look. It is the exact same look Rose and I shared moments ago. It is the look of people staring into an abyss and realising the abyss is staring back.

"We'd better get back to the sisters and deliver the news," Luca says. His deep voice sounds hollow, empty of its usual authority. "I think we also need to find a new, secure location for the rest of our pack to hide out in. I can't see the Harpers wanting our people around once we tell them their sister might be dead."

He pauses, his expression twisting into something raw and pained. "This also perfectly explains why the mate bond vanished so violently."

Luca looks truly, profoundly heartbroken when he mentions the severed bond. He looks like a man who just realised he threw away a winning lottery ticket seconds before the numbers were drawn, only to find out the ticket was burned in a fire.

We made our excuses to Chief Hawk for not sticking around to interview Su Ling. The drive back to Luna Falls feels like wading through wet cement. Every mile is a struggle. The interior of our Tahoe is suffocatingly silent, save for the rhythmic click of the turn signals and the soft, guttural sounds of Pickle crying quietly in the back.

Her tiny sobs punctuate the silence, cutting through me like a knife. I catch her constantly checking her tiny wrist, her face scrunching into a look of absolute confusion every time she peeks under the small leather strap she wears there.

What are you hiding, little one? I wonder, but I don't have the energy to ask.

When Sam finally turns the heavy SUV off the main road and onto the gravel drive leading to the Harper property, my heart plummets into a new, bottomless level of despair. I really do not want to do this. The thought of it makes me feel physically ill. I do not want to look Freya and Maya in the eyes and tell them their sister has been dragged to hell.

As soon as Sam shifts the car into park, Beastie and Pickle completely vanish through the rear door. They are gone before the engine even stops humming. I should have anticipated that; Pickle is an emotional creature, and she is going to blurt out the horrible truth to the sisters before we can even put our boots on the front porch.

For a long, cowardly moment, I refuse to move. I sit in the passenger seat, staring at the dashboard, my hands gripping the upholstery so hard my knuckles are white. I am the last one to slide out of the vehicle.

"It's going to be okay, Ava," Rose says softly.

She steps close to me, wrapping her strong arms around me in a fierce, protective hug. She smells of safety and strength, but right now, it feels like a lie.

"How on earth is this going to be okay?" I demand, my temper flaring suddenly.

I push her away slightly, shooting her a dark, accusing glare. Rose has never liked Reya, and while I love Rose with everything I have, I have seen a cold, prejudiced side of her lately that I absolutely despise. The way she views Reya sometimes makes my skin crawl.

Before we even make it to the front steps, the heavy oak door flies open with a crash that echoes across the yard.

A very pissed-off Freya stands in the threshold. Her eyes are blazing with righteous fury, and I can almost see the sparks of fire magic dancing in her pupils. She looks like a goddess of war on the verge of a massacre.

"This is your fault!" Freya screams, pointing a shaking finger at us. "You were supposed to protect her! If you had just gotten her out of that cage sooner, this never would have happened!"

Sam steps forward, ever the diplomat, raising his hands in a placating gesture. He uses that soft, measured CIA voice, the one designed to calm panicked assets. "Freya, please. Before we heard the bad news, we actually managed to convince the Chief of Police in Jackson that Reya was completely innocent. He was going to help speed up her release. We can still craft a narrative where she was forcibly kidnapped by people wanting revenge for Jacob."

"That's a lovely legal strategy, Sam," Freya spits, her sarcasm dripping like acid. "Truly impressive. But how in the hell do we actually get her back from demons?"

"That," Sam responds, his shoulders slumping in defeat, "I don't know."

A reckless, dangerous idea sparks in the back of my brain. It is a soldier's instinct. if you can't find the target, attack the source.

"What if we go hunting?" I suggest, my voice gaining strength. "What if we go after these demons in Jackson and manage to capture this Devika woman? Maybe whatever ancient demon is possessing her can give us the answers on where Reya has been taken. Only a high-level demon can give us the coordinates we need."

I don't know if it was the sheer audacity of my suggestion or just the overwhelming grief, but Freya doesn't argue. She simply spins on her heel and shoots straight back into the house without a single word.

We all share a weary, defeated look before silently agreeing to follow her inside.

The living room is a scene of utter heartbreak. The air is thick with the smell of old parchment and extinguished candles. Pickle is sobbing openly now, clinging desperately to Maya, who is also crying silent, steady tears that track down her pale cheeks. Jenny is nowhere to be seen, likely hiding in another room to avoid the emotional fallout.

As Luca steps inside, Elijah appears silently from the rear door, joining them to hear the update on the disaster at the prison. He looks solemn, his presence a quiet weight in the corner of the room.

A bizarre moment of dark comedy breaks the tension. Suddenly, two chaotic fox cubs storm into the house, yipping and tumbling over each other. They are being chased by Reya's stuffed panther, which has become a permanent, animated golem due to Freya's failed spell. The plush predator, with its button eyes and soft fur, lunges at the cubs with surprising agility. It chases them right back out the rear door, leaving us in a heavy, oppressive silence.

I move toward one of the plush armchairs, trying my best not to disturb the weeping pile of Pickle and Maya on the couch. As I lower myself onto the cushions, it happens.

A sudden, violent wave of vertigo hits me.

The world tilts forty-five degrees to the left. The edges of my vision fray, turning into a fuzzy, static black, like an old television losing its signal. I lose my footing entirely and collapse into the chair like a broken ragdoll, my limbs feeling heavy and disconnected.

"Ava! What's wrong? Is it your back?" Rose rushes over, her hands hovering over me in panic, her green eyes wide with terror.

"No," I gasp, pulling in a deep, shaky breath as the dizziness slowly recedes. "I just... I felt incredibly dizzy. It's nothing. I'm fine."

"I do not believe you," Rose insists. She reaches out and touches my forehead, her expression grim. "You don't look well at all. You're pale, Ava. You shouldn't have pushed yourself so hard today."

Before I can argue or push her away, Freya comes rushing down the wooden staircase. She hits the landing and comes to a sliding, frantic stop, her breathing heavy.

"I know how to find Reya," she announces, her voice ringing with desperate hope.

She holds up a small, dark clump of hair between two fingers.

Maya and Pickle both gasp, understanding its significance immediately.

"Madi, we need your help. Please help us," Freya commands.

The crossroads demon Madi steps smoothly out from the deepest shadows near the bookcase. She doesn't walk so much as glide, folding her majestic, dark wings behind her back with a soft *whump*. Her eyes are ancient and knowing.

"You summoned me," she says, her voice smooth and dangerous, like velvet over steel. "What is wrong?"

"Reya has been taken by demons," Freya demands. "Can you go down there and get her back?"

Madi's expression shifts into profound mournfulness. She looks at Freya with a pity that feels almost insulting. "I cannot do that. I am so sorry. I cannot cross the threshold into the Underworld. My origins prevent it. To enter is to be erased."

"What are we supposed to do now?" Freya cries out, throwing her hands up in defeat, her voice cracking.

Suddenly, Madi's head snaps toward the dark corner behind my chair.

Sera materialises from the gloom. The shadow demon's purple eyes are blazing with lethal intent, her form shimmering like oil on water. She looks absolutely ready for a bloodbath, her claws extending as she prepares to launch herself at Madi.

I am the first to notice her impending attack, as the distraught sisters are preoccupied and the rest can't see Madi. Everyone else sees only a dark corner.

"Sera, stop! She isn't an enemy!" I yell.

Madi drops into a defensive crouch, her massive wings spreading to shield herself. The sudden display shocks Luca and Sam, who still cannot see the shadow targeting the demon. They only see Madi reacting to something invisible.

'Are you absolutely sure this demon isn't an enemy, Ava?'

Sera's cold, echoing voice violently invades my mind. It is not a sound, but a thought that feels like ice water being poured into my skull.

I jump in my chair, startled. I completely forgot that Reya was supposed to be the only one able to communicate with her.

"Yes, I am completely sure she isn't an enemy," I say aloud to the empty air. "Freya called her here to help us find Reya."

The room falls dead silent. Every eye in the room turns toward me.

"Did she just speak to you?" Rose demands, her voice dangerously quiet. She steps closer, her eyes narrowing with a mixture of confusion and suspicion. "How in the hell is Reya's personal shade able to talk directly into your mind?"

My stomach plummets. I can feel the lie forming in my throat before I even consciously decide to tell it. Telling Rose that Sera can talk to me because Reya's blood runs in my veins will end in a fight I am far too exhausted to have.

"I think it must have something to do with the specific magic Reya used to save me," I lie smoothly, leaning back into the chair. "Whatever she did to heal me... whatever that transfusion was... it must have given me the temporary ability to hear her frequency."

"Why didn't you tell me this was happening?" Rose demands, her eyes flashing with hurt. "We are partners, Ava. Why keep this from me?"

"We have had a hell of a lot going on, Rose," I deflect, my voice growing tired. "Anyway, we should leave the sisters alone for now. But Freya, if you come up with a plan, call us."

I attempt to push myself up from the chair, intending to end the conversation and escape the oppressive atmosphere. But as I move, a bizarre, tingling sensation erupts across my right hand. It feels like thousands of tiny needles pricking my skin.

A sharp, metallic *clink* echoes through the silent room.

The dizziness slams back into me like a speeding truck. My vision fractures violently. one second I see the living room in its warm amber light, and the next everything dissolves into black static. Panic claws at my throat, and I feel myself slipping away again, until a pulsing energy washes over my eyes. It feels like a cool, thin film of water settling over my corneas.

The room snaps back into brutal focus.

Everyone is staring at the floor in absolute, stunned silence.

I lean forward, following their gaze. I look at my right hand, expecting to see the heavy, magical silver ring Papa Legba gave me. the one that is permanently charmed to be invisible to my own eyes, the artefact that allows me to see the unseen.

The ring isn't on my finger.

It is sitting innocently on the scuffed wooden floorboards, gleaming brightly in the afternoon light. It looks small and insignificant, a simple band of silver.

I look up, and I freeze.

I am staring perfectly at Pickle. I can see the iridescent shimmer of her wings and the salt stains on her cheeks. I can see Sera, the shadow demon, standing in the corner with her purple eyes glowing. I don't seem to need the ring anymore.

The magic is gone, but my sight has returned. Or perhaps, something much more terrifying has taken its place.

CHAPTER 12

The Metamorphosis of Blood

I stare at the heavy silver ring resting innocently on the scuffed wooden floorboards. Its polished surface catches the afternoon light, throwing a brilliant glint across my vision in a way that feels like a mockery. My brain absolutely refuses to process the sight. It is a small thing, a simple loop of metal, yet its absence from my finger feels like a limb has been severed.

I am trying desperately to maintain my composure. I focus on keeping my breathing steady and my expression neutral, but the room is spinning on a tilted, sickening axis. The world wobbles, the walls leaning in as if they are curious about my collapse. Then, the heat hits. A vicious, unnatural fever spikes through my veins, an internal combustion that makes my skin feel like it is roasting from the inside out. It isn't the external heat of the Mississippi sun anymore. this is a biological fire, as if my very blood has been replaced with molten lead, heavy and searing, pulsing through my arteries with every thud of my heart.

What is happening to me?

The biggest problem is that every single person in this room just watched me collapse into this armchair like a puppet with its strings suddenly cut. The silence that follows is suffocating, broken only by the ragged sound of my own breath.

Rose, naturally, is hovering over me in full protective panic mode. Her presence is a constant, high-voltage hum of anxiety that I can feel vibrating against my skin. She doesn't just stand near me. she envelops me, her scent of rain and wild flowers becoming oppressive in her desperation.

"Honey, what's wrong?" Rose demands.

Her voice is tight, bordering on a scream. Her hands are frantic, checking my face, tracing the line of my jaw and the pulse in my neck for any sign of injury. Her touch is soothing because it is hers, but it is also terrifyingly insistent, as if she is trying to hold me together by sheer force of will.

"Why has the ring fallen off? Has it run out of magic?" She snaps her head up, her glowing green eyes scanning the room with a predatory intensity. She is silently demanding answers from anyone brave enough to speak, her body coiled like a spring ready to snap.

"I just feel a little dizzy. I'm okay," I lie through my teeth.

I force a strained, brittle smile that feels like it might crack my face in half. My voice sounds hollow, distant, as if I am speaking from the bottom of a well. "And I have absolutely no idea why the ring fell off."

Right. Totally fine. I tell myself, while my internal monologue screams in terror. *I'm just spontaneously rejecting divine artefacts because my DNA is currently undergoing a chaotic rewrite.*

"You are changing," Madi states.

The crossroads demon steps closer, her movement fluid and eerie, as if she is gliding through the air rather than walking on floorboards. Her dark eyes study me with a mixture of deep concern and a morbid, clinical fascination that makes my skin crawl. She looks at me not as a person, but as a specimen under a microscope.

"That ring was specifically forged for a human vessel," Madi explains, her voice smooth and devoid of judgment. "It rejected you because it seems you are no longer human. The frequency has shifted. Your essence is vibrating on a plane that the metal can no longer anchor to." She tilts her head, a small, knowing smile playing on her lips. "Papa Legba will certainly want to hear about this development."

Freya steps right into the demon's personal space. She doesn't care about the danger; she is driven by a grief so potent it has turned into a weapon. Her fists are clenched so tightly at her sides that her knuckles look like white stones.

"You are not going anywhere until you help us get our sister back," Freya snarls, her voice low and dangerous.

Madi doesn't even flinch at the aggression. She has lived for eons. a human girl with power in her veins is barely a flicker to her. "I cannot cross into the Underworld to retrieve her, Freya. As I already explained, my wings will not allow it. The threshold of the Pit is anathema to my kind."

She pauses, her gaze softening slightly. "I will ask my contacts to see if I can get any news. I would be quick if I were you. Don't waste time. If you want answers fast, I highly suggest you capture some of the lower-level demons currently terrorising Jackson. Torture them. Break their spirits. See if you can force them to talk. It would be infinitely quicker than waiting for a diplomatic response from the void."

Maya pales, her hands trembling against the fabric of her floral skirt. She looks as though she might faint just at the mention of torture. "Why do we have to be quick?" she whispers, her voice small and fragile.

Madi's beautiful, imposing face softens with a flicker of genuine pity. It is a look that makes me feel even more vulnerable. "I am not one hundred percent certain on the exact math, as I've never been to the Underworld myself, but time flows differently down there."

She looks directly at the sisters. "For every single month that passes in our realm, roughly a year passes in the Underworld."

The blood drains completely from Freya's face, leaving her looking like a ghost. The fire in her eyes doesn't go out, but it is suddenly eclipsed by a sheer, blinding horror.

"Are you fucking kidding me?" Freya whispers. "A year? You're telling me she could be there for years while we're just... sitting here?"

"We have much more important things to deal with right now," Rose snarls, completely ignoring the horrifying revelation of time dilation. Her focus is entirely on me. She glares daggers at Madi, her body coiled and ready to strike. "What exactly do you mean, Ava isn't human anymore?"

"As I said, she is fundamentally changing," Madi replies smoothly, her voice as calm as a stagnant pond in the middle of a forest. "I can literally feel the shift in her energy from all the way over here. Her aura... it is shifting colours, blending into something new. It feels vaguely familiar yet completely alien at the same time."

Madi steps even closer, leaning in to sniff the air around me. I feel like a piece of meat being appraised by a gourmet chef. "It is a fascinating metamorphosis. I honestly cannot wait to see what you finally transition into, Ava. The bridge between species is always so volatile." She pauses, her eyes narrowing. "How did this even happen to you?"

I keep my mouth clamped shut, my jaw aching from the tension. I can feel Rose's gaze on me, searching for a truth I am not ready to give. I know exactly why this is happening.

The metallic, copper taste of Reya's blood still haunts the back of my throat like a lingering ghost, a memory of desperation and survival. I remember the way it felt sliding down my throat, the sudden explosion of power that had stitched my organs back together. There is absolutely no way I am telling anyone in this room the truth. If I utter a single word about drinking a witch's blood to stay alive, Rose will lose her mind. She is already protective; if she finds out I've been "tainted" by the very woman she distrusts, she might actually tear the sisters apart in a blind, protective rage.

But my gorgeous, hyper-observant girlfriend has already connected the terrifying dots.

"Whatever Reya did to you in that battle is what is causing this mutation," Rose states. Her voice is trembling with barely suppressed fury, and I can see her pupils dilating, her inner panther rising to the surface. She looks back at Madi, her eyes burning. "Is there a way to stop the process? Can we reverse it?"

"The change is occurring on a deep, genetic level," Madi explains casually, as if she were merely discussing the weather or a change in the tides. "It is written into your very being now. So, no. It cannot be stopped. But really, isn't this vastly better? Look at her."

Madi gestures toward me with an elegant hand. "She will likely become much stronger, faster, more resilient. She won't be quite so fragile and easy to kill. You are trading your mortality for something... durable."

Gee, thanks. I think bitterly. *I love being reminded of my mortal squishiness while I feel like I'm melting into my chair.*

"Reya had absolutely no right to alter her like this," Rose growls.

Suddenly, the shift happens. Rose's panther teeth and fangs fully extend, pushing past her lips in a display of primal aggression. Her voice drops an octave, becoming a guttural snarl that vibrates through the floorboards. She looks lethal, a predator who has found something to kill.

"Rose, calm down," Luca orders.

His Alpha tone bleeds into the room, heavy and commanding. It is a physical weight that forces the air out of the conversation. Rose freezes, her shoulders tensing under the pressure of his authority.

"I actually agree with the demon," Luca says, his voice firm. "This can only be a tactical advantage. We are entering a war we don't fully understand. If it makes Ava stronger and harder to kill, then we accept it. Whatever Reya did, she did it to save Ava's life."

He looks at Rose, his eyes softening but remaining stern. "Tell me, Rose, would you honestly prefer she had just let her bleed out in the dirt? Would you rather have a dead human or a living... whatever she is becoming?"

Rose shrinks back slightly, the fight draining right out of her. The fangs retract, and her expression crumbles into one of utter defeat.

"Luca, how can you say that? Of course, I didn't want her to die," she whispers. She looks at me, and for a moment, I see the raw terror in her eyes. the fear that the woman she loves is slipping away, replaced by something strange. "I am just so incredibly frustrated that we are completely flying blind here."

I reach out, wrapping my hot, trembling fingers around Rose's wrist. Her skin feels cool compared to my feverish heat. I stroke the soft skin with my thumb, trying to anchor us both in the storm.

"It will be okay," I promise softly, locking my eyes with hers. "I am going to be okay. Please stop stressing. If whatever is happening to me makes me stronger, then I am entirely on board. I really, truly do not want to experience dying ever again."

I sound incredibly confident, the External Warrior projecting strength for her partner. But deep down, a cold knot of pure terror is twisting in my gut. *I am turning into a monster.* A literal, supernatural anomaly. I don't know where this road leads, but I can feel the human part of me receding, like a tide pulling away from the shore.

Sam clears his throat, ever the practical tactician, breaking the emotional tension. "Well, since the ring rejected you, I guess you are no longer going to be able to see the demons and warn us of incoming attacks?"

I blink as the realisation hits me. I am no longer our secret weapon. Amid the searing fever and existential dread, I hadn't even noticed the visual anomaly. My heart skips a beat. If I can't see the enemy, I am useless in a fight. I am just a target.

I look down at my bare finger, and I suddenly realise Sam's statement is wrong.

I stop. I blink once, twice. I can still see Pickle and Sera; if I had lost my sight, then I wouldn't be able to see them anymore.

I scan the room to make sure what I saw after the ring fell off is still true. As I look at Pickle's last known location, I see the shimmering, iridescent glow of her wings, clear as day. When I turn to look at Sera, I see the oppressive, swirling darkness of Sera lingering in the corner. Her purple eyes are watching us with detachment. The world hasn't gone grey. If anything, the colours are more vivid, more saturated.

"Actually," I say, my voice breathy with shock. "Whatever is mutating my DNA is apparently doing the exact same job as Legba's magical ring. I can still see Pickle. And I can clearly see Sera."

"Really? You can still see and hear me?" Pickle gasps.

She launches herself off Beastie's massive back, where she had been quietly crying since we returned. She flutters straight over to my face, her wings humming with a sudden burst of energy.

"Yes, Pickle. I can see you perfectly," I reply, offering her a tired, weary smile.

"Oh, good," she sniffles, her tiny hands grabbing handfuls of my black shirt, pulling herself close to my neck. "I would have been so incredibly sad if I weren't able to talk to you ever again." She presses her tear-stained cheek against my collarbone in a fierce, tiny hug.

"I would be deeply sad as well," I whisper, lifting one hand to carefully, gently hug her back.

"Can I see the ring, please?" Freya asks suddenly, stepping forward. Her grief is still there, but it is being overtaken by an intense, academic curiosity.

The request catches me completely off guard. "Sure."

Pickle releases my shirt and zips back over to the hellhound. I lean forward, fighting through the painful stiffness in my healing spine, and reach for the silver band on the floor. The absolute second my bare skin makes contact with the metal, a blinding, searing agony shoots up my arm.

It isn't a burn; it is an electric shock of pure repulsion. It feels like I just grabbed a white-hot coal directly out of a blazing furnace.

"Ouch! Son of a bitch!" I curse, snapping my hand back. I shake my fingers in the air, trying to cool the blistering, phantom heat radiating from my skin. My fingertips are pulsing red, though there is no actual mark on the flesh.

"Did that ring just burn you? Let me see," Rose demands.

She drops to her knees and snatches my right hand. Her fingers feel like ice against my burning skin as she starts probing the flushed, sensitive flesh, her brow furrowed in confusion.

"It did. It burned like pure fire," I grit out, wincing at the lingering sting.

"Why on earth did it do that?" Rose demands, glaring at the innocent-looking silver loop as if she wants to crush it under her boot.

I can't help but glance up at Madi. The demon is watching the entire exchange with a smug, knowing glint in her dark eyes. She isn't surprised. In fact, she looks delighted. She knows infinitely more than she is sharing, and the secrecy makes me itch. I make a mental note to corner her later, to interrogate her when my overprotective panther isn't hovering within earshot.

"It burns because it is no longer necessary," Madi says, looking incredibly smug. "Your body is now doing the job the ring was doing. You have developed your own internal 'Sight'. It is like the two frequencies of the ring and what your body produces are overloading your system when you touch the metal, creating a dissonant magical feedback loop. Hence, it burns you."

Madi straightens her posture, preparing to depart. "Anyway, I need to leave now. I am being summoned by another crossroads entity."

She lifts one elegant hand to her dark, flowing hair. With a brutally sharp, elongated fingernail, she casually slices off a thick lock of her own hair. She rolls the severed strands between her palms, and a brilliant, blinding flash of violet light erupts from her hands. When she opens them, the hair is neatly bound together with a pretty, dark silk ribbon.

"You essentially wasted the last token, considering I cannot physically enter the pit to help you. Take this replacement," Madi says, extending her hand to Freya.

Freya accepts the demonic token with a curt nod. Madi bids the room a brief, formal goodbye. Her dark, calculating gaze lingers heavily on me for one last, terrifying second, as if she is trying to predict exactly what I will become. Then, she spreads her massive, leathery wings.

The air behind her rips open with a sound like tearing silk, revealing a terrifying, swirling black void of pure nothingness. She steps backwards into the abyss, and the portal snaps shut instantly. The heavy, rhythmic beating of her wings echoes in the room for a heartbeat, accompanied by the bizarre, faint sound of rhythmic, upbeat jazz music.

Okay. That was weird. I blink. *Does she have a soundtrack?*

Freya carefully tucks the enchanted hair into the front pocket of her jeans. She turns her attention back to the floor, stepping up to my chair and crouching down to retrieve Papa Legba's artefact.

"Please be careful, sis," Maya warns, her voice laced with anxiety.

"I will," Freya promises. She extends one finger, cautiously tapping the side of the silver band. Seeing no reaction, she pinches the metal and lifts it into the air. The absolute second the ring rests fully in her palm, Freya gasps, her eyes widening into massive, shocked saucers.

"Oh my gods," Freya whispers, staring at the metal. "I think I know exactly how this was created. It is like the magic inside the metal just instantly downloaded the instructions right into my brain."

A wild, frantic excitement replaces her grief. The switch is sudden and jarring. "I will be right back! I read something specific in that ancient book we picked up from New Orleans. I think I can replicate this!"

Without waiting for a response, Freya sprints for the wooden staircase, taking the steps three at a time in her desperate rush.

Sam raises a hand, his tactical mind never shutting off. Even in the wake of supernatural chaos, he is thinking about gear and logistics. "I have a serious question."

"What is it, Sam?" I ask, rubbing my temples to soothe a budding headache.

"If you don't have the protection of the ring anymore, does that also mean your weapons and your tactical harness are no longer cloaked from human eyes?"

My stomach drops. That is an incredibly valid, terrifying point. The ring was the only thing hiding my lethal arsenal from the mundane world. If I walk into a store with a short sword on my back, I'm going to be arrested within minutes.

"I guess they won't be invisible," I admit, groaning in frustration. "Damn it. I wish I hadn't left all my gear locked in the SUV. I just didn't think it was wise to strap all that heavy tactical weight onto my healing spine right now."

"I can run out and grab it for you, just so we can test the theory," Sam offers, already moving toward the door.

"Don't bother, Sam," I sigh, slumping back into the cushions. "I know for a fact it won't be cloaked. It is going to be exceptionally difficult to carry a massive, silver short sword down the street without causing a city-wide panic."

Maya steps forward, her chin lifted high. A new, fierce determination radiates from her. She isn't the trembling peacemaker in this moment; she looks like a woman who has found her purpose. "Go get her harness and her sword, Sam. I can help with this. I can cast a rune to ensure it cannot be seen by anyone."

She looks more confident and commanding than I have ever witnessed. It is almost unsettling.

Sam doesn't need to be told twice. He jumps into action, slipping out the front door to raid the vehicle. If the witches can actually solve this tactical nightmare, it would be a massive relief.

I am a little confused, though. Why are they suddenly so willing to assist us? They explicitly told Sam and Elijah repeatedly that they wouldn't lift a magical finger to help our team unless Reya was safely out of prison. The shift in attitude is palpable.

A heavy, pregnant silence settles over the living room as we wait. Freya is the first to reappear, practically vibrating with manic energy. She rushes past us and blows straight out the back door toward the garden without uttering a single word.

A moment later, Sam returns, his arms full of my black leather tactical harness and the heavy, leather-wrapped sword. He hands the gear directly to Rose. She gently helps me manoeuvre my sore arms through the straps, securing the heavy rig over my back. The leather is cold and smells of gun oil and old blood. Even though I fully anticipated the result, a bitter wave of disappointment washes over me when I look at the team's faces.

The cloak is completely gone. I am standing there in full combat gear, looking like a mercenary who took a wrong turn into a suburban living room.

Rose reaches for the buckles to strip the heavy gear off my aching back, but Maya holds up a hand. "Leave it on her for now. I just need to go downstairs and gather some specific supplies."

I watch in absolute bewilderment as Maya walks straight toward a solid, blank stretch of drywall. Instead of colliding with the plaster, she simply vanishes right through it, her body merging with the wall like water into a sponge. A second later, the distinct, heavy creak of a wooden door opening floats through the illusion.

Elijah notices our completely dumbfounded expressions. "They have a massive basement," he explains casually. "They cast a powerful illusion over the entrance, completely blocking the door from view. Only those they specifically invite can actually see the physical door."

"Are you serious? That is incredibly clever," Sam notes, his eyes wide with professional appreciation. He's probably already imagining how to use that for CIA safehouses.

"It really would," I agree, my mind spinning with tactical possibilities. "I can instantly think of about a dozen past black-ops missions where an invisible door would have saved me a lot of bleeding."

I sit down as the dizziness starts up again, while Rose perches on the arm of the chair. She slides her arm around my shoulders, gently pulling me sideways until my head rests comfortably against her ribcage. She opens her mouth to lecture me about the risk, but she stops the second my skin presses against hers.

"Ava, you feel significantly colder than normal," Rose notes, her brow furrowing in alarm. "Do you think you are coming down with something? Or maybe fighting off a severe infection from the wounds?"

"I feel perfectly fine, Rose," I assure her, leaning into her intoxicating scent of storm clouds and rain. "Honestly, I don't even know how you can accurately gauge my temperature considering your shifter body runs like a literal blast furnace."

From across the room, Elijah takes everyone completely by surprise. A wicked, incredibly cheeky grin spreads across his handsome, rugged face. "Well, she would definitely know all about how hot you run, wouldn't she?"

A loud, completely undignified snicker bursts out of my mouth. I can't help it; the absurdity of the moment is too much. Rose, on the other hand, does not find the sexual innuendo amusing. Her eyes flash a dangerous blue, and her lip curls.

"Do you want a severe, painful beating, EJ?" she threatens softly.

Elijah just shrugs in response.

The two sisters reappear in the living room at the exact same moment. Maya emerges through the illusory wall carrying a thick, leather-bound book and a small, ceramic tub filled with a dark substance that smells of sulphur and ancient dust. The back door slams open, and Freya marches inside, her arms full of freshly cut, thick brown vines from the garden.

"What are you doing?" Freya asks, eyeing the ceramic tub in Maya's hands.

"Ava's tactical harness isn't invisible anymore since the ring rejected her," Maya explains, dropping the heavy book onto the coffee table with a thud that sends a cloud of dust into the air. "There is a specific rune in this text that can help cloak her gear. It will be infinitely more permanent and stable than a standard ward because it binds to the user's essence."

"That is an incredibly smart idea," Freya responds in approval.

Maya gestures toward the dining area. "Ava, do you mind moving over to one of the wooden kitchen chairs so I have better access to work on your harness?"

"I can just take the whole rig off," I offer, already reaching for the chest buckle.

"No, leave it on," Maya instructs firmly. Her voice has a new edge to it, a command that doesn't brook argument. "The magic needs to be cast while the object is physically attached to your body, so I can magically tether the illusion directly to your aura. Otherwise, the harness will become completely invisible to your eyes as well, which makes drawing a sword rather difficult. I am also going to need a few drops of your blood to anchor the spell."

"You want to use blood magic on Ava?" Rose snarls, leaping off the arm of the chair. Her protective instincts are now at a fever pitch. "Over my dead body."

Luca steps forward, his massive frame radiating suspicion. "Your coven practices blood magic?"

"Calm down. It is not true, forbidden blood magic," Maya sighs, rolling her eyes at their dramatic overreaction. "It is ancient rune magic. When crafting permanent runes on inanimate objects, you simply use a tiny drop of blood from the caster to add a raw power source and a few drops from the wearer to permanently link the magic to their specific soul."

"I still highly dislike this," Rose mutters, her hands fidgeting nervously at her sides.

I ignore her paranoia. I am tired of being treated like a fragile piece of glass. I push myself out of the armchair, my joints popping, and slowly make my way over to the kitchen table. When I glance back over my shoulder, Rose is glaring at me with an expression that promises a very long, very intense argument later tonight.

Freya, completely ignoring our domestic drama, plops down cross-legged on the floor. She drops her pile of freshly cut vines next to her and cracks open her own ancient-looking textbook. “Alright, who wants to be my magical guinea pig?”

“What exactly are you planning to do?” Luca asks, his arms crossed over his chest.

“I am hoping to artificially recreate the exact magical frequency that Papa Legba’s ring uses,” Freya explains, her fingers tracing the faded text of a diagram. “But I am modifying the spell so it will bind to non-human biology. If this charm works, hopefully, every single one of you will be granted the Sight. You will be able to see and physically fight the shadow demons when we launch a rescue mission to get our sister back.”

Ah. There it is. I think. *That perfectly explains why they are suddenly so eager to arm and upgrade our squad.* They aren’t doing this out of the goodness of their hearts; they know they can’t save Reya alone. They are forging an army.

“You can test the prototype on me,” Elijah volunteers without a second of hesitation. He takes a step toward Freya, but abruptly pauses, shifting his gaze toward Luca. He is silently requesting his Alpha’s tactical permission to undergo untested witchcraft.

Luca’s jaw ticks. He looks deeply troubled by the concept, his protective instincts warring with the need for victory. Eventually, he gives a slow, reluctant nod.

Elijah drops to the floor, sitting directly across from Freya while she flips to a specific, heavily illustrated page in her book.

Meanwhile, Maya is busy setting up her workspace on the kitchen table. She pops the lid off the ceramic tub and scoops a pile of fine, jet-black ash into a stone mortar. The smell is pungent, like burnt bone and wet earth. She pulls a menacingly sharp, sterile silver needle from within the tub as well.

She holds out her hand, her palm facing up. “Hand, please Ava. I literally only need a few drops to bind the spell.”

I hesitate. My heart hammers a frantic rhythm against my ribs. A cold sweat breaks out on the back of my neck. *What if my blood is black? What if it looks like molten lava?* Pushing down my rising panic, I bravely place my left hand into her waiting grip. Her skin is soft, but her hold is firm.

Maya wastes no time. She lines up the sharp silver needle and presses the tip firmly into the pad of my index finger.

Or, at least, she tries to.

The needle doesn't pierce the flesh. It bounces off. Maya frowns, applying significantly more pressure, grinding the sharp metal against my skin until, finally, with a sickening little *pop*, the tip breaks through the surface.

"Well, that is fascinating," Maya murmurs, her eyes wide with genuine surprise. "It seems your cellular structure has drastically mutated. Your skin has become incredibly tough... almost like I guess you would call Kevlar."

"Has her skin really become noticeably tougher, or are you just incompetent and not holding the needle, right?" Rose snaps rudely from the living room.

"Rose, please stop being rude," I chastise her, wincing as a thick drop of crimson wells up on my fingertip. "She is right. She actually had to push the metal much, much harder than any normal human skin would require."

"Okay, fine. I'm sorry," Rose mutters defensively, crossing her arms over her chest.

Almost every single person in the room turns to shoot a scathing, judgmental glare at the hostile panther. Rose shifts uncomfortably under the collective weight of their stares, looking like she wants to disappear into the floorboards. "I said I was sorry, alright?"

A massive wave of relief washes over me when I look down. The liquid welling from my puncture wound is still a rich, vibrant, normal red. It isn't black or glowing; it just looks like blood. Maya guides my hand directly over the stone mortar and gives my finger a firm squeeze. We both watch in silence as three heavy, crimson drops fall, soaking instantly into the black ash.

Satisfied, Maya releases my wrist and reaches for the pestle after she also pierces her own skin and adds a few drops of blood to the mixture. A single, tantalising bead of blood remains perched on the tip of my finger. Operating on pure, deeply ingrained instinct from a childhood of scraped knees and minor cuts, I pop the injured digit into my mouth to suck away the blood.

The absolute second the metallic, coppery liquid hits my tongue, my entire world violently tilts.

A massive, explosive shockwave of pure, predatory adrenaline detonates inside my chest. It is not like a rush of energy. it is an invasion. It feels like I just injected a thousand volts of pure electricity directly into my brain. An agonising, bone-deep thirst rips through my throat, making it feel as if my oesophagus has been packed with dry, burning desert sand.

I want more.

The thought isn't mine; it is something deeper, something primal and hungry. *I need more.*

I rip my finger out of my mouth, my eyes wide with visceral, undeniable horror. I can feel a hunger clawing at the back of my throat, a craving for that metallic taste that makes me want to scream.

As usual, Rose's hyper-sensitive predator instincts do not miss a single micro-expression. "Ava, are you okay?" she demands, taking a step toward the kitchen, her nostrils flaring as she scents the air. "You look utterly shocked and completely terrified."

I force my heart rate down, swallowing hard against the burning need. I can't let her see this. Not now. "I'm totally fine," I lie smoothly, offering a weak, dismissive wave of my hand. "I didn't mean to worry you. I just had a momentary panic attack. I thought that if my genetics were mutating, maybe my blood would taste completely alien. I've always sucked on my cuts since I was a kid. It turns out, it still tastes exactly the same. The realisation just startled me."

Rose studies my face for one long, agonising second. She doesn't look entirely convinced, but she slowly nods. "Okay. If you are absolutely sure."

I turn my attention back to the table, desperate to distract myself from the monstrous hunger gnawing at my insides. I watch in silent fascination as Maya vigorously grinds my blood into the dark powder, creating a thick, metallic-smelling paste. She grabs a narrow, wooden spatula, scooping up a dollop of the magical ink. With practised, elegant strokes, she begins copying an intricate, jagged rune directly from the book onto the thick leather shoulder strap of my harness.

When she finishes painting the final slash, her lips begin to move silently, her eyes scanning the ancient text on the yellowed page. Once she memorises the incantation, she turns her bright blue eyes up to meet mine.

"Are you ready for this?" Maya asks softly.

"Yeah. Hit me," I say, bracing myself.

Maya hovers her right hand directly over the freshly painted blood-rune. She steps closer, pressing the flat of her left palm firmly against the centre of my chest, directly over my racing heart. The very first sensation is an incredible, soothing heat radiating from her palm, sinking straight through my ribs and wrapping around my soul like a warm blanket. Then, her voice rings out, strong and melodic as she chants the ancient spell.

"Protect thou this tool so none may see, only its wielder doth hold the power to perceive, make this ward shield all it binds to thee, by blood and ash, so mote it be."

A brilliant, blinding crimson flare erupts from beneath her right hand, the blood-rune igniting with violent magical energy. A strange, phantom sensation ripples across my skin, a heavy, invisible weight settling over the leather straps. For one bizarre, dizzying second, an exact, glowing blueprint of the tactical harness burns itself directly into my mind's eye. It is permanently tethered to my consciousness; I can feel exactly where every buckle and strap is without looking.

As the crimson light slowly fades into nothingness, the heavy leather straps vanish completely from existence. Maya pulls her hands away and turns to face our stunned audience, but as I continue to look, slowly the harness returns to my sight. It is like a slow-fade transition in a movie.

"Apart from my sister, can any of you currently see Ava's weapons or her harness?" Maya asks, a proud smirk playing on her lips.

I look over at everyone. Every single jaw in the room is practically resting on the floor. Luca, Rose, Sam, and Elijah all shake their heads in absolute, stunned silence. I am sitting here in a T-shirt and leggings, appearing completely unarmed.

"That was absolutely incredible to witness," Sam breathes, completely awestruck by the display of raw power.

"Thank you, Maya," I say, running a hand over my chest. I can feel the solid leather beneath my fingers, and I can see the harness again, though I look completely harmless to everyone else. "That chant actually rhymed. I always assumed rhyming spells were just cheap tropes used in Hollywood movies. I really didn't expect authentic witchcraft to be so poetic."

"It technically doesn't have to rhyme," Maya chuckles, wiping the remaining paste from her spatula. "I guess whoever originally authored this specific spell centuries ago just really enjoyed a good rhyming couplet."

Well, I am eternally grateful this nightmare is sorted. Walking around with a massive medieval short sword in plain sight would have ended in my immediate arrest and probably a psychiatric hold.

"Alright, I am completely prepped and ready on this end," Freya announces from her spot on the living room floor.

Luca narrows his eyes at the pile of greenery. "So, what exactly is the procedure here? What are you intending to do with those pieces of garden vine?"

"According to this specific book, powerful protective charms can be physically forged using living, natural items," Freya explains, tapping the yellowed page. "Legba's ring is essentially a complex mixture of a physical charm overlaid with deeply carved runes to grant it multiple, layered functions. I am hoping the natural charm I weave will successfully grant Elijah the Sight. If the magic takes hold, a distinct rune should organically manifest within the wood of the vine itself."

She looks up at Luca. "The text also mentions something specific about the charm having a bonding phase if the charm is being applied to non-human biology."

"Well, that vague description is certainly incredibly convincing," Elijah laughs, flashing a charming, reckless smirk. "It fills me with absolute confidence that you know precisely what you are doing."

"Of course I don't know exactly what I am doing," Freya retorts, completely unashamed. "My sisters and I are still incredibly new to all this power. But I refuse to sit around and let paralysing fear hold me back while my sister is locked in hell. As long as my mental intentions are absolutely pure and focused, we should be totally fine."

"Are you absolutely positive you want to risk this, Elijah?" Luca asks, his protective Alpha instincts flaring. He doesn't like the idea of untested magic being grafted onto his pack.

"Yeah, boss. I am sure," Elijah says easily. "Since we arrived in this town, these women have done nothing but impress me. They definitely do not fit the stereotypical mould of wicked, cackling hags stirring bubbling cauldrons. Not that I have actually known many real witches to compare them to, but still."

"You haven't known a single witch in your entire life, EJ," Rose teases, flashing a cocky, razor-sharp smile.

Elijah shoots her a dark glare. "What have I explicitly told you about calling me that ridiculous nickname?"

"That you secretly love it," Rose fires back without missing a beat.

"You two sound exactly like Reya and Freya arguing," Pickle

pipes up from her spot on the back of Beastie, her bell-like giggle cutting through the tension. "It's just like when they annoy Maya by calling her ma-ma, or when they call Reya Ragey."

"We do not sound like that!" Freya and Maya protest loudly, speaking in perfect, defensive unison.

The synchronised, sisterly denial shatters the heavy gloom in the room, making everyone bark out a genuine laugh. It is the first moment of levity we've had in hours, and it feels precious.

Maya huffs indignantly, turning back to the table to scrub the blood-ash paste from her mortar. Meanwhile, Freya boldly snatches Elijah's massive right hand and begins tightly coiling a thick piece of vine around his wrist.

"Hey, if you permanently wrap that around my wrist, I am going to have to remember to unbuckle the thing every time before I shift," Elijah points out. "Otherwise, the expanding muscle mass will snap it like a twig."

"That is exactly why I purposely selected living vine instead of leather or metal," Freya counters smoothly, tying off a complex knot. "The magic infused into the organic plant matter will allow the vine to rapidly stretch and grow right alongside your body when you shift."

"I will take your word for it," Elijah sighs.

"Hold completely still," Freya orders, her face shifting into a mask of intense concentration.

I watch in absolute awe as Freya presses the two severed ends of the green vine together. It is mesmerising watching her channel her raw earth-magic. She wills the plant to grow, and I can see the cells dividing and fusing in real time. The severed ends reach out and fuse together seamlessly. The thick vine literally slithers and tightens against his skin, moving with the eerie, fluid grace of a living snake.

Once the organic bracelet is securely fastened, Freya wraps her left hand tightly over Elijah's wrist, fully covering a section of the vine. She holds Papa Legba's silver ring aloft in her right hand, using it as a magical tuning fork to set the frequency. She begins rapidly whispering a low, guttural incantation that I cannot quite decipher, but it sounds like wind rushing through an ancient canyon. Just like the spell Maya cast, a brilliant, emerald-green glow erupts beneath her palm. Seconds later, the entire circumference of the vine illuminates with a pulsing, radioactive light.

Elijah's entire body violently tenses. He looks like a cornered animal desperate to fight its way out of a trap. A heavy sheen of sweat breaks out on his forehead, and I can hear his teeth grinding together as he battles the excruciating pain to remain seated. Just as Freya's breathless whispering reaches a crescendo, I clearly catch the final, binding phrase.

"So mote it be."

Freya snatches her hand away, breaking the physical connection, but the vine continues to pulse with an aggressive, blinding green light. Then, the horror begins.

The plant actually starts moving on its own. It is horrifying to witness. Dozens of tiny, razor-sharp roots violently erupt from the underside of the vine, piercing through Elijah's skin in a dozen different places.

Elijah's suppressed animal side violently surfaces. A deep, bone-rattling snarl rips from his throat, and he grips the fabric of the couch so hard that the wood beneath begins to crack. The magic is aggressively invading his biology, stitching itself into his nervous system.

"Elijah, talk to me! Are you okay?" Luca barks, his concern a raw, deadly thing.

Rose's reaction is far less diplomatic. "Stop this spell right now, witch!" she screams, her claws fully extending as she lunges forward.

"I literally cannot stop it! I think this is the bonding part!" Freya yells back, holding her ground with shocking confidence despite the chaos.

Slowly, the blinding emerald glow begins to fade, revealing the gruesome reality of the spell. The tiny, jagged roots extending from the vine are actively burrowing deep into Elijah's flesh, weaving through his muscle and bone. As the final remnants of the light recede, a dark, complex rune is left permanently scorched into the bark of the vine, looking as if it had been branded by a hot iron.

Elijah lets out a massive, ragged gasp of air and slumps backwards against the fabric of the couch, his chest heaving with exhaustion. He looks like he just ran a marathon through a thorn bush.

Freya immediately grabs his thick wrist, clinically examining the horrific, magical fusion. "Look over your shoulder," Freya commands, her voice trembling slightly. "Tell me, can you clearly see Pickle?"

I instinctively glance over at the dark corner where Sera had been lurking, thinking the massive shadow demon would be a vastly easier target to spot. However, the corner is completely empty. The shade has vanished into thin air; I have absolutely no idea when she silently slipped out of the house.

I hold my breath, waiting anxiously for Elijah to confirm the success of the brutal ritual. He turns his head, his eyes glancing in the direction where the tiny pixie is nervously hovering.

Elijah blinks, a heavy frown creasing his brow. His next words completely shatter all our rising hopes. "I am sorry, guys. I still can't see her."

"I knew this was a waste of time," Rose spits, throwing her hands up in absolute disgust.

Before a screaming match can erupt between Rose and the sisters, Elijah's massive frame begins to sway. The disoriented, glazed look in his eyes is terrifyingly reminiscent of the exact moment Legba's ring rejected my body.

Thankfully, the agonising fever and dizziness within my own system have finally begun to subside, leaving me feeling strangely energised, as if I've just woken up from a long sleep. Even better, Rose is so distracted by the unfolding drama that she seems to have completely forgotten about my suspicious medical emergency.

Elijah shakes his heavy head, squeezes his eyes shut, then opens them abruptly. He leans forward, focusing intently in Pickle's direction. His expression resembles that of someone staring so hard that they might go cross-eyed, attempting to coax a hidden image out of one of those dot-based pictures.

"Wait," Elijah whispers, his voice trembling with disbelief. "I see something. I... I think I see what looks like red hair."

"Yes! I have red hair! Can you actually see me?" Pickle shrieks, doing a frantic, joyful loop-the-loop in the air.

Elijah flinches, clapping a hand over his ear. "I think I heard her," he says excitedly.

Slowly, the magical block in Elijah's mind completely dissolves. It takes a few more agonising minutes of focus, but his vision finally shifts, allowing him to perfectly, fully perceive the shimmering pixie hovering in the living room.

For the next few exhausting hours, the living room is transformed into a brutal, magical assembly line. Freya painstakingly recreates the organic, burrowing charm for every single member of the shifter pack. Of course, this only happens after Luca orders Elijah to fully shift out back, verifying that the magic vine successfully stretches without causing catastrophic nerve damage or shattering.

Luca and a highly reluctant, endlessly complaining Rose are the absolute last holdouts to submit to the agonising branding process. Rose fights it until the very end, her eyes flashing with hatred for the vines, but eventually, she succumbs to Luca's command.

Pickle is over the moon with this new reality. She spends time with each member of the pack, properly introducing herself. However, she avoids Luca and especially Rose, purposely stating so they can hear, "I don't need to get to know them, it's not like they are accepting of us, so why should I bother."

By the time Jenny finally returns home from her mundane shift at work, we are all exhausted. We crowd around the kitchen table, heavily briefing her on the catastrophic prison break and the terrifying fact that Reya has been dragged into the Underworld. The look of horror on Jenny's face is a reminder of how far beyond the normal world we have fallen.

Before packing away her ancient book, Freya magically carves the sight-granting rune into a plain silver band she found in a jewellery box, ensuring she has a master template to work from if she ever needs to forge more in the future.

The final, ultimate test of the evening is determining if the original ring will successfully bond again with an ordinary human like Sam. He cautiously taps the silver metal first, verifying it won't instantly sear his flesh as Papa Legba's artefact did to mine. When the metal remains cool to the touch, he slides the band onto his right pinky finger, as the delicate jewellery is far too small to fit over his thick knuckles.

The very second the metal slips past his knuckle, the ring vanishes completely from existence. I genuinely thought my newly mutated vision would allow me to pierce the illusion, but I am staring at bare skin. Even the shifters, armed with their incredibly painful, root-infused vine bracelets, cannot perceive the cloaked artefact. Only Freya and Maya, possessing the inherent magic of their coven, can still see the silver band resting on his finger.

Now, Sam can conceal weapons on his person just as easily as I can. We are finally armed, cloaked, and ready to plan our next move. But as I look at my reflection in the dark window, I wonder how much of "Ava" is left, and what exactly is staring back at me from the glass.

CHAPTER 13

The Blood of the Dead God

Luca and Rose head out through the back door with Elijah to coordinate with the rest of the pack. The air in the room feels suddenly thinner, as if their presence had been providing a structural support I didn't know I needed.

Before she crosses the threshold, however, Rose lingers. She pauses, her body angled toward me, and for a moment, the world shrinks until it is only the two of us in the oppressive silence of the house. She leans down, her movements fluid and predatory even in their tenderness. When she presses a kiss to the crown of my head, it isn't just a gesture of affection; it is an anchor. Her lips are soft, lingering against my skin, and I can smell her. a heady mix of wild rain and something primal, something that smells like deep forests and midnight hunts.

Her fingers brush against the sensitive skin of my neck, a feather-light touch that sends a jolt of electricity straight to my core. It is a silent promise. *I am coming back for you.*

I lean into her preternatural warmth, closing my eyes as I let that panther shifter energy seep into my pores. It feels like liquid gold flowing through my veins, momentarily soothing the frayed ends of my nerves and silencing the screaming alarms in my head. For one fleeting, blissful second, the terror of the last few days vanishes. There is only Rose.

Then, she steps away. The door clicks shut behind her, and

suddenly everything reaffirms itself as reality, overwhelming me once more.

The warmth vanishes, replaced by a sudden, biting chill that makes me shiver. I opt to remain seated in the plush armchair because the mere thought of moving feels like a death sentence. I try to shift an inch to the left, and my entire world narrows down to a single point of agony.

A sharp, radiating pain shoots down my lumbar spine, a brutal, jagged reminder of the trauma I just endured. It isn't just a dull ache; it is a visceral, white-hot assault. The muscle spasms are relentless, throbbing with rhythmic cruelty around what feels like deep tissue contusions and severe damage to my vertebrae. Every time I breathe, I can feel the misalignment in my lower back, as if my spine has been replaced by shattered glass and rusted nails.

It is more than pain; it is a total sensory overload. It feels like my neurological pathways are literally on fire, sending sharp, electrical shocks straight up my spinal column every time I even think about shifting my weight. My breath catches in a bruised lung, and I can taste the metallic tang of old adrenaline at the back of my throat. That's when I realise I am feeling worse because my body is healing quicker while I'm here within the sisters' protective wards that also help with healing.

God, just kill me now. Preferably quickly and without the spinal combustion. I've fought insurgents in war zones, but I think I'm actually being defeated by a chair.

"So, Ava. How are you really feeling?"

Freya's voice breaks through my internal spiral. It is soft, lacking its usual sharp edge, but her eyes are tracking my every micro-expression with surgical precision. She is reading me like a tactical map, looking for the tell-tale signs of shock or collapse. I can see the concern etched into the corners of her mouth, though she tries to mask it with a neutral expression.

"Obviously, I am thrilled to have survived," I reply. My voice sounds hollow to my own ears. I try to inject a note of my usual sarcasm into the words, attempting to sound more casual than I feel. I carefully shift my hips, trying to ease the crushing pressure on my lower back, but a fresh spike of agony makes me grit my teeth so hard I think they might crack.

"But," I continue, my tone shifting as the warrior in me takes over, "I'm a little concerned about what is actually happening to my body. I like the fact that I seem to be getting stronger, but I've noticed a few... weird physiological things that have me on edge."

"Like what?" Freya asks.

As she speaks, she shoots Maya a highly loaded look. It is one of those silent, sisterly communications that practically screams they are sitting on a mountain of secrets. The glance is brief, but it is heavy with shared knowledge and hesitation. It makes the hair on my arms stand up. I hate being the last person in the room to know why my own biology is betraying me.

"I've noticed a slight change to my hair and eye colour," I say, the words feeling heavy on my tongue. I think of the reflection I saw earlier, the subtle shift that didn't look entirely human. "And I've been getting these bizarre, unquenchable thirst moments where I literally cannot seem to drink enough water. It is like a void has opened up inside me, and no matter how much I swallow, I am still parched."

There is one thing I am absolutely not going to tell them. I keep the memory locked behind a steel door in my mind. the taste of my own blood. The way it had tasted not like copper or salt, but like something intoxicating. Something powerful. The memory makes my skin prickle with a dark, confusing heat that pools in my gut.

Instead, I pivot, pushing the discomfort aside to focus on the mission. "Are you guys fully aware of how Reya saved me?"

Freya bites her bottom lip, her expression darkening. The playful spark she usually carries vanishes, replaced by a brooding intensity. "I saw what she did to save you," she says softly. "I've been trying to research it feverishly since then, diving into every text we have, but I haven't found anything concrete. The only historical texts I found suggest that something like this would result in almost immediate physical changes and a complete, sudden shift in personality."

A cold pool of dread settles heavily in my stomach, weighing me down more than the pain in my back. *Great. Fantastic. So I'm not just healing; I'm transforming into some kind of paranormal freak.*

"So, we have absolutely no idea what is happening to my cellular structure?" I ask. I can feel the frustration bleeding into my voice, giving it a sharp, dangerous edge. I am a woman of action and facts, and "we don't know" is an answer that makes me want to put my fist through a wall.

Freya looks to Maya again, exchanging another one of those silent communications. The air between them is thick with tension, a tangible web of hesitation that makes me want to scream.

"Can I ask one crucial thing before I continue?" Freya asks.

"Sure," I snap. *Just spit it out already before I lose what's left of my mind.*

"Did you die? Even if it was just for a few seconds or a couple of minutes?"

I freeze. I search my memory, trying to claw back the moments after the attack, but all I find is a suffocating haze. I remember agonising pain, the smell of ozone and blood, and then a crushing, absolute darkness that felt like being buried alive in cold velvet.

"Not that I am aware of," I say slowly. "No one has mentioned me flatlining. Why?"

"Okay. That is very good," Freya exhales, her shoulders dropping as she sounds genuinely relieved.

"Why is that good?" My patience is officially paper-thin now. The pain in my spine is throbbing in time with the beating of my heart, and I am reaching my limit.

"I decided to read through our sister's translation of the old diary she discovered, the one Papa Legba left for her," Freya explains, her voice becoming clinical, as if she is reciting a report. "As I read the detailed lore about the ancient gods from which all paranormal beings are descended, I noticed a terrifying similarity. It detailed the powers of one of the children of the original gods... and those powers match Reya's."

Freya pauses, her eyes wide with a mixture of fear and hesitation. She looks at Maya, clearly debating if she should drop this particular bomb on me while I am already physically compromised.

"Whatever it is, just tell me," I demand. My heart kicks up a chaotic, frantic rhythm against my ribs. *Thump-thump. Thump-thump.* It feels like a trapped animal trying to claw its way out of my chest.

"There was a god called Thanatos," Freya begins, her voice dropping an octave, becoming low and solemn. "He was the embodiment of death. He used his blood to create the very first vampires when he experimented on the dead. He also created the first demons from the human spirits sent to the underworld. He put a dark spell, a curse, on the realm so that, over time, those human spirits would mutate. If they drank blood or fed on ambient magic or life force, it would accelerate their changes and make them infinitely stronger."

I stare at her, my mind spinning in dizzying circles. The room seems to tilt slightly. "Are you trying to tell me I am becoming a vampire?"

"No, no! As you just said, you did not die," Freya says quickly, waving her hands as if she could physically push the idea away from me. "The text explicitly stated that the first vampires created from his blood were completely out of control, mindless, aggressive monsters. The vampires we see in the modern world were created from their victims, assuming they even survived the feeding. It acts as a kind of aggressive biological infection."

I don't know if I should be relieved or terrified. A part of me is grateful that I won't turn into one of those feral, mindless creatures we fought back in Pittsburgh, but another part of me is horrified by what this means. If I am not becoming a vampire, then what exactly is mutating inside my veins? What did Reya's blood do to the fundamental architecture of my genes?

"Do you honestly think Reya knew what she might have turned me into by feeding me her blood?"

A spike of genuine hurt pierces through my chest, sharper than any spinal injury. The idea that Reya would knowingly infect me, even to save me, is deeply disturbing. We are sisters in arms, bound by a trust I thought was unbreakable. To think she might have treated me like a laboratory experiment makes my stomach churn.

"I really do not think she did," Freya reassures me, leaning towards me from her spot on the couch. "In her translation, she wrote copious notes in the margins. Most seem to be about the visits she received from Cat in her dreams. One specific note mentions, 'Cat said my blood can heal.' I don't think Reya pieced together what I have just discovered. We were all too distracted by the chaos of the attacks and learning that we have magic and everything else going on."

I let out a harsh, dry chuckle that turns into a wince as it jars my back. "Fine. I will hold off on kicking her arse when we finally get her back, then."

The sisters and Pickle chuckle, the tension breaking just a fraction. The sound is small, but it is welcome. Beastie, however, does not find it funny. The hellhound lets out a low, rumbling growl from his spot on the floor, his eyes fixed on me. He clearly does not appreciate my threat toward his missing owner.

"That leads me to another pressing question," Freya says and continues. "Now that we have helped you, and Luca and his pack members have the sight to see demons and fight them," her eyes locking onto mine with intense seriousness, "will you help us go after the demons in Jackson? We need to get our sister back."

"Of course we will. I gave you my word," I say firmly. My voice is no longer hollow; it is the voice of the Captain. "I do not agree with the others who suggested we should move on just because they lack a conventional way to fight demons. We don't leave our own behind."

As soon as the words leave my mouth, Pickle practically torpedoes through the air. The tiny pixie moves in a blur of iridescent wings leaving behind that same watery trail, slamming her small body against my collarbone in a fierce hug.

"Thank you, Ava! Whatever you are becoming, I am absolutely sure it will be amazing because you are a fundamentally good human. So do not worry... okay... honey?"

Her tiny voice vibrates against my skin, high-pitched and earnest. Despite everything, I can't help but smile. The fierce loyalty of this little creature is unexpected, but heartwarming. She is about the same size as a barbie doll, but she has the heart of a warrior and the mouth of a sailor.

The weight of Freya's revelation is still heavy on my mind, an unanswered question that refuses to stay buried, so I press her further. "You mentioned that Reya's powers are similar to those of Thanatos. Are you trying to say Reya might be some kind of god?"

"No, of course not! There's no way," Freya says quickly, looking almost offended by the suggestion. "I'm just saying their powers are similar. From what I understand, all the powers the gods used to have are now split between their descendants. For example, your shifter friends out back, their ability to shift came from the gods because the gods could shift too."

Before we can dissect my impending biological crisis or the origin story of Reya's powers any further, the heavy oak door swings open. Luca, Rose, and Sam step back inside, bringing with them the scent of pine and cold air.

They all freeze simultaneously, their eyes locking onto Pickle. They look entirely startled to see a winged pixie actively hugging my neck. It doesn't help that Freya and Maya look incredibly guilty, as if we were caught plotting a murder in the middle of the living room.

Rose immediately crosses the room, her movements a blur of athletic grace. Her brow is furrowed with concern, her green eyes searching mine for any sign of distress. She rests a warm, steadying hand on my shoulder, her thumb gently stroking my skin in a rhythmic, soothing motion. The touch is electric, grounding me and pulling me back from the edge of my anxiety.

"Everything okay in here?" Luca asks. His dark eyes scan the room with sharp, alpha precision, noting every shift in posture and every flicker of emotion. He doesn't miss a thing.

"Yeah, everything is perfectly fine," I say, trying to ignore how much I want to lean into Rose's touch, to let her pull me out of this chair and carry me away from all the madness. "I was just telling them that now everyone can visibly see the demons, we are going to help go after the ones in Jackson. We need to capture this Devika girl and hopefully beat some answers out of her about getting Reya back."

Luca's jaw ticks, a sign of mild annoyance at the mention that I have made plans without him, but he doesn't seem surprised. "Of course, we will help. I am still not entirely convinced, though. Just because we can suddenly see these creatures does not mean we can physically touch them, let alone fight them in close-quarters combat."

Pickle decides she has heard enough. She detaches herself from my neck, her tiny wings buzzing with furious, high-pitched energy. She flies straight across the room, a miniature missile of indignation, hovering dead in the centre of Luca's vision. Then, pulling her arm back with all the might her tiny frame possesses, she swings her hand and slaps him squarely on the side of his face.

The moment drags in slow motion. The sheer audacity of this tiny creature attacking a massive, deadly shifter is staggering. The sharp *smack* echoes loudly across the silent room, a sound so absurd it feels surreal.

I instantly tense, my muscles locking up with worry. I prepare to jump between them, terrified of how his volatile alpha instincts might respond to being physically assaulted by a pixie. My heart hammers against my ribs, a frantic drumbeat of panic. *Please don't kill her, please don't kill her.*

Luca takes me completely off guard. He blinks, slowly reaching up to touch his cheek where the tiny hand had connected. A low, rumbling chuckle escapes his chest, sounding like distant thunder.

"Point well taken. I like you, Pickle. I am glad I can actually see you now." His expression turns thoughtful. "Magic is a fickle thing, though. Just because I can see you, how does that translate into physical combat with a demon?"

"I think it is mostly because I am just completely amazing!" Pickle declares. She hovers proudly in front of Luca, striking a perfect superhero pose with her tiny fists planted firmly on her hips and her chest puffed out.

Everyone except Rose snickers at the display. Rose is still watching me with total focus, her protective instincts flaring so high I can almost feel the heat radiating from her body. It is an oppressive, comforting warmth that wraps around me like a blanket.

As we laugh at Pickle's brazenness, Jenny comes padding down the stairs. Her hair is damp from a shower, and she's swapped her gear for an oversized T-shirt and comfortable sweats, looking far more like a normal civilian than anyone else in this house.

"What exactly have I missed?" Jenny asks, looking between our grinning faces with genuine confusion.

"Just Pickle being Pickle," Freya explains, her eyes dancing with amusement.

"Oh, man, I missed it! I love it when she does that."

The levity fades as quickly as it arrived. Luca shifts back into business mode, the alpha taking over his posture. His presence expands, filling the room with an undeniable authority. "We had better start packing up. Before we can assist with the demon issue, we desperately need to change locations. Our current property is simply not big enough and is too hard to defend. The demons have already ransacked our motel rooms in town."

"How do you know for sure that demons ransacked your rooms?" Freya asks, tilting her head in curiosity.

"The smell they left behind," Luca replies, his lip curling in pure disgust. "Everything absolutely reeked of raw sulphur from where they touched our belongings. It is a scent that clings to everything, an olfactory stain that doesn't wash off."

Freya nods slowly, then offers something completely unexpected. "When you find a new secure location, let me know. Maya and I will come out to set up some magical protection wards and a perimeter warning signal in case anyone tries to cross the boundary."

"Thank you," I say, genuinely touched by the offer. It is a step toward true alliance, a merging of our tactical skills with their mystical ones.

"I am sorry for how I reacted before," Freya admits, looking down at her hands. "I was furious about Reya's situation and completely single-minded about getting her back at any cost."

"It is okay. I completely understand. We are going to need each other if we are going to survive the war that is brewing in our world," I say. Around the room, everyone nods in grim agreement. The air feels heavy with the shared knowledge of the coming storm.

"I have already scouted a few suitable fallback locations. Hopefully, we can decide on one tonight and start moving out at first light tomorrow," Sam chimes in, tapping through a digital map on his phone with professional efficiency.

"If you want that timeline to happen, we really do need to get moving," Luca says, gesturing toward the door. "Once we secure the new base and the wards are established, we can finally formulate a tactical plan to hunt the demons."

We exchange quick goodbyes and head toward the front door. I move slowly, every step a battle against the agony in my spine, but the adrenaline of a new mission is starting to mask the worst of it.

The very first indication that something is horribly wrong is the deep, vibrating sound of Beastie growling. It isn't his usual playful huff; this is a guttural, primal warning. The hellhound's hackles are fully raised, his lips pulled back to expose vicious, deadly teeth and gums the colour of raw meat.

Suddenly, Sera materialises. The shadow guardian lands

heavily on the ground right in front of us, facing the driveway. She spreads her massive, inky wings, blocking our view of whatever threat is approaching. Her presence is like a void of light, a sudden eclipse that plunges the porch into shadow.

The sudden appearance catches Luca, Rose, and Sam off guard. They flinch back, hands already shifting into claws, their instincts screaming danger. I push through the agonising protest of my spine and descend the veranda steps, ignoring the white-hot flare of pain in my lower back so I can get a clear line of sight around Sera's shadowy form.

The first thing I register is the massive, slate-grey feathered wings. At the wing joints, sharp, deadly-looking claws protrude menacingly, glistening in the afternoon sun. My eyes track downward, taking in the fiery red and silver hair that whips in the wind and those luminous, terrifying black eyes that seem to swallow all light.

Devika.

My instincts kick in before my mind does. I am already holding my tactical harness and my enhanced silver sword. The moment I recognise her, my combat training overrides the pain. The world sharpens into crystal clarity; the noise of the others fades into a dull hum. I drop the heavy leather harness to the dirt. In one fluid motion, I adjust my grip on the hilt of the sword, bringing the blade up into a defensive guard.

The others join me a heartbeat later, fanning out into a tactical formation. Beastie aggressively shoves his way between Sera and me, snapping his jaws at the winged hybrid. He shifts back to his original form faster than I have seen any of the shifters do. His hellhound form is a sight to behold and very scary if this is the first time you have seen him. As black flames roll over his body and he opens his jaws to reveal deadly teeth, showing how enraged he is, I expect him not to hold back and to lunge for our visitor's throat, so I'm honestly surprised when he stands with us, waiting.

"Well, this is going to make things significantly easier," Devika says. Her voice is calm, carrying a terrifyingly cynical edge that makes my skin crawl. She looks at us with an expression of profound boredom.

"Make what easier?" I demand, keeping my sword steady. My knuckles are white against the hilt, the metal cold and reassuring in my palm.

"I have been sent here as a courtesy to warn you. Right now, Reya is considered the absolute property of our king. He will do with her exactly as he pleases as punishment for her crime of stealing one of his hellhounds." She shoots a filthy, venomous glare at Beastie before turning those black eyes back to me. "It has been decided that since the king now possesses Reya, he has graciously agreed to let the rest of you live. This amnesty only applies as long as you stay completely out of our business and quietly live your pathetic mortal lives. Do you fully understand the message?"

"I do not care about your bloody king or your message! We want our sister back!" Freya shouts, stepping out from behind Luca's protective bulk. Her voice is trembling with rage, her eyes flashing.

"Well, we cannot always get what we want in life," Devika sneers, the expression twisting her beautiful face into something monstrous. "You should feel incredibly lucky that you are being allowed to walk away. Normally, anyone who is not part of the grand plan is brutally destroyed."

"We are not scared of you," Freya spits, her fists clenching as her power begins to crackle and hum in the air around her, small sparks of energy dancing between her fingers.

"Maybe you are not scared of me. But you should be absolutely terrified of the one who has returned," Devika warns, a dark smirk playing on her lips.

"And exactly who is that?" Luca demands, his alpha aura flaring outward, thick and oppressive like a physical weight pressing down on everyone in the yard.

"For now, he wants to keep his identity a fun little surprise. You will find out exactly who he is when he decides he wants the whole world to know. Assuming, of course, that you manage to survive until then."

Before a single person can formulate a response or launch an attack, Devika flexes her knees. She beats her massive grey wings once, sending a violent shockwave of displaced air over us that nearly knocks me off my feet. She leaps into the sky, rocketing upward at a speed that defies physics. Within seconds, she is nothing but a dark speck against the clouds.

Chaos erupts instantly. Everyone is shouting, voices overlapping in a frantic mess of questions and accusations. I ignore them, turning directly to Reya's shadow guardian.

"Sera! Can you track her again? Follow her and confirm if she returns to the exact same location as before, then report back to me."

I quickly relay our current coordinates. Sera gives a sharp, decisive nod, her form dissolving into a pool of ink before rocketing after the demon.

The yard falls into a stunned, heavy silence. The only sound is the distant chirping of birds and the ragged breathing of the group. But when I look back at them, nobody is looking at the sky anymore. They are all staring blankly toward the edge of the lake.

I follow their collective line of sight. Standing near the water's edge is a young girl. She is translucent, her form shimmering like a heat haze in the sunlight. I have definitely seen her before.

The memory of who she is suddenly flashes in my mind; her name is Kracis.

I take point, stepping forward slowly with my hands raised in a non-threatening gesture. I don't want anyone's aggressive posturing to scare her away; she looks fragile, like a piece of glass about to shatter. "It is Kracis, right?"

The shade takes a tentative step toward us, her form flickering. "Have they really taken Reya?" she asks, her voice echoing with a hollow, soul-deep sadness that vibrates in the air.

"Yes, I am afraid they have," I say, my heart aching for her.

The sight of such profound loneliness is almost unbearable. "But we are planning an assault to get her back. Can you offer us any help?"

"You really need to get her out of there. That horrible place changes you. It twists your soul and makes you do horrific things that you would never want to do." The spirit pauses, looking down at her ghostly, shimmering hands as if she can still see the stains of the past on them. "I have finally remembered my true name from before they broke me and turned me into Kracis."

"What is your real name? I do not want to keep calling you Kracis if that is not who you truly are," I say softly. A heavy lump of sympathy forms in my throat, making it hard to swallow.

"It is Damaris. I believe my parents were Greek, but they were tragically killed in a shipwreck off the coast of England. I do not understand how I survived, but I ended up completely alone on the brutal streets of London," Damaris explains. She looks profoundly devastated, as if those centuries-old memories are happening right now, playing out in a loop of agony.

"I am so incredibly sorry." What else can I even say to a traumatised ghost? There is no comfort for the dead, only acknowledgement.

"To answer your previous question, yes. I can help you navigate their territory, but only on one strict condition. You must promise not to hurt Devika. You have to help me find a way to exorcise the demon out of her," Damaris pleads, her eyes wide and desperate.

"That aligns with our plan. We were actually hoping the demons could be coerced to help us get our sister back," Freya interjects, though she sounds sceptical.

"I will help you, but I do not think the demons will ever cooperate. Devika, however, might be able to. Her unique wings grant her the incredibly rare ability to travel freely between the Underworld and what humans call Heaven. That is exactly why they kidnapped her. They are actively using her as a portal to smuggle demons straight into Heaven. Their grand plan is to systematically turn all the pure, resting spirits in that realm into demons as well. All I know is that they used her to transport someone to the realm. When they brought them back, they started sending demons there. It actually takes a lot out of Devika to travel there, so they haven't sent many demons so far. I'm just not sure what they did on that first visit."

"They are doing what?!" I shout, the words tearing from my throat in raw horror.

A sudden, blinding wave of panic crashes over me, more suffocating than any physical injury. My brain immediately jumps to the worst-case scenario. *My parents.* Their souls are supposed to be resting peacefully in the light, away from the violence and blood of the world they left behind. The thought of demons infiltrating that sanctuary makes my blood run cold.

"We will capture Devika and stop them. I swear it."

"Thank you," Damaris whispers, her form flickering like a candle in a draft. "I just wish I could find Hecate; she would help with Devika, as she cares about her. I haven't seen her for years now, after Devika, and I left the coven." Damaris suddenly jerks her head towards the sisters, suddenly looking guilty.

I wonder what that's about.

I look over my shoulder at the others, silently debating if I should drop the brutal truth on this fragile spirit about the fate of Hecate. Rose meets my eyes, her expression sombre, and gives me a barely perceptible nod. Freya mirrors the gesture. We are all thinking the same thing. some truths are too heavy to carry when you are already breaking.

I turn back to the young girl, bracing myself. "I am so sorry to have to deliver this news, but we have strong reason to believe Hecate is dead. Her spirit has briefly visited a few of us in our dreams. I believe her soul is currently in hiding to avoid complete destruction," I say softly.

"What?!" Damaris recoils, looking utterly distressed. If it were physically possible for a shade to cry, I know tears would be pouring down her translucent cheeks right now. She looks as if she has been struck.

Since spirits cannot weep, I desperately try to distract her from the grief before she fades away from the emotional shock. “Who exactly was Hecate to you?”

It takes a long, agonising moment for her to compose herself. When she finally speaks, what she says makes my own chest ache with the urge to cry.

“She saved me. A high-level demon had captured me and was forcing me to do unspeakable, horrible things... which is what eventually mutated my soul into a shade. Hecate saw my suffering. I have no idea why a Goddess would care, but she ripped me away from that monster. She gave me safe jobs here and in the Underworld that did not involve hurting innocent people, like keeping a watchful eye over Devika.”

“That was incredibly kind of her,” Maya offers gently, stepping forward with a soft expression. “I am absolutely sure that if she manages to visit one of us in our dreams again, we will make sure to let her know that you are safe and okay.”

“Thank you,” Damaris whispers, her form flickering.

Just like I did with Sera, I give Damaris our location, where we are staying until we officially move out. Freya quickly adds that the shade is welcome to come to the sisters’ property whenever she needs sanctuary.

With a final, solemn nod, Damaris fades completely from view, dissolving into the golden afternoon air like a dying ember.

We stand in the yard, rapidly discussing the terrifying new intelligence for a few tense minutes before deciding we need to go begore its gets too late. The threat is too immediate; the amnesty Devika offered feels more like a trap than a mercy.

As we head toward the vehicles, I clench my teeth, my breath coming in short, ragged gasps. I absolutely cannot wait to sit down again. The adrenaline that had been sustaining me is finally crashing, leaving me hollow and exposed. The deep tissue trauma in my back returns with a brutal, sickening vengeance, each step feeling like a hot iron being pressed into my spine, underneath the pain, though I start to feel something shift within me, something is happening, I am in too much pain to care.

I'm going to kill Devika, I think, the darkness of the thought surprising even me. *And then I'm going to find this King and show him exactly what happens when you touch one of mine.*

CHAPTER 14

MY HEARTBEAT IS A SUGGESTION

When we finally make it back to the safe house, the world is nothing more than a blur of grey concrete and the rhythmic thrum of the SUV's engine. Every bump in the road feels like a personal assault on my nervous system. By the time the vehicle comes to a halt, I am not just tired, I am depleted. I feel as though someone has reached inside my chest and scooped out everything but the raw, jagged edges of my exhaustion.

I do not waste a single agonising second. The moment the door opens, I don't so much walk as I do gravitate toward my makeshift hospital bed. My movements are clumsy, mechanical. Each step is a battle fought against gravity, my muscles screaming in a discordant symphony of protest. When I finally collapse onto the mattress, crawling backwards into the sheets, a heavy, involuntary sigh of pure relief escapes my lips.

It is a sound of total surrender. The moment my aching spine meets the mattress, the tension snaps. It feels as if my skeleton is finally settling back into place, though the relief is laced with a dull, throbbing heat that radiates from my lower back up to my shoulder blades. I stare up at the ceiling that I am now very familiar with, as I mentally tell myself. *My body is officially on strike; it has decided it's had enough of my stubbornness for one lifetime.*

"Your back is really hurting, isn't it?"

Rose's voice is a low, melodic hum that cuts through the fog in my brain. I shift my gaze slightly. She is hovering near the edge of the bed, her brow furrowed with a depth of concern that makes my chest tighten for reasons that have nothing to do with my injuries. Her presence is a warm, protective weight in the room, filling the space with the scent of rain and something primal, something feline.

I try to put on my Captain's face. stoic, detached, professional. I try to tell her I'm fine. But as I attempt to shift my weight, a sharp, electric bolt of pain shoots through my lumbar region, causing me to hiss through my teeth and arch my back involuntarily. The facade shatters instantly.

I cannot lie to her. Not when the way I hobbled from the SUV into the house made it blindingly obvious that my body is currently held together by nothing more than spite and sheer, unadulterated willpower.

"Yeah," I admit, my voice sounding raspy and thin even to my own ears. "It aches like crazy. I think venturing out to the Harpers for the first time was pushing it a bit too far."

I close my eyes, imagining the damage. I can almost feel the inflammation, the way the tissues are swollen and angry. *I am a liability,* the internal warrior whispers. *A soldier who can't walk is just a target.*

"I desperately need to start working out again," I mutter, more to myself than her. "I need to get my body back into actual fighting shape."

Preferably before the next apocalypse drops on our heads and finds me as useless as a screen door on a submarine. The thought brings a flicker of a smile to my lips, though it feels more like a grimace.

Rose sighs, her posture softening as she sinks slightly toward me. The predatory edge she usually carries, that constant readiness to spring into action, melts away, replaced by a tenderness that still catches me off guard. She reaches out, her movements slow and deliberate, and gently interlaces her warm fingers with mine.

The contact is electric. A spark of comfort surges through my weary nerves, momentarily silencing the screaming pain in my spine.

Her skin is hot, an anchor of vitality against my own shivering coldness.

"I have decided to stop fighting with you about everything," she says softly.

I blink, looking at her. *Wait, what? Did I hit my head harder than I thought?*

"Watching you today with the Harpers and Pickle..." Rose continues, her green eyes searching mine. "I realised you are never going to leave them or stop supporting them. You have this... this fierce, quiet loyalty that I can't compete with. So I am going to promise you that when we get Reya back, I will actively work on my attitude towards her."

My chest tightens, but this time it is genuine emotion, a swell of gratitude that threatens to choke me. It is a strange sensation, feeling this much warmth and hope while my physical form feels as if it is crumbling into ash.

"Thank you, Rose," I whisper. "It means a lot to me." I pause, struggling to find the words for something that defies military logic. "I cannot fully explain it, but they just feel like family. Like something I didn't know I was missing until I found them."

I squeeze her hand, anchoring myself to the reality of her touch, the only thing in this chaotic world that feels certain.

"I can see that," Rose replies softly.

She leans over me, her hair falling like a golden curtain around our faces, shielding us from the rest of the room. When she presses her lips to mine, it is a tender, lingering kiss. She tastes of vanilla and longing, a grounding force that pulls me out of my own head and back into the present moment. I lean into her, craving the heat of her body, the scent of her skin, the sheer *fact* of her.

"Your happiness is all that matters to me," she murmurs against my lips, her breath warm on my skin. "Most of the time, I don't notice any strong emotions coming from you through our bond... well, unless we are under attack or in bed together."

A small, genuine laugh huffs out of me. *Well, at least my libido is still functioning.*

"But I definitely notice how you feel when you are around them," she continues, her voice dropping an octave. "Especially when you were around Reya. There was a resonance there, Ava. A connection."

Well, she did literally pour her lifeblood down my throat, I think sardonically. *Hard to miss the emotional fallout on that one.*

I look up at her, feeling a sudden surge of playfulness despite the agony in my back. I offer her a tired, cheeky wink, though it's more of a slow blink. "Why don't you climb into this bed with me while I take a nap?"

Rose doesn't hesitate for a fraction of a second. There is no hesitation, no doubt. She slips under the covers with a fluid, feline grace, manoeuvring her body carefully so she straddles my hips. She is mindful of my injuries, distributing her weight in a way that provides an overwhelming sense of closeness without putting any pressure on my shattered vertebrae.

Her warmth seeps into me, acting like a heating pad for my soul. I can feel the steady thrum of her heart through her chest, a rhythmic beat that begins to synchronise with my own. She is a shield, a sanctuary. In the circle of her arms, the war, the demons, and the terrifying uncertainty of my future feel miles away.

"I love you, Rose," I murmur, my eyelids already drooping heavily, the darkness calling to me with an irresistible pull.

"I love you too," she whispers, kissing my forehead. "Now get some rest so your back heals faster."

"Yes, boss," I say, a sleepy smile curving my lips as the world fades to black and the heavy curtain of sleep finally falls.

I don't know how long I drift for. Time becomes a fluid, meaningless concept. For a while, there is only the sensation of floating in a warm, golden ether. But then, the current shifts.

The transition isn't gentle. It is a violent descent into a suffocating dream where I am suddenly, terrifyingly stripped of my sight. The darkness that envelopes me is absolute. It isn't just the absence of light, it is a physical entity. heavy, thick, and vast. It feels as though I am buried under miles of cold, black earth, the weight of the world pressing down on my chest until I can no longer draw a full breath.

Then, the silence is shattered by a sound that makes my heart actually stutter in my chest.

"Ava, wake up! You need to wake up! Can someone get the doctor, NOW!"

The scream is visceral. It is Rose. But her voice sounds distant, as if she is shouting from the bottom of a deep well, or perhaps I am the one at the bottom, listening to the world above.

What the hell?

I struggle to pry my eyes open, yet it's as if I lack eyelids altogether. As I assess myself, a chilling realisation dawns—I can no longer feel my body. All I know in this moment is that I am floating somewhere, hearing the world around me as if at the end of a shadowy tunnel. No matter what I try, I am met with complete silence, as if my mind has severed all connection to the physical realm. My brain screams for clarity, fires panic signals that reverberate through the void, but everything remains muffled and distant. It's as if I am submerged in an ocean of icy, crushing molasses.

Why is Rose screaming? Have the demons found us? Is the safe house compromised?

The soldier in me takes over. I command my arms to move. *Move, damn you! Reach for the sidearm. Get up. Protect the pack.* But there is no response. My limbs are completely paralysed, dead weights attached to a torso that refuses to obey. There is no sensation of touch, no feel of the sheets against my skin, just this crushing, oppressive weight pinning me to the mattress.

"Ava, please, wake up! Come back to me, I can't lose you.

Please, I need you to come back."

Rose is begging now. Her voice cracks with raw, unfiltered terror, and the sound slices through my mental fog like a jagged blade. The sheer desperation in her tone triggers a surge of adrenaline, but it has nowhere to go. I am a prisoner in my own mind. Then something dark crosses my thoughts. Is this what it's like for Devika? Have I been possessed? No, I can't be. If I had been possessed, Rose would be reacting very differently.

Come back to her? I am right here! I'm trying, Rose! I'm fucking trying! I scream internally, the words echoing in the silence of my mind. *I'm not gone! Just... open my eyes! Let me out!*

It feels exactly like severe sleep paralysis, that horrific state when the mind awakens before the body, but the panic radiating from Rose suggests something infinitely worse than a bad dream. Then I notice feelings I know aren't mine; it must be our bond. We are still connected, so I concentrate on it to try to gather as much information as possible about what is happening to me. Even though I can't feel it, I suddenly sense through the bond that Rose is shaking me in desperation. Then I feel her warm palms cup something very cold, which sends Rose's emotions spiralling even further into a desperate abyss.

"Ava, please do not leave me. You need to come back to me!"

Through the bond, I sense someone approaching, then I hear the heavy wooden door to the room slam open, rebounding loudly off the wall with a crack that echoes in my mind like a gunshot.

"What is going on? What's wrong?"

Doctor Stevens. His voice is commanding, though laced with an underlying current of alarm. I can hear his footsteps rushing across the floorboards, the rapid *tap-tap-tap* of professional urgency.

"It is Ava!" Rose cries out, her voice now a frantic, breathless sob. "I was lying here with her. I couldn't sleep, so I was just listening to her heartbeat. And then it just stopped! That is when I noticed her hair. I have tried everything to wake her, but I can't. I have only felt and heard her heart beat a few times since it stopped!"

The words hit me with a devastating blow. *Wait. My heart stopped.*

The thought should terrify me. It should send me into a spiral of absolute panic. But in this void, it just feels... distant. Detached. As if she is talking about someone else entirely. *That's impossible. I can think. I can hear. If my heart stopped, I wouldn't be here to wonder why my heart stopped.*

"Move aside, Rose. Let me examine her," the doctor orders. His clinical authority cuts through the panic, a sharp contrast to Rose's emotional wreckage.

I am officially freaking out now. The detachment vanishes, replaced by a cold, biting fear. *What does she mean my heart stopped? I am alive! I am thinking! This has to be some kind of mistake. I'm just having the world's worst hangover from Reya's blood!*

Again, through the bond, I sense Doctor Stevens pressing his cold fingers firmly against my radial pulse at my wrist. I wait, straining to feel the pressure, but there is nothing. Then his fingers slide up to my carotid artery in my neck. I push every single ounce of my willpower into waking up, fighting the suffocating black void that wants to swallow me whole. I imagine myself as a diver, swimming upward through the molasses, fighting for a breath of air.

I sense his hands gently peel one of my eyelids open. I desperately expect to see the harsh overhead light of the room or the doctor's concerned face.

Instead, I see absolutely nothing.

My vision is gone. It isn't blackness, because that would imply the presence of an eyelid or a shadow. It is just... empty. A void where sight should be.

"There is something happening to her pupillary response and her corneas as well," Doctor Stevens notes. His professional tone is now laced with deep, unsettling bewilderment. He sounds like a man looking at a medical textbook that has suddenly started writing itself in a language he doesn't understand.

"What do you mean?" Rose asks, her breath hitching in a way that makes my non-functioning chest ache.

"Her eyes have turned an icy white with a distinct blue tint to them, just like her hair. Medically speaking, this should not be possible. She has only been back for four hours. Sudden, complete depigmentation like this cannot happen in four hours."

What? My hair changed colour? I feel a surge of absurdity. *Great. I've gone from Captain to a geriatric ghost in record time.*

"Let me see," Rose demands. I sense the mattress dip through our bond as she crowds in beside the doctor. Through Rose, I know he is pressing his stethoscope to my chest. I should be feeling the cold metal against my skin, as I have so many times before. Again, I feel nothing except what I'm feeling through the bond. If we didn't have it, I would be in a complete meltdown by now.

"What the hell is going on with her?" Rose's voice is trembling now. "She looks severely cyanotic. She is deathly pale, her hair and eyes have turned stark white... she looks dead."

Dead? I look dead? What the actual hell is Reya's blood doing to me? The panic returns, sharper this time. I am trapped in a body that is mutating into something unrecognisable, something that looks like a corpse, while the mind inside remains screamingly awake.

"What is going on in here?"

A deep, rumbling voice asks from across the room. Luca. His presence is heavy and commanding, his alpha energy vibrating through the air even though I cannot see him. I can feel what it is like for Rose when her alpha is present.

"Her heart suddenly stopped, and her hair and eyes have completely changed colour," Rose explains rapidly, her words tumbling over one another in her haste.

"Doctor Stevens, what exactly is happening to her biology?" Luca asks. His voice is tight with a tension that suggests he is barely holding back his own panic.

"I honestly do not know," Doctor Stevens admits. He sounds

defeated, his clinical confidence shattered by my impossible medical chart. "None of this aligns with standard human physiology. She is in severe bradycardia. She does have a heartbeat, but the intervals are massive. It is as if her body is hovering precariously on the absolute brink of death, simply refusing to cross over. I cannot explain it, nor do I understand it."

The cold terror finally begins to sink into my mind. I am trapped in a failing, mutating shell, and no one has a map to get me out.

Yet, strangely, as the fear peaks, I don't feel the familiar symptoms of a panic attack. My breathing doesn't spike, mostly because I can't feel myself breathing at all. Instead, there is just an intense, oppressive pressure. It isn't a physical weight on my chest, but a heavy, static pressure pushing directly onto my mind. It feels like a radio frequency humming at a volume that threatens to shatter my skull.

Then, the source of that pressure makes herself known.

"What the fuck!" Luca curses loudly, his usual composure completely shattering.

"What is that doing here?" Rose snarls. Her voice instantly shifts from grief to aggression, dripping with hatred and predatory instinct. I can almost hear her teeth baring.

"What is going on? What is here?" Doctor Stevens asks, his voice darting around the room in confusion.

"It is a shade," Rose spits out. "It belongs to the witch who did something to Ava to try and save her."

"Why can't I see it, but you can?" the doctor asks, sounding genuinely perplexed.

"We couldn't see them before today," Luca explains, his voice tight. "One of the other witches gave us these magical root bracelets. It grants us the Sight."

"How can I acquire one? Wait, are those actual plant roots digging right into your skin?" The doctor's medical curiosity temporarily overrides the crisis, and I can almost hear him leaning in to inspect Luca's wrist.

"They are. I really wish I could talk to her," Luca murmurs, his tone shifting into something deeply sorrowful, a weight of regret that fills the room.

'What is wrong with you?'

The voice isn't heard with my ears. It rings directly inside my head, cold and echoing, like a stone dropped into a frozen lake.

Holy crap. I wish this worked both ways, mentally saying to myself, *I do not know what is wrong with me! I wish I could answer you properly! I can't move! I can't see!*

'I can hear you just fine, Ava. What is wrong?'

The voice belongs to Sera, the shade created from Reya's essence. Her mental tone is calm, almost clinical, but there is a flicker of curiosity there.

'Oh my gods, this is amazing!' I mentally say, the excitement momentarily overriding my terror. *'Can you tell... crap, you can't talk to the others. I have no idea what is happening to me, Sera. Rose says my heart stopped. It is apparently still beating, but incredibly slowly. The doctor says I am on the verge of death, but I am not actually dying.'*

'Very interesting,' Sera muses. I feel a shift in her energy, a ripple of something dark and ancient moving closer to me. *'There is a distinct difference. When I was near you before, I felt absolutely nothing from you. You were a blank slate. But now, as I move closer, I feel a terrifying, ancient fear radiating deep inside of me. A fear I have never felt before.'*

'Well, that is definitely not a comforting diagnosis,' I reply, the sarcasm returning as a defence mechanism. *'Anyway, while I can still communicate with you, do you have any news from your scouting mission?'*

'I do,' Sera replies, her voice becoming focused. *'I followed the winged demon. She returned to the exact same property in Jackson. There is a massive congregation of demons there, and I also spotted several vampires. It looks like they are actively building a substantial army.'*

The tactical brain in my head clicks into gear, overriding the paralysis. *That is catastrophic news. 'So, before we go blindly charging in after Devika, we need to formulate a plan to drastically reduce their numbers first. We can't walk into a meat-grinder.'*

'I completely agree. I had better return to my sisters to ensure they remain safe.'

'You see them as your sisters?' I ask, genuinely surprised. I had assumed Sera was just a magical construct, a tool created for a purpose.

'I do,' Sera replies, and for the first time, her voice is tinged with dark sorrow. *'I possess all of Reya's memories... well, up to the exact moment I was magically created. So yes, they feel exactly like my own family. Even though they will likely never see me as anything more than a shade only created to protect them, I am entirely okay with it. I'm okay with why Reya created me.'*

'I am so glad they have you looking out for them right now,' I say, feeling a genuine warmth for the entity currently haunting my mind.

'Hopefully, we will get Reya back soon. I really miss her as she was the only one I could talk to.'

'I miss her too,' I say.

Sera then changes the subject, '*Actually, you can pass on a vital message for me to Freya and Maya. Tell them to keep a very close eye on their house. Something strange is happening with it. It feels like the structure itself is actively watching me sometimes.'*

'I will definitely pass that on. Do you have any theory on what might be causing it?'

'I have had some time to analyse it. Reya inscribed a powerful rune on the house to absorb magical attacks, ensuring the physical structure does not get destroyed during combat. That specific rune has been working overtime. It has absorbed several magical assaults, and Maya has continuously used healing magic on the property. I strongly believe all that residual magic is pooling and lingering deep within the foundations of the house.'

'That is incredibly fascinating,' I respond. *'Do you think it*

might put them in danger if the house continues to absorb that much raw power?'

'I do not think so, but I am going to keep a very close watch regardless.'

'Okay, I will definitely let the sisters know. You can actually help me with something before you leave. You cannot speak to anyone else, but they can clearly see you. Can you point directly at me, and then give them a thumbs up so they know I am conscious and okay? Please.'

'I can certainly try,' Sera replies. *'I hope you feel better and get back on your feet soon, Ava. We desperately need you.'*

'Hopefully. Thank you, Sera.'

I hold my mental breath, listening intently to the reactions in the room.

"What exactly is it doing?" Rose demands, her voice laced with suspicion and a hint of that panther growl.

"It seems to be pointing directly at Ava..." Luca starts, his voice trailing off in utter disbelief. "Now it is giving us a thumbs up. I think she is trying to tell us that Ava is okay."

I feel the heavy, static mental pressure lift from my mind, vanishing entirely as Sera departs. The silence that follows is heavy and thick.

"Do you really think that means Ava is okay?" Rose asks. She sounds desperate, clinging to this shred of hope like a lifeline in a storm.

"I think it might," Luca reasons. "Shades communicate strictly via the mind. So maybe she was able to establish a link with Ava, which would definitely mean Ava is awake inside her own head and was able to ask her to do that."

"Do you really believe that?"

"I do. Also, you haven't mentioned the fact that your prime bond has gone completely silent," Luca points out gently.

"You are right," Rose admits. "I do still feel the bond between us, but my own sheer panic has been completely overwhelming me. I don't think I have felt anything radiating from her end. Except, right before the shade left, my blinding feeling of panic suddenly reduced. So maybe Ava was panicking just as badly as I was, and the shade managed to calm her down?"

Nailed it, I think. *Rose is still the smartest person in the room.*

"That sounds highly plausible," Luca says. "I also think you should really stop calling her 'it' or 'a shade'. Her name is Sera."

"Why are you suddenly so accepting of what Reya did by creating it? I mean, creating Sera," Rose challenges.

"Losing the mate bond made me realise a very harsh truth," Luca admits, and his voice is thick with heavy regret. "If I hadn't been so incredibly pig-headed, if I hadn't let old prejudices completely rule my judgment, maybe if I had just given it a chance... we wouldn't have lost Reya. It does seem she might actually still be alive, though. If she is alive, why has the bond vanished? Maybe there are other magical ways to sever it that we do not know about."

"I am trying to be much more accepting," Rose sighs softly. "It is just incredibly hard when all you have been taught before these attacks is that black witches are inherently evil. I am finally starting to realise that just because Reya utilises dark magic does not automatically mean she is a bad person."

"Maybe if our lives hadn't been violently turned upside down by these attacks, we might have learned acceptance much sooner," Luca replies.

"I think you may be right."

"I am very sorry to interrupt this profound moment of growth," Doctor Stevens interjects, his tone dry and clinical, though I can detect the exhaustion in it. "But if the shade thing successfully communicated that Ava is mentally okay, then all we can currently do is strictly monitor her physical condition. Because I have absolutely no medical idea how to treat her."

"I will not leave her side. I will keep a constant eye on her," Rose vows fiercely. Her voice possesses a lethal edge now, the panther claiming its mate.

"I know you will, Rose. However, I would still like the nurse and myself to keep a close watch. You may not know the specific physiological changes to look for that would indicate she is returning to us, or..."

"Do not even say it," Rose snaps, her voice vibrating with lethal energy. "We will not lose her."

"I truly hope you are right. Anyway, I am going to re-attach the telemetry monitor and EKG leads so we can closely track these massive cardiac intervals," the doctor says.

Again, I still can't feel the cold, sticky patches being pressed onto my chest as the sensors would cling to my skin. I miss the feeling, a reminder that I am currently more of a specimen than a soldier.

I continue to listen for a long while. Rose remains steadfast by my side, and I sense her hand now clenching mine, her voice a constant, soothing anchor in the dark void. She talks to me softly, keeping me updated on the chaotic world outside my paralysed body.

She tells me that Sam went out with half of our backup tactical team to officially secure our new operational base. It is an old, abandoned commercial building, she explains, but it has an attached dwelling and excellent lines of sight. It is secluded, meaning if a massive fire-fight breaks out, we won't have innocent civilians caught in the crossfire.

Slowly, the world begins to fade again. The rhythmic, incredibly slow *beep... beep...* of the heart monitor becomes a hypnotic lullaby, and the soothing cadence of Rose's voice blends into a warm melody. The exhaustion dragging at my mutating cells finally wins, pulling me back down into the deep, healing darkness. This time, I don't fight it. I let the void take me, hoping that when I wake up, I will be something more than a ghost.

CHAPTER 15

THE PREDATOR'S AWAKENING

For days, I have been trapped in the suffocating prison of my own mind. It is a claustrophobic existence, a sensory deprivation chamber where the only company I keep is the echo of my own frantic thoughts. Unlike the last time, when my body was shattered, filled with lead and a weakness that dragged me under like a rusted anchor in a storm, this time is entirely different. There is no agony, no screaming nerves, no feeling of being dismantled piece by piece.

Instead, there is a hum. A low, thrumming vibration of raw, unadulterated power that resonates in the void.

Since the darkness swallowed me, the world has continued to turn without my permission. From the fragmented sounds and hushed tones that bleed into my consciousness, I know my team has packed up and moved us to a new location. Rose, predictably, has been a wreck. I can feel her anxiety through our bond, a jagged, pulsing frequency of worry that tastes like salt and desperation. She nearly panicked over the logistics of transporting my comatose, defenceless body, fearing every bump in the road might further damage whatever is happening inside me.

I wish I could reach out and tell her I am not defenceless. I'm just... resting. Like a predator waiting for the perfect moment to strike.

To secure our new base, the heavy hitters came out in full force.

I can hear the rhythmic chanting of Freya and Maya, their voices weaving together in a harmonic cadence that makes the air vibrate. Beside them, Pickle and Sera are standing guard over the sisters along with Beastie. Together, they wove a dense, shimmering web of protective wards around the perimeter, a psychic fortress designed to keep the world out.

One by one, they shuffle into my room. Through my bond with Rose, I can smell them. Freya's scent of damp earth and ozone, Maya's soft fragrance of vanilla and dried herbs, and Pickle's sharp, sugary scent that reminds me of spun cotton candy. And of course, Beastie smells of a burning fire. They stand around my bed in a heavy silence, their breaths shallow. Then comes the question, the same exhausting, repetitive loop. "Does anyone know what is actually happening to her?"

Of course no one knows. You're all grasping at straws in a pitch-black room.

As far as I can gather from the frantic murmurs that drift over me, not a single person has mentioned the translation from Reya's diary. There is a terrifying little footnote in those pages regarding a god's ability to create vampires from their blood, but it seems to have been conveniently forgotten or ignored.

Maybe Freya is right. Maybe I am turning into a bloodsucker. Brilliant. Just what my resume needs. 'Special Skills. Professional Assassin, Expert Marksman, and Occasional Bloodsucker.' I can see the LinkedIn update now.

Sera has been my only lifeline, a ghostly tether to the waking world. Because I can communicate with her mentally, I turned her into my personal intelligence officer the moment we settled into our new safe house. I needed eyes on the ground, someone gathering intel while I lay here playing the role of the Sleeping Beauty. I instructed Sera to have Damaris monitor exactly which humans the demons are possessing and to map out their regular hunting grounds in the city, with a specific focus on the vampires.

During one of our mental exchanges, Sera highlighted

something we should have figured out much earlier. She notes that it is strange how suddenly everyone could hear Damaris. When Damaris drank Reya's blood, it may have granted her the ability to speak like a normal ghost, mirroring Doris, the spirit Reya and Freya had mentioned back in New Orleans.

Sera has another theory that Damaris has been undergoing a gradual evolution. Her form is shifting from a hazy, translucent shade into something more solid, a recognisable spirit with weight and presence, so it may not have anything to do with Reya's blood; there's no way to know unless we run an experiment on another shade.

Sera also hypothesises that even though Damaris is changing, she still thinks that if she were to drink a tiny amount of my blood, she might be able to establish a mental link with me as well, acting as a bridge between my locked mind and the physical world.

I am an elite assassin, not a juice box, I grumble internally, but the tactical advantage is too delicious to pass up. If it gives me a voice, I'd let her drain half my arm.

Today, the air in the room feels cool and stagnant. Sera and Damaris hover in the shadows, waiting with that unnerving, supernatural patience for Rose to finally leave my side. The moment the door clicks shut and the echo of Rose's footsteps fades, Damaris approaches. As usual, I feel nothing, except for a sudden, strange feeling washing over my mind. Of course, Sera keeps me updated on what is happening, which makes me realise that when Damaris is drinking my blood, it coincides with that strange feeling.

Heavy, rhythmic footfalls from someone approaching suddenly break the quiet. I recognise the sound as Luca's. I tell Sera to leave, but she refuses, as Damaris needs just a little more if this is to work. He doesn't knock. He bursts into the room, his presence hitting me like a thunderstorm in a small space.

"What the hell are you two doing to Ava?" Luca growls.

His anger floods the room, thick and suffocating. He is by my side in an instant, his protective instincts flaring from seeing a demon hovering over his Beta's mate.

Oh, perfect timing, Luca. Really helpful. You're a real ray of sunshine.

Thankfully, Sera's insane plan worked. Damaris's voice suddenly echoes through the dark void of my mind, clear as a ringing bell in a silent cathedral. I quickly project a wave of calm toward her, feeding her the exact words I need her to say, tailoring the tone to be just convincing enough. Finally, I have a mouthpiece.

"Luca, Ava asked Sera to bring me here," Damaris says aloud. Even through my mental link, I can hear the tremor of intimidation in her voice. Luca's presence is overwhelming. "Sera had a theory. She believed that if I drank a small amount of Ava's blood, I might be able to mentally talk to her, even though I have changed and am no longer a shade. It worked. I can hear her right now."

Damaris pauses, waiting for my next mental instruction. I push the information forward with clinical precision.

"Ava told me to tell you that you were guided by a voice to seek out Agent Moore," Damaris relays. "She says the voice told you to work with him to try and save our world."

I can practically hear Luca's jaw drop. The oppressive weight of his anger vanishes, replaced by a sudden, sharp intake of breath.

"You really can talk to her?" he asks. His voice has lost its aggressive edge, replaced by a desperate, raw kind of hope that makes my heart ache.

"Yes, we both can," Damaris confirms.

Luca steps closer, his boots heavy on the floorboards. I can imagine him looking down at me, his dark eyes searching my still face for any sign of life. "Is she okay? Does she know what is happening to her?"

I feed the response to Damaris instantly, keeping it professional and steady.

"She says she is fine," Damaris relays. "She isn't entirely sure what is happening. The only thing she thinks is that if she is going through some kind of cellular mutation, she might be stuck in this state temporarily. Like a caterpillar turning into a butterfly."

A highly lethal, heavily armed butterfly, I add mentally, though Damaris wisely leaves that bit out.

"So, Ava thinks she is turning into something good?" Luca asks, a weary, shuddering sigh escaping his chest. "We have been out of our minds with worry. We thought whatever is happening to her might turn her into a monster. Something... different."

"I can guarantee you from my short conversation with her, Ava is the exact same person," Damaris says, and I can hear a hint of a smile in her voice. "She can hear everything you talk about in her presence, and she is incredibly frustrated that she cannot fully wake up."

"That is a massive relief," Luca mutters. Somehow, even with not being able to see, I can picture him rubbing the back of his neck in that awkward, humble way he does when he's not playing the Alpha. "Does Ava have anything else she wants to pass on?"

I immediately push my next thoughts forward, letting the emotion bleed through the mental command.

"Ava has asked if you can tell Rose she loves her," Damaris says, her voice softening significantly. "And that she desperately needs her to stop worrying." I pause, then add the tactical layer. "She also asked me to tell you that she has got Sera and myself to start tracking the demons and vampires in the city. That way, when she wakes up, you can start picking as many off as possible before you try to capture Devika."

"That is a damn good tactical plan," Luca admits, his voice regaining its authoritative clip. "Anyway, I can hear Rose returning. You two had better go. If Rose sees you hovering over Ava like this, she is likely to shift and tear your throats out. She is beyond stressed."

Even through the haze of my slumber, I hear it. the familiar, rhythmic padding of Rose walking down the hallway. Sera and Damaris quickly murmur their goodbyes and vanish into the ether, leaving a vacuum of silence behind them.

The door swings open with a soft thud. “Who were you talking to?” Rose asks, her voice breathless and thin. “Wait. Has Ava woken up?”

I hear the shift in her gait, the sudden transition from a walk to a frantic jog as she rushes toward the bed. I feel it then. a sharp, blooming ache as her profound disappointment radiates through our bond when she realises I am still trapped in this silent slumber. It is a wave of grief so potent it nearly knocks me back into the darkness.

Luca gently guides her to a chair and sits her down. He carefully explains the encounter with Damaris and Sera, leaving no detail out, and passes on my messages. Rose, being wonderfully, fiercely Rose, completely freaks out at first. The idea of a demon drinking from me sends a spike of raw panther fury through the room. As Luca calms her down and the reality of my message sinks in, her frantic energy shifts into an overwhelming sense of relief that feels like a warm blanket.

She moves to the edge of my bed. Through the bond, I can feel how cold my skin is as she holds one of my hands and, with the other, cups my face. “I love you too,” Rose whispers, her voice thick with unshed tears. “Please, baby, wake up soon. I am not sure if you are going to like your new look, but we can fix it. Maybe you can wear coloured contacts and dye your hair if you want to. Honestly, I have to say your new look is striking. You are a little pale, but make-up can fix that. Not that you ever use any.”

Do I look like a Victorian ghost with an attitude problem?

A desperate surge of willpower floods my mind. I focus every ounce of it on moving my hand so I can touch her face. I picture it. the tension in the tendons, the contraction of the muscle. I push against the void, this invisible barrier that keeps me paralysed, fighting it like a physical weight, a mountain I have to move with a single finger.

As usual, I feel absolutely nothing. No movement, no sensation. But then, Rose jerks violently. I feel the sudden, shocked movement of her body through the bond.

"Luca, get the doctor!" Rose shouts, her voice cracking with wild, unrestrained excitement. "Ava just squeezed my hand!"

"Ava, baby, can you squeeze my hand again?" she begs.

I am completely stunned. I actually broke through. The thrill of it sends a phantom rush of adrenaline through my mind, an electric spark that lights up the void. I immediately gather my focus and try to clench my fist, pouring everything I have into that one movement.

"Come on, Ava, try to squeeze my hand again. Please," Rose pleads. A second later, she mutters under her breath, "I really wish that Damaris were here so she could give me some actual answers."

I am slightly taken aback by that admission. Rose actively wishing for a demon's presence? Maybe she really is adapting to this chaotic new world we live in. Or maybe she's just that desperate.

Heavy footsteps echo in the hallway, and I recognise the distinct, hurried gait of Doctor Stevens. He breaches the doorway, his breath slightly laboured. "What happened?"

"Ava squeezed my hand. Does this mean she is finally waking up?" Rose asks, practically vibrating with hope.

"Let me run a few neurological tests," Doctor Stevens replies, his tone professional but laced with cautious optimism. "It might have just been an involuntary muscle spasm in her hand. We have seen that happen in her lower extremities a few times over the past forty-eight hours. This might be a similar localised reflex."

"It did not feel like a spasm," Rose argues, her tone leaving no room for debate. "It felt like a deliberate squeeze, and it happened precisely after I told her I loved her."

"Okay, okay. As I said, I will run a few diagnostics," Doctor Stevens says, moving closer to the bed. I hear the rustle of his stethoscope and the snap of latex gloves. "I will start with the CRS-R tests to check her auditory and motor function. If that doesn't produce definitive results, I will run another EEG. I know you refused the transport last time, Rose, but it really might be worth taking her to the local hospital for a full MRI."

"We will discuss it," Luca interjects firmly.

For the next few agonising hours, Doctor Stevens pokes, prods, and tests my reflexes. He taps my knees, shines lights into my eyes, and speaks in that monotonous clinical voice. Rose continuously begs me to squeeze her hand again. I push against the mental wall with everything I have, straining until I feel like my mind is going to fracture. It is infuriating. I am screaming inside my own skull, a prisoner in a silent tomb.

By the time the doctor finishes his barrage of tests, I feel mentally and physically drained. The effort of trying to communicate has exhausted me.

"What is the result?" Rose asks, her anxiety bleeding through the bond and wrapping around my heart like barbed wire.

"There is a marked increase in alpha wave response on the EEG telemetry," Doctor Stevens explains, his voice tinged with genuine surprise. "I believe she is starting to surface. She is currently in a condition very similar to locked-in syndrome. Her brain is functioning perfectly, processing external stimuli, but her motor pathways are completely inhibited. She cannot move her body, but she is in there."

I hear a sudden, tearful gasp, followed by the rustle of clothing. I am certain Rose just threw her arms around Doctor Stevens in a crushing hug. A moment later, she returns to my bedside. She grips my hand like it is the only thing tethering her to the earth. It is a strange feeling through our bond, knowing she is holding my hand.

Now that she knows from Damaris that I can hear everything, Rose begins to talk. She doesn't stop. She tells me stories of her childhood, of the pack, and of the stupid things Luca used to do when they were younger, when he first found her on the streets. Her voice is a rich, soothing melody that washes over my frayed nerves, pulling me away from the clinical coldness of the doctor's tests. Exhausted and fragile, I let the cadence of her words draw me down into a deep, dreamless sleep.

The first thing I notice when I drag myself back to consciousness is the heavy, comforting weight of an arm draped across my waist. I have no concept of how long I have been asleep, but a deep, primal instinct tells me it is the dead of night. The room is bathed in a soft, indigo shadow.

Everything feels... amplified. The silence of the house is not actually silent. It is a symphony of tiny sounds. I can hear the faint, rhythmic squeak of a floorboard two rooms over as someone paces. I hear the low, rumbling vibration of someone snoring down the hall. I can even hear the distant hum of electricity in the walls.

The heavy lethargy that kept me pinned to the mattress is entirely gone. In its place is a vibrant, crackling energy that courses through my muscles like liquid lightning. I can feel the absolute, terrifying strength coiled in my arms and legs. My back, usually tight with residual aches from the attack, feels loose and perfect, as if every scar has been smoothed away.

"I can tell you are awake," Rose whispers softly into the dark. "I have been focusing intensely on our bond. I finally figured out the subtle shift in your energy when you transition from sleep to wakefulness. You fell asleep on me earlier. Are my stories really that boring?"

'I love your stories. All the damn tests the doc performed just drained me,' I say casually, wishing fiercely that she could actually hear my voice.

"I am so sorry about the tests, baby," Rose murmurs, her fingers tracing soothing circles on my hip. "I was just so sure you squeezed my..."

Rose stops dead.

I feel her entire body stiffen before she shoots straight up in the bed like she has been electrocuted.

Panic spikes instantly in my chest. *Threat.* We are under attack. The instinct is so deeply ingrained it bypasses conscious thought. I try to force my heavy limbs to react, preparing to defend her.

The next thing I know, the world blurs into a dizzying smear of motion. A rush of cold air hits my face. I am no longer lying down. I am standing perfectly upright on the hardwood floor, my eyes wide open and pupils dilated, scanning the dark corners of the room for a target.

Nothing. The room is completely empty, save for the two of us.

I whip my head around and finally see Rose. She is kneeling in the centre of the mattress, the sheets tangled around her legs. Her eyes are wide as saucers, her jaw slack as she stares at me in absolute, unadulterated shock.

"Are we under attack?" I demand.

My voice sounds foreign to my own ears. It is deeper, carrying a strange, melodic resonance that vibrates in my chest, like a low-frequency hum.

"Why in the hell would we be under attack?" Rose breathes out, looking entirely bewildered.

"You stopped talking mid-sentence and practically launched yourself off the mattress," I say, my brows knitting together in confusion.

"I stopped because I realised you just answered me. Out loud," Rose says, her gaze sweeping over my face, taking in my altered features.

It takes a full three seconds for her words to process in my brain. I look down at my bare feet, grounded firmly against the cold floorboards. I look at my hands, flexing my fingers. I am standing. I am awake. I do not even remember the physical act of getting out of bed. It happened faster than humanly possible. a blur of motion that defies every law of physics I have ever known.

I do not waste another second trying to understand the mechanics of it. I launch myself back towards the bed, desperate to feel her against me, to kiss the worried crease from her forehead.

Only, my new body does not obey the laws of gravity and inertia I am used to.

I move with terrifying, explosive velocity. I misjudge the distance completely and collide with Rose's chest like a freight train. The sheer force of my momentum carries us both backwards, tumbling right off the opposite edge of the mattress. We crash onto the floor in a tangled, chaotic heap of limbs and blankets.

We both lie there on the floor for a long, stunned moment, waiting for the pain to register. But there is no pain. Just the heavy, rapid thud of Rose's heart against my chest, sounding like a war drum in the silence.

A sharp knock raps against the bedroom door. "Is everything okay in there, Rose?" Commander Rodriguez calls out, his voice laced with sudden authority. "Is there an issue with Ava?"

Rose and I look at each other, our faces mere inches apart. A bubble of pure, ridiculous joy rises in my throat.

"We are totally fine!" we both yell out in unison.

The absurdity of the moment catches up to us, and we both start to giggle like schoolgirls, a sound of genuine levity that feels alien in this dark house.

"Oh, okay. Glad you are back with us, Ava. See you in the morning," the Commander says, chuckling softly before I hear his heavy boots retreat down the corridor.

Rose and I laugh again, a sound of pure relief, before we slowly untangle our limbs. We climb back onto the bed, and this time, I move with extreme, hyper-focused caution. My body feels like a loaded weapon with a hair-trigger. It seems I have some serious adjusting to do if I don't want to accidentally demolish the furniture.

Once we are settled beneath the covers, the laughter fades into something much heavier, more intimate. I look down at Rose, her stunning green eyes locked onto mine. The overwhelming tide of love I feel for her nearly brings me to my knees; it is a physical weight, a crushing devotion. I carefully frame her beautiful face with my hands, my thumbs tracing the curve of her cheekbones.

I lean down and crash my lips against hers. I kiss her like the world is burning around us, like we are the last two people left on earth. This might be the last time we get to do this, so I can't help but pour every ounce of fear, relief, and desperate longing into the connection.

Rose responds instantly, her hands tangling in my hair. She pulls me flush against her body, her mouth opening hot and demanding under mine. The kiss deepens, turning frantic and bruised. Her tongue sweeps against mine, tasting of coffee and vanilla, igniting a fire low in my belly that has nothing to do with my supernatural changes.

I groan, shifting my weight to straddle her hips. Her hands roam eagerly over my back, mapping the new contours of my strength, pulling me closer until there isn't a millimetre of space between us. Every brush of her fingertips against my skin sends a jolt of electricity straight to my core. I trail open-mouthed kisses down her jaw, my lips grazing the sensitive skin of her neck, savouring the soft, breathy gasps escaping her lips.

The heat between us is suffocating, a beautiful, intoxicating friction. I grind my hips down against hers, revelling in the sharp arch of her spine and the whimper that vibrates in her throat. She is so soft, so warm, so perfectly alive beneath me.

But as my mouth moves over the smooth column of her throat, something terrible shifts inside me.

Beneath her intoxicating scent, the musky aroma of arousal, a new scent violently breaches my senses. It slices through the haze, sharp, bright, and undeniable. It is raw metal and wild honey, overwhelmingly rich, coating the back of my throat with a dark promise.

My eyes snap open. The dimly lit bedroom blurs, everything fading into shadow except for one singular focal point. the frantic, erratic flutter of the thick blue vein pressing against the translucent skin of her neck. *Thump. Thump. Thump.* Her racing heartbeat ceases to be a comforting lullaby. It amplifies, drumming against my eardrums like a frenzied, driving bass, practically begging me to tear it open.

A blinding, agonising ache erupts deep within my gums. My skull throbs as if my jawbone is being forcibly split open from the inside out. A heavy, molten pressure builds behind my incisors, a deep, searing burn that demands violent, immediate release. In a heartbeat, my throat turns to ash. It contracts with a vicious, clawing thirst, a desperate drought that instantly obliterates love, reason, and every remaining shred of humanity in my head.

The predator doesn't ask permission; it just takes the reins. I don't even realise I am moving.

My mouth falls open as the agony in my teeth crests into something brutally sharp. I bury my face into the soft, fragrant crook of her neck, feeling the desperate flutter of her pulse against my lips for one fleeting second. Then, I bite down hard.

Hot velvet explodes across my tongue. The copper taste of her blood is devastatingly, impossibly sweet, flooding my mouth like liquid sunlight. It is the most exquisite, decadent thing I have ever consumed. But the initial swallow is just gasoline poured over a raging inferno. The starvation spikes, rabid and demanding. I draw desperately at the wound, my fingers digging into her bare shoulders, pinning her down to the mattress with a terrifying, effortless, and entirely unnatural strength.

"AVA! STOP!"

The scream is ragged, shattering the euphoric, bloody haze enveloping my mind. The pure, unadulterated terror in Rose's voice cuts through the monstrous hunger like a serrated blade.

Reality crashes over me in a bucket of freezing water. *Oh my god. What am I doing?*

I manage to yank myself back, a guttural, wet sound of self-loathing tearing from my throat. Simultaneously, Rose slams both of her hands against my chest. Driven by blind panic and her own volatile shifter strength, the impact hits me hard. harder than I have ever felt.

I am launched backwards, flying completely off the edge of the mattress. I slam into the hardwood floor, the impact jarring my bones, but I scramble instantly onto my knees. I am trembling uncontrollably, my entire body seized by an icy shock. I drag the back of a shaking hand across my chin. It comes away slick, smeared thick and wet with brilliant crimson.

Her blood.

Rose has scrambled backwards, pressing herself flat against the solid wood of the headboard. Her chest heaves with ragged, shallow gasps as her hand clutches frantically at her neck, dark red already seeping through her trembling fingers. Her brilliant green eyes are impossibly wide, the pupils blown out with a gut-wrenching mixture of sheer horror and devastating heartbreak. She isn't looking into my eyes. She is staring directly at my mouth.

Trembling, I slowly run my tongue over my teeth, tasting the metallic ruin left behind. There, resting heavy and razor-sharp against my bottom lip, are two elongated fangs.

What the hell is happening to me? Have I become a monster?

CHAPTER 16

THE TASTE OF LOVE AND HATE

I remain frozen, glued to the floor. My knees ache against the firm surface, a dull pain that pales in comparison to the agonising void ripping through my chest. It feels as though someone has reached inside me with a rusted hook and carved out my heart, leaving a cavern of echoing silence and shame.

I gaze at Rose.

She is huddled back against the headboard, her breath coming in shallow, jagged hitches that sound like breaking glass. Her vivid green eyes are wide, the pupils blown so large they almost swallow the iris. They are overtaken by an expression I never imagined I would see aimed at me.

Terror. Pure, unfiltered, soul-crushing terror.

No. No, no, no. Please, not this. Anyone but her.

I silently plead with the universe, with whatever cruel gods are currently playing dice with my existence, to tell me she is only frightened by the situation. I want to believe she is scared of the suddenness of the attack, or the sheer chaos of the moment. *Please, gods, do not let her be afraid of me.*

The metallic tang of her blood still coats my tongue, heavy and cloying. It is a damning, copper reminder of my complete loss of control, a taste that lingers like a sin I cannot wash away. My mouth feels tight, the skin stretching in ways it shouldn't, and the phantom sensation of something sharp still pressing against my gums makes me want to scrub my tongue raw.

I have to speak. *Come on, Ava. Move. Breathe. Say something. Anything.*

I need to explain the inexplicable, but as I open my mouth, the words die in my throat. What the hell am I supposed to say? It is not as if I possess a tactical manual for whatever biological nightmare is currently unfolding inside my veins. How can I possibly help Rose understand when my own mind is a swirling vortex of confusion and self-loathing?

I just bit her. I sank my teeth into the woman I love, and I liked it. Oh god, why did that feel like the only right thing in the world for three seconds?

I debate with myself for a few agonising seconds. The silence in the room is suffocating, thick as wool and twice as heavy, broken only by Rose's ragged breathing. She looks so small, despite her strength, clutching her neck with a trembling hand. Finally, a pathetic, broken whisper escapes my bloodstained lips.

"I am sorry."

It is the absolute worst thing I could have said. The apology does not soothe; it confirms. It shatters the fragile quiet like a grenade detonating in a confined space, turning the tension into raw, screaming panic.

"LUCA! LUCA, WAKE UP!" Rose screams at the top of her lungs.

I flinch violently, my entire body jerking as if I have been electrocuted. Her panicked shouts do not just echo in the small room. they pierce my eardrums like physical needles, stabbing deep into my brain. The volume is astronomical, a sonic assault that makes the walls seem to vibrate.

I slam both hands over my ears, desperate to block out the unbearable noise, but it is useless. Even with my palms pressed tightly against the sides of my head, my new, hyper-sensitive hearing picks up everything. I can hear the frantic rhythm of Rose's heart, a drumming panic that sounds like a war march. I can hear the settling of the house, the creak of floorboards three rooms away, and the distant, muffled sounds of the world outside.

The whole building is waking up. I can hear the shift in breathing from the other rooms, the sudden movements of people startled from sleep. The only exception is Johnson, still snoring rhythmically up in the attic where we banished him for his nocturnal noise pollution. The sound of his nasal whistling is suddenly an irritating, rhythmic thud in my skull.

Heavy footsteps thunder in the corridor outside. Our backup team is preparing to move, their boots striking the floor with a precision that usually comforts me, but now it sounds like a stampede. I hear Rodriguez's rough voice shouting orders, telling the puzzled team members to go back to their quarters until he knows what is really happening. His heavy boots march purposefully towards our door, each step vibrating through the hardwood and into my knees.

Luca and Sam intercept him in the corridor. Even through the walls, I can hear them. Luca's deep, commanding resonance and Sam's clipped, professional tone. They are assuring Rodriguez they will manage the situation, their voices a low hum of authority that usually signals safety. But now, it just feels like a countdown to judgment.

A moment later, a sharp, urgent knock rattles our bedroom door, the sound echoing like a gunshot in my hyper-tuned ears.

"Rose, what is going on?" Luca demands through the solid wood. "Has something happened to Ava?"

"Luca, get in here!" Rose shrieks, her voice cracking with raw hysteria.

The door crashes open with a fierce bang that makes me wince again. Luca charges into the room, a towering wall of shifter strength and instinct. He fills the doorway, his presence dominating the space, with Sam close by his side, looking alert and confused.

"What is wrong?" Luca begins, his dark eyes darting around

the room in a tactical sweep before settling on me. “Oh, Ava. You are back with us.”

For a split second, a flicker of genuine relief crosses his face. “This could have waited until the morning...”

His voice trails off, the relief instantly vanishing from his commanding presence. The air in the room grows icy, the temperature seeming to drop ten degrees in an instant. Luca’s nostrils flare, catching the scent. He knows that smell. We all do. Copper and iron. Blood.

“Wait. Is that blood? Rose, what is wrong with your neck?”

“You need to secure Ava right now,” Rose commands. She is pressing a trembling hand against her bleeding throat, her eyes never leaving mine. There is no warmth there anymore, only a cold, hard edge of survival. “She is turning into a vampire.”

A vampire? What on earth is she talking about? I’m a soldier, not a creature of the night.

“Look at her, Luca! Look at her!” Rose demands, pointing a trembling finger in my direction.

I am still paralysed by fear, staring at the visceral evidence of my attack on the woman I love. I look down at my hands and see them shaking, but it is not just fear. My body trembles with a terrifying, unfamiliar energy. It feels as though I have gulped down a hundred energy drinks while being struck by lightning at the same time. Every nerve ending is practically singing with excess voltage, a humming current of power that makes me feel like I might actually explode if I don’t move, run, or kill something.

Luca moves cautiously to my side, his movements slow and deliberate, as if he is approaching a wounded predator. Sam remains stationed by the bedroom door, his posture stiff and tactically alert, his hand hovering near his weapon. Since Rose has stopped screaming, I slowly lower my hands from my ringing ears, feeling the silence rush back in like a tide.

“Ava, are you alright?” Luca asks. His voice drops to a soft, calming murmur, the kind of tone he uses to settle a panicked shifter.

"What is happening?"

I desperately want to reply to him, but I cannot find the words. My throat feels tight, and something strange and deeply unsettling is occurring inside my mouth. There is a pressure, a sliding sensation in my gums that makes me feel nauseous. As Luca closes the narrow gap between us and the bed, I catch a glimpse of utter shock on his face.

He can clearly see the crimson smeared across my chin, the bright red stains painting my mouth. He can see my teeth. I haven't been able to close my mouth properly since I pulled away from Rose's throat because something is in the way.

"Are those... elongated canines?" Luca asks, his brow furrowing in deep confusion.

"I told you! She is turning into a vampire, Luca," Rose states. Her tone is laced with a venom that makes my stomach physically churn. It is not just anger; it is revulsion.

"Rose, take a breath," Luca replies. His Alpha command slips into his voice, a calm, stabilising frequency designed to override panic. "Ava does not look like any vampire I have ever seen. If she were truly transforming into a turned vampire, her soul would be actively fracturing. She would be completely feral, attacking everyone in this room. She certainly would not be kneeling on the floor, utterly frozen in fear."

I had anticipated Luca would overreact. I expected him to go into full protective mode, perhaps even pinning me to the floor for the safety of the team. Instead, he is analysing the situation with cold, tactical precision. He is looking at me not as a monster, but as a puzzle to be solved.

"Explain this, then," Rose snaps, jabbing a finger at the puncture wounds on her neck. The blood is still seeping through her fingers, staining her skin in long, dark streaks.

"Should I get the medic?" Sam asks from the doorway. His eyes are darting between the blood and my pale face, his professional mask slipping to reveal genuine alarm.

"No need," both Rose and Luca say in perfect, tense unison.

"Ava, I need you to communicate," Luca says softly, crouching down to meet my eye level. He is so close now that I can smell him. cedarwood, rain, and the underlying musk of a predator. "Can you talk to me, please?"

Before I can even try to make my vocal cords work, the strange sensation in my mouth grows stronger. The sharp pressure against my lower lip starts to lessen. It is an agonisingly slow process, a sliding shift that feels like bone moving through muscle. I can practically feel the fangs retracting, sliding back into my gums with a disgusting, microscopic shift of tissue.

I watch Luca's eyes widen as he sees the biological anomaly firsthand. He is watching my mouth, witnessing the retraction in real time.

"Please, Ava. You need to talk to me so we can try to understand what is happening to your physiology," Luca urges.

It takes an immense effort to push past the shock, to force my brain to reconnect with my voice. I feel like I am swimming through molasses, fighting against a current of pure panic. Finally, I manage to force the words out, though they sound foreign to my own ears.

"I do not know what is happening to me. I feel wired... my adrenaline is surging so intensely I could run nonstop for weeks." I swallow hard, my gaze dropping to the floor because I cannot bear to look at Rose. "I did not mean to hurt her. I was just so overwhelmingly excited to be finally awake again. I got caught up in the moment, and I completely lost control."

The disgust pooling in my gut threatens to make me violently ill. *I am a monster. I am a predator. I nearly killed her because I was 'excited'.*

"Luca, what are you doing?" Rose snaps, her voice trembling with an intensity that borders on hatred. "Find a secure room and lock her inside. We are all in danger."

I look up at her, and the air is completely knocked out of my lungs. She is staring at me with pure, unfiltered hatred. I have seen Rose angry, I have seen her protective, but I have never been on the receiving end of that specific glare. The last time I saw her look at someone like that was when she directed her fury at Reya during one of their clashes, or back in Pittsburgh, when she spoke of the vicious vampires we were hunting.

The rejection does not just hurt emotionally. it feels like a physical assault. It is a blunt force trauma to my chest. I can sense her revulsion pulsing through our bond, hitting me like a brutal blow that leaves me breathless.

If I have truly become a soulless monster, shouldn't the bond have broken by now? Why does it still hurt this much?

"Ava, come with me. Let us get you cleaned up before the rest of the team sees you in this state," Luca says. He extends a large, warm hand towards me, his expression neutral but his eyes searching.

"I can do that," Sam says, taking a half-step forward, perhaps thinking it is safer for the Alpha to stay near Rose.

"I think it is best if I handle this," Luca replies smoothly, stopping Sam with a subtle shift in his dominant stance. He doesn't even have to look at him; he just occupies the space in a way that makes it clear he is in charge.

"He does not want to put you in harm's way, Sam," I say. My voice sounds hollow and detached, as if I am speaking from the bottom of a well. "He does not think you possess the physical strength to stop me if I decide to attack you."

Sam blinks, processing the tactical truth of my statement. He looks at his own hands, then back at Luca's massive frame. "Oh!"

"If Rose requires medical assistance, please help her, Sam," Luca instructs. He then grasps a massive hand around my bicep and carefully hauls me to my feet.

His grip is firm, but not aggressive. He is guiding me, steering me away from the wreckage of the room. As we turn to leave, I cannot stop myself from glancing back at Rose over my shoulder. She is huddled against the headboard, clutching her bleeding neck, her eyes locked on me with a mixture of terror and loathing.

I immediately wish I had not looked. The image burns itself into my retinas. the woman I would die for looking at me as if I were something disgusting found on the bottom of a shoe.

Thankfully, the hallway is deserted. Rodriguez must have successfully wrangled the curious team members back into their quarters, keeping the peace through sheer volume and authority. The bathroom is just a few steps away, and Luca steers me inside, clicking the lock behind us with a definitive snap.

He guides me directly to the sink. When I finally lift my head and come face-to-face with my reflection in the mirror, my breath hitches. A strangled sound escapes my throat.

I do not recognise the woman staring back at me.

Of course, the smeared crimson blood around my mouth is the first horrifying detail, painting me like some twisted version of a horror movie villain. But it is the drastic alteration to my hair and eyes that truly captures my attention.

They resemble ice.

Not just a pale colour, but the kind of crystalline, transparent ice floating on deep water during a winter freeze, allowing a vibrant tint of piercing blue to shine straight through the frost. The visual impact is startling. It makes me appear entirely alien, stripped of my humanity. I am horrifyingly mesmerised by my own reflection, staring at the predator in the mirror.

Luca grabs a washcloth, runs it under the hot water tap, and wrings it out. He steps into my personal space, his presence warm and grounding against the coldness emanating from my own skin. He raises the cloth to my face and begins to gently, methodically wipe away the incriminating evidence of my attack.

His touch is tender, a stark contrast to the violence I have just wrought.

"What is happening to my body, Luca?" I ask, my voice

trembling.

"I am not certain... I shouldn't say just yet, as I am not one hundred per cent sure," Luca admits, his dark eyes fixed entirely on the task of cleaning my skin. "I am pulling fragments of childhood memories, so I cannot guarantee I am remembering the lore accurately."

"Please, Luca. Please tell me something that might give me a shred of hope that I am not a monster," I beg. My cold new eyes search his, desperate for some kind of anchor in this storm.

He sighs, a heavy, exhausted sound that seems to carry the weight of centuries. "Okay. When I was a child, not long before the attacks decimated my pack, I was being taught about the various vampire factions. Specifically, the biological differences between the born version and the turned."

"Please do not tell me I am actually becoming a type of vampire," I whisper, my stomach sinking into a cold pit.

"I do not believe so. Well, not in the traditional sense you are thinking of, anyway," Luca says, tossing the stained washcloth into the sink with a wet thud.

"Then what am I? What have I become?" I demand, my panic mounting again, threatening to swallow me whole.

"When I first saw your new physical markers, a very specific memory surfaced. While my father was teaching me about the vampire lineages, he showed me an ancient drawing of a hybrid. Do you remember when Rose was explaining the different classifications of paranormals to you?" he asks. "She stated there were two types of vampires, and I interrupted to correct her. I mentioned there was actually a third classification, but they were supposedly eradicated such a long time ago. That drawing I remembered looked exactly like you do right now."

I close my eyes, digging through my chaotic mind to recall the memory. *Briefings. Lore. Shifters and vamps. It all felt so theoretical then.*

"You were feeding me a hefty amount of intelligence briefing back then. I highly doubt I retained half of what you said," I admit.

"Well, this particular hybrid species was despised. Especially by the vampire courts, because these hybrids actively hunted them," Luca explains. He leans against the counter, crossing his muscular arms over his chest. "Eventually, the warring factions of vampires actually formed a temporary alliance for the sole purpose of hunting down every last hybrid and wiping them from existence."

He pauses, his expression grim. "No one has any historical record of how the very first hybrids were biologically engineered. But if a hybrid reproduced, their offspring were always a hybrid, regardless of the gender of the mortal parent. At least, that is what I recall from the lessons. I am not positive I have all the historical details perfectly aligned."

"Okay. So, did this particular hybrid classification have a name?" I ask, eager for a label to assign to this nightmare. If it has a name, maybe it can be managed. Maybe there is a way to fix it.

Luca hesitates for a brief moment. He turns away from the mirror, forcing me to look directly at him, his dark eyes solemn. "They were called Dhampirs."

Dhampirs.

The word rings in my skull like a death knell, cold and final. So, I am a kind of vampire. Just the specific type that all other vampires universally despise and fear. I suddenly understand exactly why Rose looked at me with such venomous hatred. It isn't just about the bite. it is about what I represent.

Will she ever be able to move past this? Can you love something that was designed to hunt your kind?

"There is one major discrepancy I do not understand, though," Luca adds, furrowing his brow. "I do not recall any lore suggesting that Dhampirs possessed retractable fangs or required blood consumption to survive. This is precisely why I am hesitant to confirm my theory."

"We need to find out the truth. If I cannot even trust my own instincts, how can I possibly remain with this team?" I ask. The devastating reality of my situation finally crushes my chest, making it hard to draw a full breath.

"Do not go making rash, tactical decisions," Luca warns, his voice regaining that Alpha edge.

"I have no other viable option! You saw exactly how Rose was looking at me," I argue, my voice faltering, the strength leaving me. "She looks at me like I'm a plague."

"Yes, I saw it. She will come around eventually," Luca insists gently. He reaches out, placing a hand on my shoulder. "Rose's main problem is her deeply embedded trauma related to vampires. She endured a brutal life on the streets before I found her. There was a vicious den of vampires that made her life a complete nightmare. They taunted her. They hunted her for sport. She was utterly terrified to close her eyes at night, which is exactly why she changed her internal clock to sleep during the day."

He sighs, his thumb rubbing a small circle into my shoulder. "You have triggered a major trauma response. She just needs a moment to process. She isn't seeing you right now. she is seeing every monster that ever hurt her."

He pauses, rubbing the back of his neck. "Maybe there is still a contact out there who can provide us with accurate intelligence."

A sudden spark of hope ignites in my chest, sharp and bright. "Madi!" I blurt out.

"What about the Crossroads Demon?" Luca asks, raising an eyebrow.

"She gave me a very specific, knowing look right before she departed, as if she possessed far more intelligence about my condition than she was revealing," I say, my mind racing with strategic possibilities. "If she cannot provide the answers, perhaps her boss, Papa Legba, can. He is an ancient deity, is he not?"

"I don't think Madi would really know much, as I said, the Dhampirs haven't been around in a very long time, and crossroads demons aren't immortal," Luca agrees thoughtfully. "But if anyone knows, it will be Legba. I believe he was actively ruling during the era when the hybrids roamed the earth." He frowns. "I just have no idea how to initiate contact with a Loa. And frankly, I am not convinced it is a tactically safe manoeuvre. Dealing with deities usually comes with a price that we cannot afford to pay."

"I need to know, Luca. I need to know if my mere presence is an active threat to you and Sam. And especially to Rose," I say, a fresh wave of panic threatening to drown me.

I press a hand to my chest, suddenly realising another terrifying anomaly. My heart is not racing in sync with my panic. Normally, in a state like this, my pulse would be hammering against my ribs, a frantic bird trapped in a cage. But now, it is beating slightly faster than my new normal, but the heavy thuds remain inexplicably spaced out.

It is slow. Too slow. It is almost as if my newly mutated body no longer requires a beating heart to function at full capacity.

Luca watches me intently, noticing my hand on my chest. "Ava, I need you to be completely honest with me. Right now, are you feeling any urge to sink your newly discovered fangs into my carotid artery and drink my blood?"

"What? Absolutely not!" I gasp, appalled by the mere suggestion. "There are zero intrusive thoughts along those lines. I have no biological need, no lingering want, and absolutely no craving for blood. I do not understand what went wrong."

I take a shaky breath. "I was just so overwhelmingly excited to finally be awake. I just wanted to kiss Rose, to hold her, to be intimate with her. I felt incredible. I felt alive and impossibly strong. Apparently, my body operates at a terrifying speed now. We were completely lost in the heat of the moment. Then... then I caught sight of the pulse jumping in the vein of her neck, and my higher brain functions just shut down."

I suddenly fall silent, my cheeks flushing fiercely as I realise exactly who I am revealing my sexual frustrations to. *Great. Just great. First I bite her, then I tell the Alpha about how much I want to get laid.*

"I am sorry. I have definitely overshared," I mutter, looking away.

Luca actually bursts out a sincere, short laugh. It is a surprising sound, warm and genuine. "It is perfectly alright. We shifters do not hold human reservations about sexual intimacy or nudity. It is quite difficult to keep modesty when we are constantly tearing off our clothes and shifting into naked humans around each other all the time."

His smile fades, replaced by a serious, commanding expression. He steps closer, his voice becoming that of the Alpha. "Here is the plan. For the immediate future, you need to give Rose absolute physical space. That requires separate sleeping quarters. You cannot be near her while she is in this state, and you cannot risk another loss of control."

I nod slowly, the logic cutting through my grief.

"Tomorrow, I will take you into the field and run you through intense combat training," he continues. "I am going to push your physical and mental limits to see if you are prone to losing control under stress. I am going to break you down until we find the edge of your discipline. It is highly probable that you simply need to train your mind to maintain control during states of high arousal or combat."

He looks me in the eye. "Born vampires are required to master control just as rigorously as the turned ones. If they did not, the human populace would have discovered their existence centuries ago."

He makes a solid, logical point. I am more than willing to subject myself to whatever gruelling tests he deems necessary. I will crawl through broken glass if it means I can look Rose in the eye again without her flinching. But there is one glaring issue that we are ignoring.

"Well, Reya does not exactly have the luxury of time," I point out, the heavy weight of our mission pressing down on my shoulders. "If the intelligence regarding time moving at an accelerated rate in the Underworld is accurate, it has already been weeks for her. She might have already begun to lose hope, believing we have completely abandoned her to the demons."

"We have not abandoned anyone," Luca says firmly.

"Okay. I will remain on site and be subjected to your training plan," I agree, locking my icy gaze with his dark one. "I will also stay long enough to engage the demon forces and help extract Reya from the Underworld. But if I am still losing control of my predatory instincts after that... I will have to exile myself from this team."

Luca studies my face for a long, weighty moment. The silence in the bathroom is absolute, save for the drip of the faucet. "Ava, do you still feel the bond tethering you to Rose?"

The question makes my chest ache again. *Yes. God, yes.*

"I still feel it. I can feel her raw, agonising fear of me pulsing through it this very second," I admit, my voice breaking on the final word. It is a physical cord, vibrating with her pain, pulling at me even while she pushes me away.

"Good," Luca says, his voice dropping to a harsh, gravelly whisper. "Then do not make the catastrophic mistake that I made. I stopped believing in the sacred power of the bond, and I lost everything that mattered."

He looks past me, his eyes staring at something far away and heartbreaking. "Do not replicate my failures. I still believe, with every fibre of my being, that bond is a divine gift from our creators. It does not sever easily, Ava."

I watch as the devastating ghost of his past tragedies briefly darkens his eyes, a stark reminder of just how much this fierce Alpha has lost. And it terrifies me, because I know exactly how much I stand to lose if I cannot tame the monster suddenly awakened inside me.

CHAPTER 17

WHITE HAIR AND BAD VIBES

Thump.

I wake up to the sound of my own heartbeat.

A long, terrifying expanse of absolute silence spreads across the cold room. It is not a peaceful silence. it is a suffocating void, a heavy shroud that presses against my chest and makes me wonder if the next beat will ever come. I lie there for what feels like an eternity, suspended in a state of breathless anticipation, waiting for the clockwork of my biology to resume its function.

Thump.

It is a sluggish rhythm, lazy and distant. By every medical standard I was taught in the academy, this heart rate should belong to a corpse. It is too slow, too rhythmic, lacking the frantic energy of a living, breathing human being. Yet, as I force my eyelids open and stare up at the unfamiliar, cracked ceiling of our new safe house, I feel more vibrantly alive than I ever have in my entire existence.

Every single nerve ending in my body is humming. It is an electric current, undeniable and searing, vibrating beneath the surface of my skin like a live wire stripped of its insulation. I can feel the air moving across my skin, each tiny current of oxygen feeling like a physical touch. I can hear the distant settle of the house, the groan of old timber, the faint scuttle of something small in the walls three rooms away.

The room is silent. Too silent. I am lying on a standard-issue tactical cot, the kind designed for utility rather than comfort. The mattress is brutally stiff, biting into my shoulder blades and hips, but that physical discomfort is nothing compared to the agonising void beside me.

The real pain stems from the chilling absence of Rose.

For the first time since we sealed our Prime Mate bond, her preternatural warmth is not securely wrapped around me. Usually, I wake up plastered to her, my face tucked into the crook of her neck, enveloped in the scent of storms and wildflowers and something primal, something that smells like home. Now, there is only cold linen and empty space. The bed is freezing because my body temperature is much lower now. The air in the room feels heavy, thick with the physical weight of her rejection.

I push the scratchy wool blanket off my legs and swing my feet onto the hardwood floor. The wood is ice-cold against my soles, but I don't shiver. In fact, I barely feel the cold as a negative sensation.

My body does not ache. This is the first thing that truly registers. Only a few days ago, my lumbar spine had been a wreckage of catastrophic fractures, each movement bringing blinding, white-hot agony that threatened to black out my vision. Now, there is nothing. Not a flicker of pain. Not a single lingering throb of inflammation.

I don't just feel healed. I feel like a tightly coiled spring made of weaponised titanium wire.

I stand up, and the sheer, effortless grace of the movement takes me completely by surprise. There is no stiffness in my joints, no hesitation in my muscles. I rise in one fluid motion, my balance perfect, my centre of gravity shifted into something more predatory. All I feel is a low, thrumming hum of raw, kinetic power vibrating just beneath my skin, an itch that demands to be scratched, a hunger for movement that feels almost violent.

I walk over to the small mirror fixed to the wall above a cheap plastic sink. The lighting is dim, the fluorescent bulb overhead flickering with a rhythmic buzz that sounds like a scream to my enhanced hearing. I stop.

The reflection staring back at me belongs to a complete stranger.

My usually brown hair has turned to a stark, icy white, shot through with cold blue tints that shimmer even in the gloom. It is the colour of a frozen lake under a winter moon. But it is the eyes that truly terrify me. They match the hair, radiating a piercing, luminous blue that completely washes out my pupils. I look like a ghost haunting my own life, a spectral entity carved from ice and moonlight.

I lean in closer. My breath, unlike before my change, no longer fogs the glass. I run my thumb over my gums, half-expecting to feel the sharp, lethal points of elongated canines pressing into my skin. I press hard, searching for the edge of something dangerous. Thankfully, my teeth feel normal for now. The fangs are safely hidden in my gums, retracted and dormant.

For now.

'*You are a monster,*' a dark, cynical voice whispers in the back of my mind. It sounds like me, but colder. Crueller. '*You are exactly the kind of creature you are here to hunt.*'

The thought sends a jolt of nausea through me. I splash freezing water onto my face, the droplets hitting my skin like tiny explosions. I scrub at my cheeks, trying to wash away the image in the mirror, forcing the terrifying thoughts into a dark corner of my mind. I cannot afford this. I do not have the luxury of an identity crisis when the world is tilting on its axis.

Reya is currently trapped in the Underworld, facing a fate far worse than death. The Lorcan pack of wolf shifters is building a massive army designed to slaughter everything in their path. The demons in Jackson are stirring, waiting for the signal to tear through the veil.

I cannot be broken. I cannot fall apart because my DNA decided to mutate into something from a nightmare.

I grab a clean black T-shirt and my tactical cargo trousers from my go-bag, the one Luca graciously grabbed for me during the move. I dress quickly, my movements blurred by a speed I don't yet understand. As I strap on my leather harness, I pause, taking an extra moment to ensure the physical changes haven't interfered with the cloaking spell Maya placed on it.

I run my hand over the straps. They remain visible to my eyes, but the weight is comforting, a solid anchor against my back that reminds me who I am. a soldier. A captain. A weapon.

The moment I leave the bedroom and step into the narrow hallway, sensory overload hits me like a physical punch to the gut. I gasp, clutching the wall for support as the world suddenly expands in volume and detail.

My hearing has sharpened to an alarming, almost pathological level. It is no longer about listening. it is about receiving every vibration in the environment. Two doors down, I can hear the muffled, rhythmic breathing of Sam, the slight whistle in his nostrils. Outside, I can hear the heavy, booted footsteps of our backup team patrolling the gravel perimeter, the grit grinding under their soles sounding like thunder.

More unsettling is the hum. I can sense the faint, high-pitched vibration of electricity flowing through the copper wiring in the walls, a constant, buzzing river of energy that makes the hair on my arms stand up. It is too much. It is an onslaught of data that threatens to drown me.

I force myself to breathe, counting to four, focusing on a single point of intent. the kitchen. I follow the rich, bitter aroma of brewing coffee. The scent is intoxicating, cutting through the building's stale air, but it takes a back seat to the pulsing smells of the people in the room. Humans and shifters have scents, unique chemical signatures that I can now categorise with terrifying precision.

I step through the doorway and immediately spot her.

Rose is standing near the counter, her tall, athletic frame dressed in light clothing that clings to her curves. Her striking blonde hair is tied up in a severe, practical knot, leaving the elegant line of her neck exposed. For a split second, I feel a surge of longing so intense it feels like a physical ache in my chest. I want to cross the room, wrap my arms around her, and bury my face in that scent until the world disappears.

The moment I cross the threshold, Rose becomes completely rigid.

Her spine straightens instantly, the tension radiating off her in visible waves. She does not look at me. She refuses to even acknowledge my presence with a glance. Her hand trembles slightly as she hurriedly slams her ceramic mug onto the counter, spilling hot coffee over the rim and across the laminate. The liquid splashes, but she doesn't seem to notice. She sharply turns on her heel, intending to leave before I can speak.

"Rose," I say softly.

The name is barely a whisper, a desperate plea catching in my throat. It sounds fragile, stripped of all my usual military authority.

"Keep your distance from me," Rose snaps.

Her voice oozes with a venomous, icy hostility that chills the blood in my veins. There is no playfulness here, no seductive edge, no warmth. It is the voice of someone looking at something repulsive. "I am not in the mood to be someone's breakfast."

The words strike me directly in the chest, sharper and infinitely more devastating than any physical blade I have ever faced in combat. I flinch, my shoulders hunching instinctively. I cannot hide the profound hurt flashing across my face, the raw vulnerability of a woman who has just been told she is no longer loved by her mate.

Through the invisible tether of our bond, I feel it. It hits me like a wave of freezing water. a chaotic surge of fear, disgust, and deep-seated trauma radiating from her soul. She does not just hate what I have become.

She is terrified of me.

Without another word, she marches out of the kitchen, giving me the widest possible berth, as if my mere presence could contaminate her. The void she leaves behind is deafening.

You nearly tore her throat out last night, the voice in my head sneers. *You don't get to be offended.*

"Well, that was certainly frosty," notes Sam from his spot at the small dining table.

I blink, pulling myself out of the emotional spiral. Sam is dressed in his usual smart attire, his fingers moving with mechanical precision across the keyboard of his agency laptop. He looks up at me, and for a second, I see a flicker of hesitation in his eyes, a brief moment of uncertainty as he takes in my appearance.

"Good morning, Ava," he adds, his voice returning to its professional cadence. "Or should I say, good morning to whatever entity has currently possessed our assassin and team leader?"

"I am still me," I reply flatly.

My voice sounds different to my own ears. it is lower, with a resonance that feels like it could vibrate through steel. I move to the coffee pot to pour myself a cup. I don't actually want the coffee, but I need something to do with my hands so they don't start shaking.

"I'm just... upgraded," I add, glancing at my reflection in the polished surface of the pot. "And slightly paler."

"Upgraded is a massive understatement," Doctor Stevens interrupts.

He practically vibrates with clinical excitement as he emerges from the adjacent living room. He is clutching a thick medical file to his chest, his eyes wide and obsessive behind his wire-rimmed glasses. To him, I am not a person in crisis. I am the most interesting specimen he has ever encountered.

"Agent Bekke, your biological chart is actively defying every established law of human physiology," Stevens rambles, stepping closer with an eager intensity. "I need to run a complete diagnostic workup immediately. We are talking about unprecedented cellular mutation!"

I take a slow sip of the black coffee. It tastes like hot dirt. bitter, ash-like, and completely unsatisfying. There is a strange, hollow craving gnawing at the pit of my stomach, a void that caffeine cannot fill.

"I am not a lab rat," I say, my voice turning cold. "We have a mission to plan."

"Ava, please," Doctor Stevens insists, stepping fully into my personal space, his scent a mix of rubbing alcohol and old paper. "The localised hyper-accelerated mitosis we observed yesterday was just the beginning of this anomaly. The necrotic tissue around your original bite radius has spontaneously synthesised entirely new cellular structures. Your hepatic system completely metabolised the synthetic analgesics in record time. I must monitor your cytokine levels to ensure your immune system is not currently masking a fatal cytokine storm."

I stare at him blankly, my icy blue eyes locked on his. The intensity of my gaze seems to make him blink, a flicker of instinctive fear crossing his face as he realises he is standing too close to a predator.

"Doc, I feel perfectly fine," I state. "My spine is healed. The extensive soft tissue damage is erased. I am not letting you poke me with any more needles."

"But... but... I need to understand what is happening to you!" Doctor Stevens argues, pointing a frantic, trembling finger at my chest. "Your resting heart rate has plummeted to roughly eight beats per minute! A normal human would be in stage four hypovolemic shock, completely comatose, or suffering massive neurological deficits due to cerebral hypoxia. Yet, you are standing here arguing with me coherently!"

"The answer is no," I state.

My voice drops into the cold, detached cadence of 'The Destroyer'. It is the voice I use when I am clearing a room, when there is no room for negotiation or empathy. "No more blood draws. No more tests. You are here to patch up bullet holes and treat combat trauma, not to write a groundbreaking medical journal on my freakish changing DNA."

Doctor Stevens opens his mouth to protest, but the air in the room suddenly changes. A massive, commanding presence fills the kitchen doorway.

Luca steps into the room, his broad shoulders nearly touching the doorframe. He doesn't speak at first; he simply watches me. His dark eyes lock onto mine, analysing the change in my hair, the glow of my eyes, the way I am standing. He is calculating, weighing me with the composed authority of a born Alpha.

"Leave her be, Doctor," Luca commands.

His voice is a deep rumble that seems to vibrate in the very floorboards. It is a command, not a suggestion, and it leaves absolutely no room for further argument. "Ava is clearly fully operational. We have more pressing tactical concerns today than her blood work."

Doctor Stevens snaps his mouth shut, visibly frustrated, but he knows better than to challenge Luca when the Alpha has set a boundary. He wisely retreats to the living room, muttering something about 'lost opportunities for science'.

"How are you actually feeling, Ava?" Luca asks, crossing his thick arms over his powerful chest.

The movement makes his biceps strain against the fabric of his shirt. He is looking at me not with fear, but with a professional curiosity and a hint of caution.

"I feel like I could outrun a bullet," I admit, setting my coffee mug down on the counter with a soft clink. The hollow craving in my stomach spikes as I look at him. I can see the pulse in his neck, the steady rhythm of an Alpha's heart. "I need to burn off this excess energy. I need to know exactly what my physical limits are now before we engage the demons."

Luca nods slowly, a serious, predatory glint igniting in his dark eyes. He recognises the restlessness. He knows what it is like to have power that feels too big for your skin.

"I agree completely," Luca says. "We cannot risk taking you into a hostile combat zone if you are a liability, or worse, a danger to the team. Follow me to the backyard. We are going to spar. I want you to come at me with everything you have."

"Are you absolutely sure about this?" Sam asks, looking up from his laptop. His expression is one of genuine concern. "If she is truly becoming a Dhampir as you explained to us last night, she might even outpace your shifter reflexes, Luca."

"We are about to find out," Luca says, turning towards the back door with a confident smirk.

The secure yard of the abandoned commercial property is vast, enclosed by towering brick walls that offer excellent tactical cover and absolute privacy. The ground is a harsh mixture of cracked, uneven concrete and tough, overgrown weeds that push through the fissures like desperate fingers. It is a grey, bleak space. the perfect, unforgiving arena for a stress test.

I step onto the concrete, my combat boots making no sound against the pavement. I roll my shoulders, feeling the smooth, frictionless motion of my joints. The air outside smells incredibly complex to my newly enhanced senses. I can smell the dry dust of the brickwork, the metallic tang of a rusted chain-link fence twenty yards away, and the rich, musky aroma of Luca's panther energy bleeding into the atmosphere. It is an intoxicating scent, thick with power and dominance.

I look up and notice a shadow shift in the second-story window.

Rose is standing there, partially hidden behind a dirty, frayed curtain, watching us with her arms tightly crossed over her chest. She is a silent sentinel of judgment. The sight of her isolated figure makes my heart ache, a dull, throbbing pain that completely eclipses any physical injury I have ever sustained in the field.

I will prove to you that I am still in control, Rose. I will prove I am not a mindless monster.

"Alright, Ava," Luca calls out.

He walks to the very centre of the yard, rolling his thick neck until the vertebrae pop loudly. The sound is like a series of small gunshots in the quiet air. "No weapons. Hand-to-hand combat only. I am not going to hold back, and I expect you to do the exact same."

"You asked for it, Alpha," I reply.

I drop into a relaxed, perfectly balanced fighting stance. My weight is distributed evenly, and my centre of gravity is low. I feel an odd sensation in my legs, a tension that feels like compressed air waiting to be released.

I do not wait for him to start.

I push off my planting foot, aiming to close the twenty-foot gap with a standard tactical sprint. But what happens next entirely destroys my fundamental understanding of physics.

I do not run. I simply arrive.

The world blurs into a smeared streak of grey concrete and bright blue sky. The acceleration is so violent it causes a sharp crack of displaced air, a sonic pop that echoes off the brick walls. I cross the distance in a fraction of a second. I am standing directly in front of Luca before his brain has even processed that I have moved.

His dark eyes widen in pure, unadulterated shock. He raises his enormous forearms to block, but to my altered perception, he is moving through thick molasses. The world has slowed down. I can observe the intricate flex of his biceps, the microscopic shift of his weight on the concrete, and the slow widening of his pupils.

I have all the time in the world to decide the trajectory of my strike.

I pivot on my heel and launch a sweeping roundhouse kick aimed directly at his exposed ribs. I feel the air whistle around my leg, the movement so fast it creates its own wind.

My shin hits his solid torso with a sickening, heavy thud.

The sheer kinetic force of the impact lifts the two-hundred-and-forty-pound Alpha clean off his feet. Luca sails through the air for ten feet, his body horizontal, before crashing into the overgrown weeds at the edge of the yard. He rolls fluidly to absorb the momentum and springs back to his feet in a defensive crouch, though he is breathing heavily.

He lets out a low, coughing grunt, rubbing his side where my shin connected. A fierce, competitive grin spreads across his face. "Okay, I didn't realise you had gained that much speed," Luca breathes. "That is definitely an upgrade. You hit like a speeding truck."

"I barely even put any force behind that strike," I admit, staring down at my hands in complete bewilderment.

The power is terrifying. It feels unnatural, as if I am cheating at the game of existence.

For the next two hours, the yard becomes a brutal testing ground. We clash repeatedly, the sounds of impact echoing through the abandoned complex. Luca relies on his innate, born-shifter strength, throwing devastating combinations of jabs and hooks that would have shattered my ribs in my previous life. He fights with the calculated precision of a seasoned warlord, attempting to corner me, to use his mass to overwhelm me.

Yet, I dance around him.

It is almost insulting how easily I can evade most of his assaults. I duck beneath a heavy right cross, feeling the wind of his fist ruffle my icy white hair. I slip to his blind side, launching a rapid sequence of strikes into his abdomen. Left, right, left. My fists connect with the blistering speed of a pneumatic drill, each hit landing with an explosive force that makes Luca grunt in surprise.

By the fourth hour, the physical toll on Luca begins to show. His dark T-shirt is completely soaked with sweat, clinging tightly to his muscular frame and highlighting every ripple of muscle. His breathing is heavy, his chest heaving as he desperately tries to draw enough oxygen into his lungs.

In stark contrast, I am hardly winded.

My pale skin is completely dry. The relentless heat of the afternoon does not bother me in the slightest. if anything, I feel a strange coolness settling over me. My heart rate remains a slow, steady thump, entirely unbothered by the intense cardiovascular output. I feel as if I could do this for days without stopping.

"Luca, you are too slow," I taunt.

The words slip out before I can stop them. My blood is singing with the sheer, intoxicating thrill of the combat. The power feels like a drug, an addictive rush that makes me feel invincible.

Luca spins around, roaring with pure frustration. He drops to one knee, breathing heavily, his eyes flashing with something primal. "You are right," he growls, his voice dropping an octave and resonating with a guttural, inhuman tone. "My human form cannot keep up with this mutation. Ava, if you want a real test, you are going to get one."

His eyes flash a brilliant, glowing red. The air around him shimmers with raw heat. He drops fully onto all fours.

Then comes the sound.

The horrific symphony of bones breaking and reforming fills the yard with my enhanced hearing. It is a wet, crunching noise that makes my stomach turn. His clothing shreds into useless tatters as thick, midnight-black fur erupts from his expanding skin. Within seconds, a massive, lethal panther stands where the man used to be.

The beast unleashes a deafening roar that rattles the windows of the buildings and sends birds screaming from the rooftops.

The panther does not hesitate. It charges at me with terrifying speed, a literal blur of shadow and deadly intent. It launches its massive body through the air, its heavy paws outstretched, razor-sharp claws glinting in the sunlight.

With my improved vision, the speed difference is still astonishing, though less so than before. I dive to the side, narrowly avoiding his crushing weight as he slams into the concrete where I had been standing a millisecond prior. The panther lands silently and pivots with extraordinary agility, swiping a massive paw directly at my torso.

I raise my forearms to block.

The impact is huge. it feels like being hit by a wrecking ball. The force sends me skidding across the concrete, the soles of my boots squeaking from the friction as I fight to keep my footing.

Before I can fully regain my balance, he is on me again. He weaves in a zig-zag pattern, his movements fluid and unpredictable. He swipes upwards with a sudden, vicious motion. Three razor-sharp claws cut through the fabric of my cargo pants, piercing deep into the flesh of my outer thigh.

A sharp, brilliant spark of pain erupts in my leg.

It is the very first time I have felt real pain since waking up. And it changes everything.

The heat in my veins sharpens instantly, transforming from a hum to a roar. The exhilarating rush of combat transforms into something darker, something feral and predatory. It is no longer about training or testing limits.

It is hunger.

I look down at the blood oozing from the lacerations on my thigh. The scent hits my nostrils. metallic, salty, rich. But it is quickly drowned out by the musk of the massive predator circling me.

I parry his next lunge, my forearm slamming fiercely against his thick front leg. As our skin and fur make contact, my hyper-sensitive hearing captures a specific sound beneath the roaring of the panther.

Thump. Thump. Thump.

It is the heavy, frantic pulse of Luca's heart pumping rich, boiling hot blood around his body.

My vision tunnels. The edges of the yard fade into a hazy, blurry grey. All I can see is that rhythmic, pulsing heartbeat just beneath the thick black fur of his muscular neck. It is the only thing in the world that matters.

A blinding, agonising pressure bursts behind my gums. It feels as if hot needles are being thrust violently into my jawbone, pushing outward. I gasp, and the sound that escapes me is not a human breath. it is a wet, guttural hiss.

No. Stop it. Focus! I scream at myself in the chaotic void of my mind.

But the Dhampir instinct does not concern itself with logic. It does not care about ranks, friendship, or loyalty. It only cares about becoming stronger.

The panther lunges at my throat, his jaws snapping open to reveal deadly canines. I do not dodge. I do not retreat. I step straight into the strike, gripping his huge, furry neck with both of my hands.

The impact sends a shockwave up my arms, but I do not move an inch. My grip tightens around his thick throat like a steel vice, crushing muscle and fur until a choking, wheezing sound escapes his jaws.

The panther's red eyes widen in sudden, terrifying realisation. He thrashes wildly, his heavy claws raking frantically against my arms, carving deep, bloody trenches into my skin.

I do not feel the pain. I do not care about the blood. All I care about is becoming stronger.

I yank his trapped body downward and sweep his back legs out from under him with a brutal kick. Luca crashes hard onto his back, the impact shaking the ground beneath us. Before he can even try to roll away, I am on top of him.

I straddle his broad, furry chest, using my knees to pin his front limbs to the ground with an unnatural, crushing weight. He struggles fiercely, his Alpha panther roaring for supremacy, but he cannot dislodge me. I am an immovable object.

I am the apex predator now.

I can no longer hear his growls. The only sound in my universe is the frantic, terrified drumming of his massive heart. My mouth falls open. The agonising pressure in my gums finally crests, breaking through the skin. I physically feel the sharp, elongated fangs slide down.

His scent is a maddening, intoxicating perfume. It smells of wild earth and absolute salvation. My throat burns with a dryness so severe it feels like my oesophagus is cracking open.

I lean down, my face just inches above his exposed, furry throat. I can see the pulse leaping under the skin. I open my mouth wider, my fangs fully extended, ready to sink my teeth into his jugular and tear it apart.

"AVA! STOP!"

The scream is high-pitched, laced with pure, unadulterated horror.

It is Rose.

Her voice cuts through the thick, bloody haze like a bright spotlight piercing pitch darkness. The sound of her terror acts as a psychological shock collar, snapping the leash of my insanity.

My higher brain functions slam back online with violent, nauseating force. The grey tunnel vision shatters instantly. I look down at the massive black panther pinned beneath my knees.

The beast has stopped struggling. His red eyes are fixed on my mouth in stoic, rigid fear. In the reflection of his glowing pupils, I can see myself. the icy white hair, the luminous blue eyes, and the sharp, elongated points of my own fangs dripping with saliva.

Oh my god. What am I doing?

Pure, suffocating horror crashes over me like a tidal wave of ice water. A wet, guttural sound of utter self-loathing rips from my throat. I violently throw myself away from him, scrambling off his chest as if I have been burned by holy fire.

I crawl across the concrete on my hands and knees, desperately trying to put as much distance as possible between us. I reach the rusted chain-link fence at the far edge of the yard, my spine smashing hard against the metal wiring.

I pull my knees to my chest, burying my face in my trembling hands. I am shaking uncontrollably, a violent tremor that starts in my core and radiates outward. I run my tongue over my teeth, tasting the metallic tang of my own saliva, and feel the razor-sharp tips of the fangs slowly, painfully retracting back into my aching gums.

"I am sorry," I gasp, my voice a broken, pathetic rasp. "I am so sorry, Luca. I lost control. I couldn't stop it."

Across the yard, the massive panther flickers. The bones crack and realign, the black fur dissolving into bare skin in a series of sickening pops. Luca slowly sits up in his human form, completely naked and breathing heavily. He rubs his throat where my lips had hovered seconds before.

His expression remains remarkably calm. analytical.

"Ava, it is okay," Luca says, his voice a steady, grounding rumble. "You stopped yourself. That is the most important takeaway from this drill. You felt the predator take over completely, and you pulled it back. That proves you still possess the mental discipline to control the monster inside."

I lean my head against the cold metal fence. I think I know now exactly what had broken my control. getting injured brought out the beast within. Pain is the trigger. Blood is the catalyst.

I lift my heavy head, my icy blue eyes darting immediately towards the second-story window.

Rose is no longer hiding behind the curtain. She is gazing down at me, her beautiful face pale and contorted into a look of deep, devastating revulsion. She does not see her mate. She does not see the woman she loves. She regards me as if I am the most dangerous, disgusting creature walking the earth.

She remains silent for a long heartbeat, then, without saying a word, steps back into the shadows and forcefully slams the window shut.

The sharp sound is just another rejection that ripples through the bond, a freezing, suffocating wave of terror and disgust that leaves me gasping for air.

She hates me. She truly hates me.

"Fascinating. Absolutely fascinating," Doctor Stevens breathes, breaking the heavy silence.

I glance over at the porch. Sam looks utterly pale, his hand resting as if instinctively on the grip of his sidearm. Of course, I can no longer see the gun now he is wearing the ring. I just know the stance, as if he is ready to put me down if I snap again. But Doctor Stevens is practically leaning over the wooden railing, his eyes gleaming with a chilling clinical obsession.

"Agent Bekke, the biomechanical velocity you just exhibited against a fully shifted predator is scientifically impossible!" the doctor rambles, frantically scribbling notes in his file. "The force-to-weight ratio alone... and the sudden appearance of elongated canine teeth! I must insist on a full neurological scan and a deep tissue biopsy while your adrenaline levels are still elevated!"

"Doc, shut the hell up before I throw you over that railing," Sam snaps, stepping between the doctor and the stairs.

I push myself up from the concrete, completely ignoring the doctor's frantic scientific babbling. My entire body feels hollow, utterly drained of the euphoric energy, leaving nothing but cold, bitter ashes in my soul.

"I need to be alone," I say to Luca, absolutely refusing to meet his eyes.

"Ava, we need to discuss tactical deployment based on these new parameters," Luca starts, his voice trying to pull me back into a professional headspace.

"I said, I need to be alone!" I roar.

Luca pauses immediately, recognising the dangerous, unstable edge in my tone. He gives a slow, heavy nod of understanding. "Take an hour. Clean yourself up. Then we meet in the war room. We have a rescue mission to plan."

I turn away from the yard, from the terrified stares of my colleagues, and from the agonising judgment emanating from the second floor. I walk towards the darkest recesses of the abandoned warehouse, searching for the quietest, most secluded corner I can find to hide.

I am faster than any shifter. I am stronger than any human. I am a perfectly engineered killing machine.

And gaining this power has cost me the one thing in this world I truly cared about.

CHAPTER 18

HOW TO TURN YOUR SOULMATE INTO A STRANGER IN TEN SECONDS

The air around this warehouse at the back of our safe house is thick with the smell of industrial decay and old grease, but it doesn't matter. None of it matters because the metallic, sickly-sweet scent of rusted iron and raw copper has already hijacked my nervous system. It hits me long before my eyes even register the deep red liquid pooling on the cracked concrete.

We have spent the last seventy-two hours in this godforsaken yard, trapped in a cycle of torture and discipline. Luca calls it a 'method.' I call it an invitation to lose my mind.

My heart stutters. It doesn't beat; it misfires against my ribs in a frantic, double-beat rhythm that feels like a bird trapped in a cage. A violent, bone-rattling shudder rips through my entire frame, tearing away the fragile, paper-thin veneer of control I've spent years perfecting as a soldier. Suddenly, the world expands. My senses don't just sharpen; they explode into a terrifying, overwhelming intensity that makes me want to scream.

In the cavernous silence of the yard, I can hear it. the frantic, rapid-fire thumping of a rat's heart as it scurries behind rotting drywall fifty feet away. I can hear the microscopic scratch of its tiny claws scraping against wood like fingernails on bone. I look up and see the dust particles dancing in the shafts of bleak, grey light that pierce the broken skylights on the warehouse. Each one is a glittering mote, so vivid and clear that I feel I could reach out and pluck them from the air if my focus weren't currently being shattered by the scent of blood.

Focus, Ava. Just breathe. Don't let the beast win.

But the internal plea is drowned out by a deafening roar of white noise. The universe shrinks until there is only one thing that counts. the blood.

Luca stands twenty paces away in the dead centre of the dilapidated yard. He looks like a statue carved from granite, his massive hand gripping a standard, medical-grade IV bag. With a slow, deliberate motion, he slices the heavy polyurethane plastic open with a serrated tactical combat knife.

The crimson fluid drips. Drop by agonising drop.

Time stretches, snapping into a torturous slow motion. I watch a single sphere of blood detach from the plastic. It hangs there for a heartbeat, a perfect ruby globe, before hurtling toward the grey, stained floor. When it hits, there is a sickening, melodic splash. like a stone dropped into stagnant water. Crimson ripples spread across the concrete, pulsing in time with my own erratic heartbeat.

He is trying to break me.

The thought flashes through my mind, sharp and cynical. My nails dig ruthlessly into my palms, carving crescents into my skin until I feel the warmth of my own blood welling up to mix with the sweat on my hands. I use the pain as an anchor, a desperate attempt to stay tethered to my humanity while something ancient and hungry claws at the inside of my mind. He wants to see if I can control the monster. He wants to know if I am going to turn into the very feral abomination we spend our time hunting.

"Focus, Ava," Luca orders.

He doesn't just speak; he projects. His voice is a low, rumbling growl of pure Alpha authority that vibrates through the soles of my boots, travels up my spine, and settles in the hollow of my skull. He maintains a calculated, highly tactical distance, his dark eyes tracking me with the precision of a predator assessing a newly caged beast.

"You need to master the hunger," he continues, his tone unwavering. "If you lose your mind every time an artery gets clipped in the field, you are a liability. To yourself. To the team. To the entire mission."

A low, guttural hiss rips its way up my throat. It doesn't sound human. It sounds like something from a nightmare, a demon clawing its way out of a freshly dug grave, raw and wet with the promise of violence. Every mutated instinct screaming inside my altered DNA demands action. My muscles coil, my weight shifting instinctively to the balls of my feet. I want to lunge across those twenty paces, tackle a two-hundred-pound Alpha shifter to the ground, and devour every single drop of that spilt life force.

The burn in my throat is pure, unadulterated agony. It feels as if I have swallowed a cocktail of crushed glass and battery acid, each shard scraping against the raw lining of my oesophagus.

I don't understand this. Why now? I have zero thoughts about blood until it's right in front of me. Get a grip, girl. You are a trained assassin, not a rabid dog.

I squeeze my eyes shut, blocking out the crimson temptation. I force my erratic, shallow breathing into the rhythmic, four-count tactical pattern the military drilled into my skull years ago.

Inhale for four. Hold for four. Exhale for four.

The count is a lifeline, a metronome dragging me back from the edge of the abyss.

You are Ava Bekke. You are the Destroyer. You are not a feral beast.

"Open your eyes," Luca commands. His tone leaves no room for debate.

I snap them open. My vision has shifted. everything is sharper, colder. I can feel my new, terrifyingly icy eyes burning like twin suns. There is a sickening, physical shift in my jaw; an unnatural elongation of my canine teeth pressing brutally against my bottom lip. The pressure is constant and distracting, making the simple act of swallowing feel like chewing on shards of glass.

Luca tips the plastic bag further. A fresh cascade of blood spills, splattering heavily against the concrete in a macabre painting. thick, wet arcs that catch the grim light and refuse to be absorbed.

My vision swims, swallowed entirely by a dark, reddish hue. I drop to my hands and knees, the grit of the concrete biting into my palms. My muscles lock and coil like high-tension steel springs, vibrating with pent-up violence. The thick, heavy air between us practically hums with electricity. If I move, I will cover those twenty paces in less than a second.

I am faster than him now. We both know it.

That single, terrifying thought brings a twisted, cynical spike of amusement to my fevered brain. a humourless, brittle thing that shatters almost as fast as it forms. *Poor Luca. He thinks he's the apex predator in this yard.*

"Fight it," Luca says. His dark, unwavering eyes follow my every microscopic twitch. "Push the predator down."

I dig my fingers brutally into my own thighs, bruising the muscle to ground my fracturing mind. The physical sensation acts as a lifeline, cutting through the hazy, intoxicating red fog of bloodlust. My chest heaves with violent, jagged breaths. Cold sweat beads on my forehead, rolling down the side of my neck in a mocking caress, tracing paths through the grime and soot.

I force my jaw to unhinge, pulling my lips back to bare my new, deadly teeth in a defiant snarl. I am shaking, every fibre of my being screaming for the kill, but I refuse to move forward. I stay rooted to the concrete, fighting a war within myself that feels more dangerous than any battlefield I've ever known.

A loud, echoing thump reverberates through the vast space. The heavy wooden door at the edge of the yard slams shut.

Suddenly, the scent changes. The smell of fresh rain, damp earth, and intoxicating vanilla fills the air, slicing through the overwhelming coppery stench of blood like a blade. My violently thrashing mind hits the brakes instantly. The monster inside me doesn't scream this time. it purrs.

It is a familiar, beloved scent, one that is woven into my very bones. a fragrance of shared silence, stolen touches, and whispered promises in the dark. For a split second, the world feels right again. But the sweet relief is painfully, brutally brief. The vanilla is tainted. It is soured by a sharp, acrid spike of pure distress and visceral revulsion that slams through our bond like a physical blow.

Rose cautiously steps toward us.

Her stunning, vibrant green eyes lock onto my trembling, crouched form, and a massive flinch ripples through her entire body. She sees the elongated fangs. She sees the animalistic way I am poised on the concrete, ready to strike, and pure, unfiltered horror washes over her beautiful features.

The prime mate bond between us used to be a source of warmth. a fierce, unconditional love that made me feel seen for the first time in my life. Right now, it feels like a frayed, sparking live wire whipping against my bare heart. Each pulse of her fear and disgust is a searing brand.

I know why she's reacting this way. Her trauma surrounding vampires runs far too deep. Luca told me how they tortured her, how they hunted her for sport in a game of cat and mouse that left scars on her soul. And now, looking at me, she sees the exact face of her worst nightmares. a reflection she cannot unsee, a terror made flesh.

She does not kneel to comfort me. She does not offer a hand or a soothing word. Instead, she crosses her arms tightly over her chest and steps back, creating as much physical distance as the walled yard allows.

God, that hurts.

A fresh wave of sheer agony twists in my chest, and it has absolutely nothing to do with the bloodlust. It is the hollow ache of being known and rejected, the slow poison of watching the person who is your soul's mirror flinch from your reflection.

She hates me. My own prime mate looks at me like I am a walking, breathing abomination.

I want to reach for her. I want to scream that I am still the same Ava, that the monster is just a shell and the woman inside is still hers. But the words turn to ash in my throat, choked by the weight of her gaze and the sudden, crushing terror in my own chest.

I clamp my jaw shut. I swallow the beast, forcing the fangs to recede, and slowly, painfully rise to my feet. I wipe the damp sweat from my brow with the back of my hand, absolutely refusing to let her see how deeply her revulsion wounds me. I will not give her the satisfaction of seeing me break.

"Patient is showing signs she is regaining cognitive control," a nasally, deeply irritating voice announces.

The sound drifts down from the rusted observation catwalk bolted to the side of the warehouse. When we decided to move our training away from the main house to avoid endangering others, the doctor still insisted on monitoring my vital metrics. He found the elevated catwalk that runs around the perimeter, placing himself safely out of my striking range.

It is a very smart move on his part. Considering what happened on the first day. And the second. And then again on the third.

I am going to throw him off that catwalk, I think. A dry, sarcastic laugh bubbles up in my chest. *I will snap his stupid medical clipboard over his head and feed him his own diagnostic tablet, piece by piece, if he keeps talking.*

"Doc, shut up! Stay out of this before she decides to test her new supernatural speed on your fragile little neck," Sam calls out.

Our resident tech genius and top sniper steps into view beside the doctor on the rusted metal grating. Sam looks utterly exhausted. Deep, bruised purple bags hang heavily under his eyes, a grim reminder of the sleepless, nightmare-fuelled nights we've all endured. Yet, despite his fatigue, his sharp, calculating gaze remains fully alert, scanning the yard with sniper's precision.

"Come on, Ava," Sam adds softly. "Stay in control. You are getting better."

Getting better. Right. If wanting to drain a local blood bank dry is 'getting better,' I am doing absolutely fantastic.

Luca casually tosses the empty plastic IV bag into a nearby yellow hazardous waste bin. The wet, heavy slap of the plastic hitting the bottom makes my teeth ache all over again, stirring a sudden, violent urge to bite down on something living and pulsing. anything to silence the scream in my veins. He grabs a coarse cotton towel to wipe his blood-stained hands, his expression instantly hardening into the stoic, ruthless Alpha we all silently rely on.

He doesn't offer me a single ounce of pity. I respect him deeply for that. Pity is for the weak, and neither of us is weak.

"Sam, what do we have?" Luca asks. His voice is a low, commanding rumble that expects immediate, precise answers.

"Movement in Jackson," Sam replies. He taps the illuminated screen of the heavy-duty military tablet clenched in his hands, swiping to access the CCTV live feeds. Damaris provided us with specific coordinates where the demons and vampires have been operating, so Sam naturally hacked directly into the city's secure camera network. We also dispatched a few stealth team members to install additional hidden cameras to cover the unavoidable blind spots.

"Lots of movement," Sam continues. "The specific area Damaris mentioned is a warehouse district on the east side, just near the old, abandoned rail yards. The vampires have definitely created a massive feeding den. The thermal biological spikes are completely off the charts from the victims they are holding captive. It really does seem like they are actively preparing for something big."

I force my gaze away from Rose and her suffocating, agonising wall of silence. I blink hard, clearing the lingering red haze so I can refocus my eyes on the screen. Even from this distance, I can see the grainy images on the tablet where Sam has angled it to face us. The thermal imaging is horrifyingly clear. The image shows huddled, glowing clusters of orange and red figures that are packed tightly in the basement of a huge warehouse.

Some look so weak they can barely twitch, while others seem to be frantically thrashing, trying to fight their heavy bindings. My stomach drops. I recognise that exact, desperate look from many past black-ops missions where I was sent behind enemy lines to rescue prisoners of war.

I can't help but remember those past ops where I had to witness the same hollow-eyed terror, the same way the light catches the sweat on their foreheads as they strain against ropes that bite into raw flesh.

"They are getting bold," Luca mutters, a dangerous edge creeping into his tone. He closes the distance, walking over to study the small screen as Sam stands positioned on the catwalk right above him. "Vampires never grab this many human civilians to feed on all at once. They usually target one or two and drain them slowly over a few days in the shadows. Humans naturally replenish their blood over time, keeping the food source sustainable. If they are clustering together in large, organised groups, then, as you said, they must be planning something catastrophic. They must be preparing for a coordinated, massive strike that requires that much fresh blood."

"What are we going to do about it?"

A new, airy, yet profoundly sad voice echoes through the cavernous, damp yard as they step through the gate. Even though my new heightened senses tell me this visitor is familiar, my lethal tactical instincts take over completely. The shift is immediate. I drop sharply into a low, defensive combat stance, my hand instinctively reaching for the empty weapon harness strapped across my back. My fingers brush empty nylon where a blade should be.

My newly elongated canines throb painfully in my gums, demanding action.

"Stand down," Luca orders sharply. Despite his command, his massive hands clench into fists, ready to tackle me if I go rogue. "They are friendlies."

A swirling, unnatural darkness quickly coalesces in the very centre of the space. Sera manifests first, stepping out from the inky, suffocating abyss. Reya's shadow guardian is a terrifyingly beautiful construct forged from pure, solidified darkness. Her eyes are bright, glowing purple orbs that seem to pierce right through my flesh and scrutinise my bruised soul. Immediately behind her steps Freya.

The normally vibrant witch's blonde hair isn't in its normally perfect ponytail, and her usually bright, endlessly optimistic expression is uncharacteristically grim, haunted by unseen horrors.

'The Alpha speaks the truth,' Sera's ethereal voice echoes directly inside my skull. Her voice in my mind is different now. it feels like a bucket of freezing ice water trickling slowly over my raw brain matter, numbing and shocking all at once. *'We bring vital intelligence.'*

I shiver violently, rubbing my throbbing temples with the rough heels of my hands to physically dispel the strange, invasive sensation of mental communication.

"That feels incredibly strange now, hearing your voice directly inside my head," I mutter aloud, my voice still raspy from the hissing, the sound scraping my throat like sandpaper.

Freya steps forward, the soles of her boots softly crunching on the concrete. Her eyes nervously dart towards the fresh, glistening bloodstain on the floor before finally settling cautiously on me.

"Your new look is... very different," Freya says. "Damaris told us about your biological changes, and apparently, you are experiencing some severe control issues."

"Yeah, I am having some issues," I say dryly, the words tasting of iron and resolve. "According to Sam, I am improving, but it doesn't feel like it to me."

My cold, calculating tactical mind takes over entirely. It slams a heavy, reinforced steel door shut on my bleeding heartbreak over Rose and my burning physical hunger. The mission is everything. It is the only thing that makes sense in this chaotic world. I straighten my spine, regaining total, unwavering control over my posture.

"Good, because we still desperately need you, Ava," Freya says, her voice thick with desperation, her hands twisting the hem of her stained shirt. "You might literally be our only hope to permanently eliminate these demons and vampires."

"We need to extract these prisoners first," Luca states. His voice leaves absolutely no room for argument. "It might be tactically best to split into two separate strike teams. One team goes in hot after the vampires and secures the prisoners, while the other team methodically picks off the demons. Then we can initiate the plan to capture Devika, extract her to a secure location, and wipe out the entire demon strike force in the process."

"Not just wipe them out," I say quietly. The words are absolute, devoid of emotion, and coated in pure, lethal ice. "We eradicate them. I believe I should be on the team that hunts the demons. With my blade, the demons won't just be temporarily banished to the Underworld to recover and return later to terrorise us. They will be utterly, permanently destroyed. Their vile, blackened souls will burn to literal ash on the mortal plane."

"Alright," Luca says, giving a single, sharp nod.

I turn back to the group. The lingering hesitation and the blind, feral panic from the blood training are gone. I am right back in my element. I am the weapon. I am the Destroyer.

"We take the fight directly to them tomorrow," I announce. "We hit the warehouse district hard before the sun goes down. We rescue the captive humans and take out the demons. We leave absolutely nothing but scorched earth in our wake. No survivors, no traces."

Luca nods approvingly, his dark, calculating eyes assessing my renewed focus. "We need to go over the tactical blueprints tonight, then. We cannot just rush in blindly, guns blazing, and hope for a miracle. We will also need serious, coordinated crowd control to make sure no one enters our operational zones."

"I will go with the team to rescue the prisoners on the eastern flank," Rose announces immediately, stepping swiftly forward. "I am highly in the mood to take out some vampires."

It feels like a slap in the face. The declaration is directed straight at me. She still absolutely refuses to look my way. Her voice is fiercely resolute, echoing with the unwavering authority of a Beta, but beneath that tough bravado, my heightened hearing detects her heartbeat spike. a frantic rabbit's thud against ribs.

I can hear her overwhelming need to put distance between us. I don't know exactly what the vampires did to torment her, and I have no magical way to fix the trauma of her past. Now, thanks to some sick twist of fate, I have become a terrifying hybrid of the very monster that haunts her nightmares. It is clear we still have much to learn about each other. if we even can.

"Sam and I will lead Team Alpha," Rose continues, her vibrant green eyes fixed stubbornly on Luca's face. "Part of our assault team will lock down and secure the outer perimeter. Sam can easily set up a sniper nest on the old municipal water tower and take out any vamps that try to escape into the city or attempt to flank our position while most of the backup team joins me with modified wooden tipped bullets."

The words are a devastating physical blow, sharper and colder than any serrated blade. She cannot even stomach standing by my side in a fight anymore. I keep my facial expression perfectly blank, a mask of unreadable stone, locking the searing agony behind a massive wall of pure ice.

Fine. If she cannot stand the sight of me, I will do the dirty, blood-soaked work myself. I will be the executioner she cannot bear to watch.

Sam grins, tapping the reinforced tablet in his hand, completely unaware of the suffocating tension between Rose and me. "I already have the optimal firing vectors mapped out on the grid. I can easily cover three intersecting alleyways from that tower elevation and provide continuous, lethal overwatch."

"Good," Luca says. He turns his head to look directly at me, his gaze razor-sharp. "Ava, you and I are taking Team Beta. We will take a smaller, highly mobile strike team and go after as many demons as we possibly can. We will free any human souls that have been possessed, as human hosts cannot survive prolonged possession. We have to ensure the civilian population is kept in the dark."

I look back at Luca, overwhelmed by a sudden, deep surge of genuine respect. He is actually trusting me. Despite the erratic bloodlust and the horrific biological changes currently ravaging my DNA, he is throwing me right into the thick of it. He treats me exactly as I am. a weapon of mass destruction.

"I will personally handle the general and any high-level close-quarters threats," I state, my voice dropping to a lethal, flat cadence that promises nothing but absolute, catastrophic violence. "As I am the only one who can permanently destroy the demons, it is best you watch my back. And if I lose control in the heat of battle... you can then deal with me."

I meet his eyes, making it crystal clear exactly what I mean. If I go feral, he has permission to end me. to put me down like the rabid dog I fear I'm becoming.

"Deal," Luca says without a single ounce of hesitation.

That single word provokes a physical reaction from Rose. She finally turns her gaze to mine. My chest tightens as I feel a sudden, sharp surge of intense pain bleeding through our frayed bond. A white-hot lance of fear and sorrow. Fear radiates from her, a terror that she is not fully certain about our suicide plan, or what Luca will actually do to me if I lose my mind in the field.

I risk one last, incredibly painful glance at Rose. The moment has passed. She is already turning her body away, her delicate jaw set in a hard, unforgiving line, refusing to acknowledge the gaping, bleeding chasm between us. A chasm I helped carve with my own monstrous hands, well, *fangs*.

I swallow the bitter, metallic taste of rejection. The adrenaline is already singing a dark, beautiful melody in my veins, sharp and brilliantly clear. The monster inside me is wide awake, but it is no longer blindly thrashing around for a cheap fix. It is entirely focused.

"Freya, you should join us for dinner so we can go over the precise tactical layouts with you," I say, glancing back at the team, completely adopting the chilling, methodical calm of an elite assassin. "You might have some magical insights that could help. But for now, we need you to stay out of this initial strike stage. If they find out you're involved, they might come straight for you while we are distracted in the city. When we finally go after Devika, then we will desperately need everything you and the others can possibly bring to the table if we are to succeed. Every spell, every ward, every ounce of power you can summon."

Freya agrees. I then sweep my icy gaze over the group, feeling the deadly purpose lock into place. Bone-deep and absolute. "We are going to Jackson. And we are going to save the city."

Not just from the monsters out there, but from the one growing inside me. If Rose can't stand the sight of me or doesn't want to be with me, then I might as well put everything into the fight, even if it costs me my own life.

CHAPTER 19

How to Kill a Shade Without Ruining Your Boots

The heavy, rhythmic hum of the SUV's engine vibrates fiercely through the thick rubber soles of my combat boots, sending a low-frequency tremor up my spine that feels less like a machine and more like a warning. We are racing down the dark, deserted highway towards Jackson, moving like a shadow through the night, a sleek black predator cutting through the gloom. Outside, the bruised Mississippi twilight presses heavily against the tinted glass, a suffocating shroud of purple and charcoal trying to drown the small, pressurised space we occupy.

Inside the cabin, the silence is absolute and utterly deafening. It is not a peaceful silence. It is a thick, volatile tension that feels like a physical presence, something you could practically cut with a silver blade if you had the nerve to try.

Luca sits rigidly behind the steering wheel, his large frame dominating the driver's seat. His broad, muscular shoulders are coiled tight, locked in place like loaded springs ready to snap. I can see the corded muscles of his neck straining against the collar of his shirt, and his jaw is clenched so firmly that I can actually hear the faint, unnatural grinding of his teeth as he navigates the empty, winding stretches of cracked asphalt. Every movement he makes is calculated and controlled, but there is an underlying current of violence in the way he grips that leather steering wheel, his knuckles white, his predatory instincts humming just beneath the surface.

I sit stiffly in the passenger seat, my body a coiled spring of its own. My fingers run rhythmically over the familiar, worn leather-wrapped hilt of my silver short sword. The texture is gritty, comforting. A grounding constant against the absolute chaos currently swirling in my soul.

Just keep it together, Ava. Focus on the steel. Focus on the weight.

Maya's intricate cloaking rune still hums faintly against the edges of my mind. It feels like a strange, phantom weight, a psychic veil that tethers my tactical harness securely to my newly mutated, chaotic aura. To the blissfully ignorant mundane world passing us by, I merely look like an average woman dressed in a plain black T-shirt and cargo pants. We desperately need to remain completely invisible. Even to those rare beings possessing the Sight, they will only perceive me as an unarmed human with a bizarrely pale hair colour.

Luca specifically suggested I wear low-tint aviator sunglasses to effectively conceal my eyes. My eyes, which are no longer just eyes. They are glowing, icy-blue beacons that would instantly flag me as a supernatural threat to anyone paying attention. They feel hot in my sockets, pulsing with a power I don't fully understand.

Just breathe, Ava. You are in control. Focus on the mission, not the monster within.

My internal voice sounds pathetic and entirely unconvincing, a thin layer of lacquer over a crumbling wall. My newly enhanced Dhampir senses are a relentless, chaotic symphony of sensory overload that I am struggling to tune out. It is as if someone has turned the volume of the world up to eleven and stripped away my filters.

I can distinctly hear the rapid, anxious thumping of a stray dog's heart in the dense woods, several hundred yards away, as it picks its way cautiously along the side of the dark highway. I can smell everything. The rich, damp Mississippi earth after a brief rainfall earlier today, the choking acridity of the exhaust fumes from our own engine, and the sharp, musky, metallic scent of Luca's violently simmering tension. It smells like ozone and old blood, the scent of an Alpha on the edge of a hunt.

My biological upgrades are both a spectacular gift and a horrifying curse. Out of all the overwhelming scents flooding my nasal cavity, what I miss most is the intoxicating, perfect blend of rolling storms and fresh wildflowers.

I miss Rose.

The thought hits me hard. A sharp, hollow ache violently twists deep inside my chest cavity, mimicking the exact, searing pain of a shattered rib. Her face lingers in my mind, jagged and unforgiving, each glance a cruel reminder of what we lost. I can't shake the image of her avoiding my gaze when we split into our designated strike teams back at the safe house, as if I were nothing more than invisible dust swept away by the wind.

I can still see it. The way she had practically sprinted over to Sam’s vehicle, her movements frantic, looking as though she were fleeing a predator rather than walking away from a partner. She was utterly desperate to put as many physical miles between my fangs and her delicate skin as humanly possible.

I squeeze my eyes tightly shut behind the sunglasses, viciously fighting back the brutal, acidic sting of her rejection. The memory of it tastes like copper and shame. I had almost torn her beautiful throat right out. I had tasted her blood, felt the electric jolt of her essence on my tongue, and for a heartbeat, the monster had won. She has every single right in this chaotic universe to despise me.

I am a freak. A hybrid mistake. Why would she ever want to touch me again?

The heavy silence is suddenly broken by a sharp, hissing burst of static from the tactical radio clipped to my belt. The sound is like a whip-crack in the quiet cabin, making me jump.

“Beta Team, this is Alpha Team. Do you copy?”

It is Sam. His voice is incredibly tight, clipped, and entirely focused on the logistics of our operation. There is no room for emotion in his tone. Only the cold, hard facts of a CIA operative in the field.

I snatch the radio from its pouch, my body reacting with a speed that still surprises me, my movements blurring slightly. "Copy, Alpha Team. What is your current status, Sam?"

"We are locked in position at the abandoned warehouse district," Sam reports. I can hear the faint, whistling wind rushing past his microphone headset, suggesting he is exposed to the elements. "I have successfully established a highly concealed sniper nest on top of the old municipal water tower. I currently have clear, unobstructed lines of sight on all three intersecting alleyways leading directly into the main vampire den. Damaris was entirely accurate with her intelligence and will assist in tracking vampires as they start to leave."

Luca leans his massive frame slightly closer to my seat, his dark eyes never leaving the dark road ahead, though his focus has shifted entirely to the radio. "Have you started to engage the hostile targets yet?" he asks.

"Negative."

Rose's voice suddenly cuts sharply across the channel.

My mutated, sluggish heart gives a pitiful, involuntary flutter at the exact sound of her voice. The severe bradycardia I have been experiencing since my transformation seems to disappear only for her. My pulse still doesn't return to normal. It just produces an extra heartbeat that, for some reason, makes my body feel weird. I don't know how to explain it, as I have nothing to compare it to.

But as she continues, the hope is crushed. Her tone is sharp, terrifyingly professional, and completely devoid of the blazing, unconditional warmth she used to reserve solely for me. It is like listening to a stranger who happens to have her voice. There is no flirtation, no hidden softness, just the cold efficiency of a soldier.

"We are strictly holding the outer perimeter," Rose continues, her breathing remarkably steady despite the impending slaughter. "Damaris is currently sweeping the interior, waiting for the first vampires to leave. She believes they will start to move in and out of the structure in small, disorganised clusters. As planned, we will intentionally let the stragglers leave the main building. We are about to engage them and methodically pick them off quietly in the security blind spots exactly as planned, long before they can hit the populated city streets. Damaris indicated just before we made contact that four hostiles are about to head out now. It's twilight."

"Excellent," Luca says, his deep tone radiating firm approval. "Keep yourself safe out there. Do not take any unnecessary risks. Keep me constantly updated. Do not breach the main warehouse to rescue the human captives until you possess a massive, undeniable tactical advantage. If things go sideways for even a fraction of a second, you pull the team back immediately. That is a direct order."

"Understood," Rose replies sharply.

A brief, painfully tense pause lingers heavily on the encrypted frequency. For a few seconds, neither of them speaks, and the air in the car feels like it has been sucked out by a vacuum. I hold my breath, praying for something. anything. A slip of the tongue, a soft sigh, a sign that she is as miserable as I am.

"Ava. Watch his back out there."

The radio goes completely dead, leaving a hollow, ringing hum in my ear.

I sit silently and simply stare at the cold, black plastic device resting in my pale hand. My thumb brushes the edge of the casing. It was certainly not a romantic or affectionate sign-off. It wasn't a "miss you" or an "I love you." But it was a clear acknowledgement of my ongoing existence. It was a thread, thin and frayed, but it was there.

I will take it. I will gladly accept any pathetic, tiny scraps of affection I can scavenge from her, even if they are wrapped in ice.

"She still cares deeply for you," Luca says incredibly softly. He keeps his intense dark eyes locked on the white lines of the road ahead, giving me the privacy of my own grief. "She just desperately needs time to mentally process your sudden biological changes. Your new anatomy is a lot to take in."

"I know," I lie smoothly, the words tasting like ash. I deliberately shove the radio back into its tactical pouch on my hip with a sharp snap. "Let us just focus entirely on the mission at hand. We have souls and a city to save."

Rose and her team didn't have far to go to reach their target. We had to head farther south to reach our target area, so we are only just breaching the city limits of Jackson. The atmosphere shifts drastically. The transition is almost physical, like crossing an invisible border into a diseased land. The air suddenly tastes foul on my tongue. It is heavily laced with the biting, metallic tang of industrial smog and the subtle, gag-inducing stench of pure sulphur.

It is the smell of the pit. The demons are incredibly close. I can practically feel their malevolent energy scratching at my newly awakened Dhampir senses like a thousand tiny needles trying to find a way under my skin. Every instinct in my body begins to scream, urging me to draw my weapon and start killing.

Without any warning, a violently swirling pool of inky, freezing darkness erupts right in the centre of the vehicle's dashboard. It looks like a hole ripped into the fabric of reality. Sera gracefully materialises from the pitch-black shadows, her terrifyingly beautiful, winged form rapidly coalescing into solid, breathing night. Her glowing, vibrant purple eyes immediately lock onto mine, piercing straight through my skull and into the deepest recesses of my thoughts.

'They are moving,' Sera's cold, echoing, ethereal voice rings directly inside my mind.

I suppress a shiver at the invasive telepathic contact; it feels like a sliver of ice being slid into my brain.

'A concentrated cluster of lower-level demons is currently terrorising a crumbling block of abandoned tenements exactly three streets over from our current location. They are actively hunting human strays. They are sadistically feeding on their mortal fear before they finally kill them. They are specifically hunting those humans possessing darkened, corrupted souls so they can build a much larger army to send

down to the Underworld.'

"Take a sharp, hard left at the very next intersection, Luca," I command.

The transition is instantaneous. My clinical, tactical mind seamlessly takes the driver's seat, shoving all my romantic grief and longing into the dark, locked corners of my mind where they belong during an operation. The warrior replaces the woman. "Sera currently has a demonic cluster pinned down," I relay to Luca.

Luca twists the leather steering wheel, aggressively throwing the heavy SUV around the sharp corner with a loud, protesting squeal of rubber against pavement. We instantly switch off the bright headlights, opting to roll entirely silently down a shattered, debris-filled alleyway bordered on both sides by decaying, crumbling brick buildings that look like they are holding each other up by sheer will.

Luca completely cuts the engine so we can roll up to the building we want in silence. The resulting silence of the abandoned city block is unbelievably dense, heavy, and utterly oppressive. It feels as though the city itself is holding its breath, waiting for the slaughter to begin.

I swiftly unbuckle my seatbelt and step out into the muggy, humid night air. As I place my feet on the ground, I seem to know instantly where to step so I make no sound as I am forced to walk over broken glass; my senses are so heightened that I can feel the exact placement of every shard before I even touch it.

My mutated body feels impossibly, dangerously light. I am wound extremely tight, heavily coiled with that terrifying, crackling kinetic energy that fiercely urges me to rip something apart with my bare hands. It is a hunger for combat, a biological imperative that makes my skin itch and my fangs ache in my gums.

"Sera, guide us to the target," Luca whispers softly. I hear the wet, sickening sound of his bones popping slightly as he deliberately shifts his human hands into lethal, curved panther claws. He looks at me, his eyes glowing with a predatory light that mirrors my own.

Sera smoothly glides through the heavy air using her massive, shadowy wings. She is a beautiful yet terrifying phantom of pure vengeance, leading us directly towards a decaying apartment complex that looks like a skeletal remnant. She won't be involved in the take-downs. She needs to stay out of sight, ensuring that if any demon escapes, they can't report back that the Harpers were involved in the operation.

We gave the two backup team members who accompanied us the job of making sure no one enters this area, so there's no chance of innocents getting hurt. Except if you're in this area at night, I'm guessing they wouldn't be so innocent.

As we approach the heavy, rotting wooden front doors, we find they have already been violently smashed inward, leaving a gaping, dark maw waiting to consume us.

'There are three active hostiles currently on the second floor,' Sera transmits sharply into my mind. I can't help but wonder just how far this form of communication can go. If we get a spare moment after the blood stops spilling, I might ask her to do some distance tests. *'They have not yet possessed any physical human hosts. They currently exist solely in their ethereal shade forms. It will not be long until they either slaughter the trapped humans or possess them. If they do kill them, Reapers will turn up to transport the souls to the underworld. You do not want to go up against those while you are still getting used to your new sense of self. The humans know something is hunting them, but of course, they can't see them.'*

"We have three shades upstairs," I quickly relay, softly whispering to Luca as I draw my weapon.

The weight of the silver sword feels right in my hand, an extension of my own arm. "Stay incredibly close to my six."

We methodically breach the dark building while the two heavily armed backup team members we brought with us secure the outer perimeter, making absolutely certain no innocent civilians inadvertently wander into the operational area. The interior wooden staircase is a complete, rotting hazard. planks are missing, and the air is thick with the smell of damp mould and ancient dust.

However, my brand-new, terrifying Dhampir reflexes instantly allow me to geometrically calculate exactly which decaying wooden planks will support my body weight in a split second. I don't even have to think about it; my brain simply processes the structural integrity of the wood as I move. We quickly ascend the stairs, appearing just like a pair of silent, lethal ghosts in the dark.

The ambient temperature drops sharply the moment we reach the gloomy upper landing. It is an unnatural chill that seeps through my clothes and bites at my skin. Usually, a sudden drop in temperature would affect me, but now my body doesn't really notice the change. The atmospheric pressure also shifts, growing denser and more suffocating as we approach the shades' exact location at the end of the narrow hall. It feels like walking underwater.

I adjust my grip on the hilt of the sword as I prepare myself. The worn, leather-wrapped hilt feels absolutely perfect and balanced in my firm grip. My mind briefly flashes back to the day Reya Harper gently took this very blade from my hands. I vividly remember the intensely focused, fierce look burning in her incredible eyes as she somehow transformed the sword at a molecular level. I watched in pure awe as she fed her raw, crackling magic directly into the cold silver of the sword, and the word *Destroyer* magically scorched itself right down the centre of the metal blade.

I channel my chaotic, hyper-focused energy directly into the cold metal. The enchanted blade responds instantly to my violent intent as I activate it. A brilliant, violently crackling aura of pitch-black hellfire erupts spectacularly along the razor-sharp edge. The dancing dark flames do not emit any actual thermal heat, but they aggressively radiate a pulse of pure, unadulterated, destructive magic that makes the normal shadows lingering in the hallway physically recoil in terror, as if the darkness itself is afraid of the blade.

I do not bother knocking. I forcefully kick the rotten door clean off its rusted hinges with a thunderous crash, making the humans in the next room cry out in shock and terror. I can now hear their frantic breathing, the rapid-fire pounding of their hearts, and the scent of their raw fear. it smells like salt and sour sweat.

The interior space is cloaked in complete, suffocating darkness, but my newly mutated eyes cut through the thick gloom effortlessly, casting the room in sharp, predatory contrast. Three towering, writhing silhouettes of pure, concentrated malice gradually turn to confront our intrusion. They are shades. Wisps of smoke and hate given form. Their glowing eyes burn like hot, radioactive coals, filled with hateful, starving malevolence.

They do not hesitate for a single second. They launch themselves aggressively across the confined room in a highly synchronised, terrifyingly silent wave of impending death.

They arrogantly expect a fragile, squishy human. They fully expect slow, pathetic, easily breakable mortal reflexes.

They are fundamentally and catastrophically wrong.

The entire world around me instantly slows to an agonising crawl. This is the rush. The adrenaline surge that turns seconds into minutes. I casually watch as the lead demon stretches its smoky, wickedly clawed hands directly toward my exposed throat. My vision is so incredibly sharp that I can see the individual, writhing tendrils of thick darkness forming its ethereal yet physical shape, like ink swirling in water.

I move smoothly and gracefully inside its broad guard, stepping past the reach of those claws with a fluid motion that feels effortless. I swing my arm backwards, then with a fluid motion, I swing the sword in a fierce, sweeping upward arc. The hellfire-imbued silver blade cuts effortlessly and cleanly straight through the centre of the demon's shadowy torso, slicing through essence as if it were silk.

The vile creature does not even have the microscopic moment needed to scream in agony. The magical black fire fiercely consumes the entity completely from within, igniting its very core. It violently erupts into a dense, choking cloud of fine, greasy grey ash that rains heavily onto the decaying wooden floorboards.

The second shade, now enraged, lunges for Luca. He skilfully ducks beneath the attack with remarkable, fluid agility, his body twisting in mid-air. He viciously slashes his elongated panther claws horizontally across its shadowy kneecaps, successfully loosening its physical hold on this realm. The shade awkwardly stumbles forward, its form flickering like a dying lightbulb.

A fierce grin spreads across my face; this is the very first time he has ever managed to physically injure a demonic enemy, all thanks to the magical root bracelet Freya gave him.

I pivot on my heel, executing a dizzying, impossibly fast spin that generates a terrifying amount of kinetic momentum. I feel the wind whip past my ears as I move. I brutally drive the razor-sharp tip of my sword directly through the dead centre of the stumbling shade's chest cavity. The ravenous black flames immediately erupt outward from the wound, entirely incinerating the dark entity in a blinding, spectacular flash of violent, witch-born magic.

The third and final demon finally recognises its catastrophic, deadly mistake. It frantically turns to flee, desperately trying to dissolve its form back into the solid brick wall to escape my wrath. It thinks it can hide in the stone.

I do not run. I practically teleport. Or at least, that is exactly how the insane speed feels to my brain. a jump from one point in space to another. The sheer, explosive kinetic force of my sudden acceleration violently cracks the thick floorboards right beneath my combat boots with a loud *snap*. I stand squarely between the terrified demon and its escape route long before it can even formulate a coherent thought.

I fiercely seize it directly by its icy, spectral throat. My pale hand makes firm, bruising contact with the freezing mist. My newly mutated Dhampir biology effortlessly enables me to physically grapple with the supernatural realm, my fingers digging into the shade's neck as if it were solid flesh. I do notice, though, that when I touch the shade, a strange coldness starts to seep into my fingers, making them almost feel numb, *strange*.

"This is for Reya," I hiss. My voice drops into a deep, almost demonic cadence that genuinely startles even me.

I brutally drive the blade straight up through its shadowy jaw, violently pinning its skull directly to the plaster ceiling. Thick, greasy ash cascades heavily over my face and shoulders as the miserable creature is permanently, violently erased from existence, its form dissolving into nothingness against the ceiling.

I smoothly draw my sword free from the ceiling, breathing heavily. I am definitely not winded from the physical exertion, but rather from the deeply intoxicating, magnificent, adrenaline-fueled rush of the slaughter. The monster roaring inside my veins feels utterly, terrifyingly glorious. For a few seconds, the pain of Rose's rejection is gone, replaced by the pure, cold clarity of the kill.

Luca simply gazes at me from across the ruined room, his broad chest rising and falling slightly as he absorbs the rapid extent of the carnage. He looks at the ash on my shoulders and then into my glowing blue eyes.

"That was... terrifyingly efficient," he comments, his tone tinged with a mix of alpha respect and mild horror.

"I explicitly told you I would handle the close-quarters threats," I reply. My lips involuntarily curl upward into a cold, undeniably arrogant smirk. The warrior is still in control, and she loves every second of it.

'Do not celebrate your victory just yet,' Sera's icy voice cuts sharply through my swelling arrogance, pulling me back to reality. *'I followed a fourth shade. It successfully entered a residential home and possessed a human host exactly two blocks east of your location. The demon will desperately need physical rest to acclimatise to the flesh before it heads back out into the night to harvest more human souls.'*

"We currently have a possessed human host located exactly

two blocks east," I tell Luca, sharply flicking my wrist to shake the thick residual ash from my glowing blade.

I look at him, the lethal, focused *Destroyer* fully in command, the hunger for the hunt still screaming in my blood.

"Let us go save a soul."

CHAPTER 20

CHASING SHADOWS AND SOUL-FIRE

The two deserted blocks ahead of us feel less like a city street and more like a sprawling, concrete graveyard. A suffocating, heavy silence drapes over the neighbourhood, clinging to my skin like damp wool in a storm. It is an oppressive kind of quiet, the sort that doesn't just signify an absence of noise but feels like it is actively trying to swallow us whole.

We move through the urban decay with practised, lethal precision. I keep my weight on the balls of my feet, hidden deep within the shadows cast by decaying brickwork and the skeletal remains of steel fire escapes. As we proceed, we blend into the grayscale misery around us, while our two backup guys head to the entrance of the road to block any passage. We chose to walk for two reasons. I wanted to burn off some energy, and we needed to ensure there was no trouble circling the building during our approach, which we couldn't tell if we just drove to the end of the road.

I really hate this part. The creeping. The waiting. It's the anticipation that gets you, the way your brain starts inventing monsters in every dark alleyway because it's bored with the actual silence. The funny thing is, I'm good at this part, really good. It's also the reason I was so good at my job. No one ever saw me coming.

Every step feels heavier than the last, as if the atmosphere itself is thickening, resisting our progress. Despite the mental drag, I don't dare slow down. My eyes are locked on our target. A small, spectacularly dilapidated residential house. It sits in the centre of a weed-choked, abandoned lot, looking less like a home and more like a festering wound in the earth.

The front windows aren't just broken. They are heavily boarded up with moisture-warped plywood that looks grey and sodden. The wood is so degraded it feels as though it might disintegrate if I breathed on it too hard. But through the splintered cracks, faint, sickly slivers of jaundiced yellow light seep out. They don't shine; they pulse. It is a slow, rhythmic throb, like the dying heartbeat of something that refuses to stay dead.

Because nothing screams 'easy extraction' quite like a creepy murder house filled with raw sewage and questionable life choices. I should have stayed in bed. Or moved to a tropical island where the only things trying to eat my soul are overpriced cocktails.

"Sera says there is only one target inside," I whisper. My voice is barely a vibration in the air, a ghost of a sound that barely reaches Luca's ear.

We are crouching low behind the rusted, hollowed-out shell of a gutted sedan. The metal smells of old rain and oxidised iron, a sharp, metallic tang that cuts through the smell of damp earth. I can feel the grit of the pavement pressing into my knees.

"It has possessed a human male," I continue, my eyes never leaving that pulsing yellow light. "We need to incapacitate the physical host without killing him. If we can force the demon out while there is still a window of opportunity, we might actually save this human. Even if he has a dark soul, it's better than letting the entity do irreparable damage to the vessel."

Luca shifts beside me. His presence is a warm, grounding weight in the oppressive dark, a beacon of stability that keeps me from spiralling into my own hyper-vigilance. I can feel the heat radiating off him, the sheer physical power of a shifter held in check by a thin veil of discipline.

"I'll grapple with the host and pin him down," he murmurs back. His voice is deep, a low rumble that I feel in my chest as much as I hear it.

I glance at him and meet his eyes. They are no longer human. They glow like golden orbs of predatory intensity. He has no need to use his alpha eyes on me, so it's a pleasure to see his beautiful golden eyes for once. He is scanning the dark perimeter, his pupils slit, cutting through the gloom with an Alpha's precision. He is searching for anything or anyone lurking at the periphery that my eyes might miss.

"You use your blade to threaten the entity," Luca adds, his gaze returning to me. "Maybe having your hellfire sword shoved directly in its face will be enough of a terrifying deterrent to force the shade to abandon its meat suit."

I give him a sharp, singular nod. I don't need words to tell him I agree. My fingers tighten around the hilt of my sword, feeling the familiar texture of the grip. The dark magic within the blade hums against my palm, a restless, hungry vibration that mirrors the thrumming in my own veins. It feels like a living thing, an extension of my own will that is just as eager for blood as I am.

Let's get this over with before I start imagining the ghosts of previous tenants judging my ponytail.

We move. We aren't fast. We are purposeful. Every movement is calculated, every breath timed to avoid detection. We close the distance to the decaying front porch, our boots barely making a sound on the cracked pavement. As I step onto the wooden porch, the damp steps groan painfully under my weight. It is a shrill, protesting sound, a wooden scream that twists my stomach with an instinctive dread. There is no other quick way in, so we have no choice. We don't have time if we're going to save the possessed human.

We don't halt. We can't.

Luca doesn't bother with subtlety once we reach the threshold. "It's my turn," he whispers. He doesn't knock; he doesn't check for traps. He simply raises a heavy, combat-booted foot and kicks the front door clean off its rusted, failing hinges.

The sound is explosive. The thick wood slams into the interior hallway wall with a deafening, echoing crash that vibrates through my teeth and rattles my skull. For a split second, the world is nothing but the sound of shattering timber and the smell of ancient dust.

We surge into the dimly lit living room, and immediately, my lungs rebel.

The stench hits my heightened senses, making me feel like I want to retch. It is an overwhelming, nauseating cocktail of advanced decay, rotting drywall, and the sharp, stinging scent of raw sewage that has backed up into the floorboards. The smell is cloying, thick enough to taste, striking the back of my throat with a chemical bitterness that makes me want to gag.

Then I see him.

A lone man stands perfectly still in the dead centre of the ruined room. He is horrifyingly gaunt, his frame so skeletal it looks as though he might snap under the weight of his own skin. His clothes are rags, clinging to a body that has been wasted away by something parasitic.

His skin isn't just pale. It is a sickening, necrotic shade of jaundiced yellow. It is the colour of acute hepatic failure, the hue of a body that has ceased to process toxins and has simply begun to rot from the inside out.

Why would a demon even want this wreck? It's like picking the most expired piece of meat in the freezer and deciding it's a delicacy.

The man's eyes are rolled back so far into his skull that only the bulging, bloodshot whites are visible. He is staring at nothing, seeing things that exist on a plane beyond my sight. Thick, pulsating black veins spiderweb across his neck and jawline, looking like an aggressive, toxic infection crawling just beneath the surface of the skin, throbbing in time with that same jaundiced light from outside.

He slowly opens his mouth. There is no greeting, no plea for help. Instead, a guttural, rattling hiss escapes his throat, sounding like steam escaping a cracked pipe. His joints begin to pop and snap with a sickening, wet crunch, the sound of cartilage being forced into unnatural positions as he contorts his body, preparing for an attack.

Luca doesn't hesitate. He moves with the brutal, breathtaking speed of a born apex predator, a blur of motion in the gloom.

He tackles the possessed man around the waist, driving him hard into the peeling, mouldy wallpaper. The brittle drywall crumbles into grey dust under the impact, filling the air with a chalky haze. Luca uses his massive, muscular weight to pin the man's violently thrashing limbs.

"Get the hell out of him!" Luca roars.

I watch, mesmerised and horrified, as Luca's human features begin to warp under the strain. His teeth sharpen into deadly points, his nose reshaping into a powerful panther snout. The Alpha nature is surging to the surface, not fully shifting yet, but asserting dominance over the parasite in the room. He is trying to out-alpha a demon, and the raw power radiating from him is electric.

I step forward, my movements sharp and decisive. I raise my sword, and with a thought, the blade ignites. Crackling black flames erupt along the blade, singeing the oxygen in the air between us.

I hold the edge of the burning blade directly to the man's exposed throat.

"Vacate the host immediately," I command. My voice drops into a low, dangerous register, the tone I use when there is no more room for negotiation. "Or I will literally burn you out of his veins."

The thrashing stops instantly.

The man tilts his head to the side in a grotesque, jerky motion that defies every law of human anatomy. His neck snaps at an angle that should have severed the spinal cord, but he doesn't flinch. He stares blindly up at me with those white eyes, and then, his chapped, bleeding lips curl into an impossibly wide, genuinely horrifying grin.

"You walked straight into the trap, little mortal," a dark voice rasps from those torn vocal cords.

The voice is wrong. It doesn't sound human. It sounds like

grinding tombstones, like the crushing of old bone beneath a heavy boot. It is a sound that vibrates in the marrow of my bones, triggering an ancient, primal alarm in my brain.

"I was connected to one of the other shades," the entity sneers through the man's mouth. "So I summoned some help."

Well, that is just wonderfully cliché. Why are demons always so fond of the 'it's a trap' monologue? Can't they just attack and get it over with?

Suddenly, the temperature in the room plummets in a fraction of a second, turning my blood to slush in my veins. The shadows in the corners of the room begin to stretch. They don't merely shift with the light. They peel from the walls like strips of rotten, blackened flesh ripped from a carcass. The frost spreads rapidly, blooming across the cracked windowpanes in crystalline patterns of ice.

It isn't just one demon.

Seven towering, massive, ethereal shapes emerge from the pitch-black darkness. They surround us in a suffocating, freezing ring of swirling black smoke and blazing, hateful red eyes. I feel a surge of anger. They managed to mask their presence from us, concealing themselves perfectly, using this wretched, dying host as nothing more than bait to lure us into a kill box.

"Luca!" I say, spinning on my heels to face the overwhelming threat.

"I'm ready," he responds.

The seven shades attack simultaneously.

There is no time for elegant tactics or military precision. There are no formations here, no strategic retreats. This is pure, chaotic, bloody survival.

I swing my burning sword in a desperate, wide arc, the black flames whistling through the freezing air. The blade slices through the smoky chest cavity of the closest demon. The creature performs the physical act of shrieking, a silent, agonising spasm that ripples through its ethereal form, before it erupts into a cloud of greasy ash.

But victory is short-lived. The gap closes instantly as two more monsters surge forward to fill the void, their red eyes locked on my throat.

Suddenly, I feel it. A heavy, freezing ethereal claw rakes across my back.

The pain is a brilliant, blinding white flash of pure agony. The claws shred through my shirt and slice into my skin, carving deep furrows into the muscles of my shoulder and spine. I feel the cold of the demon's touch burning worse than fire, an icy poison that seeks to freeze my heart in its tracks.

The sheer force sends me crashing forward. I hit a rotting wooden coffee table with a sickening thud. The wood shatters into lethal, jagged splinters directly in my face, driving shards of timber into my stomach. Luckily, I manage to close my eyes and shield my face in time.

I gasp, the air leaving my lungs in a ragged sob. For a moment, the world goes grey.

"Ava!" Luca's voice is raw with panic. It is a sound I have rarely heard from him. Genuine, unadulterated fear.

He releases the host, throwing a frantic, looping punch that connects squarely with an attacking shade. The strike sends the entity flying backwards in a spray of shadow, but he is already pivoting, his eyes wide as he tries to reach me through the swarm.

The possessed man isn't out of the fight, either. He scrambles to his feet, his movements jerky and insect-like. He snatches a rusted iron fireplace poker from the hearth and swings it wildly at the back of Luca's skull with murderous intent.

"LUCA, SHIFT!" I scream at the top of my lungs, my voice cracking. I watch in horror as Luca manages to move just in time before the poker connects.

I scramble to my feet, ignoring the hot, sticky sensation of blood coming from the injury in my shoulder, back and stomach and soaking into my gear. Every movement feels like a thousand needles are being driven into me.

I duck under a sweeping shadow claw, the wind of it chilling my skin, and drive the heavy silver pommel of my sword into a demon's faceless visage with everything I have. There is a satisfying crunch as the silver impacts the entity. The monster stumbles, disoriented by the purity of the metal, giving me a heartbeat of space.

I pivot on my boots, slicing through the torso of another entity attempting to flank me. The resulting cloud of ash fills my lungs, making me choke on the bitter, acrid taste of sulphur and burnt hair.

Luca lets out a deafening, feral roar that shakes the very foundations of the house.

His body expands violently. I hear the sound of seams bursting and fabric tearing as his muscles swell, shredding his civilian clothes in a spray of cloth. Within seconds, a massive, terrifyingly lethal black panther stands where my partner once was. He is a mountain of sleek, midnight-black muscle and predatory grace.

With one heavy, clawed paw, Luca swats the possessed man aside. The impact is brutal; the man is sent crashing into the kitchen wall with a sickening thud of breaking ribs. He goes limp, sliding down the wall, finally neutralised.

But four shades remain. And they are converging on me like a localised storm of hate.

They swarm.

Ethereal hands seize my arms, my legs, and my throat. Their touch is unnaturally cold, a freezing magic that doesn't just chill the skin but seeps into my veins, attempting to induce immediate cardiac arrest. I thrash, my muscles straining against the crushing weight, but it's no use. I am outnumbered and injured.

Their touch feels lethal. My body starts to feel sluggish, making it hard to fight them off. Even though I came close to dying before, I actually feel like I'm dying in this moment.

My fingers go numb. The grip on my sword fails, and the blade clatters uselessly to the filthy floorboards, the black flames flickering out.

I am slammed against the cracked plaster wall. A massive shadow looms in front of my face, its jaws opening to reveal a swirling vortex of absolute nothingness. It isn't just going to kill me. It is ready to swallow my soul whole.

And then, something happens.

The freezing magic pulsing from their grips hits something ancient and primal deep within my mutated DNA. It is as if the cold has acted as a catalyst, triggering a biological failsafe I didn't know existed. A fierce, predatory override snaps my consciousness into a new reality.

Adrenaline floods my heart, but it isn't normal adrenaline. It is a powerful mixture of intense anger and an evolutionary survival drive that overrides every shred of my human morality. Time appears to slow down. The world shifts into high definition.

I catch my reflection in a cracked mirror across the room. My eyes are now on show, as the glasses I was wearing were knocked off when I crashed into the coffee table, and they are no longer just a luminous blue. They are glowing with a radioactive intensity. The static noise of fear in my mind disappears, replaced by a single, thunderous drumbeat.

Hunger.

It isn't a thirst for blood. Not exactly. I look at the dark mass pinning my throat and I finally see it for what it truly is. It is just a battery. A concentrated, delicious mass of leftover human life force and crackling dark magic.

The pressure building behind my gums becomes unbearable, an aching throb that demands release. Then, it bursts. My fangs slide down, razor-sharp and aching with an unholy need to feed.

I don't reach for my sword. I don't attempt a punch.

I lunge.

My jaw nearly unhinges as I sink my elongated fangs into the smoky, freezing shoulder of the shade. The creature screams. It is a silent, absolute, unadulterated agony that ripples through its entire form.

It shouldn't be possible. I am biting a ghost. But the moment my teeth pierce its ethereal membrane, a pressurised geyser of pure, crackling energy floods my mouth.

It tastes like raw, striking lightning mixed with thick, dark honey. It is an overwhelming, intoxicating, euphoric rush of god-like power. The sensation is better than any drug, more addictive than any high I have ever known. I suck desperately at the wound, my throat working rhythmically as I drain the essence of its stolen life force directly into my veins.

Instantly, the agony in my back vanishes.

I can feel it happening. rapid cellular regeneration. The deep lacerations are closing; torn muscle fibres are knitting together with a tingling heat, and the bleeding stops in a heartbeat. The splinters are pushed out of my skin by the sheer force of the healing process.

The shade thrashes, trying to tear itself away, but I have the unyielding grip of a god. I hold it tight, mercilessly draining it until, within three seconds, the massive demon collapses inward. It is sucked into the void of my hunger until nothing remains but a lingering scent of ozone.

The three remaining shades freeze.

They stare at me with pure, horrific disbelief. They have never seen a mortal consume one of their own. In their moment of hesitation, they release their grip on me.

I drop to my hands and knees on the filthy floor, trembling violently. My entire body is radiating an intense, internal heat that threatens to incinerate everything around me. The wounds on my back and stomach are gone, replaced by smooth, new skin. I feel invincible. I feel like a walking, breathing deity of destruction.

They turn to flee.

I am a blur of kinetic motion. I don't even think. I just act. I catch the first fleeing shade by its throat and rip its entire form in half with my bare hands. The magic dissipates into the air like smoke in a gale.

I snatch my silver sword from the floor, executing a dizzying spin that decapitates the second demon in a gorgeous arc of hellfire. Luca lunges forward, his massive panther form pinning the final shade just long enough for me to drive my burning blade straight through its skull.

Silence falls over the room. It is broken only by the heavy, wet breathing of the unconscious man in the kitchen.

I stand in the centre of the wreckage, chest heaving, fangs still extended and dripping with residual, glowing black energy. My icy blue eyes burn with a feral, radioactive glow. I slowly lick my lips; my body screams for another taste. The hunger is still there, simmering just beneath the surface.

Luca shifts back into his human form. He stands naked amidst the debris, his chest heaving, staring at me with a look of profound, terrifying realisation.

"Ava," he breathes, his voice trembling. "It isn't blood."

I glance at him, my mind still swirling in a euphoric high, the world feeling soft and malleable around the edges. "What?"

"You didn't want my physical blood during training," Luca says, taking a cautious, slow step toward me, as if he is approaching a wild animal. "You wanted the raw magic running through my shifter veins. You just fed on a demon's pure energy. You aren't drawn to the blood, Ava. You are drawn to the life force locked inside it."

I stare at my trembling hands. I can still feel the lightning humming in my fingertips. He is right. The blood is just the vessel, the packaging.

The truth crashes into me with a weight that almost knocks me over. I am a predator of magic. I consume the very essence of the soul. I am a monster that feeds on monsters.

Before the isolation of that reality can crush me, my tactical radio erupts with a piercing burst of static from the floor near the coffee table.

"Beta Team! Beta Team, come in!" Sam's voice screams over

the channel, frantic and raw. In the background, the deafening, rhythmic roar of automatic gunfire tears through the transmission. "We have a situation. Alpha Team is in danger. We need help!"

The feral haze snaps. The hunger doesn't vanish, but my training overrides it. I snatch the radio from the debris.

"Sam, talk to me! What's your status?"

"A massive, unknown demon just dropped into the centre of the vampire den!" Sam yells, pure terror bleeding through the speaker. "It's ten feet tall, heavily armoured, and immune to everything! It's tearing the building apart to get to us!"

"Where is Rose?" Luca demands, snatching the radio from my hand. His control is fracturing; his Alpha authority is gone, replaced by the desperate panic of a man whose beta is in danger.

"She's pinned inside the main feeding floor!" Sam shouts over another blast of gunfire. "The armoured demon cornered her! She shifted into a panther, but it's too strong! You need to get here now or she's dead!"

The radio cuts out with a sickening crunch of static and the sound of shattering glass.

Luca looks at me, his eyes wide with unadulterated panic. He is paralysed by the tactical nightmare, staring at me—his highly unstable, magic-drunk assassin—aware that I am buzzing with volatile, uncontrollable energy.

My heart stops.

Rose.

The thought of that beautiful, vibrant woman being killed, of her light being extinguished by some armoured monstrosity, sends a wave of dread through my system. Then, the dread turns into something else. A violent, protective rage consumes every rational thought in my head. My fangs ache again. My blood boils.

Nobody touches my mate. Nobody.

"Luca," I say, my voice dropping into a cold, lethal whisper that promises nothing but slaughter. I tighten my grip on my sword until the knuckles of my hand turn white. "We are going to save her. And I am going to utterly destroy that demon."

CHAPTER 21

Something Borrowed, Something Bloodthirsty

The ruined living room is a symphony of devastation. Splintered wood and shards of glass litter the floor like fallen stars in a graveyard, reflecting the dim, flickering light of the dying evening. But the loudest sound in the space isn't the crackle of my hellfire sword or the distant wail of sirens. It is the wet, ragged breathing of the human host bleeding out on the kitchen tiles.

I remain frozen in the centre of the wreckage. Time doesn't just slow; it feels as if it has curdled, sticking to me like thick syrup. My chest heaves with an exertion that makes my lungs burn, but the adrenaline coursing through my mutated veins has absolutely nothing to do with physical tiredness.

It is pure, unfiltered euphoria.

Gods, I feel electric.

My fangs are still fully extended, aching and heavy in my gums. My eyes burn with a feral, radioactive glow that pulses behind my lids every time I blink. I slowly run my tongue over my lower lip, savouring the lingering heat of the magic. My newly hijacked biology isn't just satisfied; it is screaming for another sweet, intoxicating hit of that dark energy. It feels like a drug, a narcotic that has stripped away every layer of my military discipline and left only the raw, pulsing nerve of a predator.

Luca, back in his human form, stands completely naked amidst the ruins. His broad chest rises and falls heavily, his skin glistening with a sheen of sweat that makes his muscles ripple under the light. He is appraising the broken man on the floor with a cold, calculating precision that makes my skin prickle. He isn't looking at a person; he's looking at a tactical problem.

"His injuries are catastrophic, Ava," Luca states. His deep voice carries a grim, heavy finality that usually grounds me, but right now, it sounds distant, as if he's speaking to me from the bottom of a well. "He has severe bilateral femur fractures from the impact against the wall. His chest cavity is caved in. He won't survive even if we manage to extract the demon. If we aren't already too late."

I observe the broken man. His skin is an awful, ashen yellow, a sickly hue that screams of organ failure and shock. It is painfully clear he was already dying before the parasite took up residence. His lips are tinged with the bruised blue hue of severe cyanosis, the oxygen fleeing his blood. He is drowning in his own fluids, a slow, suffocating death that fills the room with the scent of decay and iron.

I know the mechanics of this. If the demon stays, it might eventually knit the flesh back together, weaving its own necrotic energy into the man's cells to create a more efficient vessel. But by then, there won't be enough of the original human left to save. He will just be a skin-suit for something ancient and hateful.

"Destroy them both, Ava," Luca commands softly. "Then we can get to Rose and Sam to deal with this new problem."

He gestures toward the heavy silver sword gripped tightly in my right hand. The leather wrap of the hilt is damp with my sweat. As his eyes meet mine, I see it. a flicker of concern, a shadow of doubt. He sees the glow in my eyes. He knows I'm not entirely here.

"Remove the demon from this world and bring peace to the human," Luca repeats.

Give him peace.

The thought is rational. It is the merciful thing to do. It is the tactical objective. My mind, the part of me that was trained by the best in the CIA and military and all the private trainers I hired, tells me to step forward and end it. I tighten my grip on the blade, preparing to deliver a clean, swift strike to the heart.

But as I shift my weight, the intoxicating high of the demon magic continues to short-circuit my higher brain functions. My senses aren't merely heightened; they are hijacked. The man smells foul, but beneath it all, I catch the copper, salt, and raw, unfiltered energy. It is the most delicious thing I have ever encountered in my life.

Suddenly, the parasite living inside my body violently awakens. It doesn't whisper; it screams, clawing desperately at the inside of my skull with invisible talons.

Feed.

The command is primal. It bypasses every moral compass, every oath of service, every shred of humanity I have left.

I need more. Just a little taste. Just one drop to quiet the noise.

My sword arm drops limply to my side. The blade, which had felt like an extension of my will seconds ago, now feels heavy and useless, a piece of scrap metal that has no place in this moment. I don't raise it to strike. Instead, I drop into a low, predatory crouch, my centre of gravity shifting with a fluid, inhuman grace. My muscles coil like high-tension steel springs, humming with a lethal energy that threatens to burst through my skin.

A guttural, inhuman purr vibrates deep in my throat, a sound I didn't know I could make. I stalk toward the bleeding man, each step silent and deliberate. I can see it now. the frantic, erratic flutter of his carotid artery, struggling to pump the last remaining drops of blood through his failing system. The vein is a pulsing blue line against the yellow skin. It looks so... vulnerable. So inviting.

"Ava!" Luca warns.

His tone shifts instantly from tactical command to sharp, jagged alarm. He recognises the look in my eyes. He knows the predator has replaced the soldier. "What are you doing? Use the sword!"

I ignore him. I can't hear him, not really. The rational, human part of my brain is screaming from behind a thick pane of soundproof glass, watching in horror as I move closer. But the monster has entirely taken the wheel. I reach the human, leaning down until my shadow swallows his trembling form. My jaw unhinges slightly, my elongated canines zeroing in on that pulsing vein.

"Ava, stop!"

A massive weight slams forcefully into my side.

Luca tackles me away from the dying host with every ounce of his shifter strength. The impact is brutal. We crash hard onto the splintered floorboards, rolling through a sea of debris and broken glass. I feel shards slicing into my skin, but I don't care about the pain. The interruption triggers a blinding, white-hot rage.

I am no longer Ava Bekke. I am a creature of teeth, hunger, and instinct.

I twist my body with terrifying velocity, kicking out with my combat boots to break his hold. My heel connects with his ribs with a sickening thud, but Luca grunts and absorbs the blow. His dense shifter muscles refuse to yield. He scrambles to gain the upper hand, pinning my shoulders firmly to the ground with his heavy knees. He uses his weight as a physical anchor, trying to drag me back from the ledge of insanity.

I snarl, thrashing wildly against him. My hands grip his forearms, and I am momentarily astonished by my own strength. I can literally feel the dense bones in his arms beginning to bend under the crushing pressure of my grip.

"Snap out of it!" Luca roars. His dark eyes are blazing with a mixture of terror and fierce determination. "You are not a monster! Fight it, Ava! Fight the hunger, the need."

"Let me go!" I hiss. The voice isn't mine. It is deep, dark, and utterly demonic, sounding as if it were being dragged through gravel and blood.

"Think of Rose!" Luca screams.

His voice cracks with desperate authority, the name acting like a thunderclap in the silence of my mind. "Think of exactly what Rose would see right now! Do you want her to look at you and see a feral beast, feeding on a dying innocent? Not only that, Rose is also in danger! She needs you to pull yourself together!"

Rose.

That single, beautiful name hits me like a jolt of pure electricity, racing through my faltering heart. The suffocating, blood-red haze that had clouded my vision dissipates instantly, shredded by the thought of her. The memory of her brilliant green eyes floods my mind. I can't help but recall the moment I sank my new fangs into her neck.

The shame is immediate and crushing. It hits me harder than Luca's tackle ever could.

I stop fighting. My body goes entirely limp against the ruined floor, the tension draining out of me as if a plug had been pulled. A ragged, devastating sob tears its way up my raw throat, tasting of salt and failure.

"I am sorry," I gasp, squeezing my eyes shut. Hot tears burn my cold cheeks, carving tracks through the dust and blood on my face. "Gods, Luca. I am so sorry. I completely lost control."

Luca instantly releases my shoulders, stepping back to give me space. He wipes a hand down his face, his chest heaving as he tries to regulate his breathing.

"It is the magic," he says, his voice returning to that calm, Alpha cadence. "It acts like a highly addictive narcotic on your new system. You have to lock that craving down. Deep down. If you let it in, it will eat everything you are until there is nothing left but the hunger."

I push myself up onto my hands and knees, trembling violently. Every muscle in my body feels overstretched, like a rubber band about to snap. In the kitchen, the human host takes one last, gurgling exhale. The sound is small, pathetic, and final. His erratic heartbeat ceases completely.

I watch with a hollow feeling as the demon within the body

begins to stir. No longer held back by the dying man's will or biological functions, it starts to ripple under the skin. It is a grotesque, restless movement, like maggots shifting under a layer of wax.

I move swiftly, grabbing my sword where it lay discarded in the dust. Without hesitation, I thrust the blade through the man's heart. I feel the resistance of the ribs and then the slide of silver into necrotic flesh. In a burst of white light, both human and demon dissolve into a cloud of silent ash.

Yet, even as the darkness settles and the room goes quiet, a traitorous part of me whispers in the back of my mind. *What a waste of energy.*

I swallow the bitter taste of ash and self-loathing. I can't look at Luca. "I need to get you some clothes," I mutter, desperately seeking any task, any routine, to calm my chaotic mind. "You cannot run around the city naked. I will go to the SUV."

"Be careful," Luca warns, slowly rising to his feet and shielding his modesty with a piece of wreckage. "Our backup team is securing the perimeter. Do not let the scent of their blood trigger another episode."

I nod sharply. I turn toward the shattered front door and activate my mutated physiology. The world around me instantly slows to an agonising, beautiful crawl. It is a cinematic shift; dust motes hang suspended in the still air like tiny diamonds frozen in amber. The sound of Luca's breathing stretches into a deep, distorted drone, like the humming of a distant engine.

I propel myself forward. The sheer, explosive speed is breathtaking. I am a blur of motion, gliding silently past the rusted gates of the property. As I move, I notice two backup agents maintaining their tactical positions near the alleyway entrance. They are statues in my world, their eyes frozen in mid-blink.

My heightened senses immediately lock onto them. I can hear it. the rhythmic, pulsing sound of their hearts. Thump. Thump. Thump. The scent of their warm, living blood wafts toward me on the hot evening breeze, a siren song that makes my fangs throb with a painful, phantom ache.

No.

I grit my teeth, forcing myself to focus on the image of Rose's smile. *You are the Destroyer, not a parasite. You are a soldier. Get it together, Bekke.*

I force my gaze away, sealing a mental iron vault over the hunger. I rush past the agents so quickly they might only feel a faint gust of displaced wind rustling their tactical vests. I reach the SUV in a fraction of a second, grab a pair of dark trousers and a black T-shirt from Luca's duffel bag, and sprint back into the house before they even have time to register that something has moved.

I toss the bundle of clothes to Luca. He dresses swiftly, his face a mask of intense focus. He doesn't thank me; he knows I did it for my own sanity as much as for his modesty.

"Are you mentally secure enough to proceed?" he asks, his dark eyes searching mine for any sign of the beast.

"I am locked in," I confirm. My voice has returned to its familiar, cold, and detached cadence. The warrior is back on duty. "Let us go hunt some vampires and a demon."

We exit the building at a normal pace, joining our team members who are still scanning the perimeter with their rifles raised. We pile into the car, and Luca floors the accelerator, the engine roaring as we speed toward Sam's position across town.

As we navigate the dark streets of Jackson, we are forced to switch on our official lights. The red and blue strobes paint the city in jarring colours, signalling law enforcement that we are on official business. We race through red lights at well over the limit, the world blurring outside the windows.

I retrieve my phone from my tactical pouch and type a message to Rose. My fingers tremble slightly as I hit send, even though I know she won't receive it while she is in her panther form.

We are coming, stay safe.

I stare at the screen, watching the "delivered" icon appear, waiting for a response that I know won't come. A cold realisation settles in my gut. Rose is more than just a partner or a romantic interest. She is my anchor. She is the only thing keeping me from drifting into total, abyssal darkness.

As I sit in the car with nothing to occupy my mind but the hum of the tyres on the asphalt, a sudden wave of emotion crashes over me. It isn't mine. It is cold, sharp, and absolutely terrifying. Through our bond, I feel her fear. It's not the fear of death, but the fear of something overwhelming, a suffocating pressure that makes my own breath hitch in my throat.

"Hang on, Rose," I whisper to the empty air. "I'm coming for you."

We spot Sam crouched behind a rusted dumpster near the loading docks of the meat-packing plant. The area smells of old blood and industrial cleanser, a cloying scent that makes me want to gag. He is clutching his suppressed rifle, eyes scanning the dark warehouses. Normally, he'd need night-vision goggles to navigate this gloom, but because he's wearing the magical silver ring—a gift from Papa Legba—he can see perfectly in the dark.

My new mutated eyes track him even better than the ring ever could; I can see the heat radiating off his skin and the slight tremor in his hands.

"Took you long enough," Sam whispers as we approach, his voice tight with tension. "I was beginning to wonder if the Alpha decided to take a naked stroll through downtown Jackson."

"Very funny, Sam," Luca deadpans.

Without another word, Luca begins to strip his clothes off again. He doesn't do it for show; he does it because the shift is more efficient without fabric in the way.

"What is the tactical layout?" Luca asks.

"Thermal imaging shows a cluster of eight cold signatures inside the main warehouse," Sam reports, his tone turning crisp and professional. "Vampires. Definitely. No human hostages in this sector. It looks like a staging area. We were just finishing off the last vampires when Rose was trapped with our team in the room between the hostages and the reinforcements. Since that demon showed up, more vampires have arrived to bolster their numbers."

"At least eight targets. No collateral damage to worry about," I say, rolling my shoulders to loosen the tension. I reach back and draw my sword. The metal sings softly as it leaves its sheath, a high-pitched chime that signals the start of the slaughter. "We breach fast and hard. Leave no survivors."

Luca's shift begins. It is a violent process, his body expanding with a series of wet, heavy cracks. His bones snap and reform, his skin darkening into sleek fur. Within seconds, a massive midnight-black panther stands where the man once was.

I move forward with Sam at my back. We approach the steel service door, the metal cold and pitted with rust. I carefully slide it open. Trying to be as quiet as possible. I fail as the old door makes a screeching noise, so I just yank the door to the side and rush in.

The cavernous room seems empty for a heartbeat, and then eight vampires surge from the shadows like ink spilt on paper. Their faces are contorted into feral masks of rage, their lips pulled back to reveal jagged fangs. None of them seem to be "born" vampires; they all appear turned, their eyes glowing a sickly, necrotic crimson beneath the flickering fluorescent lights that buzz overhead.

"Take them!" the lead vampire shouts, launching himself through the air with unnatural speed.

He is quick, but I am something else entirely.

The world reverts to that glorious, slow-motion crawl. I glide effortlessly to the side, avoiding his outstretched claws by a hair's breadth. The wind of his passing ruffles my ponytail. In one fluid motion, I swing my silver blade in a brutal, upward arc. The metal slices through his collarbone and neck with zero resistance, as if he were made of wet paper.

His severed head hits the concrete with a dull thud, and his body instantly combusts into ash before he even realises he is dead.

Sam opens fire from the doorway. The suppressed pop-pop-pop of his weapon echoes through the room. He uses specialised wooden rounds coated in silver nitrate—perfect for dealing with most shifters and vampires. Two more vampires take multiple rounds to the chest, their bodies jerking violently as the wood burns them from the inside out before they collapse into piles of grey dust.

Luca's massive form crashes into a female vampire with the force of an articulated lorry. He pins her to the concrete, his enormous jaws clamping ruthlessly around her throat. There is a sickening snap of vertebrae as he breaks her spine in one fluid motion.

I engage three more hostiles at once. The combat is a beautiful, deadly dance of shadow and flame. I duck beneath a swipe from a towering male vampire, spinning on my heel to drive the glowing blade straight through his heart. The hellfire erupts upon impact, licking my skin, familiar and comforting.

I rip the sword free, pirouetting to face the next threat. A female vampire manages to grasp my arm, her unnatural strength trying to hurl me across the room. I don't even flinch. I seize her wrist, twisting it with a sharp, brutal torque until the bone audibly shatters. She screams in agony, a high-pitched sound that is cut short when I drive the hilt of my sword into her temple. Before she can fall, I finish her with a precise thrust through the chest.

Within thirty seconds, the room falls silent. Piles of smouldering ash are the only evidence they ever existed. The air is thick with the smell of burnt ozone and sulphur.

"Clear," Sam announces, lowering his smoking weapon. "That went better than I expected."

Before we can even draw a breath to celebrate, the atmosphere shifts. A roar echoes through the far wall, a sound so primal it vibrates in my bones and makes my teeth ache. Then, the reinforced concrete wall explodes.

A dark mass hurtles through the debris, sending dust and rubble flying everywhere. My heart stops. Through the settling grit, I see the features of a panther.

"Rose!" I scream.

The demon must have caught her and thrown her like a rag doll. My stomach drops into a void of pure terror. *Please, gods, let her be alive. Please don't let her be broken.*

"Sam, I think that was Rose! Check on her!" I yell, my voice cracking with an emotion I can no longer suppress.

I feel the shock ripple through Luca and Sam. Even Luca's panther form lets out a low, mournful whine before he braces himself. I drop into a defensive stance, raising my sword to guard my chest just as a colossal figure steps into the flickering light of the warehouse.

My breath hitches.

It is a demon unlike anything I have ever seen. Standing over ten feet tall, its entire body is encased in thick, black armour engraved with glowing, blood-red runes that pulse with a malevolent rhythm, like a beating heart of fire. A heavy, horned helmet obscures its face, leaving only two burning amber eyes visible through the narrow visor.

"I am Eligos," the demon rumbles. Its voice is a catastrophic earthquake, vibrating with the echoes of a thousand tortured souls. "A Great Duke of the Pit. Summoned from the deepest trenches of despair."

"I do not care about your royal titles," I spit. My bravado is a thin veil masking a spike of genuine, icy fear. I can feel the power radiating off him; it makes the air feel heavy, as if we are underwater. "You die today."

I don't wait for a response. I propel myself forward at maximum speed, swinging my sword with every ounce of my newly acquired Dhampir strength in a lethal, decapitating strike aimed at the demon's neck.

The silver blade connects with the armour, and then the world breaks.

A deafening, concussive shockwave erupts from the point of impact. The magical hellfire coating my blade clashes against the red runes, but instead of burning them, the runes flare brilliantly, absorbing the fire and snuffing it out instantly. It is as if he just inhaled my attack.

The recoil is devastating.

A brutal, jarring vibration shoots up my arm, shaking me to my core. I hear the sickening, sharp crack of my radius and ulna fracturing under the immense pressure. A scream of pure agony rips from my throat as the silver sword is violently deflected, flying from my numb fingers to clatter uselessly across the concrete floor.

"Pathetic," Eligos scoffs.

The demon swings a massive, armoured backhand. The strike hits me directly in the ribs, thankfully he didn't use the weapon he is holding, that looks like something a modern caveman would use. It feels like being hit by a tank. I am launched through the air, crashing into a thick metal support pillar twenty feet away.

I hit the concrete hard. Pain, bright and blinding, explodes across my entire left side. I spit a mouthful of thick, coppery blood onto the floor, watching it splatter against the grey stone. My ribs are definitely shattered; I can feel the jagged edges of bone grating against each other with every shallow breath.

"AVA!" screams Sam.

Luca charges, leaping through the air to deliver a crushing bite to the demon's shoulder, but Eligos barely notices the attack. He reaches up with one massive, iron-clad gauntlet, grabs the panther by the scruff of his neck, and hurls him across the room like he weighs nothing. Luca crashes into a stack of wooden crates, shattering them into splinters and hits the wall.

Sam opens fire, but the bullets merely spark harmlessly against the black armour, bouncing off like pebbles. Eligos raises a hand, sending a shockwave of dark, kinetic energy that knocks Sam off his feet, sliding him across the floor into the far wall with a dull thud.

"The one you know as Devika sent me," Eligos rumbles, taking a slow, menacing step toward my broken body. "She feared your little coven was involved, so she summoned me to ensure no other witches with hellfire could interfere. Little did she know that an extinct race was in their midst."

The demon pauses, his amber eyes narrowing as he looks down at me.

"How, after all this time, are you here? Dhampirs don't exist anymore. I thought your kind was stronger than this. I don't see why so many feared you."

I struggle to lift myself, my fractured right arm hanging limply at my side. My body is desperately trying to repair the damage, burning through energy reserves and knitting flesh, but it isn't fast enough. The pain is a white-hot roar in my ears.

"She has every right... to be terrified," I gasp, coughing up another dark splatter of blood.

"Perhaps," Eligos chuckles, a sound like grinding stones in a landslide. "But I am not here to alleviate her fears. I am merely here because I am hungry. And your mutated soul... it smells absolutely divine."

CHAPTER 22

THE DUKE OF RUIN

The heavy, oppressive stench of raw sulphur and fresh, coppery blood brutally assaults my newly heightened senses. It is not just a smell; it is an olfactory assault that feels physical, like a thick, greasy film coating the inside of my nostrils. My lungs burn with every jagged inhale, the toxic air scraping against my throat like shards of broken glass. I stand perfectly still, facing off with this walking nightmare, my chest heaving in a rhythmic, desperate struggle for oxygen. The air settles in my throat like liquid lead, heavy and suffocating.

Luca and I had raced across the dark city in a blind, feral panic after I got my shit together. When Sam's radio transmission abruptly cut out in a sickening crunch of static, I should have been out the door without a second thought. Instead, all I cared about was getting another hit. I can't help but dwell on the fact that Rose is now hurt because of my delay, and it keeps running on a loop in my mind. Now, the absolute, horrifying reality of the tactical situation completely paralyses my normally hyperactive assassin mind. For once, I am not thinking three steps ahead. I am not calculating exit strategies or identifying cover. I am simply trying to remember how to breathe.

Get it together, Ava. Breathe. Just fucking breathe.

The jagged hole in the wall through which the demon hurled Rose offers a gruesome window into the room beyond, where her team was trapped. The scene is utterly heartbreaking, a tableau of carnage that makes my stomach churn with a violent surge of nausea. It looks less like a battlefield and more like a slaughterhouse.

Before we arrived, the demon and its vampire lackeys clearly managed to decimate our elite backup team with surgical cruelty. I can see Commander Rodriguez slumped heavily against a cracked concrete load-bearing pillar. His Kevlar vest, designed to stop high-velocity rounds, is shredded like wet paper, hanging in useless strips across his torso. He is desperately clutching his left shoulder, and I can see the bright crimson blood coating his thick fingers in a slick, glistening sheen. He looks pale, his eyes glazed, likely slipping into shock.

A few yards away, Johnson is completely buried beneath a massive, jagged pile of shattered cinderblocks and twisted rebar. His weak, rhythmic groans echo pitifully through the cavernous space, sounding like a dying animal trapped in a snare. Every sound he makes is a wet, bubbling rasp that tells me his lungs are likely punctured. Several other team members are scattered across the blood-stained floor, either unconscious or severely wounded, their rifles lying discarded and utterly useless against an ancient, supernatural threat that doesn't care about ballistics or tactical training.

I turn my gaze back to Rose.

My heart ceases to beat. For a moment, there is a vacuum in my chest where my soul should be. A cold, suffocating dread violently floods my veins, temporarily overshadowing the crackling, radioactive energy rushing through them. It was definitely Rose who crashed through that wall; now she is trapped beneath the ruins of the brickwork and steel.

A massive, collapsed steel structural beam lies across her lower half, pinning her. She has been forcefully reverted to her human form, the trauma of the impact stripping away her panther skin. Her beautiful blonde hair is matted with grey dust and dark, drying blood. Her skin is terrifyingly pale, almost translucent in the flickering, dying light of the warehouse, and her breathing is painfully shallow. Each gasp is a visible struggle, her chest barely rising against the oppressive weight of the world pressing down on her.

The sheer, unadulterated thought of that vibrant, fiercely loyal woman being crushed to death injects a lethal dose of pure, toxic adrenaline directly into my system. It hits me like a lightning strike, scorching every nerve ending. My fangs ache with a sudden, violent pressure behind my gums, demanding release. My blood practically boils, turning into a pressurised stream of white-hot heat that makes my skin itch.

Nobody touches her. Nobody gets to take her from me.

Standing between me and the woman I love is a walking, breathing fortress of evil.

The towering demon takes another heavy, deliberate step toward me. The reinforced concrete floor actually trembles beneath his weight, sending rhythmic vibrations up through the soles of my combat boots and into my marrow. His iron armour clanks with a sickening, metallic finality, a horrific, grinding sound that actively grates against my highly sensitive eardrums like a serrated blade being dragged across bone.

He is an absolute juggernaut, entirely encased in thick, rune-carved iron. The glowing red symbols pulse across his heavy breastplate with a rhythmic, nauseating light, radiating waves of pure, concentrated malice that feel like a physical weight pressing against my skin, trying to force me to my knees. He is completely, undeniably immune to the hellfire sword, the weapon that has always been my ultimate trump card.

Panic, cold and sharp as a surgeon's scalpel, tries to claw its way into my mind, whispering that I am finally outmatched. I shove the terror down, locking it away behind a massive, reinforced steel door inside my psyche.

Think, Ava. You are a highly trained tactical assassin. You are not some helpless victim waiting for the slaughter. Every single suit of armour possesses a weak point. Every impenetrable fortress contains a fatal breach just waiting to be exploited.

My right arm hangs useless at my side, a testament to my arrogance. My initial strike against his glowing breastplate was a costly error, born of desperation. I had swung with all my new Dhampir strength, expecting to cleave the demon in two. Instead, the enchanted iron absorbed the force and rebounded it back into my own limb, fracturing the bones and draining my energy in one singular, violent snap. My sword lies twenty feet away, mocking me with its silver glint on the concrete. I lack the strength for a knockout blow, and I certainly don't have the reach.

Note to self. Hitting magical iron with a metal sword is a terrible life choice. Also, stop being an idiot and thinking you're invincible.

I am going to have to dismantle this walking tank piece by painful, microscopic piece.

"Your fear is a truly delicious appetiser," Eligos taunts. His voice is not human; it is a vibrating, demonic rumble that rattles my teeth in their sockets and causes the fine hairs on my arms to stand at attention. It sounds like two mountains grinding together, heavy with an ancient, sadistic glee.

He gradually lifts a heavy, spiked iron gauntlet. Pure, dark energy sharply crackles across his metal fingertips, emitting the thick, cloying smell of burning sulphur and ozone. It is a terrifying display of raw, unfiltered magical power that makes the air around him shimmer with heat, distorting the image of the ruins behind him.

"I am not afraid of an overgrown, pathetic walking tin can," I spit. I wipe a thick smear of crimson blood from my chin with the back of my good left hand, my voice steady despite the chaos in my chest. I force a smirk, even though every nerve in my body is screaming for me to run. "Is that all you have, your grace? I expected a Duke of Hell to hit a little harder. My grandmother swings a heavier purse."

Eligos releases a guttural, mocking laugh that sounds like tectonic plates shifting beneath the earth. "Brave words from a fragile, broken little insect. I will thoroughly enjoy peeling the flesh from your bones before I consume the souls of your pathetic friends. Your mutated blood smells fascinating, little Dhampir. Devika will reward me handsomely for your severed head."

He lunges.

Despite his enormous, hulking size and the ridiculous, crushing weight of his heavy iron armour, he moves with a terrifying, unnatural speed that defies physics. He is a blur of black iron and red light. He sweeps his massive, armoured arm in a brutal, horizontal arc, aiming to completely crush my skull into fine, bloody powder.

Time slows to a thick, viscous crawl. The world around me sharpens into high-definition, hyper-focused clarity. I can see the individual sparks of dark energy dancing off his knuckles like dying stars. I drop completely flat onto the concrete floor, feeling the violent, roaring rush of displaced air whistle right over the top of my head.

The sheer force of his missed strike shatters a nearby wooden crate into a million tiny splinters that rain down around me like lethal confetti. The sound is an explosion of wood and nails. I roll rapidly across the gritty, blood-slicked floor, sliding smoothly right past his heavily armoured legs, the smell of old oil and demon sweat filling my nose.

I spring to my feet on his left side, my eyes scanning for any vulnerability in the iron shell. My right arm is still useless, the bone actively fusing together in a haze of burning nerve pain that makes me want to scream into the void. I rely entirely on my left hand and my rapid, evasive footwork, dancing on the edge of death.

I pivot sharply, driving a lightning-fast left hook directly into the exposed, unarmoured joint of his elbow. The impact is jarring; I feel the cartilage crunch beneath my knuckles like dry twigs. Eligos grunts, his massive arm flinching slightly, his swing going wide and smashing into a concrete pillar instead. The pillar cracks, spiderwebbing under the force, but it is a victory nonetheless. A tiny, microscopic fraction of damage, but it's more than I had a second ago.

He backhands blindly in retaliation. I duck underneath the

massive iron fist, the spiked knuckles grazing the very top of my scalp with enough force to make my vision swim with white spots. I instantly retaliate with a brutal, driving kick to the back of his ankle, specifically targeting the vulnerable Achilles tendon just below his heavy greave.

Pain shoots violently up my own tibia, my bones actively screaming under the intense pressure of the impact, but the demon actually stumbles. His footing is compromised for a heartbeat, his massive weight working against him.

Death by a thousand tiny, annoying papercuts. You can do this, Ava.

Eligos roars in raw, unfiltered frustration, a sound that vibrates through the very foundations of the warehouse and makes the remaining glass in the windows shatter. He ceases his slow, sweeping strikes and starts violently stomping the concrete floor, desperately trying to crush me under his massive boots like an insect.

I dance backwards, my movements fluid and feral, tapping into the predatory instincts that come with my blood. I weave between his clumsy, heavy attacks, darting in to deliver rapid, shallow strikes wherever I find a gap in the rune-carved iron. A sharp jab to the armpit. A sweeping kick to the inner thigh. A brutal, open-palmed strike to the side of his heavy knee.

Every single hit sends a shockwave of agonising pain rebounding through my healing body, but I relentlessly push the agony away. I am completely running on toxic adrenaline and the desperate, burning need to protect Rose. If he breathes one more word about her, I will find a way to rip his heart out through his throat.

My breathing is ragged, tearing violently through my throat as if I'm inhaling shards of glass. My muscles scream in protest as my shattered ribs continue their miraculous, excruciating regeneration. I can feel the bone knitting together, the friction causing an internal heat that feels like a fever. I am bleeding from a dozen tiny lacerations, my clothes are torn and ruined, but I am keeping the monster entirely focused on me.

I am the bait, and I will play the part until he's dead.

"Stand still, you wretched pest!" Eligos bellows. He swings both massive fists downward in a devastating, hammer-like blow that permanently shatters the concrete floor where I was standing a mere microsecond ago. The impact sends a cloud of dust and pulverised stone into my eyes, blinding me for a heartbeat.

As I throw myself backwards to avoid the crushing impact, my newly heightened auditory senses detect a subtle, distinct change in the chaotic environment. Beneath the ringing of metal and the groans of the dying, I hear a familiar, rhythmic sound.

A heartbeat.

It is incredibly strong, rapidly accelerating, pumping highly oxygenated blood through a massive, powerful frame. I inhale deeply, completely ignoring the toxic sulphur, and catch the distinct, musky scent of a panther. It is a smell of rain-soaked earth and predatory power.

I glance quickly out of the corner of my eye toward the large, splintered pile of wooden shipping crates to my right. Luca had been buried there, temporarily stunned from that brutal backhand earlier in the fight.

Through the thick haze of dust and debris, I can see him. His eyes are completely open and look feral, golden and glowing in the gloom like two miniature suns. He is awake. He is actively watching the fight, his intense gaze tracking my every rapid movement with lethal, predatory intelligence. He is utterly motionless, hiding his newly restored consciousness from the raging demon currently tearing up the floor.

A silent, tactical understanding instantly passes between us. No words are needed; we've done this a hundred times in training, mirroring each other's movements until we were one entity. He is the heavy hitter. I am the distraction. He just needs a clear, unprotected target.

Time to finish this, buddy.

I stop dancing away. I deliberately plant my combat boots firmly onto the cracked concrete, directly in the monster's path. I make myself look vulnerable, a tempting target for his rage, dropping my guard just enough to entice him.

Eligos sneers, his glowing eyes flaring with triumphant, sadistic joy. He thinks he has me. He raises a heavy iron boot, fully intending to kick my fragile body entirely across the cavernous room hoping to shatter my body in the process.

I wait until the very last possible millisecond. As his massive leg starts its forward movement, shifting all his considerable weight onto his remaining standing leg, I move.

I drop extremely low, using my new speed to its full, terrifying maximum. I slide effortlessly beneath his raised boot, aiming for the pivot point of his stance. I pivot sharply on my heel, harnessing every ounce of my remaining body weight and momentum into a single, devastating blow. I forcefully drive my heavy left combat boot into the back of his standing knee joint.

The force of the impact is utterly staggering. It feels just like kicking a solid, reinforced concrete pillar at sixty miles an hour. Sharp, blinding pain shoots violently up my tibia, threatening to completely fracture my leg, but the precisely calculated strike hits the tiny, unarmoured gap perfectly.

Eligos releases a wet, guttural grunt of shock. His thick, armoured leg buckles under the immense pressure. He completely loses his balance, his heavy knee slamming into the concrete with a loud, cracking thud that reverberates through the entire building.

I refuse to give the ancient monster even a fraction of a second to recover his footing. I aggressively leap onto his broad, iron-clad back, wrapping my legs tightly around his waist to secure my grip. I grasp the heavy, horned helm with my functioning left hand, digging my fingers into the gaps of the metal. My right arm is now mostly healed, the deep bone ache fading to a dull, throbbing burn, so I raise that hand as well, gripping the cold iron horns with both hands.

I need to reveal the vulnerable, pallid flesh of his throat concealed beneath the thick metal gorget. If I can just pull it back an inch, we have him.

"Get off me, you pathetic insect!" Eligos roars, thrashing his massive body violently from side to side in a desperate attempt to shake me off him like I'm a flea.

He throws himself backwards with terrifying speed, slamming his armoured back forcefully against the nearest structural metal scaffolding. The brutal, unforgiving impact instantly crushes the limited breath right out of my healing lungs, pinning me between the cold, unyielding steel beams and the armour on his back.

My vision flashes a blinding, brilliant white as fresh, searing agony washes through my body. I can actually hear another healing rib snap under the immense, crushing pressure, the sound like a dry branch breaking in winter. I absolutely refuse to let go of his helm. My knuckles are white, my muscles screaming, but I hold on.

I am Ava Bekke. I am the Destroyer. I do not yield to anyone, especially not some arrogant, oversized demon who thinks he can brutally slaughter my team and touch my mate.

I channel every ounce of the terrifying, feral energy currently simmering hot in my veins. I summon the same dark, predatory strength that nearly made me violently tear Rose's beautiful throat out days ago. I fully embrace the monster lurking inside me, letting it take the wheel. I concentrate all that chaotic, lethal power into the muscles of my arms and hands.

The ancient, enchanted metal of his helmet actively groans under the immense, inhuman pressure I am applying. The glowing red runes flare a blinding, angry crimson, aggressively trying to magically repel my physical touch with bursts of heat. But his demonic magic is specifically designed to absorb magical attacks, not raw, unadulterated, physical force.

Physics wins today, you ugly bastard.

With a sickening, high-pitched metallic screech, the thick iron rivets securing the heavy gorget to the breastplate completely snap under the immense strain. The heavy horned helmet is wrenched backwards, finally exposing a thick, vulnerable band of pale, sickly grey flesh at the demon's throat.

"LUCA!" I shout, the loudness straining my vocal cords and making them raw.

The large pile of splintered wood across the floor suddenly erupts in a massive shower of sharp debris. The colossal black panther catapults his highly muscular body high into the dim, dusty air, a shadow blocking out what little light remained. Luca effortlessly covers the twenty feet between us in a single, devastatingly beautiful leap, his powerful jaws wide open in a silent roar of pure fury.

He aims his lethal, precision strike directly for the exposed, fleshy gap I just forcefully created. His powerful jaws clamp down incredibly hard, delivering thousands of pounds of crushing, lethal pressure directly onto the demon's exposed jugular. The sickening, wet crunch of tearing thick cartilage and snapping cervical bone echoes loudly through the cavernous warehouse, completely drowning out the pained groans of our injured team members.

Eligos emits a wet, gurgling, horrific shriek that sends a freezing, jagged shiver racing swiftly down my spine. The towering Duke of Hell collapses heavily to his knees, the fight leaving him in an instant. His armoured hands immediately release his weapon, desperately clawing at the panther's thick, muscular neck, frantic to dislodge the Alpha's lethal, locked grip.

I instantly drop from the demon's broad back, landing heavily but perfectly balanced on the thick soles of my combat boots. A quick internal diagnostic scan confirms my right arm is now mostly healed; the fractured radius has magically fused back together, though the surrounding traumatised muscle tissue actively screams in burning protest with every tiny movement. I simply do not care. The pain is just a temporary, highly annoying distraction.

I sprint across the blood-stained, slippery floor, dropping into a smooth, low tactical slide to retrieve my discarded sword. I can feel the grit of the concrete scraping against my hip, but it doesn't matter.

I quickly snatch the worn leather hilt directly from the gritty concrete, the familiar, comforting weight of the weapon instantly grounding my chaotic thoughts. I don't attempt to summon the crackling hellfire again; the magical flames are entirely useless against his rune-carved armour. But the pure silver of the blade itself is still a highly lethal weapon against his ancient demonic flesh.

I charge back towards the struggling, groaning behemoth. Luca stubbornly maintains his brutal, suffocating grip, entirely pinning the demon's heavy head backwards to keep the pale throat exposed. He looks like a god of death in that moment, sleek and merciless.

"Time to go back to hell," I snarl.

I draw the sword backwards, then drive the gleaming silver blade straight upward in a flawless, lethal arc. I bypass the heavy iron breastplate entirely, thrusting the razor-sharp sword directly up into the soft, unarmoured gap located right beneath the demon's thick, fleshy jawline. The blade slides effortlessly deep, piercing straight through the soft palate and directly into his demonic brain matter.

Eligos goes terrifyingly rigid. His glowing, crimson eyes widen in absolute, unadulterated, stunned shock. The pulsing red runes carved deep into his heavy armour rapidly flicker, dimming like dying embers in a rainstorm, before fading completely to dull, lifeless, ordinary iron.

I press a heavy, blood-soaked boot firmly against his massive chest as I grip his chest plate with my left hand and tear the blade free with a wet, sickening suck. The towering demon collapses onto the concrete floor with a thunderous, earth-shaking crash that jars the building, sending more debris down on us all.

Thick, foul black ichor quickly spreads around the ruined helmet, emitting a strong stench of rotting flesh and ancient decay. Interestingly, the body does not immediately turn to ash as lower-level demons do; perhaps his enchanted, heavy armour is actively preventing rapid magical decomposition, or high-level demons just don't turn to ash, but the dark, ancient entity inside is undeniably and permanently dead.

I heavily drop to my knees, my chest rapidly heaving as I desperately drag much-needed oxygen into my burning lungs. The bloody sword slips from my exhausted, trembling grasp, clattering loudly against the concrete floor. My entire body is shaking violently from the overwhelming adrenaline dump and the lingering, burning agony of my rapid regeneration.

Across the lifeless corpse, Luca fluidly shifts back into his human form. He kneels heavily on the floor, completely clad in his birthday suit, aggressively spitting a thick mouthful of foul, toxic black demon blood onto the concrete. He looks absolutely wrecked; his broad, muscular chest is heavily covered in dark purple bruises and deep, bleeding lacerations from the demon's heavy claws, but he is breathing. He is alive, and that is all that truly matters right now.

Sam slowly limps over to our position, tightly clutching his left side with a grimace of pure agony. His usually pragmatic, calm face is deathly pale, heavily covered in a fine sheen of cold sweat, but a profound wave of relief significantly softens his rigid features.

"Well, that was entirely too close for comfort," Sam gasps out, his voice a hoarse, ragged wheeze. "I really thought we were all going to die when our weapons did absolutely nothing to that thick armour."

"Are you okay?" I ask, watching him try to avoid putting weight on one leg.

"I'll be fine, had worse," he replies, showing the typical stoicism of an agent.

"We need to report this massive escalation to Agent Moore immediately," Luca says. His deep voice is a harsh, breathless rasp as he reaches blindly for a discarded tactical jacket lying nearby to quickly cover his nakedness before he looks for his clothes. He wipes a thick smear of black ichor from his strong jawline, his dark eyes fixed intently on the dead Duke. "Whatever ancient, malevolent entity is currently possessing Devika, can actually summon high-ranking Dukes of Hell into our world. She is infinitely more powerful and strategically more connected than our initial intelligence ever indicated."

"Whatever she is planning in this city, we need to end it as soon as possible," I add, pushing myself slowly to my feet. Every single joint pops in loud, painful protest, a symphony of clicking bone. "She is bringing in the heavy artillery. This is a wake-up call."

Luca pauses, looking out over the devastated warehouse floor. "If we do not move on her location soon, we will completely miss our tactical window. If we give her any more time to prepare, she might summon a dozen more Dukes. Or worse, she might actually possess the dark power to summon an actual Prince of Hell. Whatever catastrophic, world-ending operation they have going on here in Jackson is much bigger than we originally anticipated. We will never get close to Devika if she surrounds herself with an entire legion of these heavily armoured bastards."

I stare blankly at the lifeless, iron-clad corpse leaking toxic sludge onto the floor. We actually survived. We won this specific, brutal battle through sheer luck, desperate tactical evasion and teamwork. The horrific, overwhelming reality of the hidden war we are actively fighting settles heavily onto my aching shoulders like a thick lead blanket soaked in icy water. We are continuously dancing on the bleeding edge of a razor blade, and it feels exactly like every single tactical victory only brings us one step closer to our own absolute annihilation.

"Let us get the hell out of here," I mutter, turning my frantic gaze away from the massive demon and scanning the destroyed room. My immediate focus zeroes in on the far brick wall. "We desperately need to get Rose some medical help. Sam, please go check on Commander Rodriguez and Johnson. We need a full casualty report."

"I am on it," Sam replies. "Rose seems okay; I think she was just knocked out from the impact," he says as he begins limping towards the fallen Commander, quickly retrieving a small trauma medical kit from his tactical bag.

I rush across the slippery floor towards the fallen steel beam where Rose lies. *Please be okay,* I tell myself as panic starts to choke me, more terrifying than any demon. My head is ringing from the brutal impact against the steel scaffolding; my heightened hearing is completely gone, replaced by a high-pitched whine. I can't hear her heartbeat, and I can't feel a single damn thing radiating through our bond because of the overwhelming static of my own terrifying fear.

For the very first time since my terrifying transformation, the sudden thought of Rose does not evoke a suffocating wave of anxious dread or the sickening fear of her rejection. Instead, it sparks a fierce, desperate, clingy hope. We have just survived a literal Duke of Hell. If we can overcome that monstrous impossibility, we will surely find a tactical way to endure whatever impossible nightmare lies ahead.

I drop to my knees beside the heavy steel beam. Thankfully, it didn't crush her; luckily, some of the debris from the wall stopped the beam from flattening her completely. "Rose," I say urgently, my trembling hands hovering over her pale face, afraid that touching her might break her further. "Rose, baby, can you hear me?"

Her beautiful green eyes flutter open, completely unfocused and hazy with deep pain. A weak, bloody cough escapes her dry lips, spraying a small amount of red on her chin. "Ava? Did you... did you kill it?"

"We killed it," I assure her, gently brushing a lock of dirty blonde hair away from her sweaty forehead. My hand is shaking, but my voice is tender. "You are safe now. I am going to get this beam off you. It is going to hurt, but I need you to stay completely still."

She gives a tiny, almost imperceptible nod. I wedge my hands beneath the cold, unforgiving steel, feeling the metal bite into my palms. I brace my combat boots against the concrete floor, ignoring the screaming protest of my recently healed arm and a few ribs, and the biting pain as my remaining broken ribs dig in. I tap into that dark, feral well of supernatural strength, feeling it surge from the base of my spine to my fingertips.

With a loud, grinding screech of metal violently sliding against concrete, I heave the massive beam upward. It is incredibly heavy, several tons of dead weight, but my mutated muscles flare with unnatural power, lifting it just high enough for someone to slip through.

Luca is there in a fraction of a second, his strong hands gently grasping Rose's shoulders and rapidly pulling her out from under the beam. The second she is completely clear, I let the heavy steel beam drop back to the floor with a loud, ringing crash that makes us all jump.

"Are you okay?" I ask frantically, scrambling over to where Luca has laid her carefully on the ground and wrapping a towel around her from Sam's bag to stop the shivering.

"Nothing feels broken," Rose gasps, tightly clutching her bruised ribs with a wince. "My panther absorbed the worst of the brutal impact. I am just incredibly bruised."

A massive, profound wave of relief washes completely over me, washing away the lingering traces of deep fear and leaving me feeling hollowed out and exhausted. I gently lean down and press my forehead against hers, closing my eyes. "I thought I lost you," I whisper, my voice cracking with raw, unfiltered emotion.

"You cannot get rid of me that easily, Destroyer," she murmurs back, a weak, beautiful smile gracing her lips. She lifts a trembling hand and rests it softly against my cheek, her thumb gently stroking my skin. The simple, affectionate touch sends a warm spark of pure electricity straight to my beating heart, anchoring me to the earth.

"Commander Rodriguez is stable," Sam calls out from across the room, interrupting our quiet moment. "His shoulder is severely dislocated, and he has a deep muscular laceration, but his pulse is strong. He will live. Johnson has a compound fracture of his left leg and a punctured lung, but he is conscious. I have released the pressure in his chest, but he will need surgery as soon as possible. The rest of the backup team sustained minor injuries, mostly concussions and severe contusions, but there are no actual casualties."

"Thank the gods," Luca sighs, running a hand through his messy dark hair, looking every bit the exhausted Alpha.

I carefully help Rose sit up, wrapping my arm securely around her waist to support her weight. The affectionate, grounding physical contact is exactly what my frayed nerves desperately need right now. I can feel the heat of her body against mine, and it's the only thing that feels real in this nightmare.

"Sam, call for Doctor Stevens to come here and to bring transport," I order, my voice easily returning to its usual, crisp tactical cadence. The soldier is back, but she is holding onto the woman she loves with everything she has. "We need to get our people out of here and scrub this site completely clean before the local authorities catch wind of what happened here and turn up before we get rid of anything we need to keep secret."

"You mean like a massive dead Duke. On it, boss," Sam replies, tapping furiously on his encrypted phone.

I glance around the utterly ruined warehouse once more. The air remains heavy with the metallic smell of blood and the stale, foul odour of demonic magic. We have survived the Duke of Hell today, but the chilling truth of Luca's words echoes grimly in my mind. Devika is actively worsening this bloody conflict. She is purposefully ripping holes in the fabric of our reality, summoning immensely powerful, ancient monsters into our world.

We are completely outgunned and severely outmanned. If we do not permanently shut down this demonic operation soon, we will not only lose the city of Jackson but also the entire world.

"What are we going to do with that?" Rose asks as I help her towards the door, nodding toward the iron corpse.

"I have an idea. Luca, can you help Rose for a minute, please?" I ask.

"Sure," Luca says, stepping in to support her while I head off to retrieve my sword.

The demon lies motionless before me, its armour finally dull and lifeless after its demise. I grasp my sword tightly, anticipation coursing through me as I approach the body.

With the phrase *Reya setup*, I activate the sword, the blade igniting into vibrant flames that seem to dance with a mind of their own. I hold it near the demon, watching closely for any signs of a reaction from the armour. When nothing happens, I breathe a sigh of relief and carefully bring the tip of the blazing sword toward the demon's flesh.

As I slide the blade past the armour, it glides effortlessly, and I thrust it deep into the demon's body. The moment the blade makes contact, an unexpected rush of heat radiates from the wound. The flesh ignites spontaneously, flames consuming the body with a ferocity that takes me by surprise. It's as if I've poured gasoline onto a fire; the flames spread rapidly, engulfing the demon in moments, turning the black ichor into steaming vapour.

A sharp *woosh* fills the air as the body disintegrates into nothingness, leaving only the empty, charred armour behind and a large pile of grey ash that settles on the ground. I step back, watching as the last remnants of the demon fade away, as the smell of smoke and sulphur lingers in the air like a ghost.

I follow Luca and Rose outside and sit next to where Luca deposited her so he can head back in to help Sam with the rest of the team; the other two members of our team that were with us have also come to help and are going to help the captives in the basement of the warehouse.

"Lead them out the other side of the building, please. I will message the Chief of Police to meet you there to help them," I say to the guys as they head in. I pull out my phone and send off a message to the Chief with a quick explanation saying a gang of cultists held some prisoners, and we have just rescued them, and they need help. It is a lie, but it's a lie that keeps the world spinning.

"We'd better remove the armour before the locals get here," I say to nobody in particular.

"I'll make sure it's done, just look after Rose for now and rest, you were badly injured in there," Luca says as he reappears with another team member.

"You're injured?" Rose asks as she scans my body, her eyes searching for the wounds I'm trying to hide.

"I will live, I seem to heal quickly now, wish I did when that wolf almost killed me," I say and give her a small smile, though it doesn't quite reach my eyes.

"Thank you… Sorry, I've been a bitch. Are you sure you're okay? Everyone is bloody, and you're not reacting?" Rose asks, looking a little worried as our team members are brought out covered in blood, their faces masks of shock and pain.

"We discovered earlier that my true longing wasn't for the blood itself, but rather for the magic that courses through it. Being surrounded by so much of it in that warehouse and feeling a surge of panic over your safety, I somehow managed to close a door on my new body's needs and wants for now. It's almost comical when I think about it. Luca merely had to lock me in a blood-soaked room and threaten your life, and suddenly, I felt oddly at ease. It's as if my desire to protect you superseded everything else."

I half-joke about it, but the unease wells up within me as I glance at Rose, anxious about how she'll take my twisted sense of humour. I am a monster who finds peace in threats and blood; I wonder if that is something she can ever truly love.

She leans heavily against my side, her bright green eyes vividly reflecting a mixture of deep exhaustion and fierce, unyielding determination. "I don't really think you would have believed Luca would hurt me… just give me some time, please."

"Take whatever time you need, I will always wait for you," I say, groaning to myself at my cheesy line. *Who am I? A romantic novelist? Get a grip, Bekke.*

Rose, of course, snickers, well, tries to, but it causes her to wince in pain, and we just sit in silence, our shoulders touching as the sirens begin to wail in the distance.

CHAPTER 23

RIBS, REGRETS, AND REALLY BIG CATS

The air inside the cramped transport van is a suffocating, putrid cocktail of spilt copper, burnt fur, and the acrid, lingering stench of that Duke demon's sulphurous breath. It clings to the back of my throat, thick and oily, coating my tongue in a taste that reminds me of rotting eggs and ancient graves. Every single jolt of the heavy tyres against the uneven Mississippi roads sends a fresh, blinding wave of white-hot agony ripping straight through my torso.

My ribs don't just feel broken. They feel as if they have been ruthlessly pulverised into a collection of jagged glass shards, currently staging a violent, bloody protest against my bruised lungs with every rhythmic bump in the road. Each breath is a gamble. One moment I am inhaling, and the next, it feels like a serrated knife is being twisted between my fourth and fifth ribs.

If I never see another high-tier demon as long as I live, it will still be several lifetimes too soon. Seriously, who designed these things? Too many teeth, far too much sulphur, and an absolute lack of manners.

I lean my heavy head back against the freezing metal panel of the van, squeezing my eyes shut as I desperately try to regulate my ragged breathing. Each shallow inhale is a brutal battle, a fight for oxygen that feels like swallowing sandpaper. My vision swims in rhythmic pulses of grey and red.

Beside me, Rose is a flawless statue of coiled tension. Even without looking at her, I can feel the heat radiating off her body, a predatory warmth that usually makes me want to curl into her. Her intoxicating scent, usually a comforting, perfect blend of wildflowers and rolling storms, is currently completely masked by the heavy, metallic tang of fresh blood.

Even though we had a moment, a fleeting glimpse of something real between us before the doctor and local police turned up, she has gone back to refusing to look at me. I can hear the rhythmic, shallow click of her breathing. Her stunning green eyes are fixed stubbornly on the grimy floor of the van between our boots. I catch a glimpse of her knuckles. They are stark white where she grips the plastic edge of the seat with terrifying, panther-like strength. She is vibrating, not with fear, but with a suppressed energy that feels like a live wire humming in a puddle.

We have endured the slaughter, but the crushing silence spanning between us feels infinitely heavier than the physical weight of my injuries. The tension is a living thing, thick and suffocating, pulsing in time with the throbbing in my chest. It is a wall of ice that I don't know how to break, especially when every movement feels like my torso is being put through a meat grinder.

Say something, Rose. Please. Tell me I'm an idiot. Tell me I smell like a dumpster fire. Just don't look at me like I'm a monster.

"We are five minutes out," Luca's voice cracks through the suffocating gloom of the cabin.

He sounds exactly like he has been gargling gravel and broken glass. I do not even need to open my eyes to know he is an absolute mess. Being the Alpha naturally means carrying the unbearable weight of every wounded team member in the back of this transport, and tonight, that weight is astronomical. He absorbs the psychic echo of their pain, a burden that would snap a lesser man.

He really shouldn't take it all upon his own massive shoulders. Technically, I am officially the team leader. Except that I have been rather distracted lately. You know, by either almost dying or violently mutating into what appears to be an extinct paranormal entity. Just a typical Wednesday in my glamorous life.

The heavy van finally screeches to a violent, jarring stop outside our makeshift headquarters, the abandoned business and homestead we recently commandeered between Lunar Falls and Jackson. The sudden deceleration sends me sliding forward, and I let out a strangled, wet gasp as my ribs shift.

The rear doors groan open with a piercing metallic shriek, instantly letting in the damp, cool evening air. It is a chaotic, bloody symphony of pained groans and sharply barked orders as the extraction begins. The smell of rain and wet earth clashes with the gore inside the van.

"Move! Let's go, let's go!" Sam shouts.

His usually immaculate tactical gear is completely shredded and heavily stained a deep, ominous crimson. He moves with a frantic, disciplined energy, his face pale but determined as he helps get those who can't walk by themselves out of the van even though he still has a slight limp himself. He looks less like a G-man and more like a survivor of a trench war.

Doctor Stevens knew he couldn't treat those with the worst injuries here, so we took a slight detour to drop off Johnson and the Commander at the local hospital. The loss of manpower is a blow, but the priority now is stabilisation.

My body screams in protest as I try to move. My muscles are locked in a spasm of agony, and my vision flickers. Still, I keep my face a mask of professional indifference. I refuse to let them see me crumble. Not here. Not in front of the team.

I grit my teeth and try to slide towards the exit, but my legs immediately decide they are unwilling to cooperate. They feel like leaden weights, useless and trembling. When the adrenaline stopped running through my system, the true extent of my injuries started to show. Just as I begin to tilt, a warm, incredibly strong hand catches my elbow, instantly steadying my swaying frame.

I look up, fully expecting Luca, but it is Rose.

Her green eyes are heavily guarded, flickering intensely with a dark shadow of the fear that has haunted her ever since she witnessed what I truly am. She isn't looking at me with the love we almost touched; she is looking at me as if I am a puzzle she can't solve, or a predator she doesn't recognise.

"Do not be a hero, Ava," she mutters. Her voice is incredibly low and tight with suppressed emotion. It's a warning, but there is an underlying plea in the tone, a desperate need for me to just stay still and be okay. "You can barely stand upright."

"I have definitely had worse," I chuckle.

The cocky words come out as a pathetic, pained wheeze that makes my ribs grate together. The sound is sickening, a wet click of bone on bone that sends a fresh jolt of nausea rolling through my stomach.

Rose snorts, a tiny, brilliant spark of her usual fiery spirit returning to her exhausted expression. "Right. Because getting tossed around like a ragdoll by a Duke is just another typical day for the great Ava the Destroyer."

It's a sharp jab, but there's absolutely no malice behind it. It's an olive branch wrapped in sarcasm. I would gladly take her witty snark over that terrified, suffocating silence any day of the week. For a heartbeat, our eyes lock, and I see a flicker of the woman who wants to pull me close, fighting against the warrior who is afraid of what I've become.

We stagger painfully into the sprawling house, which has been swiftly transformed into a grim, chaotic triage centre by Nurse Philips. The smell of bleach and rubbing alcohol fights against the scent of blood and sweat. Doctor Stevens is already in constant motion, his pristine white coat serving as a stark, glaring contrast to the utter carnage around him. He looks like a beacon of order in a room full of broken bodies.

His nurse, a genuinely kind woman I currently only know as

Nurse Philips, is rapidly ripping open sterile gauze packs with military-grade efficiency. The sound of tearing plastic and the clink of surgical steel instruments create a rhythmic, clinical soundtrack to the suffering.

"Over here!" Stevens commands, pointing sharply at a modular medical bed in the corner. "Ava, sit down immediately. Sarah, I need a full vitals sweep and a comprehensive trauma panel. She has sustained significant blunt force trauma directly to the thoracic cavity."

So her first name is Sarah.

I genuinely feel a sharp pang of guilt for never asking, especially since she kept my very embarrassing, pain-induced fall in the bathroom a secret and has been so kind while I was bedridden. In this world of monsters and demons, her simple kindness feels like a luxury.

I collapse heavily onto the rigid mattress, grinding my teeth as the doctor's gloved hands move clinically over my battered chest. Every touch is an electric shock. When he presses down on my sternum to check for stability, I nearly black out. My breath catches in a bruised lung, and I can taste copper in the back of my throat.

"I am perfectly fine, Doc. Please, go tend to the others," I protest.

My raspy voice lacks any real conviction. It sounds like I've been smoking for forty years and shouting into a windstorm.

"You have multiple compound rib fractures, a suspected pulmonary contusion, and god only knows what kind of severe internal haemorrhaging," Stevens snaps. His intelligent eyes are sharp and entirely devoid of humour. He looks at me not as a person, but as a medical problem to be solved. "You are absolutely not fine. You are a walking medical anomaly that should technically be in a deep coma, yet your resting heart rate beats at an impossibly slow rhythm. Any kind of sudden, severe chest injury could stop your heart entirely."

Nurse Sarah Philips steps forward, uncapping a saline bottle to carefully clean a deep, jagged laceration on my shoulder where a spike had ripped through my clothing and skin. As she sponges away the blood, she pauses. Her eyes widen in genuine shock, and she leans in closer, her brow furrowed.

"Doctor, you need to look at this," she whispers. "The margins of the wound are already starting to close. The epithelial tissue is literally regenerating right before my eyes."

I tilt my head, watching in morbid fascination. The angry red line on my pale skin is pulsing. Slowly, impossibly, the edges of the wound begin to knit together. It looks like a time-lapse video played in real-time. I watch in morbid fascination as my flesh closes until it is just a patch of fresh pink skin that smooths over into a seamless surface.

It is captivating and deeply repulsive all at once.

Is this the new me, or is it the energy I siphoned from that demon?

I honestly do not know if what I drained from the shade is still humming beneath my skin like a live electrical wire, actively forcing my cellular biology to mend at a speed that defies every single law of human medicine. Or, perhaps, this is just exactly how my brand-new, mutated reality operates. I still feel a strange, cold thrumming in my veins, a power that feels alien and hungry.

Rose stands a few feet away, her arms crossed defensively over her chest. She is watching the miraculous biological process with a complex mixture of awe and lingering, deep-seated unease. Her nostrils flare, as if she can smell the unnaturalness of the healing. When she catches me staring, she quickly averts her gaze, focusing intently on a wounded team member across the room. That man is currently being prepared by one of the team's medics to have a small, jagged piece of rebar extracted from his thigh, and the sound of his muffled scream fills the room.

"Is she going to be alright?" Rose asks.

Her voice is barely a fragile whisper, stripped of its usual confidence. She isn't asking about the ribs. She's asking about *me.* About the soul behind the ice-white hair.

"Physically?" Stevens replies, shining a blinding penlight directly into my dilated pupils to check for neurological deficits. I blink rapidly, the light searing my retinas. "She will be entirely combat-ready in twenty-four hours if she continues to regenerate at this impossible rate. Mentally? That falls completely outside my medical jurisdiction. But she desperately needs uninterrupted rest. Her metabolism, I can only logically guess, is aggressively burning through calories like a jet engine just to fuel this spontaneous cellular synthesis."

A whole day passes in a hazy, disorienting blur of restless sleep. My dreams are fragmented. flashes of blood, the sound of Rose's voice calling my name, and the feeling of cold, dark water filling my lungs. I wake up several times, broken only by the steady, rhythmic, metallic sounds of the tactical team preparing for whatever nightmare lies ahead. The clatter of magazines being loaded and the sharp scent of gun oil seep through the walls of the triage room.

By the evening, the 'Great Healing' has perfectly completed its work.

I stand in front of a small, cracked mirror in the bathroom, staring at my reflection. The horrific, deep purple bruising that had once mapped my torso has faded to a faint, sickly yellowish hue. I take a deep breath, expanding my chest fully for the first time in days. There is no pain, only a lingering tightness.

I still can't get over how I now look, with my hair now a shocking, luminous ice-white with a tint of blue, and my eyes are no longer the colour they were. They are vibrant, glowing icy blue, like glaciers under a winter moon.

I look like some kind of high-fantasy villain. Or a very expensive hair-and-eye-treatment commercial gone wrong.

The makeshift war room is stiflingly crowded. Luca's entire pack is present, their combined presence filling the cramped space with an overwhelming, buzzing energy. Shifters have a way of taking up more space than humans, not just physically, but energetically. The air feels thick and heavy, charged with a predatory anticipation that makes the hair on my arms stand up.

Freya and Maya are huddled close together in the far corner. Their beautiful faces are etched with grim determination, though they look fundamentally incomplete and deeply out of place without their sister, Reya, standing fiercely beside them. The void Reya left is a physical thing, a gap in their formation that no amount of tactical planning can fill.

"We absolutely cannot wait," I announce, stepping firmly into the dead centre of the room.

I can instantly feel the heavy, expectant weight of every single eye locking onto me. Some looks are filled with respect, others with curiosity, and a few are laced with an unmistakable flicker of fear. I am no longer just the Captain. I am something else. Something unknown.

"Devika is currently fortified in a property just north of Jackson," I continue, my voice regaining its command. "If we do not hit her location now, she could summon more of those Dukes. Next time, we will not be nearly lucky enough to just walk away."

Luca nods slowly, his strong jaw set like carved stone. He looks exhausted, but his eyes are clear. "My pack is ready. We mobilise tonight. But we desperately need an ironclad tactical plan. That specific property is a literal fortress crawling with demons and vampires. It's not a house. It's a kill-box."

Freya steps forward, crossing her arms firmly over her chest. Her expression is fierce, her eyes flashing with that characteristic Harper stubbornness. "Maya stays at our property. Along with Pickle and Sera."

"What!" Maya begins to protest, her blue-streaked hair whipping around as she shakes her head. Her voice trembles, the old anxiety bubbling to the surface.

Freya cuts her off instantly with a sharp, lethal glare that could freeze boiling water. "No, Maya. You are not a frontline fighter. You and Pickle will remain safely behind the property's protective magical wards. I refuse to risk you in a direct, bloody assault. Sera stays to help physically protect you both and guard our home. That is the very reason Reya created her in the first place."

Maya looks frantically at her sister, then down at the massive hellhound sitting obediently at Freya's feet. Beastie lets out a low, guttural, vibrating growl that rattles the floorboards. A terrifying flicker of actual hellfire licks dangerously at the dark corners of his massive jaws, smelling of ozone and charcoal.

Maya feels deeply betrayed by Freya's unilateral decision, her lower lip trembling slightly, but she wisely chooses not to argue the point in front of the entire assembly. She knows that when Freya enters 'Protector Mode', there is no reasoning with her.

"Beastie comes with us," Freya declares firmly. "His demonic fire is one of the very few things those creatures actually fear. We are going to need every single bit of it."

Beastie lets out a deep, rumbling chuff in agreement, his tail thumping once against the floor like a sledgehammer.

I turn my gaze to Rose. She is scanning the crowded room with a deep sense of worry, her instincts clearly screaming that this mission is a gamble. Like Luca and me, she managed to heal overnight thanks to her shifter biology, though I suspect she's still feeling the psychic drain.

She looks up, her striking green eyes finally meeting mine as I move over to her location. The air between us suddenly feels electric, the tension shifting from fear to something more visceral, more desperate.

"Are you truly ready for this?" I ask quietly, stepping into her personal space.

Rose offers a small, beautifully tilted smile. It is the very first genuine one I have seen grace her lips in days, and it hits me harder than any demon's blow ever could. "I am a panther shifter, Ava. Hunting monsters is exactly what I do. Even if I am… currently dating one."

I feel a sharp, sudden tug deep within my chest. It is a potent blend of spreading warmth and a sharp, bittersweet longing. I do not take her snarky remark to heart. Instead, I reach out, my pale fingers gently brushing the bare skin of her toned arm. Her skin is hot, vibrant, and alive.

I will keep you safe. Always.

I don't say the words aloud, but I project them into the world with every fibre of my being, a silent vow that if anything tries to take her from me, I will rain down hell on them until there is nothing left but ash.

She does not pull away. Instead, she leans in incredibly close, her breath a hot, comforting caress against my ear. The scent of wildflowers returns, stronger now, grounding me. "Just do not do anything stupidly heroic and get yourself killed out there. I am absolutely not done being mad at you yet."

"Understood," I murmur, a touch of my usual dry wit finally returning to my voice. "I will carefully reserve the dramatic, bloody sacrifices for another day."

We spend the next few exhausting hours meticulously examining the structural details of the property on a digital map. We vigorously debate the exact direction from which each tactical team will assault the fortified compound, weighing the risks of ambush against the need for speed.

Eventually, we decide once again on split teams. The shifters are evenly divided to maximise their flanking capabilities. Luca will command the primary entry team, acting as the anvil, while Rose and Elijah will jointly lead the flanking units to act as the hammer.

I have personally decided to take a slight step back from the main formation.

I am currently a highly unstable wildcard.

The thought is a cold reality in my mind. I absolutely cannot be relied upon for precision teamwork, especially if I suddenly lose control of this dark side again. The memory of the blood-lust, the feeling of power overriding morality, still makes me shudder. I need to be utterly certain I do not accidentally slaughter our own people in the heat of the moment.

I will be infiltrating alone, moving through the shadows and striking from the blind spots. However, to everyone in this room, I have verbally agreed to stick closely with Luca's team, which will also include Freya and Beastie. It's a lie of necessity. I am confident that, with their combined magical and physical firepower, they will be perfectly capable. I just cannot risk fighting shoulder-to-shoulder with them.

The combat will be intensely chaotic, and the chances are extremely high that, at some point, I will completely lose my grip on the monster coiled inside my skull.

After the meeting, most of us attempt to get some much-needed physical rest and consume high-calorie nourishment before we deploy around midnight. I find myself eating mechanically, the food tasting like cardboard, my mind already miles away in Jackson. We are also anxiously awaiting Damaris's return from her spectral scouting mission, desperate to confirm that our darkest fears have not already been realised.

Maya has stayed a little longer as she is worried about leaving Freya. When I finish my small snack, I get Maya's attention, "So Maya, how are things going with Duncan?"

Maya's cheeks go a little red, a soft blush that makes her look far too innocent for the war we are fighting. It's Freya who answers me, rolling her eyes. "We have had to ward our rooms. Not all of us want to hear how well it's going."

Maya's jaw drops open in shock, her expression one of pure indignation. "Hey, not so loud!" She turns back to me with a nervous smile. "To answer your question, Ava, things are going well. He has had many questions about Reya; of course, I don't know how to answer. He shocked me by asking if it was a witchy thing. I still can't believe Reya told him we are witches."

She sighs, her expression softening. “I’ve decided that when he returns, as he’s currently working one town over on a big job, I’m finally going to sit him down and tell him everything. With the situation with Reya and it being all over the local news about her arrest, it’s time.”

“It will be okay,” Freya says, her voice softening as she places a hand on Maya’s shoulder.

“I haven’t met him yet, but I’m sure he will take it well,” I add. “If he didn’t run after what Reya hinted to him, then I think you’re good.”

I pause, a thought occurring to me from my observations over the last few weeks. “I actually had a thought the other day when we were at yours. I have noticed Jenny has been kind of close to Reya… you know,” I say, trailing off meaningfully.

Before I can elaborate, Freya cuts in, her eyebrows shooting up. “You think Jenny has a crush on Reya?”

“Well, yeah, I did,” I admit. “But after the pack’s reaction to Reya, I was wondering if she is having an effect on Jenny too, as she is descended from witches.”

“Oh my god, I never thought of that, you might have a point.” Freya looks thoughtful, her pragmatic mind already whirling. “When we return, I will have to ask Jenny about it. I still don’t understand why Reya has this effect on them.”

“I actually might have an idea why that is happening,” I say quietly. “It’s something Luca told me, but we don’t have time now to discuss it. When we have a moment, I will tell you what he said.”

“Sure, sounds good, I can’t wait to hear it,” Freya says, and Maya nods in agreement, the brief moment of normalcy providing a necessary respite from the looming violence.

When Maya is ready, a few of our heavily armed team members escort Maya safely back to Luna Falls. The atmosphere is heavy as she leaves, a sense of parting that feels far too permanent for my liking.

Damaris finally returns; she doesn't walk so much as glide into the room, her spectral form shimmering like moonlight on water. Her presence always brings a sudden drop in temperature, a chill that settles in the room.

She confirms she has seen absolutely no sign of any more Dukes or anything worse. However, her report isn't entirely positive. She mentions that the ancient entity currently possessing Devika looks incredibly worried. The demon has actively dispatched several hunting parties to search for the missing Duke, its frustration palpable even to a ghost.

If that monster is worried, then it will surely soon start considering summoning more of those unstoppable demons.

We really do not want to face them again. Well, not right now anyway, not while I am still struggling to learn the lethal mechanics of my new abilities.

We also specifically asked her to see if she could determine exactly which ancient demon is possessing Devika. Unfortunately, Damaris shakes her head, her translucent features clouded with disappointment. She still cannot confirm its true identity.

When the men return from escort duty, we begin to file silently out of the front door, heading purposefully towards the idling convoy of blacked-out SUVs parked in the gravel driveway. The overall mood is deeply sombre but lethally determined.

Those brave operatives who were too severely injured to fight, the ones still sporting heavy white bandages or limping awkwardly on aluminium crutches, stand stoically by the door. Their pale faces reveal a complex mix of bitter frustration and silent, unwavering support. They are soldiers without a war to fight tonight, and it eats at them.

I carefully inspect my weapons, feeling the comforting, familiar weight of the enchanted silver blade strapped securely to my back. I can feel the cold bite of the metal through my gear. I am also carrying my full set of lethal firearms and tactical knives.

I made a huge, nearly deadly mistake last time by only bringing my sword into the fight.

The memory of being outmatched and outgunned flashes through my mind. I absolutely will not make that foolish mistake again. The cold steel of my guns offers a deeply familiar, grounding comfort, a reminder of who I was before the mutation, before the magic. It is the only thing in my life right now that feels predictable.

My dark side is still very much present, coiled tightly at the base of my skull like a sleeping viper. I can feel it pulsing, patiently waiting for the right moment to unleash itself and feed on the chaos.

Stay down, I command it silently. *Just a little longer.*

I just desperately hope I can contain its violent urges long enough to achieve our main objective. If the monster takes over before we find Reya, I might be the one who puts the final nail in her coffin.

As I smoothly climb into the driver's seat of the lead vehicle, sliding in right next to Rose, I glance back at the illuminated house. Doctor Stevens and Nurse Philips are standing beside our battered team members, watching us from the porch, their faces pale in the silver moonlight. They look like ghosts watching a funeral procession.

We are heading straight into the storm's very centre. We are driving right towards an ancient demon actively attempting to tear the human world apart, and a manipulative goddess who sees each of us as nothing more than disposable pawns on a chessboard.

If I ever meet the divine spirit of Hecate, we will definitely have some sharp words.

The thought makes my icy blue eyes flare. She should have done much more to protect her bloodline, not play sick, twisted games with innocent lives. Reya is rotting in the Underworld precisely because of her divine inaction.

I shift our vehicle into gear, the transmission clicking with precision. My gaze is fixed intently on the dark road stretching out ahead, a ribbon of black asphalt leading us toward oblivion.

"Let us go give the demon currently possessing Devika a very good reason to regret ever crossing our path," I say.

My voice rings cold, hard, and entirely devoid of mercy. It isn't just the Captain speaking anymore; it is the Destroyer, the side of me that earned the nickname because of how deadly I can be.

As I accelerate away from our makeshift headquarters, the tyres spinning on the gravel with a violent spray, I turn slightly to Freya sitting in the back seat. "Do you truly believe Maya can magically reinforce that spare room enough to securely hold the demon until we can figure out exactly how to extract it?"

"Yes, absolutely," Freya replies, her tone ringing with fierce sisterly pride. "She has been practising her warding just as much as I have been practising my combat magic. She is going to layer so many heavy wards on that specific room that not even a microscopic fly will be able to escape it."

Freya leans forward, her eyes shining. "Regarding actually getting the demon out, Nathaniel explicitly mentioned Maya might possess another one of his angelic abilities. She might actually be able to perform the exorcism herself."

Even as the massive V8 engines roar to life, inside the car, we can't hear them; all we can feel is a slight vibration through the chassis as we speed towards Jackson. I really do love this modified car, Agent Moore gave us. It's a beast of a machine, built for stealth and power.

When we contacted him to update our situation, he sounded very worried and asked Sam to keep an eye on me.

My hearing is better than they realise.

I heard the tremor in his voice, the genuine concern that transcends professional boundaries. Agent Moore said he would coordinate with the Chief of Police to keep the area clear of all law enforcement for our mission, and that any calls that come in would be ignored until we radio that it's all clear. He wasn't happy to be left out of the action, but Moore stated that our mission is for national security, which he couldn't really argue with. It doesn't help keep them on our side; we just have no other choice. We are operating in the grey now. Agent Moore also mentioned that he is going to try to find more agents and soldiers he can trust to join our team, as it seems the threat is much bigger than he realised.

I carefully check the side mirrors to ensure our entire tactical convoy is maintaining pace. I definitely do not want to encounter an operational issue before we even reach the combat zone.

In the reflection, I see a sleek, perfectly lined-up line of mechanical shadows slicing ruthlessly through the humid night, heading straight north towards Jackson. We look like an army of ghosts.

CHAPTER 24

THE BREACH OF THE WEEPING STONE

I feel like a loaded weapon, with the safety off and my finger close to the trigger, twitching from an almost uncontrollable impulse. It's a physical sensation, a humming vibration that begins in my bones and spreads outward, making my skin feel too tight. The urge isn't only about the mission—it's something more primal and ravenous, deep in the hollow parts of my chest.

That single, terrifying thought loops endlessly in my mind as our heavy, armoured SUV crawls through the dark like a predator stalking its prey. We are navigating an abandoned dirt track in the heart of Mississippi, and the night is thick. Suffocatingly so. The humidity is a physical presence, clinging to my skin like a damp, weighted shroud. It carries the cloying scent of rotting vegetation and the sharp, metallic tang of impending violence that makes my teeth ache.

My new Dhampir senses are vibrating right out of my skin. It is unsettling, this hyper-awareness. I can hear the rapid, anxious thumping of Sam's heart from the car trailing us. It sounds like a trapped bird beating its wings frantically against a cage. Every breath he takes is a ragged staccato in my ears. From the rear seat, I catch the distinct, musky scent of Luca's mounting tension as he sits next to Freya and Beastie. His scent is heavy, thick with the smell of old leather, rain-drenched earth, and adrenaline.

But above all, overshadowing the darkness and the dread, I feel Rose.

She sits right beside me, her presence a warm, golden glow in the oppressive gloom of the cockpit. Her hand rests near mine on the centre console, our fingertips brushing in a deliberate, grounding rhythm. The primal bond between us pulses. a chaotic cocktail of fierce, all-consuming love and a deep, lingering anxiety that tastes like copper in my mouth.

I know she is still struggling to accept the literal monster I have become. I can feel it in the way her breath hitches when I move too quickly. My icy blue eyes, now piercing and luminous in the dark, and my stark white hair serve as a constant, glaring reminder of my terrifying physiological transformation. Even my resting heart rate is an affront to nature. a sluggish, echoing thump so slow it causes Doctor Stevens to have a daily existential crisis while trying to study my vitals.

Rose reaches out, her warm fingers sliding over my pale knuckles. The contrast is jarring. Her skin is flushed with life, mine is the colour of moonlight on a tombstone. She is my anchor in this storm, the only thing keeping me from drifting into the red haze of the predator. I turn my head, meeting her eyes in the shadowed space of the car. Her green eyes are shimmering, searching my face for the woman she knows beneath the veneer of the creature.

"You are thinking entirely too loudly, Ava," she whispers.

She leans in close, and for a moment, her intoxicating scent of rain and crushed wildflowers manages to mask the acrid stench of engine exhaust and damp soil. "I can practically hear the gears grinding into dust inside your skull."

"I am just running through the tactical variables," I lie.

The words are smooth and professional, but my soul is jagged. *Tactical variables? Please. I'm actually wondering if I managed to use enough force and speed, could I jump over that tree line in a single bound like Supergirl?*

The slight, knowing twitch of her full lips tells me she sees right through my absolute bullshit. She has always been too good at reading the spaces between my words.

"You are worried about losing control again," she states softly. It isn't a question. It is an observation delivered with a tenderness that makes me want to scream and weep simultaneously.

I swallow hard, feeling the phantom pressure of my fangs press painfully against my gums. They are eager, restless things, pulsing with a hunger that has nothing to do with food and everything to do with the kill. "I almost tore your throat out a few days ago. Please forgive me if I am not entirely confident in my own impulse control right now."

Rose shifts her weight, closing the narrow gap between us until there is no air left. The heat radiating from her body is an invitation, a sanctuary. She cups my pale cheek, her thumb tracing the sharp line of my jaw with a reverence that makes my chest ache.

"We have been over this," she murmurs, her voice dropping into that low, seductive register that always turns my brain to mush. "You stopped yourself. You fought the feral instincts, and you won. I trust you with my life, Ava. I just need you to start trusting yourself."

She leans forward, pressing a deep, lingering kiss to the side of my mouth. It is a slow, deliberate claim, her lips soft yet firm against my skin. A jolt of pure, crackling electricity shoots straight down to my toes, momentarily silencing the predator in my mind. For one heartbeat, I am not a weapon. I am just a woman who loves another woman with a desperation that frightens me.

"Alright, break it up, you two," Luca interrupts.

His voice is bone-dry, utterly devoid of any romantic appreciation. He doesn't even look at us, his gaze fixed on the road ahead, but his Alpha authority permeates the car. "It's time to get this started. We are sitting two miles out from the primary target zone. We have more important things to worry about than you two making up."

God, someone kill me now, I think, though my heart is still racing from her touch. Well, beating just slightly faster. maybe nine beats a minute instead of eight.

The rest of our tactical vehicles pull up behind us with ghostly silence, the engines cutting out in unison. We step out into a secluded, overgrown clearing where the trees lean inward as if trying to eavesdrop on our plans. The humid air immediately clings to my tactical gear, making the Kevlar feel heavy and restrictive against my skin.

The backup team joins us, moving with practised efficiency as they cover the vehicles with thermal camo netting. We cannot afford any mistakes. One rogue vampire or wandering demon spotting our exit route could turn this into a lethal ambush. I scan the perimeter, my eyes cutting through the darkness, noting every snapped twig and rustle of wind in the canopy.

Elijah stands near the front, looking like a genuine Viking warlord prepared to pillage an entire continent. His presence is imposing, his gaze hard as flint. Beside him, Freya emerges from behind our vehicle with Beastie.

Beastie emits a low, vibrating chuff of greeting that rattles my ribs. His fake canine glamour, whatever dark magic he uses to mask his true form, ripples and distorts around the edges of his massive paws like heat rising off asphalt in mid-July. It is a glitch in reality, a shimmering reminder that nothing here is as it seems.

Freya looks lethal tonight. Her blonde hair is braided tightly against her scalp in intricate warrior knots, and she has an expression that says she is ready to break something. preferably something that screams. I suspect Elijah's influence has rubbed off on her. She carries that same edge of calculated violence. A wicked-looking combat knife is strapped to her thigh, its hilt worn from use.

Most striking are the living, pulsing vines wrapped tightly around her arms and torso like organic armour. They seem to breathe in sync with her, their deep green leaves shivering despite the lack of wind. Since we had no intelligence on the local flora at the estate, she brought her own biological weapons. With a flick of her wrists, those vines can grow at terrifying speeds, crushing bone or strangling breath from lungs.

She joked earlier that creeping vines were created by the gods solely for tactical strangulation. Looking at her now, with that predatory glint in her eyes, I am inclined to believe her. *Remind me never to get into a gardening dispute with Freya.*

Luca steps into the centre of the group. As Alpha, his presence is a physical weight. an invisible pressure that commands absolute silence. Even the wind seems to die down as he speaks.

"Gather round," Luca orders. His voice carries easily over the nocturnal chirping of the forest, deep and resonant. "We are hitting Devika's fortified estate tonight. Recon indicates the property is crawling with low-level demons and turned vampires. This requires a highly coordinated, simultaneous strike."

I cross my arms tightly over my chest, forcing my twitching muscles to stay still. My blood is singing with toxic adrenaline. a high, screeching note that demands release. The feral instinct inside me is begging me to sprint the remaining two miles and slaughter everything with a pulse. It is a vicious, clawing hunger for life force that makes my frontal lobe feel like it is under siege.

Stay in control. Don't let the monster drive. Just for an hour.

This is exactly why I handed operational control over to Luca. I cannot trust my own judgment when the predator wants to play. I might forget where the enemies end and my allies begin.

"We are splitting into three squads," Luca continues, pulling up a glowing digital blueprint on Sam's tablet. The blue light casts ghostly shadows across his face. "Team Two and Team Three will be commanded by Rose and Elijah. You two will take the remaining shifter pack members and our federal agents. Your objective is to secure the outer perimeter and lock down all flanking routes. Nothing gets in or out without, alive."

Rose nods sharply. The warmth I felt in the car is gone, replaced instantly by cold, calculating combat mode. It is an impressive transition. From lover to soldier in the blink of an eye. "Understood. We will form a lethal net around the boundary."

"Sam," Luca says, turning to our resident CIA sniper.

Sam stands straight, his G-man neatness still intact despite the swampy environment. "I have already selected a lovely, sturdy oak tree with a spectacular view of their main courtyard," Sam replies smoothly, patting his heavy rifle case with genuine affection. He treats that rifle like a pampered pet.

"That leaves Team One," Luca says, his dark eyes shifting to me, then Freya, then the massive hellhound. "Ava, Freya, Beastie, and myself. We are the primary breach team. We infiltrate the main house and go straight after Devika. Ava, you are on point for close-quarter threats. Take their heads before they can react."

I give a sharp nod. My silver sword rests heavily against my back, concealed by Maya's intricate blood rune. The weight of it is comforting. A physical promise of death for anyone who stands in my way. I have my standard tactical loadout secured to my vest and thighs because, in my experience, having multiple lethal backups is the only way to survive an apocalypse.

"Check your weapons, sync your radios, and move out," Luca commands.

As the teams disperse, I take a deep breath of the damp night air. It tastes of ozone and decay. Luca's plan is solid, but I have a secret. An arrangement I made with Damaris. If I lose my mind during the breach, if the scent of demonic life force short-circuits my brain and sends me into a frenzy, I cannot risk harming Luca or Freya.

I have to do this alone, I think grimly. I'll draw the fire away from them. Be the distraction. Be the monster.

We advance through the thick woods, moving in a staggered formation. The grand estate slowly emerges from the mist like a nightmare made manifest. It is a sprawling, gothic monstrosity of dark, weeping stone and rusted iron that looks less like a house and more like a decaying tooth jutting violently out of the earth. The architecture is oppressive. Sharp spires reaching up to scratch the belly of the clouds, windows like vacant, staring eyes. Our research shows that an older gentleman with no family owns the property, and as far as we could find, no one has seen him in a long time. I'm guessing he is either dead or possessed.

I stay on Luca's right flank, matching his predatory stride. My Dhampir vision cuts through the gloom with crystal clarity. I can see every microscopic dewdrop on the leaves, the intricate patterns of spiderwebs, and even the faint scuff marks on the distant stone walls.

We stop at a cluster of weeping willows about two hundred yards from the gates. Their long branches hang down like curtains of grief.

Luca raises a clenched fist. Silence falls over us, absolute and heavy.

"Bravo Team is in position," Rose's voice crackles in my earpiece, her tone clipped and professional.

"Charlie Team is locked and loaded," Elijah adds.

"Overwatch is online," Sam says coolly. "I have multiple heat signatures inside. A few possessed human hosts and a cluster of cold, demon signatures moving erratically on the ground floor."

We had wondered whether he could actually see the demons through his thermal scope. It turns out that although they are cold, they still register as anomalies against the background temperature, appearing as void-shaped holes in the heat map.

"Copy that," Luca whispers. "Alpha Team is preparing to breach the western wall on my mark."

This is it. The moment of no return.

While Luca scans the perimeter with his binoculars, I let my physical form slip backwards into the shadows. My Dhampir speed is a blur. An explosion of motion. One moment I am standing three feet from the Alpha. Next, I am a ghost in the undergrowth, moving through the ferns without disturbing a single leaf.

I sprint toward the secret rendezvous. A crumbling, ivy-choked stone gazebo that looks like it hasn't seen a visitor in a century.

'*Damaris,*' I call out mentally.

The telepathic projection feels cold and invasive. Like ice shards sliding through my brain and scraping against my consciousness. '*I am at the gazebo. Where is the alternate entry point?*'

The air in front of me shimmers, warping like a reflection in a disturbed pond. A sudden, drastic drop in temperature signals her arrival. Damaris materialises, but she isn't the composed, ethereal spirit I expected. Her translucent form is trembling. Her eyes are wide with unfiltered panic, her ghostly fingers twitching.

'Ava! Thank the gods you are here!' Damaris's voice rings inside my head like shattering glass. *'Everything is wrong!'*

'What do you mean?' My hands drop to my combat knives, the steel cold against my palms. *'Is it an ambush? A Duke of Hell?'*

'No! It is the demons!' she screams mentally, the force of her emotion nearly knocking me off my feet. *'They are abandoning the property! The lesser shades are fleeing!'*

My tactical mind stutters. Leaving? Who leaves a fortified position? *'Why would they abandon their post now?'*

'You don't understand!' Damaris cries, her form flickering violently. *'The demon possessing Devika... it's not a high-level threat! It's just a bottom-feeding shade! They bluffed us into thinking it was powerful because of the followers it commanded. The real authorities in the Underworld have lost trust in this operation and recalled the forces. They are fleeing in terror because there is no real power behind Devika! Especially after she lost a Duke.'*

Devika isn't the powerful commander we thought she was. She's a host for a parasite that got lucky by possessing a powerful hybrid. The Lorcan pack's prize is nothing but a terrified puppet, a shell of a girl being used as a shield for a coward.

'Are the vampires leaving too?' I ask, my mind racing to recalculate the entire mission in seconds.

'They are furious!' Damaris confirms. *'They realised they've been played. They're planning to leave any minute to find a different*

party. They mentioned something about a promised territory. So they are trying to see if they can get back on track with a different group!'

"Not on my bloody watch," I snarl aloud, the sound guttural and dangerous.

I don't waste another second. I turn my comms back on and tap the external button to send a message to our teams. My voice cuts through the channel's silence like a blade. "All teams, this is Ava. Be advised. The vampire forces are abandoning the property en masse. They realise they've been played. They are volatile and dangerous. Engage all hostiles on sight. Do not let a single leech escape. I am breaching the main building now to secure Devika."

"Ava, wait!" Luca's voice barks through the radio, thick with protective panic. "Do not go in there alone! That is an order!"

I ignore him. *Sorry, Alpha. But the monster wants out.* My mutated blood is singing. a lethal, crackling energy that demands release. The hunger is no longer a whisper. it is a roar.

The safety is off. Time to go hunting.

I launch myself from the gazebo, my body a blur of impossible motion. I cross the courtyard in a heartbeat, the wind whipping past my ears as a roar. I leap over the high stone wall, bypassing the gates entirely and landing with a silent thud on the manicured lawn. The massive oak doors of the rear entrance loom ahead. towering monoliths of dark wood and iron.

I don't look for a handle. I don't wait for backup.

Instead of taking the door off its hinges, this time I crash through the window next to the door, as it will give me a quicker entrance. I tuck my body in tight just after I launch myself at a decent speed.

The window shatters violently, like a bomb detonating, revealing the hallway beyond in a chaotic spray of glass shards and splintered wood from the frame. The sound echoes through the hall, revealing my location to the whole house. I don't wait for the dust to settle; I launch myself through the house to find my target.

When I reach the front foyer, it is a chaotic, writhing mass of fleeing shadow-demons and panicked vampires. The stench is overwhelming, a mix of rotting sulphur, cheap cologne, and stale blood that makes my eyes water and my stomach churn. Three lower-level demons, grotesque masses of shifting shadow with elongated, needle-like claws, launch themselves at me.

My heart executes a single, heavy thump.

I draw my sword in one smooth arc, the blade singing as it slices through the stale air. The first demon leaps high, its maw opening to reveal rows of jagged teeth. I duck effortlessly, feeling the wind of its passage, and pivot on my heel. I drive the fire-drenched blade straight up into its dark chest, piercing the core of its manifestation. It shrieks. A soundless vibration that rattles my very molars before it explodes into a cloud of greasy, foul-smelling ash.

The other two attempt to flank me, their movements erratic and desperate. I don't even blink. With predatory precision, I snap a brutal roundhouse kick into the knee of the demon on my left. I feel the manifestation shatter beneath my boot like glass. As it falls, I spin, reverse my grip on the sword, and drive the blade through its chest. Then I twist and drive the heavy silver pommel directly into the skull of the next demon. It disintegrates instantly, leaving nothing but a smudge of soot on the marble floor.

"You pathetic, mutated freak!" a voice snarls from the top of the grand staircase.

I look up slowly, a cold, mirthless smile touching my lips. A vampire stands there, his skin unnaturally pale against the rich mahogany panelling of the walls. His eyes are a sickly, glowing crimson, and his fangs are fully extended. He feels old. Older than any of the fledglings we have hunted so far. His aura is oppressive, heavy with the weight of centuries of cruelty.

He moves with terrifying speed, leaping from the balcony in a blur of black silk and pale skin to crush me under his weight.

He's fast. But I am faster.

I sidestep him by a fraction of an inch, letting him crash onto the marble floor where I stood a millisecond before. The impact is immense. The stone cracks beneath him like an eggshell. Before he can even gasp, I am on his back. I grab a handful of his dark hair and wrench his head back with a sickening pop, exposing the pale line of his throat.

In one swift, clinical motion, I draw the silver blade across his neck.

He gurgles wetly, hands clawing at the wound as hellfire begins to char his flesh into ash from the inside out. It is cruel. It is excessive. But I have too much anger burning in my veins, and this vampire is the perfect outlet. I need this release.

He collapses onto a lavish Persian rug, twitching in agony as the fire consumes him.

Outside, the silence of the night is shattered by the roar of automatic gunfire and the guttural roars of shifters. Rose, Elijah, and the teams are engaging the fleeing horde. Sam's rifle barks in the distance. a rhythmic, heavy thunder that signals the systematic removal of every threat on the perimeter.

I step over the dead vampire, not even glancing back at the ash. I march toward the living room at the rear of the estate, my boots clicking rhythmically on the marble. The double doors are swung wide.

Devika stands alone in the centre of the room.

She looks tragic. Her silver eyes are wide with terror, and her fiery red and silver hair is a tangled mess against her sweat-slicked face. She is shivering, her small frame trembling under the weight of the possession. As she sees me, her eyes turn an inky, terrifying black, swallowing the iris and pupil entirely. The parasite is back in control.

"Stay exactly where you are!" Devika screams.

It is a horrific duality. The high, terrified pitch of a girl layered over the raspy, guttural hiss of a monster. It sounds like two people screaming from the same throat.

She raises her hands, and I watch as her fingernails elongate into slate-grey claws. A flickering pulse of soul-fire dances across her palms before condensing into an ethereal, glowing scythe. It is a terrifying sight for a human. It would be enough to make most soldiers flee in terror. But to me? In my current state?

It is laughable.

"It is over," I state, my voice dropping into a cold, merciless cadence. "Leave Devika's body right now and tell us how to get Reya back. Your friends have abandoned you. The Duke is dead. Stand down, or I will make this painful."

With a savage scream, she lunges, swinging the scythe in a wide, untrained arc that whistles through the air.

I don't even use my sword. I let it clatter dismissively to the floor. The sound of steel on wood echoes like a gavel. As she closes the distance, I step inside her guard, neutralising the momentum of her swing. I grasp her wrist, twisting the joint sharply until I hear a sickening pop, and sweep her legs out from under her with a brutal kick.

She crashes to the floor, her breath exploding from her lungs in a pained gasp. She lets go of the weapon, and it vanishes as quickly as it appeared. I made sure not to touch it, as the Harpers told me about the Reaper attack and what their weapons do.

I immediately pin her shoulders to the wood, using my full weight and strength to hold her down. She thrashes beneath me, her black eyes glowing with rage, even attempting to use her wings to slash at my face. But I have her pinned so precisely she cannot reach me; I am a mountain of muscle and will.

"Get out of her, now!" I growl, staring into the shadows behind her eyes. "Leave her, or I swear to the gods, I will surgically carve you out of her, piece by bloody piece."

The shade shudders beneath me, its voice a trembling hiss. "I cannot! He will kill me if I return without the body! She is already gone anyway... she is dead inside!"

"What exactly do you think I am going to do to you?" I whisper, my voice dripping with malice.

Before I can reach for my blade to begin the interrogation, the doors blow off their hinges in a spray of oak shards.

Luca charges in, fully transformed into a massive black panther. His muscles ripple beneath a sleek, obsidian coat, his paws thudding heavily on the floor. Beastie bounds beside him, a hellhound wreathed in blazing, black fire. Freya follows, her hands glowing with vibrant, emerald Fae magic.

She sees my murderous expression and the way I am struggling to hold the demon down. The look of a predator who has forgotten how to stop.

"Oh no, you absolutely do not!" Freya shouts.

She slams her glowing hands onto the floor. The response is violent and spectacular. Thick, thorny vines burst through the wood like striking vipers, erupting with a sound of splintering timber. They lash around my waist, yanking me off the demon with a force that sends me skidding across the room, while other vines bind Devika's wrists, ankles, and throat in an instant. A living wall of greenery rises between me and the girl, blocking my path back to the shade.

The demon screams in agony as the plants constrict its host, squeezing the air from her lungs. The possessed woman goes limp, her head lolling to the side.

The feral fog in my mind clears instantly, leaving me shaking and gasping for air. Through the gaps in the vines, I see Devika's silver eyes roll back as she passes out from the trauma.

I stand up slowly, my chest heaving as the adrenaline begins to ebb, leaving behind a cold, hollow ache. Luca shifts back into his human form, casually wrapping a discarded throw around his waist. His dark eyes settle on me. sharp, perceptive, and laced with concern.

"Are you injured?"

"Not a single scratch," I reply, rolling my shoulders to ease the tension. "It was a low-level shade, Luca. A bluff."

Freya walks over, examining the unconscious girl. The vines recede slightly, allowing her to check for a pulse. "This is really her. The one they kidnapped. She looks so... heartbreakingly young."

"She was a victim," I say softly, the predator in me finally retreating into the dark corners of my mind.

"What exactly do you mean by 'was'?" Freya asks, her eyes narrowing.

"The demon said there is nothing left inside her to save," I relay grimly.

I watch the hope drain from Freya's face, replaced by a flicker of stubbornness. "It's a demon, Ava. It was lying to get you to stop. We are still going to try to save her. Reya made a promise." She looks at me then with profound disappointment, as if I had given up too easily.

I feel like an idiot. If my head had been clear and steady, as it normally would be for missions, I would have seen the lie for what it was, a desperate attempt at survival.

My comms crackle, breaking the heavy silence of the room. "Beta Team reporting," Rose's voice says. She sounds breathless. exhilarated. "All hostiles neutralised or fled. Zero casualties on our side."

Relief washes over me like a cool wave, drowning the remaining fire in my veins. We actually pulled this off.

"Copy that, Rose," Luca replies. "Target secured. We're heading back to Luna Falls with the package. Sam, call the authorities for clean-up."

I walk out of the ruined room, stepping into the refreshing night air. The violence is fading, replaced by the gentle rustle of the Mississippi woods and the distant sound of sirens.

Rose is standing near the courtyard, hurriedly adjusting her clothes, which she has just pulled on. As I approach, she looks up, her green eyes scanning me frantically for wounds. When she sees I'm unhurt, a wave of relief washes over her face. A look so beautiful it makes my heart ache with a physical intensity.

"You tried to be a stupid, reckless heroine tonight, I see," she says softly, a tiny, playful smile playing on her lips.

"I did heavily hint that I would," I reply, stopping a few feet away, suddenly afraid to push my luck after the carnage I just unleashed.

Rose closes the gap herself. She wraps her arms around my waist, drawing me close and burying her face in my shoulder. I sink my hands into her soft blonde hair, close my eyes, and finally allow myself to feel the radiant warmth of our bond. She still smells the same, of storms and wildflowers, with a hint of vanilla.

"Let's get her back safely," I murmur, pressing a kiss to her cheek. "We have a lot of questions for the demon. It's going to give us every single answer we need to get Reya back."

CHAPTER 25

THE WEIGHT OF BROKEN RULES

The journey back to Luna Falls is an exercise in suffocating, absolute silence.

It isn't just a lack of noise; it's the kind of heavy, profound quiet that only raw trauma and looming consequences can produce. It settles into the chassis of the heavy SUV, seeping through the leather seats and pressing against my eardrums until it feels as if I'm travelling miles underwater. Every inch of asphalt that disappears beneath the tyres feels like a thousand miles of bad road. Outside the tinted windows, the bruised Mississippi twilight has fully surrendered to the pitch black of night. The dense, sprawling trees flanking the highway look like jagged teeth reaching up to swallow the moon, their branches casting long, skeletal shadows across the road, as if they're reaching out to grab the demon lurking in the back. I can feel its weight, a presence that thickens the air.

In the back seat, we have Devika. A demon-possessed hybrid, restrained by magical vines. I keep my eyes fixed on the road ahead from the passenger seat as Rose drives us back.

Because nothing says 'relaxing road trip' quite like transporting a high-risk prisoner who might decide to possess you the moment you hit a pothole.

My mind was still reeling, caught in a chaotic tempest of residual adrenaline, the coppery scent of blood lingering in the air, and the terrifying, exhilarating high of the fight we had just had to capture the demon.

I can feel the phantom weight of the silver sword in my grip, the horrifying yet satisfying vibration of demonic flesh yielding to my newly awakened Dhampir strength. It struck me how much I had genuinely relished it. How easily I had slipped my leash, disregarded my disciplined training, and allowed the Destroyer to take the wheel.

But every action has its consequences, and in the twisted supernatural hierarchy I had so recklessly trampled, those consequences were now breathing heavily behind me in the back seat, staring at my back with a glare of disappointment.

I glance at Rose, her grip on the steering wheel white-knuckled. The tension radiating from her is so potent it practically chokes the air in the cabin. Her jaw is locked tight, muscles jumping rhythmically beneath her skin. Rose sits rigidly, her usual comforting, intoxicating warmth replaced by a simmering chill of anxiety. I can hear her pulse racing—a frantic bird battering against the cage of her ribs, through the bond, I can feel a mix of emotions being broadcast, relief that I am alive alongside a deep terror at the monster I have become, along with the fear of the demon and where we are taking it.

I reach across the centre console, my movement slow and deliberate, letting my fingers trace the warm, familiar skin of her forearm. The contact is electric. Even through the exhaustion, the simple touch sends a vital spark of grounding energy through my system, momentarily quieting my overthinking mind.

Rose lets out a shaky breath, a sound that melds a sigh with a sob. She adjusts her hold, intertwining her fingers with mine, her palm warm and slightly damp. Despite the sweat, her grip feels like a lifeline, grounding me in the moment. Without uttering a word, our connection resonates with a steady, soothing rhythm beneath my skin—a small, radiant beacon of comfort.

As a Captain of a joint task force trained for the world's harshest environments, I find myself clutching a woman's hand like a frightened child, the only thing preventing me from descending into darkness.

When we finally crunch onto the gravel driveway of the Harpers' property, the sound echoes like a gunshot in the silence of the vehicle. The house looms ahead—a yellow-painted beacon of domesticity, jarring against the war-torn soldiers sitting in the driveway. Rose cuts the engine, and the stillness that follows feels heavy, irrevocably final.

Before I can even reach for the door handle, Luca shifts in his seat. The sound of leather groaning under his weight is the only warning I get before his voice fills the dark space.

"I am fully within my rights to eject you from the pack."

His voice drops into a low, deadly register—a primal, vibrating rumble that bypasses my human ears and resonates directly in my spine. It makes the fine hairs on the back of my neck stand at absolute attention.

"That would then force Rose to make a devastating choice," Luca continues, his dark eyes meeting mine in the rearview mirror. They are bottomless pits of Alpha authority, blazing with an ancient, uncompromising power. "A choice about whether she wants to stay with her family, the people who raised her and bled with her, or leave with you into exile. You would effectively tear my Beta from me or force her to tear herself away from you."

My breath hitches, and the air suddenly feels too thin to breathe. The thought of Rose being forced into that kind of agonising ultimatum—choosing between her soulmate and her pack—is a jagged knife twisting directly in my chest. I glance at Rose. Her beautiful face is pale, her emerald eyes wide and fixed on her lap. She isn't arguing. She knows the ancient laws that bind her kind. She is a panther shifter, and the pack is the foundation of her entire existence.

"Except," Luca sighs, the lethal edge of his voice softening just a fraction, though I can still feel the steel beneath it, "we aren't living in an ideal pack society right now, and our situation is completely fucked."

He leans forward, broad shoulders filling the space between the front seats. "So, this once, I'm willing to overlook it. Hear me clearly, Ava. If you pull a stunt like that again—abandoning the tactical formation, going rogue, and risking the lives of my people because you can't control your new impulses—I won't care that my pack is barely functioning. I'll eject you from it. I'll take my people far away from here, and you will never see us again. Do you understand me?"

I sit in shock for a moment. The harsh, unyielding reality of his words strikes me like a physical punch to the sternum. In my world—the structured, rigid hierarchy of the CIA and the military—rank is everything. I am the Captain. I make the calls. I formulate the strategies, and people follow them or face a court-martial. But here, in the hidden, bloody architecture of the paranormal world, pack loyalty and Alpha authority are the absolute, uncompromising laws of survival.

I can't even pretend that my military rank supersedes his pack authority. Since I woke up changed, I haven't been my usual self, especially not a Captain in the US military. I have openly undermined him in front of everyone. I've treated a sacred, ancient bond like a corporate hierarchy. God, my mind is really compromised by this Dhampir shit! I am forgetting how this new world works. My independence has become a liability.

"I am sorry, Luca," I say, my voice clear and devoid of my usual sarcastic armour. For the first time since we met, I offer him sincere, uncomplicated respect. I meet his gaze and hold it, letting him see the truth in my suddenly too-bright, inhuman eyes. "You are entirely right. I agreed to follow your rules, and I selfishly ignored them tonight. This new me... it overwhelming, but that is no excuse. It will definitely not happen again. Once more, I am very sorry."

His shoulders drop slightly. The heavy, oppressive Alpha aura that has felt like it was filling the car eases to a manageable level.

"Thank you," he murmurs gruffly. "If you want me to lead any of our operations moving forward, I am more than happy to do so. Just run things by me first. Even if you believe doing something specific is best for the team, we move as a unit. We live or die as a pack."

A heavy, suffocating silence settles over us once more, but this time it's born of mutual understanding rather than hostility. The reality of our situation sinks in like a stone in a deep well. We are racing against a clock that is ticking much faster than any of us anticipated, and we have a captive demon strapped in the back of our convoy waiting to be broken.

Even though we had firmly agreed on the plan before leaving Jackson, I can see Luca hesitating to leave. I notice it in the way his jaw tightens as he looks toward the Harper house. He doesn't want to abandon us here in this volatile environment, but our critically injured patients are recovering back at our base, and they need protection as well.

Reluctantly, Rose and I climb out of our SUV, the weight of our task heavy in the air while Luca jumps in with Sam and some of the backup team members. Leaving Rose and me, along with the rest of the pack members, to handle the protection for tonight at the Harpers'. As the SUV's taillights disappear down the gravel road, casting long, bloody streaks of red across the dark trees, we make our way up the steps to the house, following Freya and Beastie while the rest of us carry the demon inside. Damaris follows us in, looking worried for her friend.

When the heavy oak door clicks shut behind us, I'm immediately enveloped by the comforting, domestic scent of baked bread, old parchment, and dried lavender. It's a jarring, almost offensive contrast to the sterile smell of death, brimstone, and terror clinging to us as we carry the captive demon upto the warded bedroom upstairs.

I can feel the powerful, vibrating wards embedded in the walls. For a moment, I almost see a shimmering ripple in the doorway, resembling heat haze above asphalt. This acts as a visual sign of the magic protecting the space. The air inside feels dense and resistant, like walking through a wall of static electricity that pushes strongly against my skin. It makes my teeth ache from the intensity.

"This should hold," Maya says in a quiet voice.

Her voice is severely strained, resembling a frayed rope suspending a grand piano over a jagged cliff. She appears exhausted, with dark circles darkening the skin under her eyes, yet her hands keep moving with frantic, nervous energy as she inspects the room's perimeter, following the unseen lines of the wards.

Jenny waits anxiously in the hallway, her face unusually pale and gaunt from exhaustion. She has been sleeping in Reya's room ever since the impulsive witch was taken from the prison. It wasn't due to anyone's instruction; Beastie simply refused to be anywhere else. Jenny mentioned earlier that Pickle also sleeps there, cuddling close to Beastie's large, furry body with her fragile wings wrapped around herself.

The image causes my throat to tighten. Without Reya's fiery, chaotic energy filling the house, everything feels deeply, painfully wrong. I can still clearly see the spot where she used to lean against the doorframe, often with a sarcastic remark and a look that seemed to beckon giving one of her sisters the middle finger.

We need her back.

The thought is a heavy weight in my gut, cold and unrelenting. I will burn this entire world down to bedrock if I have to, but I am getting her back.

Devika is carefully and methodically transferred to the stripped mattress. She doesn't stir an inch, her head lolling to the side.

I move forward, my military field medic training kicking in immediately. I start checking the patient and their vital signs. I apply firm pressure with my first two fingers to her neck to check her carotid pulse, maintaining a calm distance I have honed over years. In the field, emotions are a hindrance; they can cloud judgment. You can't afford to get caught up in intense feelings when someone is bleeding badly or struggling to breathe.

Her skin feels unnaturally hot, burning to the touch. She is suffering from severe hyperthermia, a temperature that could easily damage a normal person's brain. I assess her breathing; it is dangerously slow, possibly only six breaths per minute, with each breath shallow and irregular. Her pulse is weak and fluttering under my fingertips.

"She is still alive," I announce to the tense room, stepping back and wiping my fingers on my tactical pants.

Now all we need is for the parasitic demon inside her to wake the hell up so we can interrogate it.

Freya and Maya proceed to methodically dismantle the temporary travel wards Freya had installed, moving in a coordinated dance of whispers and gestures, they were to prevent the demon from escaping during the journey here if it woke up. Despite everyone's reservations, Freya then cautiously removes the dense vines restraining her.

She only leaves the restraints tightly wrapping her wings. If this hybrid can genuinely journey to both the Underworld and the Realm of Angels, she could have the ability to pass through spaces just like Madi does. Instead of risking the room's wards failing to stop that kind of dimensional travel, Freya keeps the wing bindings intact. She handles them very carefully, ensuring not to damage her delicate slate-grey feathers.

I head downstairs and step into the cosy living room. The warmth wraps around me like a blanket. Rose follows closely behind, her presence a steady, radiating glow at my back. She is my anchor in this storm of mutating thoughts.

I sink onto one of the kitchen chairs, my muscles groaning in protest as the lingering adrenaline finally drains away. Rose instantly closes the gap between us, sitting so close that our thighs press together. She rests her head gently against my shoulder, and I feel her thumb begin to stroke a calming, rhythmic pattern against the bare skin of my arm. The touch is electric, sending a jolt of warmth through my freezing veins, settling the chaotic restlessness in my bones. I lean into her, silently soaking up her affection, letting the heat of her body ground me. I need this. I need her more than I can put into words.

If she were to let go of us, I genuinely feel as if I might float away into the dark, consumed by the lingering shadow of the Destroyer.

Across the table, Freya and Maya join us and sit rigidly while Jenny, Damaris and one of the shifters take first watch over the demon; the sisters gaze at me with unmistakable, intense curiosity. They are completely captivated by my recent biological changes. To them, I must look like a stranger wearing their ally's skin.

I catch my own reflection in the darkened windowpane for a fleeting second. I still can't get over how my complexion has turned almost translucent, like polished marble. There's a predatory stillness that defines my posture now, a coiled-spring tension that never truly relaxes. And my eyes—they seem to capture and reflect every flicker of lamplight in the room, glowing with an unnatural, icy luminescence.

"So," Freya begins, leaning forward with her elbows resting on the table, her eyes locked onto mine with a piercing gaze. "A Dhampir. I've heard about half-vampires during some deep-dive research I've been doing; most of what I found says you don't exist and never did. Here you are in the flesh. How does it work? Do you crave blood now? Does garlic offend you? Is it a physical compulsion, or more of a psychological craving?"

I let out a dry, sarcastic chuckle, desperate to lighten the heavy atmosphere. "Garlic bread is still a dietary staple, I assure you. I don't even know if vampires are okay with it or not, to be honest, not that I really care, but my Italian grandmother would roll in her grave if I gave up garlic." I offer a small, crooked smile, hoping it helps ease the tension.

I pause, acutely aware of how my hearing dissects the room. I can hear the distant hoot of an owl a mile away, the steady, soothing thump-thump of Rose's heart beside me, and the slight flutter of Maya's anxious pulse across the table. It's overwhelming, almost suffocating.

"But my senses... they're entirely different now," I admit, my voice softening. "Everything feels louder, sharper. My speed and strength have grown immensely. It's like experiencing the world in agonisingly high definition. Ordinary noises sometimes seem like an enemy trying to break in, turning every creak or strange sound into a possible danger."

Maya tilts her head, her vibrant blue-streaked hair catching the warm light of the living room lamps, her expression one of soft, unadulterated wonder. "It is just incredible," she breathes. "Reya will be absolutely blown away that her bl—"

Suddenly, Freya viciously elbows Maya in the ribs in a sharp movement, her wide-eyed glare practically screaming shut up. I'm profoundly grateful for the intervention. Luckily, Rose seems distracted by the television muttering in the background, her thumb continuing its steady rhythm on my arm. I hope she hasn't picked up on Maya's near-slip about Reya's blood being the direct catalyst for my transformation. The secret of how I became this abomination feels like a fragile glass ornament resting on the edge of a table; one wrong breath, and it could shatter, cutting everyone in the room.

Before I can awkwardly pivot the conversation, a sudden, explosive outburst of pure hysteria shatters the quiet of the house.

I glance over to the large, flat-screen television on the far side of the room, where Pickle is sitting cross-legged on Echo's lap, flanked by Quinn and Sage. The shifters are immersed in a massive marathon of the Harry Potter films, trying to distract themselves from the impending situation. At this moment, a particularly dark scene is playing out—something about a gloomy graveyard, a glowing cauldron, and ancient, deadly magic.

Pickle, though, she is throwing her head back and laughing so loudly that her tiny, iridescent wings vibrate with the force of it.

"I do not understand what she finds so hilarious about dark wizards murdering people," Dawn mutters as she walks into the room, carrying a tray of steaming mugs she was just preparing behind us in the kitchen. She looks at the little pixie as if she's lost her mind.

Pickle barely manages to point her miniature finger at the screen, gasping for breath between her peals of laughter. "If it was so easy to kill someone with such a simple, sparkly green spell, the bad guys would have won a millennia ago!" she squeals, wiping away a tear of mirth from her eye. "Oh, humans have such wild imaginations! A stick? They use a literal twig!"

Quinn groans, popping a handful of popcorn into his mouth before lofting a single kernel at her head. It misses by a mile, bouncing harmlessly off Echo's shoulder.

For a few fleeting seconds, the heavy dread in the house evaporates. We're just people in a room, entirely divorced from the pending doom, the blood, and the monsters lurking in the dark. It's a beautiful, lying illusion.

The levity is painfully short-lived. As Pickle's laughter dies down to occasional giggles, I can feel the grim subject of gathering information from the demon upstairs creeping back into our minds like a spectre.

Our first attempt at extracting actionable intelligence feels overly cautious in hindsight when the demon finally wakes. While Rose and I secure the perimeter, Freya tries to negotiate with the dark entity trapped within Devika's possessed form. She's searching for some point of leverage—a shred of desire or greed to exploit in hopes of uncovering where they've taken Reya. But, as expected, the demon refuses to cooperate. Instead, it meets every question with mocking silence, sinister laughter, and cryptic riddles that lead us deeper into despair.

After a brief mental break on the couch, Rose and I head back upstairs, determined to see if my intimidating Dhampir presence can convince the demon to talk. The spare bedroom is unsettling; it's stripped of all furniture except for a single wooden chair, and the sisters have somehow used runes to secure it to the floor.

I could never see them before; now I see a slight tint of the complex, glowing violet wards covering the walls, ceiling, and floorboards. In the centre of this strangely beautiful sight, Devika sits, bound tightly with enchanted vines. The air is thick and cloying, reeking of ozone mixed with something akin to rotting meat. When the demon sees us, it sneers, its black, void-like eyes leaking a tar-like substance.

"The half-breed," it hisses, its voice layered with the sounds of a hundred dying women. "You reek of the grave, little anomaly. How does it feel to be an abomination to both heaven and hell? To know your soul is slowly burning away into ash?"

"It feels like I have the strength to rip your host's arms off," I snap back coldly, stepping into the room. I can feel my fangs descend slightly, my eyes glowing an icy blue in the dim light. I project every ounce of the Destroyer into my stance. "Where is Reya?"

The demon laughs, a wet, rattling sound that sends a shiver down my spine. "Lost in the dark. Burning in the pits. Take your pick, mongrel. The little girl belongs to the king now."

What follows quickly devolves from any semblance of diplomacy into something systematic and brutal. Freya and Maya work in tandem, trying to convince the demon to provide details of the Underworld and Reya's exact location. But the demon is strong and remains tight-lipped.

As days stretch on endlessly, the atmosphere in the house thickens with despair. The air feels stagnant, weighed down by frustration and despair. We're running out of time, out of options.

We try everything. Sleep deprivation, holy water, which I felt silly about getting from a local church and of course, did nothing to the demon, and relentless questioning. Nothing breaks through. Eventually, I watch as Freya loses her patience completely. The careful, composed witch cracks, revealing the terrified sister beneath. She threatens the creature with raw, unadulterated violence—her eyes for a moment seem to glow with magical fury. Summoning thorny vines, she controls them to wrap around Devika's flesh, constricting the demon's grip on the host's lungs just enough to make a point, choking it without killing the vessel.

From my corner of the room, I stand with my arms crossed over my chest, the predator inside me calculating the most efficient way to inflict pain. It's a dark, slippery slope we're on. As the demon gasps for air, its black eyes locking onto mine with a promise of endless suffering, I realise we're teetering on the edge of something dangerous.

We've broken the rules of engagement. Even breaking the pack's rules of not performing torture. And now, we're breaking our own humanity. But as I see Freya's desperate tears and feel Rose's tense presence beside me, I know I'd gladly break every rule in the universe if it means bringing Reya home.

CHAPTER 26

THE DIVINE AND THE DAMNED

The buzz of my alarm doesn't just feel like a standard wake-up call; it's a violent, jarring intrusion. It slices through the fragile veil of my unconsciousness with a jagged, synthetic blade of noise. The vibration rattles aggressively against my skull, echoing the restless, toxic thoughts that haunt my fitful sleep.

I lie there, suffocated by the weight of the air, staring blankly at the pitted acoustic ceiling of the safe house. The stale air tastes of bleach and old dust. Why is waking up the hardest part of my day now? Perhaps it's because, in the fragmented chaos of my dreams, the world still feels somewhat recognisable. In my waking hours, however, I'm a mutating monster wrapped in human skin, navigating a shadow war that's spiralling out of control.

Finally, I swing my heavy legs over the edge of the mattress, the freezing linoleum floor grounding me, sending a shock of reality up my calves. I can already hear that Rose is awake and is in the kitchen.

When I make my way to the kitchen, I pause for a moment before I finally push the door open and enter while holding my breath until I see how she reacts to me. She stands perfectly still by the narrow window, her sleek silhouette framed by the bruised, purple light of the early Mississippi dawn.

Rose watches me, yet we are separated by an invisible chasm.

The weight of everything we aren't saying hangs between us, a suffocating shroud of unspoken fears and lingering tensions. Rose has been trying exceptionally hard to act normally around me. She still smiles, still touches my arm, but the lightness is gone. I know deep down she is still profoundly struggling with exactly who and what I am now.

We gear up in a silence so thick and profound that it feels physically suffocating, like a heavy blanket draped over us. There are no words exchanged, no gentle reassurances, no lingering touches that usually define our mornings. Instead, there's only the sharp, rhythmic click-clack of magazines being seated into sidearms, the heavy zip of Kevlar vests, and the soft rustle of tactical gear. My movements are mechanical, a flawless routine synchronised by years of military necessity drilled into my muscle memory.

Beneath my stoic, unyielding professionalism, I feel a vast, invisible chasm widening between me and the woman I love. The heavy weight of everything we aren't saying hangs between us like a funeral shroud. The memory of my feral loss of control still lingers over me, a terrifying spectre. I can't help but constantly run through the moment my Dhampir fangs had fully descended, and the intoxicating, maddening lure of bloodlust nearly drove me to rip Rose's throat out.

I can sense Rose's fierce, violent protectiveness, but with my newly enhanced senses, I also catch the lingering shadow of fear on her. I see it in the slight widening of her stunning green eyes whenever her gaze lands on my pale, translucent skin or the unnatural, icy glow in my eyes. She is terrified of what I am becoming. And truthfully, as I strap my silver sword to my back and feel the unnatural strength thrumming in my bones, so am I.

As we pile into the heavy, armoured SUV, the low, powerful hum of the V8 engine is the only sound filling the void between us. I could never hear the engine before, thanks to this Tahoe's upgrades; now, with my enhanced hearing, I can hear it just fine. I stare out the tinted window at the blurring, moss-draped landscape, my mind racing a million miles a minute. Our mission this morning is singular, desperate, and steeped in moral ambiguity. We need to know whether the Harper sisters have managed to extract any actionable intelligence from the ancient demon caged inside Devika's body. We are bringing Doctor Stevens with us today so he can give Devika's body a once-over to see where we stand with her physical condition.

The thought of her captive—trapped in her own biological skin while a malicious, parasitic entity systematically kills her from the inside out—creates a cold, hard knot of anxiety in my gut. I've witnessed the horrors of human warfare and the atrocities men commit against each other in the name of politics and religion, but this feels like a violation of the soul.

When we finally pull up to the Harper residence, the atmosphere outside feels profoundly oppressive. The air is thick and heavy, saturated with the scent of impending, violent rain mixed with the damp, earthy musk of the dense Mississippi woods. It smells of rotting leaves, ancient, desperate magic, and absolute despair.

We lead Doctor Stevens towards the house. He looks like a man fraying at the edges. He grips his medical bag so tightly that his knuckles look like polished bone against his pale skin. The backup team we brought with us take up positions outside for extra protection, as the demons might come to reclaim Devika.

As our boots hit the wooden steps of the veranda, a dull thud echoes behind us. It is immediately followed by a sharp, indignant groan of pain.

"Ow! Dammit!"

We turn as one. The good doctor stands several feet back from the veranda, furiously rubbing his nose. He looks entirely bewildered and thoroughly frustrated, blinking rapidly as he stares at a space that looks perfectly empty to the naked eye. He's hit the invisible protective barrier surrounding the property, and from the sound of it, he hit it hard.

It was as if he'd walked face-first into a wall of solid acrylic.

My voice drops into that low, professional register that usually makes subordinates sweat. "Doctor, whatever is running through that mind of yours, you had better stop thinking about it," I warn him as I cross my arms over my chest.

He blinks at me, looking entirely too guilty for a grown man. "What are you talking about? I am not thinking about anything. I am a professional."

Liar. You're practically salivating at the thought of poking and prodding things you don't understand.

"The magical protection on this property will not allow anyone to step foot inside if they harbour even a flicker of intent to harm the occupants," I explain, letting a heavy, weary sigh escape my lips.

God, I am starting to firmly believe that bringing Stevens here was a terrible mistake. Given how utterly obsessed he has been with me and my newfound biology, he is a liability. The way his eyes linger on my pale skin, the clinical hunger in his gaze as he studies my vitals as if they're ancient artefacts, is unsettling. Throwing him into a house full of actual witches and magical beings is like tossing a toddler into a candy store and telling them not to touch anything. He may want to help; he also wants to dissect.

He shifts his weight nervously, his face flushing a deep, traitorous crimson that clashes with the sterile white of his coat. "I... am not sure. Well, I do not want to... You see, I was just wishing I could... you know, study the physiological anomalies of the subjects."

Rose shakes her head, an expression of pure, unadulterated exhaustion settling over her face. She looks as if she hasn't slept since the last century, dark circles bruising the skin beneath her eyes, likely sleepless nights caused by me. "Well, stop it. Now. Before you trigger a defensive spell that knocks you into next week."

The doctor nods sharply, leaning his weight forward again. He closes his eyes, trying to force his way through by sheer willpower. Suddenly, the invisible resistance vanishes as his mental state stabilises, or perhaps he has simply forced himself into a state of professional numbness. He falls straight through the barrier, stumbling awkwardly ahead and hitting the wooden railing in front of him with a pathetic thud.

We all shake our heads in unison, utterly unimpressed by the display, and carry on towards the front door.

We come to a halt at the threshold as the entrance is blocked. Freya stands resolutely in the doorway, arms crossed tightly over her chest. She glares daggers at the stumbling doctor; her eyes narrowed with suspicion. The air around her feels charged, humming with an earthen energy that makes the hair on my arms stand on end.

"Is he going to be a problem?" she demands. Her voice is pragmatic and leaves no room for negotiation.

Behind Freya, Sam appears, "He will be okay," he reassures her, though he shoots Doctor Stevens a dark, warning glare. It's the kind of look that suggests any further 'curiosity' will lead to a very unpleasant conversation in a very small room. "He just gets a little too excited about this hidden world."

I am going to officially go on record here, I think, *and state that this man is a ticking time bomb.*

When all of this, the magic, the shifters, the monsters, is eventually taken from him or forced back into the shadows, he's going to be desperate. He has tasted the forbidden fruit of the paranormal, and men like Stevens don't forget that. Desperate men are dangerous, especially when they have medical degrees and an appetite for the unknown.

Freya narrows her eyes but gestures for him to follow.

Inside, the cheerful yellow house feels less like a sanctuary and more like a hospice for the damned. I find Luca taking up a tactical position near the base of the stairs, and Sam joins him, their faces grim and drawn tight with exhaustion; it was their turn to stay the night.

Rose stays glued to my side as we climb the creaking wooden steps, while Freya leads the doctor towards the room where Devika is being held. I quickly ask, "Did you get anywhere with-it last night?"

"Nope," Freya responds, giving me a frustrated glance. The hallway air seems colder than before, now tinged with a faint scent of ozone and stale sweat.

As the heavy oak door groans open, the smell hits my enhanced senses like a sledgehammer. The sterile, sharp scent of burning ozone from Freya's magical wards is completely overpowering with so many around the room.

In the centre of the room, bound tightly to a heavy wooden chair encircled by glowing, violently pulsing runes, sits Devika's possessed host—or rather, what is left of her. The physical toll the demonic parasite is taking on the human vessel is grotesque, a true horror show of biological degradation. Devika's once-beautiful, olive skin is flaking away in dry, ashen patches that look like burnt parchment. Deep, bruised, necrotic veins crawl up her throat and spider-web across her hollow cheeks like black ink spreading mercilessly on wet paper. Her eyes are sunken so deeply into her skull that they look like hollow, bottomless voids, leaking a constant, sluggish stream of dark, viscous fluid that stains her jawline and drips onto her collarbone.

Freya turns back to the trembling doctor, her expression impassive, almost cold. "It is safe to enter, provided you keep your thoughts strictly clinical."

Doctor Stevens simply stands there, utterly frozen in the doorway. He stares at the writhing, living vines as if they were highly venomous snakes poised to strike his throat. He does not move a muscle, his breath coming in shallow, panicked hitches.

Rose steps up right behind him and shoves him hard in the middle of his back. He stumbles clumsily into the room, nearly tripping over his own feet as he tries to regain his balance. We all turn to look at Rose; she merely shrugs, an unapologetic, wicked smirk playing on her lips.

God, I love that woman.

When the doctor finally completes his thorough examination,

he practically flees the room. He moves as if trying to outrun the very memory of what he's just seen. Freya smoothly calls her vines back. They slither away from the demon and obediently coil around her wrists once more, blending into what most would assume are merely decorative bangles.

"What is the verdict?" I ask, leaning against the doorframe. My muscles ache with a dull, constant throb, a reminder of the physical toll over the past few days. The transition to being a Dhampir has left me feeling as if my skin is too tight for my body, every nerve ending raw and exposed.

Doctor Stevens pauses in the hallway to compose himself, wiping beads of sweat from his forehead with a trembling hand. He forces himself back into a professional tone, though it wavers at the edges, thin and brittle.

"The host is in rapid, critical decline," he states. "She exhibits signs of severe malnutrition and acute dehydration. There is evidence of hypovolaemic shock beginning to set in as her fluid levels drop. Her skin is shedding significantly, with certain patches almost necrotic; it's as if the parasitic organism is consuming her very moisture to sustain its own form. She is also suffering from significant muscle wasting in the extremities."

He looks at me, his eyes wide. "Whatever parasitic organism she harbours must be removed immediately. Otherwise, there will be nothing left of her biological vessel to save. Her organs will begin to fail within days. We are looking at total systemic collapse."

A heavy, suffocating silence envelops us as reality hits hard, like a stone in a well. We're racing against a clock that's ticking faster than we expected. Luca hesitates before leaving, evident from his clenched jaw and the glances he throws my way. He's still worried I might lose control here. Initially, he offered to team up with me, but surprisingly, Rose declined, saying she needs time to adapt to our new situation if we're to stay together as a team.

Reluctantly, he and Sam head out the front door, taking the

highly shaken doctor back to safety.

Freya stands directly in front of the creature, her chest heaving with extreme magical exertion and barely suppressed, volcanic rage. Her intricate botanical magic is in full, terrifying effect; thick, thorny vines sprout directly from her wrists, wrapping aggressively and tightly around the demon's limbs and throat, squeezing just enough to inflict profound agony without instantly terminating the fragile, failing human.

I can hear Maya huddled in her room. I know she is likely sitting on her bed with her knees pulled tightly to her chest as if trying to shrink into herself. She weeps quietly, the sound a soft, heartbreaking counterpoint to the demon's wet, rattling, and arrogant chuckles.

"You are wasting your breath, little witch," the demon hisses, its voice layered with the sickening, discordant sounds of a hundred dying women scraping against gravel. "You can squeeze until this pathetic, fragile vessel pops like a ripe fruit, but I will tell you absolutely nothing. Reya is lost to you."

"WHERE IS OUR SISTER!?" Freya screams, her usually stoic composure finally shattering. Tears of absolute frustration, terror, and grief stream down her face as her hands glow with a blinding, toxic green light. The magical vines tighten violently, digging deeper into the body of Devika. "Tell me where she has been taken and how to get her back, or I swear to the Goddess I will tear your immortal soul apart piece by bleeding piece!"

The demon merely throws its head back against the wooden chair and laughs—a wet, gurgling sound that sprays black, acidic spittle across the protective violet wards. I watch in horror as the saliva hisses upon contact with the magic, sending up small plumes of foul-smelling smoke.

"Tear me apart? Oh, little flower, you do not have the stomach for what is to come," the demon mocks, its pitch-black, oozing eyes shifting away from Freya to lock directly onto mine. "But the half-breed does. I can smell the rot on you, Dhampir. I can smell the delicious, overwhelming hunger. You are one bad day, one tiny slip of control, away from eating every single person in this room."

"Shut your damn mouth, you fucking disgusting demon!" Rose snaps, lunging forward with alarming quickness. Her hands instinctively form lethal, black panther claws, while a low, vibrating growl reverberates from her chest. I manage to stop her in time before she actually does rip the demon apart and kill Devika in the process.

"The truth hurts, doesn't it, kitty?" the demon sneers, its lips peeling back to reveal rotting gums. Then it turns its malicious attention towards the door, towards Maya's room. "Your sister can cry all she wants. By now, Reya has been broken. They have systematically stripped her of her pride, her magic, and her hope. She is nothing but a plaything for our new king."

"Stop it!" Maya shrieks from the hallway, clamping her hands violently over her ears and burying her face in Freya's shoulder as she joins her sister in the hallway.

A guttural, primal cry of absolute fury escapes Freya's lips as she raises both her glowing hands to deliver a killing blow that would undoubtedly destroy both the demon and its host. Before the lethal magic can connect, Damaris moves from the other side of the room and hovers between Freya and the demon. "Reya promised me you wouldn't hurt my Devika."

Freya, her chest heaving as she gasps for air, smoothly calls her magical vines back. They slither away from the thrashing host and obediently coil around her wrists again, blending back into decorative, innocuous bangles. The sudden magical backlash fills the room with the stench of burnt copper and ozone.

An oppressive silence hangs in the air, thicker than the stench of decay that permeates the room. Damaris has barely left Devika's side; she drops to her spectral knees beside the chair, her ghostly shoulders shaking as if she's bearing the weight of her own profound sorrow. If she could cry, the room would be drowned in her despair.

We've breached every moral code, crossed lines we vowed never to, resorting to magical torture. And yet, here we are—Devika is dying, the demon triumphs in its silence, and Reya remains lost in the dark, suffering at the merciless hands of whoever is in command of the Underworld now.

We take a break, and I finally manage to get a quiet moment with Rose when I step outside to check on Reya's horse. The beautiful animal still seems entirely out of sorts. I noticed it from the window earlier, standing forlornly by itself near the tree line, while the other three horses happily graze together in a tight group. It was as if they were completely ignoring Reya's mount, treating it as an outcast.

I also notice Sera flying around the property line. I try to reach out to her, 'Sera, *can you hear me?'*

'I can, are you here again to try and make the demon talk?'

'I am, I would have thought you would be helping?' I say as I continue to walk towards the horse.

'I can't go near that room because of all the wards; they managed to create a few that would actually kill me instantly. I don't think they realise how strong they have made them.'

'Oh! Yeah, I guess you'd better stay away for now, hopefully won't be much longer,' I say, not really believing it myself.

'Ava, look after yourself. I'm worried about you.'

'Don't worry, I will get the hang of this new me, eventually. Come see me before I leave later and get some more blood, okay,' I say, making sure she gets enough to stay strong for the sisters, then I realise I haven't told the sisters about her warning about the house. I'd better get on that as soon as possible. Sera agrees, and I continue on.

I approach the horse slowly, speaking in a low, soothing tone. I am gently stroking the horse's warm, muscular neck and untangling a small knot in its mane when I see Rose walking purposefully towards me. She looks softer in the morning light, her blonde hair catching the sun, though a shadow of worry still lingers on her face.

"I didn't know you liked horses," she says softly, leaning against the tree beside me.

"Yeah, my parents used to take me to a local riding stable as a kid," I say with a small, self-deprecating smile. The memory is distant, blurred by years of military drills and blood. "Since then, I've only managed to ride a few times while deployed in the Middle East. I really miss it. Plus..." I pause, looking into the animal's sad eyes. "It seems Reya's horse doesn't have a single issue with the new, freaky version of me."

We stand in comfortable silence for a while, hanging out with Reya's horse. I give the horse one last, affectionate pat. I lean close to its ear and whisper, "I will help get Reya back. I promise."

Suddenly, the horse lets out a sharp neigh and jerks its head up and down. For a brief, wild moment, I genuinely believe the clever animal understood me perfectly. It clearly knew to seek out Reya when Jacob took her.

I wish it could magically help us track her now. I'd trade my last good bullet for a solid trail.

We head back into the house and find the sisters in the kitchen, drinking coffee. While I was out with Reya's horse, I made a decision about our situation. I face the sisters and say, "If the thing actually wanted to talk, it would have spoken by now," my arms crossed tightly over my chest as I stand rigidly against a pillar separating the kitchen and living area. My tactical mind has gone over everything, analysing the enemy's complete inaction. "It is not genuinely trapped. It is expertly executing a tactical holdout. It is simply biding its time until we inevitably make a fatal mistake. This is a psychological siege, and we are the ones running out of supplies."

Damaris glides over to us; she has barely left Devika since we brought her here. The ghost is a vision of utter despair, her form flickering like a dying candle.

"We cannot physically hurt her to get to it; it will only transfer the pain directly to Devika," Damaris says, raw panic flickering violently through her glowing, ethereal form. Her spectral edges waver unsteadily in the dim light, as if she might dissolve into mist at any moment. "Reya promised me, Ava. She swore my Devika would not be hurt. But you are actively hurting her by keeping that vile thing locked inside her. I want Reya back as well, but this demon will never give you the answers you seek. Please, just try to rip it out of her. She has suffered enough."

"We are not doing anything that will permanently hurt her, Damaris," Maya says quickly, her gentle voice laced with a desperate plea for understanding. "We absolutely will not allow that to happen. We are trying everything we can to save our sister; this demon knows something. It has to!"

The grim, unspoken truth hangs heavy in the stifling air. We are out of viable tactical options. We are at a stalemate with a creature that doesn't fear death, having already died and been reborn as a shade.

Freya finally speaks up, boldly saying the one thing everyone has been utterly terrified to voice aloud. "Maya," Freya begins, her light, airy voice trembling slightly with the weight of her words. "Nathaniel… our father said something specific to us, right before he died. Do you remember?"

The entire room falls deadly silent. The only sound is the low, rhythmic drone of the television in the other room. Freya swallows sharply, her throat clicking audibly. "He told us you might possess another ability. He said you might have inherited more of his divine traits."

Maya's face loses all colour, instantly taking on the shade of old parchment. She wraps her arms protectively around herself, shrinking back from her sister as if the suggestion itself were a physical blow.

"I heal damaged plants and animals, Freya," Maya says

automatically, denial spilling frantically from her trembling lips. "I draw protective wards. I bake pastries. I do not do... this. I am not a holy warrior. I am not a soldier. I am just... me."

"You are angel-blooded, Maya," I say quietly, locking my intense gaze firmly onto her terrified eyes. I step deliberately towards her, placing a reassuring, heavy hand on her trembling shoulder. "You are far more than just a kitchen witch. You have raw, unfiltered divine power flowing through your veins. I have seen exactly what you are capable of when you finally stop being afraid of your own shadow."

Maya lets out a shaky, rattling breath. "That does not automatically mean I can instantly exorcise a demon. What if I accidentally burn out her soul? What if I kill Devika instead of the parasite inside her?"

"It might be the only chance we have left to save her," Freya insists, stepping closer to her sister. The emotional tension in the room quickly intensifies, becoming almost palpable, a thick electric charge that makes my skin tingle. "And if there is even the tiniest chance that Devika is still alive in there, we absolutely have to try. For Reya. For all of us."

Damaris suddenly hovers into view, so she is right in front of Maya. The ghost's translucent eyes blaze with heartbreaking, desperate hope. "Please," Damaris whispers, her voice a chilling, ethereal breeze that makes the fine hairs on my arms stand on end. "If my friend is still alive in there... please do not give up on her. I'm sure she is still alive; it's as if I can feel her spirit, and she is drowning in the dark. I wish I could still talk to her mentally, but as soon as that thing took her over, my connection to her was lost."

Maya's hands immediately start to shake uncontrollably. She stares at the ghostly figure for a moment, her eyes searching Damaris's face for an answer that isn't there. Finally, she lets out a defeated sigh and reluctantly agrees to try. "Fine. But do not come crying to me complaining when this doesn't work, or when it goes horribly wrong."

Maya approaches the bed holding the demon, hesitantly. The sisters must have released the demon from the chair's confinement and from the runes they drew on the floor to keep it contained. We all gather closely behind her, as many as the small room can hold, forming a tight circle of physical and emotional support.

The first attempt fails spectacularly. Maya tentatively touches Devika's feverish brow, squeezing her eyes shut, but nothing happens. There is no light, no warmth, only the heavy silence of a failed prayer. The second attempt is equally frustrating, yielding only a faint, dying warmth that vanishes instantly, like a spark hitting wet wood.

Every time Maya desperately reaches deep inside herself to summon whatever divine spark she needs, nothing ignites. I can clearly see the problem; her own chaotic thoughts are getting in the way. It is a toxic, paralysing cocktail of pure fear and deep-seated self-doubt. She is fighting herself more than the demon.

"I cannot do it," Maya finally chokes out, staggering backwards out of the room as if she has just finished running a brutal marathon. Hot tears stream rapidly down her flushed, distressed cheeks. "I am just... I am not as powerful as you all believe I am. Nathaniel was clearly wrong about me."

It seems both sisters are still struggling with the fact that Nathaniel, an Archangel, was actually their father.

A heavy, devastating silence floods the hallway. I glance over at Rose. My mate looks just as heartbroken and defeated as the sisters, her green eyes clouded with profound sadness.

Then Freya gently reaches out and firmly takes Maya's trembling hand in her own, her grip steady and absolute.

"Stop thinking so loudly, Ma-ma," Freya says softly, using their childhood nickname to ground her. "Do not try to force it. Do not try to control it. Just... feel it. Let it flow naturally. Treat it exactly as you do when you are making the bread dough rise in the kitchen. Just lose yourself completely in the moment. Stop thinking."

Freya then gives us all a quick glance, then turns back to Maya and whispers something I can barely catch. "Find the right item in the place in your mind and use it."

"I know, I think I found it!" Maya whispers back.

What does she mean by that? The place in her mind... I'm going to have to ask her about that when I can get her alone.

Maya squeezes her eyes shut. She takes a deep, ragged, shuddering breath, and her tense shoulders visibly drop an inch. She steps back into the room and approaches the demon. I watch as she finally lets go of her paralysing fear, letting the silence of the room settle around her until the only thing left is the heartbeat of the woman on the bed.

Something ancient, magnificent, and terrifyingly pure responds to her desperate call with an immediacy that sends shivers down the spine. As Maya tentatively places her trembling hands flat against Devika's pale, sunken temples, an extraordinary phenomenon unfolds. A soft, shimmering golden light begins to seep from the very centre of Maya's palms, exuding an ethereal glow that swells with an otherworldly grace. This gentle luminescence gradually intensifies into a brilliant, blinding incandescence, flooding the dark, oppressive room with a potent, divine warmth that carries the aromatic essence of frankincense mingled with the freshness of summer rain.

The protective magical wards encircling the room respond instantly, beginning to hum in perfect, resonant harmony, their vibrations penetrating deep into my bones and sending a delightful shiver down my spine. However, this harmony is soon shattered by the demon's abrupt scream.

This is no ordinary scream; it is a horrific, soul-shattering shriek that echoes painfully through the very core of our beings. This sound is not just heard—it cuts through the fabric of the room, a visceral representation of absolute existential terror. It manifests as a raw, psychic agony that makes us flinch involuntarily, our hands instinctively flying up to cover our ringing ears against its unbearable intensity.

Maya stands resolute at the eye of this golden tempest, her dark hair streaked with blue, whipping violently around her face as though she is ensnared within the fury of a hurricane, despite the stillness of the room. Suddenly, a dense mass of putrid, suffocating darkness erupts violently from Devika's rigidly arched body. This darkness is alive, writhing and thrashing against the radiant light with pure, concentrated malice, a thick sludge of black oil intertwined with toxic smoke, permeating the air with the fetid stench of sulphur and decaying graves.

In a blinding flash, this malevolence is utterly annihilated—not just expelled but completely and atomically reduced to absolute nothingness beneath the unyielding, pure light of Maya, who looks like an angel. The golden aura surges one final time, flaring fiercely and leaving behind bright spots that dance erratically across my vision, a vivid reminder of the battle that has just been waged in this room.

Then, there is absolute, deafening silence.

Maya suddenly staggers backwards, her knees buckling. Freya catches her before she hits the wooden floor. Maya gasps for air, her eyes rolling back as she loses consciousness. Freya scoops her unconscious sister into her arms and carries her to her own bed across the hall.

I immediately turn my attention back to Devika. She lies motionless on the mattress. We all wait, our collective breath held tightly in our burning lungs.

"Devika?" Damaris whispers, her glowing form wavering with terror.

I rush forward, my fingers digging into the side of her pale neck to check her carotid artery. I press down repeatedly, silently praying for a rhythmic throb. I assess her airway and watch for any rise and fall of her chest. Her vitals are stable, though weak. Her skin is rapidly cooling to a normal temperature. She is medically alive, but behind her closed eyelids, there seems to be no one home.

"Maybe she just needs time to reclaim her body," I declare, infusing my voice with hollow confidence to stave off the despair gripping the room. "We don't know where her mind went when that demon took over. We just have to keep her stabilised."

Damaris lies on her side on top of the mattress so it looks like she is hovering above it, then just stares at her friend as if she stared hard enough, she could get Devika to wake up and finally reclaim her body.

Now we just have to wait, so I decide I'd better tell the sisters what Sera told me about the house. Before I can, there's a sudden, terrified shout that shatters the tension, echoing from the living room below. It's Echo, and dread laces his voice. "Rose! Ava! Freya! Come down here immediately, you need to see this!"

The raw panic pulls me from my thoughts, igniting my Dhampir instincts. An electric current shoots down my spine. Without hesitating, we race out of the room and dash downstairs, nearly tripping over each other in our frantic haste.

We spill into the warm, inviting embrace of the cosy living area, its air scented with the soothing lavender, just as the enormous flat-screen television flickers from a news desk, a man looking horrified, it cuts to a jarring, chaotic breaking news report. A dishevelled reporter, her hair askew and her suit tattered, stands against a backdrop of utter devastation, the ground littered with debris and the remnants of what once was. The bold banner across the screen blares ominously: NEW ORLEANS IN TERROR, a stark contrast to the tranquil surroundings where we are.

"Breaking news from the French Quarter, where we are witnessing a truly horrifying scene unfold. Eyewitness reports indicate multiple fatalities as large, wolf-like creatures are reportedly attacking armed police officers. The situation is chaotic and violent, with local law enforcement struggling to maintain control.

The military has been alerted and is en route to assist, but for now, the tragic scenario is escalating by the minute. Residents are urged to stay indoors and avoid any areas of conflict. We will continue to provide updates as more information becomes available. For now, our thoughts are with those affected by this devastating situation."

The camera swings wildly to the left. A massive, muscular wolf effortlessly tears through a reinforced steel barricade, its jaws snapping with lethal intent as it sends tactical officers flying like ragdolls. Then comes another cut. Panicked civilians fleeing as incredibly fast-moving figures rip their way through blood-slicked streets.

Vampires. They are feeding in the open, no longer caring about the shadows or the secrecy of the night. And behind them, emerging from the thick smoke of the alleys, are grotesque, nightmare demons.

The ancient masquerade is officially over. The world knows.

"Local and federal authorities have no explanation for this coordinated attack!" the reporter continues, just before a massive explosion rocks the street behind her, sending fire and debris raining down on the screaming crowd.

The screen cuts to dead static. The entire living area is plunged into a suffocating, dead silence. New Orleans. The heart of supernatural power, now being torn to shreds, live on air.

Then, without warning, my vision blurs. A sudden, agonisingly crushing pressure slams into the front of my skull, as if an invisible vice has just clamped shut on my brain. It is a highly familiar but much stronger psychic weight that causes my knees to buckle. I hit the hardwood floor hard, the entire room spinning violently around me.

'De debt, little Dhampir...is due!'

The voice echoes maliciously inside my mind, cold and ancient. I recognise it instantly, it's Papa Legba.

"Oh, no," I whisper, the blood draining from my face as a freezing wave of dread washes over me.

A swirling, localised storm of pitch-black clouds rapidly appears in the centre of the room, crackling with malevolent energy that smells of ozone and wet earth. From the centre of the vortex steps Madi, the crossroads demon. She looks horrific. Her normally pristine form is battered, bleeding, and scorched. Her clothes are rags, and her skin is marred by deep, glowing burns.

She locks her dark eyes onto mine with a predatory intensity.

"Ava, the debt you owe Papa Legba is now due. The city is falling, and he needs your unique skills to protect the quarter."

Rose is on her feet in a fraction of a second, where she had collapsed onto the arm of one of the chairs at seeing the news report. She steps protectively in front of me, her panther teeth beginning to bleed into view, her growl a low vibration that shakes the floorboards. "Fuck off," Rose snarls, her green eyes flashing with lethal promise. "Ava is not going anywhere near New Orleans."

I push myself up from my hands and knees to try and stand, my head is still throbbing mercilessly, causing a slight dizziness. My heart aches at the terror radiating from my mate; I am terrified, too. If I throw myself into an unrestrained bloodbath in a city of chaos, I fear I will lose control to the monster inside me forever. I fear the hunger will take over.

I had made a promise. I gave my absolute word to Papa Legba in exchange for the magical ring on Sam's finger—the very ring that helped keep me alive, giving me and now Sam the sight to fight the invisible. In my world, the rigid, unyielding structure of the military and the CIA, your word is your life. It is the only currency that truly matters when the bullets start flying.

"Rose," I say, my voice shaking slightly as I place a gentle, grounding hand on her tense shoulder. "I have to. I gave my word."

"NO!" Rose shouts, spinning around and grabbing me desperately by the tactical vest. Her fingers dig into the Kevlar with bone-crushing force, pulling me flush against her chest. "You are not ready for this, Ava! You are barely holding on to your humanity! If you go into that slaughterhouse, the bloodlust will take you! You will drown in it! Please, Ava. Don't do this to us. Don't leave me!"

Tears, hot, frantic, and devastating, spill over her lower lashes, leaving a trail down her beautiful cheeks. The sight of her breaking down, my fierce, fearless, lethal panther begging on the verge of hysterics, twists a jagged knife in my heart.

Freya rushes forward, completely bypassing the screaming argument. She shoves a crumpled piece of paper into my hand with an urgency that borders on sheer, unadulterated panic.

"Ava, if you go... if you are really going into that hellhole, you must find Priestess Marassa. She operates a shop in the Quarter. She is a true friend of our family. We owe her. Please, whatever you do, save her."

I grip the paper tightly, the edges crinkling in my fist, using it as a physical anchor amid the storm of my turbulent emotions. "I will find her, Freya. You have my word."

Elijah steps up beside Rose, his massive frame radiating pure, unadulterated aggression. He looks like a dark storm cloud given human form; his jaw locked in supreme defiance.

"Then take us with you," Elijah demands, glaring hatefully at the bleeding Crossroads demon, his voice brooking no argument. "We are a pack. We fight as a pack. You want our Ava, you take the rest of the pack as well."

Madi shakes her head weakly, leaning heavily on the tips of her wings, which she is using to keep herself upright. "I cannot," she rasps, breath hitching. "I didn't have enough magical energy to get here. This portal is forged from Papa Legba's direct, divine power; it will only allow transport for the Dhampir and me, because her soul is marked by his magical contract. The rest of you would be violently ripped to atoms if you tried to step through. You will have to find your own way."

"THEN SHE ISN'T GOING!" Rose screams, pulling me backwards, her grip bruising my ribs. "Ava, please. Let the city burn. Let Legba die. I don't care about any of it! I just care about you. We can run. We can hide. We can go north, as Luca suggested. Please!"

Every instinct I have—every soft, human desire to build a life, to be loved, to find peace, to wake up in a bed that doesn't smell of blood—screams at me to listen to her. I want to stay in her arms, to let the world burn to ash as long as we have each other in the dark. The cold, disciplined iron of my military training, and the dark, thrumming, predatory pulse of the Destroyer, know the brutal truth. If New Orleans falls, if the Loa die, there will be nowhere left on this earth to run.

"I have to go, Rose," I whisper, my voice breaking, shattering under the weight of my own words. I reach up, cupping her face, my thumbs memorising the sharp curve of her cheekbones, the exact shade of her emerald eyes. I pour every ounce of my love into her gaze, hoping it will be enough to bridge the distance of dimensions. "I am a soldier. I don't get to walk away when the line breaks. I love you. I love you more than I ever thought I was capable of loving anything or anyone."

"Ava, don't..." she sobs, her hands desperately clutching my wrists, as if her physical strength can tether my soul to the room.

"I will come back to you," I vow, though as I look at the terrifying vortex, I have absolutely no idea if it's a promise I can keep.

Before Rose can argue further, before she can physically restrain me or shift to stop me, Madi lunges forward. Her clawed, blood-stained hand closes vice-like around my forearm, her grip agonisingly tight, piercing my skin. She beats her massive, leathery wings once, generating a massive, concussive blast of wind that knocks Elijah, Rose and Freya backwards with the force of an explosion.

Madi pulls me forcefully, violently, into the swirling, roaring storm of dark clouds. The very last thing I see before the portal swallows me whole is the utterly devastated, broken face of Rose. Her beautiful features are twisted in a mask of pure, unadulterated agony, her fingers grasping uselessly at the empty air where I stood only a microsecond before. Her scream of denial echoes through the bond, shattering my heart into a thousand irreparable pieces.

Then, the world vanishes into a terrifying, roaring black void, leaving me entirely alone with the demon.

CHAPTER 27

JAZZ, DEMONS, AND THE ART OF NOT DYING

The swirling vortex forged by Papa Legba's ancient power does not simply close once I am pulled through; it violently, catastrophically collapses around me.

The transition is a sickening, bone-jarring wrench that feels as if my entire molecular structure is being gripped by colossal hands and twisted like a wet rag. One moment I am suspended in a chaotic, roaring blur of iridescent purple light and screaming, supernatural wind that is deafening. The next moment, the universe simply decides it has had enough of my presence. It spits me out like unwanted, bloody debris, slamming my body hard onto a solid, polished floor with a concussive force that knocks every single atom of oxygen from my burning lungs.

The impact is brutal. It is a jarring, heavy collision that rattles my teeth in their sockets and sends a white-hot shockwave of pain radiating from the base of my spine all the way to the tips of my trembling fingers. I gasp, my mouth opening in a silent, desperate oval as my diaphragm seizes.

But the physical agony of the landing is absolutely nothing compared to the horrific sound still echoing in the hollows of my mind.

Rose's scream.

It is a sound of absolute, unadulterated devastation. It is a jagged, rusted piece of glass tearing through the fragile fabric of the dimension we have just left. It rings in my ears, piercing and relentless, refusing to fade even as I lie there on the floor. In that scream is all her terror, all her grief, and the undeniable reality that I have just willingly abandoned her to walk into a war zone.

For one single, fleeting heartbeat, I can still feel her. I can feel the blazing, protective heat of her panther spirit, the frantic fluttering of her heart, the deep, intoxicating well of love that defines our mate bond.

Then, with the suddenness of a falling guillotine blade, the connection snaps.

The abrupt, agonising silence that follows in the wake of that severance is infinitely worse than the scream. It is a dark, suffocating void, a sprawling vacuum where her voice, her warmth, and her essence had just existed seconds before. The sudden absence tears at my chest like a physical, gaping wound. It feels as though a vital organ has been surgically removed from my body without any anaesthetic.

No. No, no, no.

I scramble frantically, pushing myself up with trembling, uncooperative arms, reaching out blindly with my mind. I claw at the empty air, searching desperately for that brilliant, warm light of our bond, that electric hum of her presence that has become my absolute only anchor in a world gone completely mad. I push my consciousness outward, throwing my mental energy against the walls of wherever I am, begging for a single spark of her to answer me.

Nothing.

The connection is entirely severed. I am adrift in a freezing sea of absolute nothingness, and the loneliness is so profound, so sudden, that it feels the same as when I lost my parents. I grab at my chest, my fingers digging so deeply into the fabric of my tactical vest that my nails ache, as if I can physically hold my breaking heart together. I can't breathe. I can't think. The isolation is a suffocating blanket pressing down on my face.

And then, filtering through the rushing static in my ears, I hear it.

Music.

It is faint at first, a soft, melancholy strain of a lone saxophone weaving through a steady, rhythmic upright bass. It is jazz. Slow, mournful, and incredibly out of place. Then comes the distinct, heavy clinking of fine crystal glassware.

I push myself up the rest of the way, so I am finally standing, my head spinning in slow, nauseating circles as the world tries to right itself. The dizzying vertigo makes my stomach churn, but years of ingrained combat training force my body to move. My hand instinctively flies over my shoulder, my fingers wrapping tightly and securely around the familiar, worn leather hilt of my concealed silver sword.

The comforting weight of the weapon is the absolute only thing that feels real in this surreal nightmare.

I am perfectly ready to draw the blade and start severing heads, but as I blink away the dark, floating spots in my vision, my eyes struggle to make sense of the bizarre environment I have just been thrown into.

The air is incredibly thick and heavy, smelling strongly of aged, spiced rum and expensive, pungent cigar smoke that clings stubbornly to the back of my throat. It is the scent of an old-world speakeasy, a place of hidden deals and dark corners. But beneath the veneer of luxury and liquor, there is a secondary scent that triggers every combat instinct I possess. It is the sharp, electric crackle of atmospheric ozone and the distinct, metallic tang of ancient magic being pushed to its absolute breaking point. It smells exactly like a lightning strike that has been forcibly captured inside a glass bottle.

Madi stands directly beside me, her presence a sudden, looming shadow in my peripheral vision.

The Crossroads demon's magnificent, leathery wings are folded tight against her back, though the dark, razor-sharp tips are twitching with violent agitation, perfectly mirroring my own internal restlessness. She looks just as battle-worn as I feel. She aggressively wipes a thick smear of black, viscous demon blood from her nose with the back of her hand, her chest heaving with exertion. Her sharp, ancient eyes scan the dim, amber lighting with lethal, predatory precision, searching for unseen threats in every shadowy corner of the room.

I follow her gaze. Behind a long, immaculate mahogany bar that stretches across the far wall stands an old man.

His skin is leathery and dark, pulled taut over a skull that looks ancient even by immortal standards. His face is deeply etched with heavy lines, resembling a weathered map of forgotten centuries and untold secrets. He looks dead, yet there is a rugged, haunting handsomeness to his features—a face carved from shadows, rum, and survival that utterly refuses to succumb to decay.

He is dressed impeccably in a sharp, timeless, tailored suit that speaks of old money and mysteries far older than the blood-soaked city he claims as his own domain. A pristine, black top hat rests on the polished counter right next to a heavy, intricately carved wooden cane topped with bone.

This is Papa Legba.

The magical silver ring he had previously gifted me through Madi—the ring that rejected me and burned my finger because I was changing—is the very reason I am here. It was a gift I accepted for a price, that price was to come when called on by Legba when he needed my help, so here I am, my heart breaking for a debt.

As I stare at him, my mind is suddenly, violently flooded with information. It is a rapid-fire download of truth and spatial awareness that makes my temples throb with a sharp migraine. I don't have the time to understand what is being given to me; I just need to get this done so I can get back to Rose.

With this new information I have been given, I know this place is not real in any physical, geographic sense. It is a manifestation, a carefully constructed pocket dimension forged deep within the folds of the Veil itself.

Out in the mortal world, Legba requires a fragile, mortal human vessel to anchor his immense, chaotic divine power so he can interact with us. But here, in this handcrafted, atmospheric sanctuary of jazz and mahogany, he possesses a true, physical body. He is the undisputed master of this space, the grand architect of the illusion.

However, as my newly mutated Dhampir eyes adjust to the dim lighting, I begin to see the cracks.

The edges of the grand mahogany bar appear to tremble, slightly out of focus, resembling a poorly tuned television. The polished wood flickers and seems to wobble, vibrating with an unsettling instability that hints at the ancient magic sustaining this dimension unravelling. Dust motes drift upward instead of downward. The soft jazz music occasionally distorts, skipping with static before resuming its mournful melody. It feels like observing a beautiful oil painting on fire from behind—the canvas blistering, peeling, and running.

He doesn't speak at first. Instead, he slowly, deliberately slides a heavy crystal glass filled with dark amber liquid across the polished wood toward me.

His old, dark eyes hold the heavy, unfathomable weight of centuries, yet at this moment, they are shrouded in a disturbing, deep exhaustion. It's a fatigue that's felt in the bones, a final weariness that goes beyond the physical and touches the spiritual. A sudden shiver runs along my spine, causing the tiny hairs on the back of my neck to stand upright.

If an immortal, divine entity like Papa Legba, the revered guardian of the crossroads and the keeper of the gates, is this tired, then humanity is utterly, completely screwed.

"De gates, dey are failing, Ava," Legba finally says.

His voice is a deep, gravelly rumble that doesn't just reach my human ears. I feel it vibrating through my ribcage, humming darkly in my bones. It sounds like heavy, ancient stones grinding together at the bottom of a deep, forgotten well.

"Someone is opening de doors from de inside, letting dem demons slip free into the waking world. When de angels fell, dis heavy burden was placed upon my shoulders. A dark ritual, chérie... a foul, unbreakable binding meant to tether my very essence to de gates to keep them shut."

He leans heavily on the mahogany bar, his shoulders slumping. He looks every bit like a weary, defeated king watching his grand empire crumble into dust and ash before his very eyes. He runs a gnarled, trembling hand over the carved bone of his cane, and I notice for the first time that the ancient, dark wood is actively splintering under his touch. Fine, jagged cracks are webbing across the surface, leaking a faint, sickly purple light.

"I brought you here because de debt, she is due," he continues, his gaze locking onto mine with a terrifying, piercing intensity that seems to effortlessly strip away all my layers of professionalism and military bravado, leaving only the raw, frightened girl beneath the armour. "But before you step into de fire, you need de brutal truth... and perhaps, another gift."

He pauses, his dark eyes narrowing into dangerous slits. "I do not know whose hand strikes our world from de shadows up above. But I know exactly what brews below, in de dark."

My grip on my sword relaxes only slightly, though my muscles remain coiled like tightly wound springs, ready for violence. In my extensive military experience, when a commanding officer or an immortal deity offers the 'brutal truth,' it is usually just a polite, poetic way of describing a suicide mission.

Wonderful. Just when I think my day couldn't possibly get any more surreal, I am getting a mission briefing from a Voodoo Loa.

"Before we begin, Madi, ma belle, return to your forces," Legba commands, his voice regaining a brief, flickering spark of its former divine authority. "Do what ya can, darlin'. I'll send Ava to join ya real soon-like."

Madi spreads her magnificent, leathery wings, the sheer span of them momentarily blocking out the dim, amber light of the bar. She gives him a sharp, deeply respectful nod, her eyes filled with an unspoken sorrow, then steps backwards into the darkness. The shadows in the corner of the room immediately rise up like living, sentient ink, swirling around her armoured ankles before swallowing her completely.

Watching her vanish in such a calm, organised, and painless way makes me profoundly wish I had arrived via the same method, instead of being slammed to the floor like a sack of wet cement.

"Belphegor now sits on de throne of de Underworld," Legba continues, his tone dropping into a dangerous, secretive register that forces me to step closer to the bar. "De old ways, de old rulers, dey are overthrown. De hierarchy of hell is broken. But hear me well, little Dhampir—Lucifer is not dead, not like poor Hecate. He breathes still."

I blink at the sheer magnitude of the statement. I have no idea who Belphegor is, but I do know of Lucifer. In the human world, he is known as the Morning Star. The original rebel. The literal devil.

You've got to be kidding me.

Well, at least I now know who has Reya prisoner. The question is: can I get to him, kill him, and then free Reya? Does this also mean that Belphegor is the one orchestrating this New Orleans apocalypse? My mind scrambles to process the theological and tactical implications. If Lucifer is still alive, would that mean that while freeing Reya, we also were to free him? Would he be able to get things back in control and end this brewing war? What hope does a human with a silver sword and a newly acquired blood mutation have?

"He is chained," Legba adds grimly. "Thrown into de darkest pit, a prisoner, just like your Reya. Dey keep him locked away because dere monsters in de deep dat only he can tame if dey ever break loose."

The fiery-tempered witch with her destructive purple flames, the sister we believed was lost to darkness, whose absence left a void in our team, is actually alive in hell. A sudden, fierce hope sparks within me, cutting through my fear and fatigue. Though small, this flame is enough. As long as she is alive, there is a path to bring her back. Her survival gives me more reasons to fight.

Legba reaches for his cane, his knuckles tightening painfully around the carved wood. "If I fall dis day, de gates will crack wide, never to close. A literal hell on earth will follow. If dat darkness comes, de only hope for dis world rests on Reya and her sisters. She is de key, Ava. She can seal de gates for good—a trick even I cannot do."

He looks at me then, his eyes peering directly into my fractured, Dhampir soul.

"She is far more dan we bargained for. Even Hecate did not see de true depths of her power. When I touched dat girl to read her, I felt a shadow inside her… something old, ancient, and it did not take kindly to my knocking."

"Dey must survive until dey are ready," Legba warns, his voice urgent, pulling me from my spiralling thoughts. "Den, Reya must take up de mantle. You will protect dem, Ava. You will see dey live to meet de violent destinies we spun for dem. Well, for Reya, at least—de spirits never planned for three of dem, but fate weaves a strange tapestry."

"I'll get her out," I say. My voice is low, a lethal, unwavering promise that rings with absolute certainty in the quiet bar. It isn't just a mission objective anymore; it is a blood oath. I will tear down the gates of hell myself if it means bringing Reya back to her family. "But what about your city? What is hitting New Orleans that has you hiding in the Veil?"

Legba's expression darkens drastically, and for a moment, the shadows in the room seem to bleed toward him, drawn by the immense gravity of his grief.

"It is not just demons, ti fi. De Loa, my brothers and sisters, dey are being wiped out. Hunted. Slaughtered. Agwé of de water, Marinette of de fire, even fierce Ogoun… gone. Snuffed out like cheap candles in a hurricane."

I feel a cold knot of absolute dread tighten in my stomach, twisting my insides. The Loa are pillars of immense, ancient power. They are gods to the people of this city. To wipe them out isn't just murder; it is to dismantle the very foundation of this region's spiritual architecture.

"Something walks de streets of my Quarter," he continues, his voice trembling slightly, betraying a fear I never thought a god could possess. "Something dat does not wake de wards. Where it steps, magic just… fades away. It dies. De world goes silent. It is an unmaking. Whatever beast dis is, it hates us simply because we are."

"What do you expect me to do against something that can effortlessly hunt and kill even you? Is it this Belphegor? Is there a chance I can take him out and get Reya back?" I ask, my heart sinking into my boots.

"No chérie, not Belphegor, he is just de puppet."

"Crap!" I can't help saying aloud. I am a highly trained soldier, a tactical expert, and a newly minted Dhampir with enhanced speed and strength, but I am not a god-killer. I am not equipped to fight such power.

"Fer now, ya just survive. Mebbe if we break de army invading my city, de master will retreat to the shadows. I have a trinket for you… something to tip de scales," Legba says, a faint, proud smile touching the corners of his mouth.

He raises his gnarled hand, waving it over the polished bar counter in a fluid, graceful motion that defies his apparent exhaustion. The crystal glassware vanishes into thin air with a soft pop, and in its wake, a suit of beautifully engraved armour materialises out of a cloud of golden sparks, resting heavily on the bar.

I freeze, my eyes widening to the size of saucers. "Is that for me?"

It appears to be of an age long past, a masterpiece of lethal elegance captured in time. I find myself holding my breath for an instant, as my tactical mind begins to evaluate the artistry before me. The armour is a stunning fusion of dark copper and gleaming gold, each piece expertly crafted to create an enchanting harmony. Intricate engravings weave across the surface in swirling, primal patterns that seem almost alive, dancing and shifting when viewed too long, reminiscent of slow-moving currents in a river flowing with gold and copper hues. The craftsmanship is so exquisite, it draws me in, each detail telling a story of ancient battles and the warriors who once wore it.

I reach out, my fingers trembling slightly, and brush the metal. It is warm to the touch, thrumming with a faint, resonant vibration that instantly syncs with my own mutated heartbeat. Across the breastplate and the articulated shoulder guards, glowing blue runes pulse with a soft, rhythmic light. The colour of the magic matches my new, icy blue eyes perfectly, as if the suit had been forged specifically for my biology, designed to resonate with the unique, hybrid frequency of my Dhampir blood.

"It is, little Dhampir," Legba says. "Dis armour belonged to de very last of your kind. I pulled it from de wreckage of dat final battle, mended de scars myself. It was no easy task; forged by ancient hands to keep de vampire plague at bay, its magic is old. De runes woven into de metal will shield you from dark arts. Put it on, and be quick. De sands in de hourglass are falling fast."

I want to grab the armour immediately, but my training screams a warning. In this world, nothing is free. Not even gifts from gods.

"What is this going to cost me?" I ask, my voice cautious.

"A gift is a gift, child. I ask for no coin, only a promise. Keep de Harpers breathing. Hecate, she thought joining dis taskforce would open your eyes slow, let you see de truth of our world in your own time. But de time for slow plans is dead," Legba says, his gaze drifting as if he's already seeing the end of the world playing out behind my shoulders.

"Fine," I mutter, picking up the metal. It is surprisingly light, almost weightless in my hands, yet it feels denser than steel. "Do you have somewhere for me to change?"

Legba waves his hand again, and a tall, antique dressing screen made of dark silk and carved ivory appears beside me.

Without needing instructions, I begin to strip off my heavy tactical vest, strapping the enchanted metal over my torso. It is surprisingly light. The moment the clasps lock into place, a surge of pure, unadulterated energy shoots through my veins, clearing lingering fatigue from my muscles as I feel the armour slowly shift to fit me perfectly, conforming to the contours of my body as if it were a second skin.

I look like a Valkyrie stepping out of a blood-soaked nightmare. I absolutely love it.

"Magnifique," Legba says, his voice filled with a grim sort of pride as he looks at the warrior he has just armoured.

Before I can ask him more about the monster stalking the Loa, or how exactly these glowing blue runes protect me from demonic attacks, Legba grips his cane with both hands and strikes it violently against the floor.

The sound is not a tap; it is a deafening, apocalyptic thunderclap that echoes as if we are inside a sealed tomb, vibrating violently through my very teeth and shaking the floor.

In terrifying, agonising slow motion, the entire back wall of the bar begins to dissolve. It doesn't break or crumble like normal architecture. It turns into floating grey ash that drifts away on a sudden, blistering-hot wind.

The tranquil, melancholic illusion of the quiet bar is shattered instantly, ripped open like a festering wound to reveal the horrifying truth.

Revealed before us is a brutal, apocalyptic nightmare. It is a street in the French Quarter, but it has been transformed into a hellscape dragged straight from Dante's Inferno.

The sky above New Orleans is no longer blue, or even the black of night; it is choked with thick, oily, toxic black smoke that blots out the stars and rains burning soot upon the ruins. Historic buildings, once beautiful, proud, and vibrant, now crumble and weep rivers of broken brick, melted wrought iron, and shattered mortar.

Then the sound hits me, a cacophony of terror that nearly brings me to my knees. The terrifying, high-pitched screams of the dying, the guttural, monstrous roars of invading demonic forces, and the rhythmic, concussive boom of magical explosions flood the room, clawing at my eardrums with savage intensity.

The blistering heat of a thousand supernatural fires blasts into the cool, air-conditioned sanctuary of the bar, searing my exposed skin and singeing the stray hairs on the back of my neck.

This is New Orleans. Or what is left of it.

"Go," Legba commands, his voice echoing with absolute, uncompromising divine authority over the sickening symphony of destruction outside. "Save de city if you can. And beware de silence."

I pull my sword fully from its sheath. The metal gleams with a lethal, cold light against the hellish, orange glow of the encroaching fires. The blade hums in my hand, vibrating with eager anticipation, hungry for demonic blood.

Another day, another impossible battle.

I tighten my grip on the hilt as my heart thumps a beat inside my new copper breastplate. At least now I will look deadly and stylish while I carve my way through the horde.

"But little Dhampir," Legba adds. His divine authority suddenly vanishes entirely, replaced by the tired, rasping, broken voice of a dying man who has seen too much death for one eternity.

"If de city falls—and de spirits whisper dat she already has—you run. Hear me? Survive. Dis is an order from de crossroads, not a request. De future needs breath in your lungs."

He pauses, leaning heavily on the splintering cane, his dark eyes softening just a fraction, showing a glimmer of genuine paternal affection.

"And if you can… keep my Madi alive. Dat one… she is my favourite."

I don't look back. I can't. If I look at his defeated face now, I might hesitate. I might remember that I am just a human girl from a broken home, playing soldier in a war of gods and monsters.

I am coming home, Rose. I promise, I project into the world one last time, closing my eyes and pouring every single ounce of my will, my soul, and my love into the mental message, hoping against all odds that somehow, across the dimensions, she might hear it.

As if sensing my absolute resolve, or perhaps as a divine reward for stepping into the fire, the severed connection suddenly sparks to life.

It is like a massive dam bursting open; a glorious, overwhelming rush of warmth, scent, and pure emotion slams violently back into my soul. I gasp, tears instantly pricking the corners of my eyes.

I can feel her. I can feel the fierce, protective, burning heat of Rose's presence. I can feel the distant, steady thrum of her heart beating as clearly as if it were inside my own chest. The ability to reach her, to feel her love, returns now that I am once again anchoring myself in the physical world of the living.

The feeling of her, is the ultimate catalyst. It instantly turns my paralysing fear into razor-sharp focus. I am not alone. She is with me, woven into the very fabric of my being.

I open my icy blue eyes, staring into the roaring apocalypse of the French Quarter. I turn my back on the fading sanctuary of the jazz bar, step over the threshold, and plunge directly into hell.

CHAPTER 28

THE ASHES OF THE CRESCENT CITY

I step through the threshold of Papa Legba's fading sanctuary and plummet straight into the gaping, burning maw of the Quarter.

The shift from the quiet, smoky, melancholic pocket dimension of the Loa's jazz bar to the harsh, unforgiving physical world doesn't just happen; it hits me like a superheated brick aimed directly at my face. It is not a magical, seamless transition. It is a violent, jarring collision with a completely unhinged reality that knocks the wind clean out of my lungs and leaves my ears ringing with the sound of a thousand nightmares.

One moment, I am surrounded by the timeless, amber glow of a quiet crossroads bar, inhaling the scent of aged rum and expensive cigar smoke. Next, the atmosphere slams into me with the force of a concussive shockwave.

New Orleans, the lively, pulsating, magical heart of supernatural refuge in North America, has been transformed into a jagged, screaming, apocalyptic battleground.

I gasp instinctively as I land heavily on the cobblestones, but the air is thick, toxic, and utterly devoid of clean oxygen, choking the back of my throat with the taste of ash. I can feel the intense, blistering heat before I even manage to open my eyes fully. It is a searing, oppressive radiance that suggests the city isn't merely burning; it is being methodically, gleefully consumed by an inferno born of malice.

When my vision finally clears, the sky above me—which should be a comforting, velvet sheet of midnight blue over the Crescent City—is completely choked by oppressive, rolling plumes of toxic black smoke. The clouds coil like massive, suffocating serpents through the air, blotting out the moon and the stars, leaving the entire world bathed in a bruised, sickly orange twilight that casts long, demonic shadows across the ruined streets.

The scent assaults my newly awakened Dhampir senses with a nauseating, visceral blend that causes my stomach to churn violently. It combines the overwhelming, sulphurous stench of the pit—the rotten-egg smell of ancient demons—with the sharp, suffocating aroma of centuries-old wood, burning down to white-hot embers. Beneath the fire and brimstone, heavy, thick, and undeniably tragic, is the unmistakable metallic scent of fresh blood—both human and supernatural—soaked deeply into the porous, historic pavement.

Welcome home, Ava, my internal voice mocks darkly. *Hope you like the smell of genocide.*

I drop immediately into a low, tactical crouch over the uneven cobblestones, my combat boots skidding slightly on something wet and sticky. I don't want to look down. I don't want to know if it's motor oil leaking from a crushed vehicle or the gore of the city's defenders.

My eyes water intensely from the stinging, smoke-filled air, but I force them wide open, scanning my chaotic surroundings with a predatory intensity that borders on manic.

The historic, beautiful architecture of the French Quarter is being systematically dismantled by forces that possess absolutely no regard for history, culture, or life. The magnificent wrought-iron balconies, those iconic, delicate laces of the city's facade, are currently twisted and melting like black wax, dripping molten metal onto the streets below. Storefronts have been brutally hollowed out, their insides gutted by unnatural, roaring fires that burn in shades of sickly green and hellish violet.

But it isn't just the physical destruction that sends a freezing, bone-deep shiver through my bones; it is the catastrophic magical fallout.

As I look around the perimeter of the surviving buildings, my Dhampir sight picks up a strange, desperate shimmer in the air. It is a frantic, vibrating distortion, resembling the heat haze you see on an asphalt highway in the dead of summer, but it is heavily charged with a buzzing, electric tension. It looks exactly like the shimmering ripple of protective magic I saw at the threshold of the warded room back at the Harper property.

The horrifying realisation hits me, settling as heavy as a lead weight in my gut. The entire Quarter is warded. Entire city blocks have been painted with ancient, protective magic, likely drawn in blood, sweat, and sheer desperation by the local covens to shield the inhabitants from this exact, world-ending nightmare.

And they are failing. Catastrophically.

I watch in absolute horror as a sickening sort of sizzling occurs in the atmosphere above a nearby club. Bursts of dying red and purple sparks shower down like morbid, magical fireworks around the buildings that have sustained heavy structural damage from the invading demons. The magical wards are fundamentally tethered to the physical reality of the stone, brick, and mortar; as the architecture shatters under the brutal assault, the magic leaks out into the toxic sky, bleeding away into nothingness.

Every single fallen brick is a gaping hole in the shield. Every collapsed roof leaves the terrified, screaming people trapped inside utterly defenceless against the monsters roaming the streets.

I hit the ground running. There is no time to formulate a grand strategy. There is no time to call for backup.

My newly mutated Dhampir muscles fire with a terrifying, explosive speed that feels almost too powerful for my human frame to contain. Every massive stride covers yards of ground, propelling me down the dead centre of the debris-strewn street. I am a blur of tactical gear and glowing, enchanted copper-and-gold armour.

I have one overriding, absolute objective burning in my mind like a physical brand. The crumpled piece of paper Freya frantically shoved into my hand before the portal swallowed me feels like it's actively searing through the fabric of the pocket I shoved it in. I can feel the edges of it pressing against my thigh, a constant, physical reminder of exactly why I am charging headfirst into this inferno.

I know exactly where I am. I realise with a sudden, sharp jolt of adrenaline that I am only a few chaotic, blood-soaked blocks away from that address.

Priestess Marassa. I must locate her. I need to save her because she is vital to the Harpers, and this has to matter to me.

As I sprint past a burning, overturned streetcar, the hair on the back of my neck stands at absolute attention. A low, vibrating growl echoes from the thick shadows of a narrow alleyway to my left. It isn't the mindless snarl of a demon; it is the calculated, predatory rumble of a hunter.

Three massive, heavily muscled beasts step out from the smoke, blocking my path entirely. They are enormous—far larger than any natural timber wolf—their fur matted with blood and ash, their eyes burning with a fanatical hatred for anything that doesn't belong to their twisted pack.

I don't even break my stride. I draw my silver sword from the sheath across my back. The metal sings a beautiful, lethal, high-pitched chime as it clears the leather, catching the hellish orange glow of the burning buildings.

The lead wolf lunges, its powerful hind legs launching it through the air with terrifying speed, its massive jaws snapping open to reveal rows of bone-crushing teeth aimed directly at my throat.

Time slows to a glorious, syrupy crawl. The Dhampir predator inside my mind takes the wheel, flooding my veins with icy, calculated focus.

I slide perfectly on my knees across the slick cobblestones, leaning back so the wolf flies mere inches above my face. As the beast passes over me, I thrust my silver blade straight upward, burying it deep into the soft, vulnerable underbelly of the creature. The momentum of the wolf's own leap does all the work, slicing it open from sternum to tail.

Hot, foul-smelling blood rains down on my armour, but I am already moving. I roll back up to my feet just as the second wolf charges.

This one is smarter. It stays low, snapping at my legs, trying to hamstring me and bring me down to its level. I parry a vicious bite with the flat of my blade, the impact jarring my wrists, and spin out of its reach. My eyes dart around the immediate environment, searching for an advantage.

Lying in the gutter, partially melted but still solid, is a heavy, cast-iron grate that had been blown off a storm drain.

I release my grip on the sword, allowing it to tumble to the ground, where it clangs against the cold, unforgiving stones. A sudden muscle cramp seizes my leg, forcing me to crouch low, my fingers pressing against the cool, rusty iron of the grate beneath me.

In that tense moment, I sense the wolf's presence behind me, its predatory instincts sharp and focused. As it lunges forward, its powerful jaws snapping with primal fury, I summon every ounce of adrenaline surging through my veins. A wild, feral roar erupts from deep within my chest, echoing into the dimness surrounding us.

The stupid mutt has fallen into my plan perfectly as I unleash all my strength with fierce determination and swing the heavy grate upwards, gripping it like a makeshift club, just in time to deflect the canine assault aimed at my face. The sickening contact of the grate against its head and jaw connects perfectly. There is a sickening, deafening crunch of shattering bone and tearing ligaments. The sheer kinetic momentum of my Dhampir strength sends the massive beast flying completely sideways, crashing violently through the display window of a burning antique shop in a spectacular shower of broken glass and splintered wood. *It doesn't get back up.*

The third wolf decides to play dirty. It attempts to flank me, darting back into the thick shadows of a narrow alleyway to get behind my guard, waiting for me to turn my back to retrieve my sword.

I don't give it the satisfaction of a sneak attack.

I spot a heavy, decorative silver-plated serving tray lying discarded in the gutter—likely looted and dropped by a terrified scavenger fleeing from a nearby high-end restaurant.

I kick it up into my free hand with a precise, lightning-fast flick of my combat boot, spin on my heel, and hurl it like a lethal, spinning frisbee straight into the pitch-black darkness of the alley.

"Fetch," I whisper grimly, snatching my sword back up from the pavement and breaking into a dead sprint once more.

The heavy silver disc slices through the smoky air with a deadly, metallic whirr. A sharp, agonised yelp echoes from the shadows, followed by a hefty, wet thud, and then absolute silence settles in my wake.

One iron grate, a silver tray, and a perfectly timed slice. Three dead wolves. If the world survives this night, I should really start charging the CIA double for my operational efficiency.

I noticed something unexpected on two of the wolves. A brand burned into their skin with the letters LP. For a moment, I wonder what they might mean, then it hits me: Lorcan Pack. They have branded their turned wolves to identify them to anyone else, so they know who they belong to.

The deeper I push into the heart of the Quarter, the thicker and more desperate the resistance becomes. Every single turn down a new street is a gamble with death. The air is rapidly becoming an unbreathable soup of falling ash and atomised blood.

As I round a sharp corner onto Bourbon Street—historically the world's most famous, vibrant party strip, now a neon-lit slaughterhouse—I am immediately forced to dive for my life.

A human body is brutally thrown from a second-story wrought-iron balcony, crashing heavily into the street just inches from where I stood, cracking a few of the cobblestones.

I roll flawlessly over my shoulder, the movement fluid and automatic, rising instantly into a defensive, coiled crouch. My icy blue eyes scan the surrounding rooftops and balconies for more threats, and I find them instantly.

Four vampires drop lightly onto the street from the fire escape. They land with absolute, feline grace, absorbing the impact without a sound, but there is absolutely nothing graceful or refined about their faces.

They are twisted, horrific masks of unadulterated hunger. Their fangs are fully extended, dripping with saliva and blood. Their eyes are completely, unnaturally red—void of any lingering humanity or intellect. These don't look like the controlled, calculating vampires we hunted back in Pittsburgh; these seem newly turned, utterly feral, and completely consumed by the blood frenzy of the apocalypse.

"Fresh meat," one of them hisses, his voice a wet, rattling sound that makes my skin crawl.

"Try it, leech," I taunt, spinning my sword in a tight, defensive arc, the silver blade humming a deadly warning.

They attack simultaneously, moving with the blinding speed of their kind. The first vampire lunges, his clawed hands reaching for me. I sidestep his clumsy, desperate grab, bringing the pommel of my sword down brutally onto the back of his neck. As he stumbles forward, I reverse my grip and drive the silver blade straight through his back, piercing his heart.

He erupts into a massive cloud of grey, greasy ash before he even hits the ground.

The next vampire throws itself around my waist from my blind spot, tackling me with surprising, overwhelming weight. We hit the ground hard, rolling chaotically across the pavement through a puddle of stagnant, foul-smelling water and iridescent demon blood.

He snaps his jaws frantically at my neck, desperate to find purchase on my pale skin, his breath smelling of copper and old, rotting graves.

I let out a frustrated, guttural growl. I release my grip on my sword, knowing it's entirely too close for a swing, and punch both my hands upward in a powerful, dual-palm strike.

I catch the feral vampire squarely under his jutting chin. The sheer, explosive kinetic force snaps his neck backwards with a loud, sickening pop that echoes sharply in the narrow street. As he lies temporarily stunned, his red eyes rolling back into his skull, I reach quickly into the tactical rig attached to my enchanted breastplate and pull out one of my specialised, hand-carved wooden stakes.

I drive it straight down through his chest with a visceral, meaty thud.

Poof. More ash explodes directly into my face. I cough violently, swatting the thick dust away from my eyes and nostrils, and snatch my stake back from the pile of discarded, blood-stained clothes on the ground.

The remaining two vampires freeze in their tracks. They are staring in absolute shock at the piles of ash that used to be their hunting members.

I stand up slowly, rolling my shoulders to relieve the tension. I retrieve my silver sword from the puddle, the metal hissing slightly as it cuts through the demon blood, and raise a single, mocking eyebrow at the survivors. I can actively see them calculating the odds, looking at the sheer carnage I've left in my wake in a matter of seconds.

"Well?" I ask, my voice echoing coldly in the street. I wipe a thick smear of soot and gore off my cheek with the back of my armoured hand. "Are we doing this, or are you going to run back to the shadows?"

They don't even bother to answer. They turn on their heels and sprint in the opposite direction, moving so fast they leave a blur in the smoky air.

I let them go. I don't have the luxury of time to chase down stragglers, and my absolute priority is still the Priestess waiting at the end of this burning road.

I push onward through the treacherous maze of smouldering cars, their charred remnants casting a grotesque silhouette against the backdrop of destruction. Collapsed masonry looms around me, creating jagged obstacles that threaten to ensnare my every step. The air is thick with an ethereal presence, the anguished wails of lost souls echoing in the ruins of this city, their spectral forms flickering like flames in the twilight. Though their sorrow tugs at my heart, I have no time to offer solace; the mission consumes me.

The oppressive heat wraps around me like an insidious fog, a relentless force that bears down on my skin and makes the metal of my armour feel as if it is searing into my flesh. My lungs cry out for fresh, untainted air, each breath a struggle against the smoky tendrils that cling to me. Yet, I steel myself against the fiery discomfort, honing my focus on the rhythmic cadence of my respiration, drawing strength from it as I march determinedly toward the objective that lies ahead, unwavering amidst the chaos.

As I approach the main junction leading to Marassa's street, I hit the front lines of the demon-possessed human forces.

I don't see the towering, heavily armoured Dukes of Hell here; I'm not actually sure if any of them are here, I'm guessing if they are, then those monstrosities must be guarding the higher-value targets or fighting the surviving Loa elsewhere in the city. This is a fundamentally different kind of war—one that is infinitely more complex, morally grey, and a thousand times more tragic to behold.

The demons here are puppeteering innocent locals, terrified tourists, and trapped residents. Their eyes burn with an infernal, sickly black light, leaking a dark, viscous fluid that constantly stains their cheeks like tears of oil. Their movements are jerky, broken, and deeply unnatural, as if they are being pulled by invisible, cruel strings. Their fragile human bodies are being pushed far beyond their biological limits by the dark entities riding them, their muscles tearing and bones fracturing from the strain.

I stop dead in my tracks, my chest heaving. I look at the makeshift mob forming an impenetrable barricade across the street—a woman in a torn floral sundress, an old man with a hunched back wielding a bloody pipe, a young couple with their faces twisted in demonic fury.

I have absolutely no way of knowing if these humans were recently possessed and are still screaming inside their own minds, or if their souls have already been shredded, leaving them as nothing more than dead, hollowed-out husks.

The horrifying, unyielding reality of demonic possession is that unless the parasitic entity leaves immediately, the host's mind is systematically destroyed. Since I do not possess Maya's divine magic and cannot perform a miraculous exorcism in the middle of a war zone, knocking them unconscious is a pointless, naive fantasy. A demon doesn't sleep, and it won't stay down just because its meat suit has a concussion.

I draw a deep, shaky breath, desperately fortifying my resolve against the absolute horror of what I am about to do. My heart doesn't race, but it does beat harder when it does actually decide to beat. *Still can't get used to it.* It feels like it might burst from my ribs, not with the thrill of battle or the fear of death, but with a crushing, suffocating sense of grief.

I'm sorry, I project into the void, hoping whatever gods are watching know I have no choice. *I'm so fucking sorry.*

The mob spots me. A dozen possessed humans shriek simultaneously with layered, nightmarish demonic voices—a terrifying mix of human screams overlaid with guttural, infernal roars—and swarm aggressively toward me.

I grip the hilt of my blade tighter, my knuckles turning white beneath my tactical gloves. There will be no non-lethal holds today. There is no alternative. This is a mercy kill on a devastating, city-wide scale.

A possessed, middle-aged man in a brightly coloured, blood-soaked Hawaiian shirt swings a heavy piece of jagged rebar directly at my head with enough supernatural force to shatter solid concrete.

I duck smoothly under the wild swing, the rusted metal whistling inches over my ponytail. I step swiftly into his exposed guard, close the distance, and drive the pommel of my sword directly into his temple, shattering the skull and ending the host's suffering instantly. The black smoke violently ejects from his mouth as the body drops, the demon banished back to the ether. I proceed to take out demon after demon as they reach me.

When one of the actual demonic brutes commanding the mob steps into my path—a hulking, crimson-skinned creature with a jaw full of razor wire instead of teeth, and arms thicker than ancient tree trunks—I don't hold back a single ounce of my power.

I let out a dark, adrenaline-fueled laugh that sounds entirely foreign, cold, and lethal even to my own ears. *Finally,* something I don't have to feel an ounce of guilt about butchering.

I draw a throwing knife from the small sheath strapped to my thigh armour and hurl it with pinpoint accuracy straight into the brute's right eye.

The demon roars in agony, a sound like grinding metal and collapsing buildings, dropping its heavy guard to frantically claw at the silver embedded deep in its face.

I use the crucial distraction to close the gap, ducking under its massive, wildly swinging fist that would have easily taken my head clean off my shoulders. I pivot sharply on my left foot, driving my silver sword deep into the soft, unprotected tissue under its ribs. I angle the weapon sharply upward, forcing the blade through the thick muscle to pierce its dark, rotting heart.

I rip the blade out with a vicious twist, resulting in a massive spray of black, viscous blood that smells intensely like burnt rubber and raw sewage. The demon's body starts to burn and dissolves into foul-smelling smoke before it even hits the ground, leaving nothing behind but a lingering stench of rot and a dark stain on the cobblestones. *I really thought it would turn to ash like my hellfire-infused blade normally does to the enemy.* I can't help but screw up my nose at the stench.

Not that I smell any better, I am entirely covered in sweat, human blood, black ichor, and grey soot. My muscles are beginning to cry out in protest, my lungs burning with every ragged breath, but I finally break through the end of the mob and reach the correct address.

Priestess Marassa's magic shop is currently under heavy, unrelenting siege.

The building itself is a charming, historic two-story colonial house with wrap-around wooden balconies hanging with weeping Spanish moss. But at this exact moment, it resembles a doomed fortress on the absolute brink of total collapse.

The front display windows are entirely shattered, massive shards of glass and hundreds of spilt, colourful potion bottles scattered across the pavement like shimmering, magical debris. The heavy, ornate wooden double doors have been brutally smashed into splintered kindling.

A vast, terrifying horde of shadowy figures, feral vampires, possessed humans, and enormous, fiery hellhounds are frantically attempting to break through a glowing, violently pulsing violet barrier that surrounds the immediate shopfront.

The defensive magic is stunning, ancient, but clearly desperate. The violet light pulses and hums with a deep frequency, fighting bravely against the pressing darkness, but I can visibly see the deep, jagged cracks forming in the shield. Sizzling bursts of red and purple sparks shower down like molten rain each time a massive demon pushes its weight against the barrier. It's exactly like watching a fragile glass dam about to burst under the immense, crushing pressure of a tidal wave.

Inside the shop, standing amidst the heartbreaking ruin of overturned tables of tarot cards, crushed herbs, and shattered crystal balls, is the woman I presume to be Priestess Marassa.

She is a profoundly formidable woman, tall, regal, and commanding, her dark skin glowing ethereally in the failing, violet light of her own wards. Her hands are raised high above her head, radiating raw, desperate magic as she struggles to sustain the barrier. Her face is drawn tight with extreme effort, sweat beading heavily on her forehead, her dark eyes wide with an exhaustion that speaks of hours of uninterrupted combat.

She is completely cornered. A singular beacon of fading light in a sea of absolute, devouring black.

I don't hesitate.

I launch myself directly into the fray, letting out a fierce, blood-curdling battle cry that pierces cleanly through the roar of the surrounding fires and the screams of the dying city.

I cleave through the vanguard of the horde like a scythe through dry wheat.

A burning hellhound snaps viciously at my legs, its massive jaws dripping with molten, acidic saliva that hisses and smokes as it hits the pavement. I slide effortlessly underneath its gnashing teeth, using my momentum to raise my blade, cleanly decapitate the blazing beast in one fluid, upward strike. *I hope it wasn't a friend of Beastie.*

I don't even pause to celebrate the kill. I spin, driving my heavy pommel into the skull of a possessed human to drop him permanently, and swiftly cut off the arm of a feral vampire trying to claw at the violet shield. I find myself grimly laughing as the screaming creature turns to dust in the wind.

The horde suddenly shifts its collective focus to me—the new, highly violent threat systematically carving a bloody trail through their rear guard.

I welcome the attention. Every single demon, vampire, or hound glaring at me is one less enemy actively breaking down Marassa's final line of defence.

I fight like a woman entirely possessed by her own dark

shadow. The Destroyer is unleashed; she is kicking arse and magnificent.

My hellfire sword is a whirlwind of pure destruction, expertly deflecting lethal claws and severing limbs before my attackers can even blink. I am not just fighting for my own survival anymore; I am fighting for my new sisters, for Rose, and for the incredibly faint, fragile *hope* Papa Legba told me still remains in this burning world.

I will absolutely not let another innocent person die in my presence today.

I finally reach the very threshold of the magic shop just as a massive, heavily scaled demon raises a rusted, blood-stained battleaxe high above its head, preparing to smash the violet shield with a decisive blow.

I jump off the dented hood of a burning, abandoned taxicab, gain some brutal, supernatural altitude, and bring both of my combat boots down hard directly onto the back of the demon's thick neck.

There is a sickening, loud crunch as its cervical vertebrae instantly collapses under my weight. The massive creature is driven face-first into the pavement with enough force to crack the solid stone beneath it.

"Marassa!" I yell, stepping forcefully over the twitching, dying demon and placing my bare hand directly against the violent, crackling hum of the defensive shield.

My mutated Dhampir senses instantly recognise the protective, ancient ward. The magical barrier ripples like disturbed water under my touch, sensing the divine intention behind my mission, and seamlessly allows me to step through the threshold and into the shop.

The ambient heat inside the building is suffocating, smelling overwhelmingly of burning white sage, scorched old parchment, and the lingering stench of brimstone seeping in from the streets.

Marassa lowers her trembling hands for a fraction of a second, gasping desperately for air as the violet light around the shop dims dangerously, the cracks widening.

"Who are you!" she breathes, her voice incredibly strained, raspy, and thoroughly exhausted from her magical effort. "You shouldn't be here, chérie! The city is lost! There is nothing left to save!"

"I'm well aware of the real estate value!" I yell back over the deafening, chaotic roar of the battle raging just inches outside the barrier. I grab her arm, my grip tight, urgent, and unyielding, immediately feeling the violent tremor of magical depletion in her muscles.

The violet shield gives a terrifying, high-pitched, glass-shattering crack. The shadows outside press harder, their horrific, demonic faces pressing aggressively against the dying magic in grotesque, starving sneers, their claws scraping against the invisible barrier.

"Freya sent me," I yell.

"Freya... do I know a Freya?" the Priestess asks, blinking through the sweat, looking as if she is about to collapse from sheer exhaustion right there on the floor. "Wait... do you mean Freya Harper?"

"Yes, the Harpers sent me! They said you helped them when they needed it most, so they owe you. We are leaving! Right fucking now!" I command, hauling her forward with my enhanced strength.

Together, we sprint for the rear of the ruined shop, navigating the overturned shelves and spilled inventory.

I kick open the heavy oak door leading to the back alley with enough force to almost take it off its hinges. I practically throw the exhausted Priestess out into the narrow, dark passageway just as a massive hellhound throws its full, burning weight against the front of the shop.

I turn back just in time to witness the inevitable.

The violet wards finally, catastrophically collapse.

The protective magic shatters into a million useless, dying sparks with a concussive sound like a military-grade bomb going off. It is a psychic shockwave that rattles my teeth in my skull and briefly blurs my vision.

The screaming horde of nightmares floods into the shop instantly. They are a tidal wave of teeth, claws, and fire, tearing apart absolutely everything in their path—the ancient crystals, the spell books, the centuries of collected magical history.

I slam the back door shut, and Marassa, moving on pure adrenaline, using magic, she quickly throws the heavy iron deadbolts just as bodies begin slamming violently against the wood from the inside.

The doorframe immediately begins to groan and buckle under the crushing weight of a dozen starving monsters.

"Keep moving!" I shout, grabbing Marassa's hand and dragging her deeper into the smoke-filled, claustrophobic alley.

We plunge deeper into the burning, chaotic heart of New Orleans, entirely unsure if there is a single safe patch of ground left in this godforsaken city, knowing that to stop moving is to die.

CHAPTER 29

WHO'S A GOOD GIRL? (SPOILER. NOT ME)

The narrow alleyway hidden directly behind Priestess Marassa's ruined magic shop is no longer a simple passage meant for discreet deliveries or quiet exits. In the wake of the city's supernatural collapse, it has been violently transformed into a suffocating, claustrophobic tunnel of absolute nightmares.

Choking, greasy black smoke billows through the tight corridor, mingling with a toxic, falling ash that clings stubbornly to the back of my throat like a wet, abrasive shroud. The air is unnaturally thick, heavy enough that I feel as though I can literally chew on it. It is saturated with the cloying, rotten-egg stench of demonic sulphur and the sharp, undeniable metallic tang of old, spilt blood. Every breath I take is a battle against my own lungs, a desperate gasp for oxygen in an atmosphere designed to smother the living.

I am dragging Marassa by her slender, trembling wrist, her dead weight pulling heavily against my aching shoulder joint. The Priestess is completely, utterly drained, having exhausted the absolute limits of her magical reserves to hold the protective wards for as long as she did. She stumbles behind me, her chest heaving with ragged, desperate gasps.

My military-issue combat boots slip dangerously on the slick, debris-covered cobblestones. I am sliding through a horrifying mixture of soot, shattered brick, and something viscous that I absolutely refuse to identify. The ground beneath us feels treacherous, a literal slip ‘n slide of apocalyptic gore.

Every single step forward is a brutal battle against gravity, exhaustion, and the oppressive, boiling atmosphere of the burning French Quarter.

Brilliant. Just perfect, my internal voice mocks, a cynical defence mechanism kicking in as my adrenaline spikes. *A romantic, midnight stroll through a literal apocalypse. I really should have stayed in bed today. Or, you know, listened to the panicked shifter, my mate, begging me not to jump through a portal to hell.*

Directly behind us, the reinforced oak door of the magic shop’s rear exit violently shudders in its frame. It doesn’t just shake; it groans under the sheer, unadulterated weight of the demonic horde that is slamming aggressively against the ancient wood.

I can hear the timber actively splintering, a series of sharp, rhythmic, bone-chilling cracks that sound exactly like suppressed gunshots echoing in the narrow, brick-lined space. The heavy iron deadbolts Marassa threw mere seconds ago are whining in high-pitched protest, the ancient hinges twisting and buckling under a supernatural force they were never designed to withstand. She must have added a little magic to them for the door to last this long.

The door is practically screaming its death throes. I know with absolute tactical certainty that it is buying us maybe a handful of precious seconds before this claustrophobic passage is entirely flooded with fanged nightmares, hellbeasts, and claws of vampires and shifters. If they breach the door before we reach the end of the alley, we will be trampled and torn to shreds in a matter of heartbeats. The narrow walls offer absolutely zero lateral movement for defensive combat. It will be a slaughterhouse.

“Keep your feet moving, Marassa!” I bark over the deafening roar of the inferno.

My voice sounds raw, stripped of its usual disciplined,

authoritative cadence. It sounds like the rasp of a lifelong chain smoker, ruined by the toxic soot filling the air.

I shove the exhausted Priestess forcefully ahead of me, positioning my own armoured body between her and the impending breach. I glance back over my shoulder, my mutated, icy blue Dhampir eyes piercing through the thick smoke to assess the integrity of our only barrier.

As my heightened vision locks onto the reinforced door, the centre panel violently, catastrophically explodes outward.

A massive, flaming paw rips through the thick oak as if it were made of wet tissue paper. The kinetic impact is immense. Burning, razor-sharp shards of splintered wood fly through the smoky air like lethal shrapnel. I'm glad we managed to put some distance between us and the door, or the shrapnel would be causing serious damage.

A hellhound's molten, dripping snout forcefully pushes its way through the freshly made, jagged gap in the timber.

The beast is a towering monument to destruction, its leathery skin coated in an intense firestorm. Its massive jaws snap wildly, dripping a highly acidic, glowing saliva that hisses and burns tiny craters into the cobblestones where it lands. The monster's eyes are glowing pits of pure, churning magma, and they lock instantly onto Marassa with a starving, malicious hunger that is almost palpable in the heavy air.

Not today, Fido. You're not getting the Priestess.

I don't even need to consciously process the tactical geometry of the strike; my newly awakened Dhampir instincts take the absolute wheel. In one fluid, blindingly fast motion, my right hand drops to the tactical sheath strapped securely to my thigh. My fingers close tightly around the leather grip of a perfectly balanced throwing knife.

I pivot sharply on my heel, the sudden, violent movement jarring my already aching hip joints, and launch the silver blade with every ounce of my supernatural strength.

The knife streaks through the thick, smoky air, a lethal, humming silver blur. It flies with absolute, pinpoint precision, burying itself straight up to the hilt directly into the hellhound's right, glowing magma eye.

The monster lets out a horrific, ear-piercing, high-pitched yelp of pure agony—a sound that vibrates right through my skull, rattling my teeth and sending a sickening shiver down my spine. The hellhound frantically thrashes backwards, its massive, bulky, burning body temporarily plugging the splintered hole it has just created in the oak door, effectively blocking the rest of the horde from pouring through the gap.

A stray, irritating thought flickers briefly through my adrenaline-soaked mind. *Why couldn't it just phase directly through the door like I've seen Beastie do back in Luna Falls?*

I don't have the luxury of time to stop and conduct a deep, theological debate about demonic phasing rules with the Priestess. The only logical tactical explanation is that Marassa has woven some kind of lasting, latent warding spell directly into the threshold itself, physically preventing the entities from shifting through the solid matter of her property line. Whatever the magical reason, the beast's agonised delay is the absolute only currency we possess right now, and I intend to spend it as quickly as humanly possible.

"Go, go, go!" I yell, grabbing Marassa's shoulder and shoving her toward the mouth of the alleyway where a faint, orange glow indicates the main street.

We burst out of the suffocating, smoke-filled brick tunnel, stumbling frantically onto a wider thoroughfare. It is a street that should look familiar from my previous operational briefings on the city, but it has been twisted into a nightmare hallucination.

The oppressive ambient heat out in the open is nothing short of apocalyptic. It isn't just the heat of a burning building; it feels as though the oxygen itself has caught fire, searing the delicate linings of my lungs with every ragged, desperate inhalation. Sweat instantly beads and pours down my face, stinging the minor cuts and scrapes I have accumulated.

I look up and feel a sudden, profound jolt of genuine, heart-stopping horror.

The majestic, intricate wrought-iron balconies that New Orleans is historically renowned for—the beautiful, dark metal lacework that defined the aesthetic of the French Quarter—are literally melting, as if some sort of magic has hit them.

The iron droops like black, weeping wax toward the ruined, blood-stained streets below, twisting into grotesque, agonised shapes under an invisible, supernatural heat that defies the laws of thermodynamics. Large, molten droplets of liquid iron rain down from the second stories, hitting the pavement with a sharp, explosive hiss, sending up plumes of white steam where they strike puddles of stagnant water and blood.

The historic storefronts, usually boasting vibrant colours and welcoming jazz, are gutted husks. Their insides burn with unnatural, roaring fires that completely ignore the building materials, burning in sickening shades of toxic green, deep violet, and putrid yellow. The very air ripples and distorts, thick with the dark magic of the encroaching Underworld.

But it is not the structural inferno that makes the blood run completely cold in my veins.

It is the sheer, overwhelming, devastating scale of the slaughter unfolding in the massive main intersection just a hundred yards ahead of us.

It is a desperate, bloody, and entirely doomed last stand.

A jagged, uneven defensive circle composed of about a dozen ragged, exhausted people is holding the dead centre of the intersection. They are standing back-to-back, a fragile island of resistance surrounded by a churning, bloodthirsty, deafening sea of absolute nightmare.

The attacking horde is a chaotic, horrific mix of the paranormal underworld. There are feral vampires, their faces twisted into monstrous visages, moving with blinding speed as they leap and slash at the defenders. There are massive, hulking Lorcan pack wolves, their fur matted with gore, snapping their bone-crushing jaws with fanatical hatred. And there are possessed, black-eyed humans, their fragile bodies being pushed to the point of breaking by the dark entities riding them, swinging pipes and machetes with reckless, suicidal abandon.

"By the Gods," Marassa whispers beside me, her voice breaking completely as she takes in the horrific scene. She leans heavily against the brick wall of the alley mouth, her dark eyes welling with tears of absolute despair. "The covens... the Crossroads demons... they are all dying."

She is right. The defenders are a desperate alliance of local New Orleans witches and tall, imposing Crossroads demons, fighting side-by-side in a desperate bid to hold the line. The witches are hurling everything they have—blasts of kinetic force, blinding arcs of elemental lightning, and classic fireballs—but their magic is flickering, weakening under the relentless, crushing attrition.

The Crossroads demons, possessing magnificent, leathery wings similar to Madi's, are wielding heavy, ancient polearms and massive swords, carving through the feral vampires with brutal efficiency. But for every monster they strike down, three more immediately surge forward from the burning shadows to take its place. It is a tidal wave of flesh and fang, and the defensive circle is rapidly shrinking.

"Stay right behind me," I command Marassa, my voice dropping an octave into a cold, lethal register. "Do not leave the radius of my blade. If anything gets past me, you run. You do not look back, you just run."

I don't wait for her to argue. I reach back over my shoulder and draw my sword.

The ancient, enchanted metal sings a high, clear, and beautiful note as it clears the leather sheath—a perfect, ringing chime that somehow slices cleanly through the deafening roar of the apocalyptic battle. The blade catches the hellish, multicoloured glow of the burning buildings, gleaming with a cold, uncompromising promise of absolute violence.

The Dhampir blood mutating inside my veins reacts to the imminent threat with a terrifying, intoxicating surge of pure, unadulterated power. The exhaustion that has been dragging at my limbs is instantly incinerated by a white-hot flash of adrenaline and the awakening of the predator within. The world around me seems to shift, details snapping into hyper-focus as the new me starts to take over, and the need for blood, the magic, starts to rise its ugly head. I can hear the erratic, terrified heartbeats of the surviving witches in the intersection; I can smell the distinct, individual scents of rotting vampire blood and wolf musk.

I transform into a relentless, walking meat grinder as I try to stay in control.

With a feral, battle-fuelled roar, I launch myself from the mouth of the alley and charge directly into the rear flank of the demonic horde.

I hit their lines with the concussive force of a runaway freight train. The element of surprise is my greatest tactical asset. They are entirely focused on the dying circle of defenders in the centre, completely unaware that the Destroyer has just arrived at their backs.

My hellfire-infused sword becomes a constant, blinding streak of lethal light against the darkness. I don't just swing the weapon; I become an extension of it, my body moving through the complex, deadly forms of my advanced martial arts training, enhanced by a supernatural speed that makes the world around me seem to move in slow motion.

A massive, grey-furred Lorcan wolf spins around at the sound of my approach, its jaws snapping open to tear out my throat. Before it can even fully turn, I slide on my knees across the slick cobblestones, driving the silver blade straight into its side. I gut the beast in just a few seconds, rolling back up to my feet seamlessly as the wolf collapses in a spray of hot, foul-smelling gore as a lung and intestines start spilling out.

"Behind us! We are flanked!" one of the possessed humans shrieks in a layered, demonic voice, pointing a rusted machete in my direction.

Four feral vampires immediately break away from the main assault and sprint toward me on all fours, moving like grotesque, oversized spiders. They hiss, their fangs fully descended, their eyes glowing with a mindless, starving red light.

I don't retreat a single inch. I step directly into their path.

The first vampire leaps at my face, claws extended. I sidestep the clumsy, feral attack with a slight pivot of my hips, bringing my heavy silver pommel crashing down directly onto the back of its neck. The spine shatters with a loud crack, and as the creature hits the ground, I drive my boot through its skull, turning it to ash instantly.

The second and third vampires attack simultaneously from opposite sides, attempting to overwhelm my guard. I drop into a low crouch, sweeping my blade in a wide, horizontal arc. The enchanted silver effortlessly shears through both of their legs at the kneecaps. As they shriek and fall to the pavement, I spin my sword in a tight figure-eight, cleanly decapitating both of them before they even register that they have lost their legs. The resulting dual explosion of grey ash coats my golden armour in a fine, morbid dust.

The fourth vampire hesitates, its feral instincts briefly warring with the sudden realisation that I am butchering its buddies with effortless precision.

I don't give it time to process the fear. I lunge forward, closing the ten-foot gap in a fraction of a second. I bypass my sword entirely, seizing the vampire by its torn collar with my free hand. I lift the creature clean off its feet, my bicep bulging, and hurl it with bone-shattering velocity directly into a burning, overturned police cruiser. The vampire hits the jagged metal frame and is instantly impaled, bursting into flames and starting to turn into ash that mixes with the vehicle's black smoke.

“Push forward!” I roar to Marassa over the din of the battle.

We fight our way slowly, methodically towards the defensive circle, bleeding and sweating for every single, miserable inch of pavement. The sheer attrition of the battle is utterly horrifying to witness up close.

Every few yards, despite my best efforts to draw aggro, I watch another brave defender fall. I see a young witch, her hands glowing with brilliant emerald light, get tackled from behind by a massive hellhound. She screams as she is dragged down into the sea of shadows, her light extinguishing in an instant. I see a towering Crossroads demon, his leathery wings torn to ribbons, finally succumb to the sheer weight of a dozen possessed humans piling onto him, violently pulling him down beneath the mob.

The tragedy is suffocating. I swing my blade until my arms burn with lactic acid, carving a bloody, ash-filled trench through the horde, but it feels like trying to empty an ocean with a teaspoon. For every monster I turn to dust, the shadows continue to vomit forth two more.

"Ava!" a familiar, desperate voice yells from the centre of the shrinking circle.

I smash the hilt of my sword into the face of a possessed woman, banishing the demon back to the Underworld inside her, and look up.

Standing in the absolute centre of the remaining defenders is Madi. The Crossroads demon looks completely ravaged. Her flawless, tailored suit is a distant memory. She is bleeding thick, black blood from a dozen deep lacerations across her torso and arms. She is still standing, wielding a massive, ancient spear that hums with dark, violent magic, thrusting it into any creature that dares step too close.

"Madi! Keep them focused on the front!" I shout back, carving my way through the last thick line of Lorcan wolves separating us.

With a final, desperate heave, I drive my sword through the chest of a massive, crimson-scaled demon, kick its dissolving body off my blade, and burst through the enemy lines into the centre of the defensive circle. Marassa stumbles in right behind me, immediately dropping to her knees on the blood-soaked road, weeping openly as she looks at the bodies of the fallen witches around us.

"You're still here, and alive!" Madi gasps, leaning heavily on her spear, her chest heaving with extreme exertion. She looks at me, her ancient eyes wide with a mixture of profound relief and absolute disbelief. "The Loa are being wiped out… I don't know how. The veil is falling."

"I know," I reply grimly, taking up a defensive stance facing the horde, my chest rising and falling rapidly. "We don't have much time. We need to fall back to a defensible position. We can't hold the open street."

"The courtyard of the old convent, just behind us!" one of the surviving witches shouts, a woman with a deep gash across her forehead, pointing a trembling, blood-stained finger toward a set of heavy, rusted iron gates attached to a high stone wall. "It's a bottleneck! They can't surround us there!"

"Move! Everyone, move to the gates!" I command, adopting the absolute authority of a military captain.

I take the rear guard, positioning myself between the retreating survivors and the advancing tide of monsters. Madi takes the front, using her massive spear to clear a path toward the convent walls.

The retreat is agonisingly slow. The horde realises we are trying to escape and intensifies their assault, abandoning all caution. They throw their bodies at us in a mindless frenzy of teeth, claws, and weapons.

I fight with relentless, precise efficiency, my mind detached from the chaos. I parry heavy axe blows from scaly demons, smoothly cut off the limbs of feral vampires, and kick large wolves back to keep our buffer zone secure. I would expect my sword to be coated in black ichor and ash, dulling its shine, but the hellfire burns away anything that touches it, so it remains bright in the surrounding darkness.

By the time we finally break through the heavy, rusted iron gates and spill into the enclosed stone courtyard of the convent, the toll is devastating.

I slam the massive iron gates shut behind us, wrapping a thick, rusted chain around the bars to temporarily secure them. I turn around and look at our forces.

Only five of us are left breathing.

Me, Madi, Priestess Marassa, and two heavily wounded, utterly exhausted local witches who look as though they have literally walked through a meat grinder. Their clothes are shredded, their skin pale from blood loss, and their magic almost depleted, but they still cast protective magic over the entrance to help protect us, even if it only lasts a minute.

The onslaught has been catastrophic. And now, after hours of relentless, brutal combat at extreme close quarters, my unnatural, mutated Dhampir stamina is finally beginning to fail me critically.

The raging, white-hot adrenaline that miraculously kept me moving at blinding speeds is swiftly burning out. As the chemical high recedes, it leaves behind a profound, bone-deep, sickening exhaustion that makes my very marrow feel as heavy as lead. My muscles tremble violently, a fine, uncontrollable shaking that travels from my calves up to my forearms. And in the back of my mind, the need to replenish my energy is growing stronger.

I had foolishly, arrogantly believed I could maintain this level of supernatural fighting forever. Now, the biological bill is due, and the price is going to be steep.

My lungs feel like they are actively burning inside my chest, and every ragged, desperate breath feels as though I am inhaling crushed glass. My vision swims dangerously, the edges of the courtyard tilting on its axis as dark spots dance across my retinas.

I am hitting the wall, I realise with a cold spike of dread. *I am running out of fuel.*

Outside the heavy iron gates, the horde is already massing. They throw their bodies against the rusted metal and magic with deafening, rhythmic clangs, their claws scraping against the bars, their glowing red eyes peering through the gaps with starving anticipation. The iron groans, the hinges protesting under the immense, crushing pressure of hundreds of monsters pushing forward while the magic sparks and rains down in what looks like mini fireworks.

"They won't hold for long," Madi states, her voice a grim, fatalistic rasp.

"Can you create a portal, one to get Marassa to the Harpers, then one to get us out of here so we can regroup?" I say, looking at her with a desperate plea for her to at least get Marassa to safety.

She drops her heavy spear completely, the ancient metal clattering loudly on the stone courtyard. "Do it now!" I shout at Madi, my voice cracking under the strain. I forcefully spin around to face the iron gates, raising my heavy, exhausted arms to hold my sword in a defensive guard. "At least get them out of here!"

Madi doesn't hesitate. She grabs Marassa and one of the wounded witches by their trembling shoulders, pulling them toward the centre of the courtyard. Her expression is focused, fierce, and utterly devoid of fear.

The Crossroads demon begins chanting loudly in an ancient, guttural, vibrating language that makes my teeth ache and the fine hairs on my arms stand at absolute attention. It sounds like the grinding of tectonic plates, a sound of profound, world-altering magic.

Her hands start glowing with a violent, tearing black light. Strangely, he reaches over to me, and with a few fingers, she scoops up some of my blood from my bleeding arm. Then, she jerks her hand towards the portal, causing my blood to spray over the black swirling clouds that are being generated.

The air directly behind them begins to violently warp and shred. The spatial distortion physically opens a swirling vortex similar to the one Papa Legba used to pull me to New Orleans. It is a jagged, unstable tear in the fabric of reality, pulsing with a dark, iridescent purple light and smelling sharply of ozone and deep earth.

"Ava! Come!" Madi roars over the deafening sound of the tearing portal and the screaming demons at the gates.

I look back at the swirling vortex. It is my exit. It is my ticket back to Rose, back to the safe house, back to a world where I am not currently standing in the epicentre of the apocalypse. Every soft, human desire I possess screams at me to drop my sword, run to the portal, and let the city burn.

As I look at the heavy iron gates, watching them bulge inward under the weight of the horde, I know the brutal, tactical truth.

If I step through that portal, the horde will instantly breach the gates. They could flood the courtyard before the vortex can fully close, allowing them to follow us through, or the portal's unstable magic might allow the demons to track the dimensional signature straight back to Luna Falls. I can't risk leading this army to Rose and the Harper sisters. I have to hold the line. I have to buy the portal time to collapse completely. Also, I can feel the need to feed rising within me; I don't want to return to the Harpers and then lose control.

"I can't!" I scream back, my voice ragged. "I have to hold the gate! Go! Take them and get out of here!"

"You cannot survive this, Dhampir!" Madi yells, her eyes wide with a mixture of anger and desperate respect. "The veil is falling! There are thousands of them!"

"Just tell Rose I love her!" I roar, my voice breaking on her name, a single, hot tear carving a clean track through the soot and ash on my cheek. "Tell her I kept my promise! Now go!"

Madi stares at me for one long, profound heartbeat. She gives me a slow, deeply respectful nod—the acknowledgement of a warrior recognising a final stand. She shoves the two witches and Marassa backwards into the swirling black void and then steps into the portal herself.

The vortex starts to shut, leaving me entirely, completely alone.

The silence inside the courtyard is sudden and profound, contrasting sharply with the deafening shrieks of the monsters just inches away on the other side of the iron bars.

I stand there, my chest heaving, the silver sword feeling impossibly heavy in my trembling grip. My human and Dhampir energy reserves are completely, utterly depleted. I am running on fumes, and the engine is about to stall.

I am going to die here, the logical, trained part of my brain calculates with cold precision. *There is no extraction. There is no backup. The perimeter is compromised.*

But as I stand there, staring at the rabid, snarling faces of the feral vampires pressing against the iron bars, something else begins to stir in the deep, dark hollows of my chest.

It is a sensation I have been desperately fighting ever since I woke up changed. It is the unnatural, pulsing, predatory hunger.

The Dhampir blood inside me, sensing the impending, absolute failure of my human biology, completely stops asking for permission and violently seizes the reins.

It feels as though a dam holding back a reservoir of liquid fire has just catastrophically burst inside my veins. A terrifying, euphoric heat floods my system, instantly incinerating the bone-deep exhaustion, the pain in my muscles, and the fear in my mind.

My heart rate gives one of its slow, deliberate, powerful, unnatural thuds. My vision sharpens drastically, the red, pulsing veins of the vampires outside the gate suddenly illuminating like neon signs in the dark. The scent of their blood—rotten, supernatural, and incredibly potent—hits my olfactory senses not as a foul stench, but as an overwhelming, mouth-watering delicacy.

I don't just feel stronger; I feel immortal.

The human woman who loved Rose, who wanted a home, who feared death—she is forcefully shoved into a tiny, dark box in the back of my mind, locked away behind a door of pure, unrestrained predatory instinct.

The Destroyer is no longer just a tactical mindset. It is my entire biological reality.

I remain perfectly, unnervingly still amid the swirling ash and the cooling blood of the innocent on the courtyard stones. I let the heavy, human fatigue completely wash away, replaced by the coiled-spring tension of an apex predator preparing to feed.

With a deafening, metallic shriek, the heavy iron hinges of the gate finally give way.

The massive, rusted doors violently burst open as the magic finally gives way, crashing against the stone walls. The horde surges into the narrow courtyard, shrieking, snarling, and tripping over themselves in their desperate haste to tear me apart. It is a tidal wave of teeth and claws.

I honestly do not feel a single ounce of fear. I feel nothing but a cold, magnificent, terrifying anticipation.

My lungs feel utterly perfect, drawing in the smoky, blood-scented air with a capacity that is far beyond human limits. The roaring bloodlust high has completely stripped away the fragile, empathetic layers of my humanity. It leaves nothing behind but the absolute, uncompromising need to slaughter and consume.

I calmly tighten my grip on the hilt of my sword. The metal feels as light as a feather in my newly empowered, clawed grip. I can feel my fangs descending, sharp and heavy against my lower lip.

I let out a dark, echoing, terrifying laugh that does not sound like Ava Bekke. It is a sound that makes the front line of vampires actually hesitate for a microsecond.

I slowly lick my lips, tasting the phantom sweetness of the blood to come, and charge straight into the hungry mouth of hell.

CHAPTER 30

I'M NOT MYSELF WHEN I'M EATING YOU

I do not know how many hours have passed since the rusted iron gates of the convent courtyard finally gave way. Time, with its neat, linear progression of seconds, minutes, and hours, has completely ceased to exist for me. It has dissolved, melting away into a relentless, crimson-stained cycle of unapologetic violence, choking grey ash, and the primal, screaming, overwhelming urge to feed.

The world is no longer a historic city filled with culture, jazz, and magic. It has been stripped down to its most basic, brutal elements. It is a hunting ground, and I am the apex predator prowling its burning streets.

The new Dhampir high is utterly overwhelming me, swallowing my consciousness whole. I can feel it like a physical, heavy tide, crashing over my mind in relentless waves of jagged, blinding euphoria. The logic part of my brain—the disciplined Captain who was meticulously trained to calculate ballistic trajectories, manage tactical assets, and assess collateral damage—is screaming in the dark that I have completely lost the reins. That voice is incredibly distant now, muffled beneath a thick, impenetrable layer of supernatural adrenaline and an insatiable, roaring hunger that makes my gums ache and my jaw throb.

Reason has become a stranger, someone I used to know in a

past life, I can no longer recall the face of. This bloodlust isn't just a passing urge or a biological necessity. It is a magnificent, terrifying, intoxicating poison. It coats my entire central nervous system in liquid fire, sending rapid pulses of electric heat through every vein, artery, and capillary. Every time my silver blade grazes a monster's skin, every time a spray of hot, foul-smelling gore hits my face, the monster inside me rejoices, demanding more.

I carve my way out of the immediate vicinity of the convent by grabbing the first creature that made it through the gate and feeding on it before it knew what was happening. After that, I left a horrific trail of butchered and decapitated creatures in my wake. Leaving the ground slick with a vile mixture of black ichor, red blood, and the oily, grey dust of destroyed monsters. I move with a speed that turns the apocalyptic landscape into a blurred smear of neon fires and collapsing architecture. My combat boots barely seem to touch the ground. I am flying on the wings of my own beautiful, terrifying damnation.

As I sprint down a narrow, burning alleyway, three vampires drop from the rooftops, hoping to catch me off guard. Their eyes are glowing pits of starving red light, their fangs fully descended and dripping with the blood of the innocent.

I do not even slow my pace. I do not raise my sword. The weapon feels too impersonal, too distant for the rage boiling inside me.

I drop the sword, letting it clatter on the ground and leap forward to meet them bare-handed.

The first vampire lunges, its clawed hands reaching for me. I duck underneath its outstretched arms, feeling the cold wind of its passing, and drive my fists directly into its ribcage. My newly enhanced strength shatters its sternum instantly. As the creature shrieks, I grab it by the throat and hurl it backwards with bone-crushing velocity. It slams into the brick wall of the alley so hard that its spine snaps, sliding to the ground.

The second and third vampires attack simultaneously, flanking me in the narrow space. The Dhampir predator inside my mind calculates their trajectories in a fraction of a microsecond. I pivot sharply on my heel, catching the second vampire's arm as it swings for my head. I twist the limb violently, snapping the bone at the elbow with a sickening, wet crunch. The vampire screams, a high-pitched sound of pure agony, but I silence it by brutally driving my knee into its face, crushing its skull. I release it, and it falls to the ground, going still.

The third vampire manages to tackle me around the waist. We crash heavily onto the debris-strewn ground, rolling through the filth and the fire. The creature snaps its jaws frantically at my neck, desperate to tear into my jugular. Its breath is foul, smelling of rotting meat and centuries of decay.

I am stronger. I am so much *stronger*.

I let out a guttural, terrifying snarl that echoes loudly off the alley walls, a sound that belongs to a beast, not a woman. I roll my hips, reversing our positions, pinning the struggling vampire beneath me. I grab its throat with both hands, my fingers digging deeply into the cold, dead flesh.

The hunger crests, breaking the dam of my restraint. The pressure in my gums becomes unbearable, and with a sickening pop, my fangs fully descend.

I do not think. I do not reason. I just react.

I lean down, my face inches from the thrashing vampire's neck, and I sink my teeth directly into its flesh.

The taste is abhorrent—a corrupted, rotting flavour of stagnant blood and dark magic—but the rush of energy that floods my system is absolute, unadulterated ecstasy. I drink, drawing the creature's supernatural vitality, feeding the void inside my chest. The vampire thrashes wildly, its red eyes widening in shock and horror as it realises it is no longer the predator; it has become the prey.

I drink until the creature begins to wither beneath me, its flesh turning dry and brittle. When I finally pull away, my chin and neck smeared with thick, dark, corrupted blood, the vampire crumbles into a pile of grey ash, blowing away in the hot wind.

I push myself up from the ground, my chest heaving, my icy blue eyes glowing with a terrifying, manic light. I wipe the blood from my mouth with the back of my armoured hand, tasting the metallic tang of my own damnation. I am not myself when I am eating you. I am the Destroyer, and I am starving.

I retrieve my silver sword from the shadows, my grip on the hilt secure and lethal, and I turn to the vampires I left destroyed, lying in the gutter. I run the sword through them and watch as the hellfire turns them to ash, then I continue my relentless march through the burning Quarter.

Eventually, the narrow alleyways spits me out onto a wider, heavily damaged thoroughfare. The street is completely blocked. I encounter a massive, makeshift barricade formed by half a dozen abandoned, overturned police cruisers, their flashing light bars shattered and dead. The defensive line is heavily manned by a dozen possessed humans and three hulking, crimson-scaled demons that look like they crawled straight out of the deepest pits of the Underworld.

The demons are towering monstrosities, standing easily eight feet tall, their thick, heavily muscled bodies covered in thick, interlocking plates of crimson scales that act as natural armour. They possess jaws filled with jagged, deadly teeth, and their eyes burn with a sickly, yellow luminescence. They wield massive, heavy battleaxes forged from dark iron, weapons that look capable of cleaving a small car in two.

They roar, their voices vibrating in my very bones, commanding their fragile, broken human puppets to attack the lone figure standing in the street, which of course is just little old me.

The possessed humans charge mindlessly over the barricade. They are a horrific sight, their bodies pushed far beyond their biological limits. Their eyes are solid, leaking black voids, and their limbs are twisted at unnatural angles. They swing heavy lengths of rusted rebar, splintered wood, and other makeshift weapons, driven by the parasitic entities riding their nervous systems.

I do not retreat. I do not seek cover. I meet their charge head-on.

I move vastly faster than their demon-corrupted minds can possibly process. I am a blur of black tactical gear, copper and golden armour, and red blood. I weave effortlessly through their wild, uncoordinated swings, my hands and feet becoming lethal instruments of blunt force trauma. I do not use my sword; the blade is reserved for the true monsters.

Snap. I shatter a possessed man's kneecap with a sweeping, brutally low kick, sending him crashing to the pavement.

Thud. I crush a woman's fragile windpipe with a targeted, explosive palm strike, the kinetic force banishing the demon instantly as the host body dies.

I seize another attacker by the waist, using his own momentum against him, and snap his spine cleanly over my knee. The sickening crunch of human bone becomes the percussive, rhythmic soundtrack to my advance.

I do not feel pity for the humans trapped inside these meat suits. I do not feel horror at the atrocities I am committing against my own kind. I only feel the absolute, uncompromising need to clear the path. I am a force of nature, a hurricane of violence tearing through the street.

As the last possessed human falls, banished back to the ether, the three crimson-scaled demons step over the barricade. They move with heavy, earth-shaking steps, their yellow eyes fixed on me with a mixture of rage and anticipation.

You should have brought a bigger army.

The three demons charge in unison, their massive battleaxes raised high above their horned heads, the iron gleaming ominously in the surrounding firelight. They plan to overwhelm me with sheer size and brute force.

They are painfully slow.

I seamlessly duck the first heavy swing, the massive iron blade whistling mere millimetres over my scalp, cutting through several loose strands of my icy white ponytail. I do not retreat; I step directly into the demon's guard.

In one fluid, lightning-fast motion, I drive my fist upward, targeting the soft, unprotected tissue directly beneath the demon's heavily scaled jaw. I push all my supernatural strength into the strike. My fist connects, and the force is so immense that it shatters the creature's lower skull completely. My hand enters its brain cavity, causing the demonic brain to pop under the pressure like an overinflated balloon.

Black, foul-smelling blood fountains explosively into the air, raining down on me in a hot, toxic shower, soaking my hair and armour in demonic filth. The smell is abhorrent—like burning rubber, sulphur, and raw sewage—but I do not even blink.

I spin on my heel, ripping my arm free as the first demon collapses. I seize the second demon by its thick, scaled throat before it can adjust its swing. I lift its massive, eight-foot frame completely off the ground, my biceps and shoulders bulging with unnatural, terrifying strength. The demon thrashes, its heavy boots kicking uselessly at the air, its yellow eyes widening in profound shock.

With a guttural, feral roar, I hurl the massive creature with bone-shattering force directly into the third demon.

The impact is deafening. The two behemoths collide, a tangle of heavy scales and iron weapons, and are sent flying backwards. They crash violently through the brick wall of a nearby burning boutique, instantly buried under tons of collapsing masonry, shattered glass, and flaming debris. They do not rise from the rubble.

I stand alone in the street, my chest heaving, my fists dripping with demon blood. I am untouchable. I am a god of monsters walking among my lesser. The high is absolute, a ringing, vibrating perfection in my mind.

Hours bleed away into nothingness. The choked sky above New Orleans turns a deeper, more toxic shade of black, as if the atmosphere itself is bruising under the weight of the invasion. The fires rage completely out of control, consuming the historic, beautiful architecture of the French Quarter, reducing centuries of culture and magic to smouldering white ash. The air is so thick with smoke that it blocks out all natural light, leaving the city illuminated only by the hellish, multicoloured glow of the flames.

I lose track of how many vampires I turn to dust, how many hellhounds I decapitate, how many possessed humans I put out of their misery. I am a machine, operating on a loop of slaughter and consumption, feeding my newly mutated cells with the corrupted energy of the fallen to sustain my impossible pace. The city is a labyrinth of death, and I am its minotaur.

Then, the atmosphere drastically, fundamentally shifts.

It does not happen gradually. It is a sudden, violently abrupt change in the atmospheric pressure, like stepping into a vacuum chamber. The heavy, ringing sound of the battle—the shrieks, the explosions, the roaring fires—seems to mute, muffled by an invisible, oppressive weight pressing down on the entire city.

The monsters around me react instantly. The vampires stop their frantic hunting, dropping to the ground and cowering in the shadows, whining like beaten dogs. The massive Lorcan wolves tuck their tails between their legs, pressing their bellies to the blood-slicked street in a posture of absolute, whimpering submission. Even the towering nightmare demons freeze, lowering their weapons and shrinking back against the burning buildings.

The blood high that has been sustaining me, the roaring, euphoric fire in my veins, stutters. The predator inside my mind, the glorious, arrogant Destroyer, suddenly recoils, shrinking back into the darkest corners of my consciousness, terrified by an unseen, unimaginable threat.

I stop walking, my silver sword hanging loosely at my side, my breath catching in my throat. My enhanced senses are screaming, a blaring, deafening alarm warning of an approaching catastrophe.

A man walks casually down the dead centre of the ruined street.

He does not emerge from a portal of fire or a vortex of shadows. He simply walks out of the smoke, his footsteps rhythmic, unhurried, and perfectly calm. He wears unique, intricately designed robes that mirror the aesthetic of my own golden armour, though his are far more ornate, woven from threads of deep gold and obsidian that seem to absorb the surrounding light.

He is the physical personification of inevitability. There is no grand, terrifying aura radiating from him, no towering demonic features, no horns or glowing eyes to mark him as a monster. He looks entirely, horrifyingly average. A man with sharp, aristocratic features and dark hair, walking through the apocalypse as if he is taking a leisurely stroll through a quiet park.

And yet, the entire demonic army parts for him in paralysed, unadulterated terror. They shrink away, desperately trying to avoid his path, their primal, ancient instincts telling them that this man is the end of all things.

He doesn't even look at me. I am standing in the middle of the street, covered in the blood of the army invading this city, glowing with Dhampir energy; it seems to him that I am nothing more than a piece of insignificant debris. I am an insect, entirely beneath his notice.

The sheer, crushing weight of his presence forces me to my knees. I try to fight it, try to raise my sword and charge, but my muscles refuse to obey. The gravity of his existence is too heavy.

He simply walks to a spot further down the road, his gaze fixed on something I cannot immediately see through the smoke.

As the smoke shifts, I finally see them.

The Loa.

They are making their final, desperate stand on the other side of the cowering horde. They aren't hiding in the Veil; they are anchored firmly to the physical world through their devoted human hosts. They stand in a defiant line across the street, their eyes glowing with specific, blindingly bright divine colours—greens, blues, and pure whites that cut through the gloom.

Other Loa have manifested through large, intricately carved wooden statues and ancient, decorated vessels, creating a desperate, vibrating line of spiritual defence against the encroaching darkness. The air around them crackles with ancient, potent magic, smelling of rum, sea salt, and deep earth.

Damballah Wedo, the ancient serpent, master of creation, intellect, and peace, stands tall in the body of a young man, radiating a blinding white light. Maman Brigitte, the fierce mistress of the dead, justice, and cemeteries, occupies the form of an older woman, her eyes burning with a relentless, punishing violet fire. There are others—gods of the crossroads, of the water, of the forge—standing shoulder to shoulder, ready to defend their city to the last breath.

For a fleeting moment, I wonder how the hell I know exactly who they are, how I can instantly recognise their divine signatures. Then I remember, through the receding haze of my bloodlust, the rapid-fire download of information I received when I entered Papa Legba's bar. The knowledge of the pantheon was planted in my mind, a parting gift from the guardian of the gates.

The man in the ornate robes does not engage in a duel. He does not offer grand words of challenge, he does not summon weapons of hellfire, and he does not make threats of conquest.

He performs a clinical, effortless execution.

He walks directly up to the line of gods, completely unbothered by the blazing aura of their combined divine magic. The Loa try to strike him. Damballah hurls a massive, blinding arc of pure creation energy; Maman Brigitte summons spiritual chains forged from the souls of the dead.

The magic hits the man and simply vanishes. It does not explode or deflect; it just ceases to exist the moment it makes contact with his robes.

He reaches out and touches Maman Brigitte's human host with a gentle, almost affectionate hand.

There is no flash of light, no concussive explosion, no scream of agony. The immortal, ancient spirit of the Goddess simply flickers out, like a cheap candle blown out at a birthday party. The host's eyes instantly revert from glowing violet to a dull, lifeless brown. The divine aura vanishes, and the human body collapses into a heap of lifeless flesh on the ground, the soul completely erased.

The man takes another step. He touches the man housing the spirit of Damballah Wedo, just like with Brigitte, he is erased from existence. He then touches an ornate carved statue housing another Loa. The ancient wood instantly, silently crumbles into a pile of fine, grey ash, slipping through his fingers. Loa by Loa they are severed from reality in a heartbeat, unmade with a casual caress.

He continues down the line, touching the hosts, tapping the statues. One by one, the gods of New Orleans fall. They don't even have time to react, to flee, or to fight back. Their magic simply evaporates. Their thousands of years of history, worship, and power are snuffed out in seconds.

I understand then, with a sudden, piercing, terrifying clarity, what I am witnessing.

The Loa are spiritual constructs, massive, complex entities sustained by the ancient magic, belief, and sacrifices of humans to safeguard the dead, maintain the veil, and balance the scales of the universe.

This man... he is not a demon. He is not a monster. He is something ancient. He is an enemy like no other. Wherever he came from, I hope there is a way to send him back.

The haze of the blood high is ripped from my vision instantly, leaving me completely, horrifyingly sober. The feral predator that had been driving me for hours recoils deep into the dark corners of my mind, defeated and exhausted, leaving me gasping for air on the pavement.

I am suddenly, painfully hyper-aware of everything I have ignored for the past several hours.

I smell the nauseating, metallic tang of blood clinging to my skin and matting my hair. I feel the oppressive, freezing weight of the gore soaking through my tactical gear and armour, making them heavy and stiff. I feel the agonising, burning ache in every single muscle fibre, the lactic acid flooding my limbs as the supernatural strength abruptly vanishes, leaving me feeling fragile and fundamentally human.

I rest my chest against my knees, my hands shaking uncontrollably against the blood-stained ground. I cannot breathe. I cannot process the scale of the power I have just witnessed.

The silence in the street is now deafening. It is a profound, unnatural quiet that signals the end of an era. In the back of my mind though, I sense there are new arrivals somewhere behind me. I don't care, I'm too distracted by what is happening in front of me to give a shit.

The man continues his relentless advance, every step carrying the oppressive weight of doom. The vibrant divine energy of the Loa stutters around him, flickering as if it cannot bear to coexist with his presence. I can feel the panic rising in my throat, a primal instinct urging me to run, cower, flee from the grasp of this horror.

As he reaches the end of the line and every Loa is dead, an invisible pull tugs at the very fabric of reality, and with a casual flick of his wrist, he rips open the Veil. The air shimmers and bends around him, an unnerving distortion that reveals the sacred bar where Papa Legba resides—a refuge hidden in the folds of existence, filled with the joyous sounds of jazz, now a stark contrast to the grim atrocity unfolding outside.

From the rift, echoes of distant melodies spill out, but they are drowned by the horror of what I know is about to happen. The man strides through the rift as if it's merely another door, moving with the same unhurried confidence that defines his every action.

I can see Papa Legba, his familiar figure, adorned with a top hat and cane, ever the guardian of the crossroads. I want to scream for him to run, whatever he can do to escape, as he doesn't stand a chance.

The man speaks before I can gather my courage. "You are not needed anymore, old man." I am stunned to hear the man talk; just like his looks, he sounds normal, like anyone you would meet on the street. The moment the man reaches out, touching Legba with that same delicate, almost tender hand, it's as if time halts in reverence to the catastrophic power he wields.

With an excruciating finality, Legba shatters like a pane of glass struck by an unseen fist. The pieces hang suspended in the air for a breath, each shard glinting with the remnants of his power and spirit. Then, like whispers of wind scattering across an open field, they dissolve into a fine ash, floating away and leaving only silence.

Suddenly, a massive, psychic shockwave ripples through the very foundation of the earth, vibrating violently through the pavement and up into my bones. It is a feeling of absolute severance, a snapping of a cosmic tether.

The bar's energy vanishes, absorbed back into the churning void that seems to expand with every moment. The delightful jazz, the warmth—they are all lost, snuffed out as if they were never real. The man stands amidst the absence, a statue of inevitability surrounded by the ash of a thousand memories, moving on, unfazed, as if he were merely walking through a fog.

I am left on my knees, the crumbling remains of the sacred enveloping me, my senses battered by the weight of loss and the overwhelming realisation that nothing will stand against him.

Papa Legba is dead. I felt the precise moment his ancient, weary soul gave out; the heavy burden of the gates has finally ended.

With Legba's death, the gates to the Underworld are completely, permanently open.

The toxic, black sky directly above us cracks with a sound like tearing sheet metal—a deafening, apocalyptic screech that forces me to clap my hands over my ears. A massive, jagged rift splits the horizon, glowing with a sickly, iridescent purple light.

The protective veil over the city of New Orleans, the ancient magical barrier that has separated the realms of the living and the dead for centuries, permanently collapses. It dissolves into nothingness, falling like shattered glass around us.

The line between life and death vanishes entirely.

Instantly, thousands of ghosts, spirits, and shades are pulled to our location and merge into our physical world, becoming fully visible to the naked eye. The air is suddenly filled with ethereal figures—some screaming in eternal agony, some weeping with invisible tears of spectral blood, some simply floating and staring in profound confusion at the burning ruins of the city they once haunted, wondering how they got here.

The man in the ornate robes who has wiped out the Loa in a matter of minutes turns slowly, looking up at the sky, then at newly manifested spirits of the dead.

He raises his hands, an expression of mild, irritated boredom crossing his sharp features. "This world was ours before it was yours. I plan to correct this mistake."

A wave of absolute, silent annihilation ripples outward from his body. As the wave passes through the air, the ghosts and spirits, just like the Loa, shatter like fragile glass in his wake. They are erased from existence, their souls unmade, leaving nothing behind but empty air.

The resistance is over. The ancient gods are dead. The last safe supernatural city in North America has completely fallen.

And as I kneel there in the blood and the ash, looking up at the terrifying, glowing void in the sky and the man who broke the world, I realise a horrifying truth.

We aren't fighting a war anymore. We are simply sitting in the dark, waiting for him to finally reach us.

CHAPTER 31

THE PREDATOR IN THE MIRROR

The blood high isn't just a passing feeling. It isn't merely a chemical rush of adrenaline, or the temporary, fleeting thrill of surviving a lethal encounter.

It feels like a living, breathing force screaming inside my mind—a dark, insidious parasite that has violently rewritten my DNA at its core. It coats my nervous system with a fiery liquid, turning each synapse into a sparking wire filled with volatile energy. The logical, disciplined part of my mind—the seasoned Captain who prioritized her team's safety—is completely gone. It has been forcibly suppressed, confined to a tiny, oppressive box, while the darkest part of my consciousness begins to reassert itself, resisting the overwhelming power radiating from this man. Soon, only the primal, instinctual roar of the apex predator remains as the Dhampir reclaims control.

I stand there in the ruins of New Orleans, surrounded by the settling ash of dead gods and the shattered remnants of the supernatural veil, and I stare at the man who did it.

He had just unmade immortals with the casual, bored touch of his hand. He had shattered the protective barriers of the city and wiped out an entire pantheon without breaking a sweat. Any rational, sane human being would look at him and feel the icy, paralysing grip of absolute terror. They would run. They would hide. They would beg for mercy.

I am no longer human, and my mutated, Dhampir biology normally doesn't recognise fear. It only recognises power. This man caused fear to enter my system for a moment, but it is returning to the fearless state. And the man standing before me is radiating a concentration of raw, divine energy that makes the air around him physically warp and hum.

The thought isn't a mere suggestion; it is a primal, absolute command that echoes through my mind with the deafening force of a thunderclap. *Feed.* I need to spill his blood. I need to tear into that mundane, ordinary chest and rip out the heart that beats with such arrogant, unapologetic calm. I want to sink my fangs into his throat and drink that divine, catastrophic essence dry until there is absolutely nothing left of him but a hollow husk of skin and bone crumbling into the ash of the city he just destroyed. I want to consume the power within him.

A raw, animalistic hiss tears violently from my throat, a sound that vibrates heavily in my chest and actually rattles my teeth. It sounds absolutely nothing like my own voice. It is the guttural, terrifying sound of a creature that has never known a name, a childhood, or love—a creature that only knows the endless, consuming void of hunger.

I lunge forward, my movements a terrifying blur of predatory speed.

My newly formed Dhampir claws are fully extended, the hardened, razor-sharp keratin slicing through the freezing, ash-laden air with a sharp, predatory whistle. I am not a soldier anymore. I am a weapon of mass destruction, completely unholstered and aimed at the end of the world. I am ready to dismantle him, piece by bloody, glorious piece, regardless of the consequences.

I don't even make it three steps.

The world abruptly and violently explodes into chaotic motion as Luca blindsides me.

The physical impact isn't just a simple tackle; it is like being T-boned by a runaway semi-truck travelling at eighty miles per hour.

Luca's massive, heavily muscled panther form slams directly into my side with devastating, uncompromising force. The sheer kinetic shock of it rattles my ribs, threatening to snap them, and sends a white-hot shockwave of agony lancing straight through my spine.

He pins me to the cracked, uneven asphalt of the ruined street with an oppressive, crushing heaviness that knocks every precious, vital ounce of oxygen out of my burning lungs in one violent, breathless rush.

I gasp, my mouth opening wide, but there is no air to be found—only the thick, metallic tang of floating ash and the heavy, earthy scent of Luca's musk of the panther.

Before my scrambled brain can even process the tackle and begin to struggle, Madi and Sera materialise directly from the thick, choking dark shadows swirling around the debris.

I see them out of the corner of my wildly darting eyes, a sudden blur of obsidian magic and profound grief. Madi's magnificent, leathery wings are heavily battered, the delicate membranes torn and weeping thick, dark fluid from her battle with the demonic horde, but her ancient eyes are focused with a lethal intensity that rivals my own bloodlust while Sera looks perfect as her shadowed form descends on me.

The Crossroads demon moves with terrifying, supernatural speed, lunging forward and grabbing my wildly thrashing legs. They both use their immense, divine strength to anchor my lower half firmly to the trembling ground, acting as a living, breathing vice made of iron and shadow. Their grip bruises my calves, an unyielding restraint.

I am trapped. I am pinned to the ground by my own allies. And for the ravenous monster currently piloting my brain, this is an intolerable, unforgivable insult.

I thrash with manic, feral desperation, my newly enhanced muscles straining against Luca's crushing weight. I snap my jaws wildly, my elongated fangs clicking against my lower teeth, inches from the panther's thick fur, desperate to tear into anything that holds blood.

"Ava, stop it!"

The voice breaks through the thick, suffocating red haze of my bloodlust. It sounds incredibly distant, distorted, as if she is frantically calling to me from the bottom of a deep, dark well.

Rose drops heavily to her knees right beside my thrashing head. The immediate scent of her hits my hyper-sensitive olfactory receptors like a physical blow. Vanilla, fresh rain and wildflowers, and the underlying, intoxicating musk of a sleek predator. Under any normal, sane circumstance, that specific combination of scents would instantly soothe me. It would be my anchor, pulling me back from the brink of whatever PTSD-induced nightmare I was drowning in.

In this mutated, feral state, the scent of vanilla and rain is entirely eclipsed by the frantic, rapid thumping of the blood rushing through her veins. Even Rose, the woman I would burn the universe down to protect, is currently registering to my hijacked brain as just another pulse. Another fragile, delicious vein waiting to be torn open.

Her frantic, delicate hands reach out, cupping my dirt-streaked face. I can feel her fingers trembling violently against my cold skin as she tries with all her might to force my wild, blown-out eyes to focus solely on her beautiful, tear-streaked features.

Her emerald green eyes are impossibly wide, swimming with a heartbreaking mixture of absolute, unadulterated terror and an agonising, profound amount of love.

"You cannot fight him! Ava, look at me! He just unmade an immortal! You will die!" Rose screams, her voice cracking, completely ignoring the fact that my jaws are snapping mere inches from her wrists.

I don't see Rose. I don't see my fierce, loyal mate. I only see a target that isn't moving fast enough to escape my reach.

The red haze returns with a vengeance, thicker and more oppressive than before, blotting out the ruins of New Orleans until all I can see is the rhythmic, tantalising throb of the carotid artery in her neck. It pulses with life, calling to the absolute darkest, most corrupted part of my soul.

I thrash with every single ounce of supernatural strength I possess, fighting exactly like a trapped, feral animal caught in the merciless jaws of a steel trap. I let out another guttural, demonic hiss, my sharp fangs seeking any available flesh, completely devoid of recognition or mercy. I am a lethal, ticking bomb, and I can physically feel the timer hitting zero. I am about to detonate on the very people I love most in this world, and the monster inside me does not care.

Realising with a crushing, devastating finality that I am entirely, completely lost to the hunger, Rose's expression undergoes a heartbreaking transformation.

Her brilliant green eyes flicker with frantic desperation before settling into a cold, resolute stare. She perceives the empty, starving void where my human soul once resided and understands with absolute certainty that if I lose my physical restraint, I will allow this mindless monster to slaughter Luca. I might tear Madi apart, and possibly Sera if I reach her in time. I could even kill her if she permits it. Following that, I will confront the man who destroys gods, risking my very existence to do so.

I see her silhouette shift in my peripheral vision. The playful, flirtatious woman who teased me in motel rooms and held me together through the nightmares, the Rose I know, vanishes, replaced by the hardened Beta of Luca's pack.

"I am so sorry, my love," Rose whispers, a single, devastating tear carving a clean track through the ash on her cheek.

She pulls her right arm back, her knuckles turning a stark, ghostly white. She doesn't hesitate. She doesn't hold back out of fear of hurting me. She knows my new biology can take the impact, and she knows it is the absolute only way to stop the carnage.

Then, she drives those knuckles brutally, flawlessly into the side of my temple with every single ounce of her formidable, supernatural panther strength.

The impact is explosive. It sounds like a gunshot going off directly inside my own ear canal. A blinding, brilliant flash of white light erupts behind my retinas, instantly short-circuiting the frantic, roaring signals of the bloodlust. The red haze shatters into a million dark, floating pieces.

The monster doesn't even have time to scream before the world violently cuts to pitch black, pulling me down into a deep, merciful, and silent abyss.

Consciousness returns not as a sudden awakening, but as a slow, cruel drip of corrosive battery acid against my brain.

A vicious, throbbing ache pounds behind my eyes, timed perfectly with the beat of my heart. Every blink feels like a struggle, my eyelids heavy and gritty. I try to reach up to rub the tender, swelling skin of my temple, but my arms are dead weight. They refuse to obey. I jerk my wrists in a sudden spike of panic, only to find them pinned securely and tightly at the sides of my body.

My eyes flutter open, fighting against a crust of dried sweat, ash, and old blood. The light is dim and flickering, the kind of oppressive lighting found in places meant for forgetting. I'm in a basement.

I realise then that I am not just restrained; I am imprisoned.

Thick, pulsing vines wrap tightly around my wrists, my waist, and my ankles, securing me flat against a heavy, unforgiving wooden table. They aren't normal plants. I can feel them breathing. I can feel the slow, rhythmic pulse of magic flowing through their stems, binding me with an intelligence that feels predatory. The unmistakable, static crackle of powerful warding magic hums in the cool, damp air, prickling sharply against my sensitive skin like a thousand tiny, stinging needles.

I pull hard against the bindings, an angry surge of adrenaline fuelling my struggle. I want to break something. I want to scream. The magical plant matter groans loudly under my strain, and in an intelligent response to my movement, it constricts even tighter around my limbs. The vines dig into my skin, bruising my wrists and ankles.

Brilliant. I am a highly trained assassin, currently being humiliated by aggressive, overachieving houseplants.

I stop fighting and lie still, breathing heavily. That's when I realise the euphoric edge of the blood high has gone, leaving behind a hollow, sickening cavern of profound guilt in my chest. *How long have I been here?*

The memories hit me like a tidal wave of freezing ice water. I remember the slaughter in the French Quarter. I remember the smell of burning flesh and the sound of screaming. Most of all, I remember the way I laughed while tearing through those creatures. It wasn't a laugh of joy; it was a laugh of pure, unadulterated hunger.

I picture Rose's face again. The horror. The way she looked at me was as if I were a stranger.

I wanted to kill them.

The thought is a physical weight, crushing the air out of my lungs. I almost let that monster erase my mate from existence simply because I couldn't leash the beast currently sharing my skin. I had become the very thing I spent my life fighting against.

God, I am a monster.

Footsteps echo softly on the wooden stairs leading down into the basement. They are cautious, hesitant. I immediately freeze, forcing my breathing to remain shallow and rhythmic. I keep my eyes reduced to tiny, deceptive slits, relying on my enhanced hearing to catch every syllable of the conversation. My ears pick up the friction of fabric, the soft thud of a footfall, the distant hum of electricity from the bulb above me.

"It takes a massive amount of effort to keep these vines reinforced," Freya says. Her usually light, airy voice is heavily strained, sounding as if she's carrying the weight of the world on her shoulders. I can hear the fatigue in her breath, the way her words clip together. "Are you sure this is a good idea? When she wakes, and if she is still in that same state as you mentioned she was in when you found her, I won't have the strength to help control her. Her new strength is absolutely terrifying, Luca. Channelling this much power to hold her is really testing the limits of my magic. It's been two days."

"Just hold her a little longer if you can. The modified sedative the doctor gave us to try should start to wear off soon, then we can see what state she is in," Luca replies. His deep, resonant voice is laced with an authority that sounds brittle, worn down by sheer, adrenaline-draining weariness. He sounds like a man who has been fighting a war for forty-eight hours straight without sleep. "We need to be absolutely certain she has come down from that feral state before we undo the wards. We barely got her out of the Quarter alive."

A heavy, incredibly anxious pause stretches between them. I listen to their hearts beating and almost jump when my own heart finally decides to beat.

"Any news on Devika?" Freya asks, her tone shifting as she tries to steer away from the grim reality of my current imprisonment.

"Devika still hasn't woken up," Luca sighs, a low rumble that seems to vibrate through the floor and into the table I'm strapped to. "Doctor Stevens and Philips arrived about an hour ago. They have her fully stabilised for now, but her condition is completely unprecedented for a born Vampire and Reaper hybrid. No one has ever seen a biological makeup like hers before, so they're flying blind. We don't know how to help her... or if there is even enough of her left inside that body to save."

"If she does wake, are we also going to have issues with her wanting blood as well?"

I recognise Rose's voice the instant she speaks. She is descending the stairs now. There is a tremor in her tone, a fragile quality that makes my heart ache. She sounds broken.

"Damaris says she has never needed blood," Freya explains softly. "She hasn't gone down that route since she accidentally killed her best friend when they were prisoners. A Lamia was feeding on the boy, and the scent of the blood was so overpowering for her—she had just started to come into herself and didn't know what to expect. She told us that ever since that day, all she has wanted to do is help others."

I strain my enhanced Dhampir senses, filtering through the

smells of the basement. I catch the subtle, sharp, clinical scent of medical antiseptic and rubbing alcohol drifting down through the floorboards from the upper levels. It's a sterile smell, cold and impersonal, clashing violently with the metallic tang of dried blood clinging to my skin. I can almost hear the rhythmic, electronic beeping of heart monitors—the steady, monotonous pulse of life sustained by wires and plastic.

"How is your friend from New Orleans doing?" Luca asks.

"She is okay. Upset," Freya responds. "She really didn't want to leave her home, but she understands why Ava forced her to leave with Madi."

Luca asks, "The other witches Madi brought here with her, are you sure it was safe to let them leave? We know nothing about them."

"Madi assured us that they are on the side of good and were safe within New Orleans during the attacks. Although they were willing to fight there, they now prefer to hide. They mentioned travelling to a different realm once their strength is restored. If such realms exist—like the one Pickle came from—we should consider visiting one of them. Perhaps we could all live better lives there," Freya says, though her tone suggests she's not fully convinced she would actually go.

"Not every realm is like ours. Some are just pockets of reality created long ago, and that doesn't necessarily make them safer. Would you really consider abandoning this world and letting it die?" Luca asks.

"No, I suppose not, but I still would like to visit one," Freya says, sounding so tired.

Rose changes the subject and asks, "Are you really going to let the demon stay here with you?" Her voice has a hint of defensiveness now, a protective instinct that I usually admire, but here it feels jagged.

"Of course we are," Freya says, sounding genuinely annoyed. "Madi has lost her home as well as everyone she was meant to protect. As long as she needs somewhere to crash, this house is hers."

"I really didn't mean anything by my question... I'm sorry if it sounded rude," Rose mumbles. I can practically feel her frustration with herself, the way she is spiralling into guilt just for asking a question.

"What exactly has the doc done for Devika?" Freya asks, redirecting the conversation.

Luca explains that he has established an intravenous drip to deliver broad-spectrum antibiotics and large amounts of hydration fluids. His tone shifts to a clinical, precise manner, possibly as a defence mechanism to detach from the emotional impact of the situation. He notes that Nurse Philips inserted a catheter to monitor her output carefully and ensure her kidneys aren't failing due to the extreme physiological stress from her possession. Additionally, a nasogastric feeding tube was placed directly into her stomach because her body is depleting calories rapidly to repair cellular damage. They are administering specialised nutrition to prevent her major organs from shutting down. If she doesn't wake soon, even modern medicine might not be able to reverse the damage caused by the demon to her brain; we can only hope she remains conscious inside and will eventually recover.

The weight of it all hits me with crushing force. Devika is dying upstairs, her body a battlefield of medical tubes and failing organs. Legba is gone, erased from existence by a man who looks like a librarian. Reya is imprisoned in the Underworld. And I am a ticking time bomb, tied to a table in a basement.

I can't stay hidden. I can't let them believe I'm still that monster and let Freya keep draining herself.

I let out a low, highly intentional groan, shifting my hips against the table to signal my awakening.

"Ava?"

Rose's melodic voice cuts through the dim space. She sounds breathless, her voice laced with raw, lingering terror and a flicker of hope.

She rushes to my side in an instant. I feel the air shift as she moves. Her stunning, vibrant green eyes scan my pale, bruised face with an overwhelming desperation that makes me want to weep. She looks as if she wants to touch me, but she looks afraid to do so.

I am here, my beautiful panther. I am so incredibly sorry. I hate how scratchy and broken my inner voice feels.

Rose lets out a shuddering, profound sigh of relief. The tension leaves her shoulders in a sudden collapse. "I think she is back," she whispers to the others, her voice cracking with unshed tears.

Luca steps cautiously forward. He doesn't rush. His eyes are hard, intensely calculating as he stares down at me, assessing my pupils, my breathing, my posture. He looks at me not as a comrade but as a threat that has been temporarily neutralised.

"Are you going to try and rip my throat out if we let you go, Destroyer?"

"Only if you critique my blood-stained combat boots while I am doing it," I rasp.

My throat feels as if I've swallowed a handful of broken glass and coarse sand. Every word is an effort. I force a dry, sarcastic smirk onto my lips, though it feels more like a grimace of pain. "I am clear, Luca. The high has completely gone."

He gazes at me in silence for a moment, assessing my words. He searches for any hint of the predator within me, any flash of that crimson hunger in my eyes. At last, he nods to Freya.

The exhausted-looking blonde waves her delicate hand towards the table. Instantly, the thick green vines loosen, slithering away from my bruised skin like retreating snakes returning to the earth. The oppressive, buzzing pressure of the containment wards lifts, leaving the air thin and empty.

I sit up very slowly, rolling my incredibly stiff shoulders. Every muscle fibre in my body protests with a dull, heavy ache that radiates deep into my bones. I feel as if I've been run over by a fleet of tanks. Before I can even attempt to swing my legs over the edge of the table, Rose is hovering by my side, her presence a warm, grounding force.

I look down at myself and realise I am still coated in a gruesome layer of dried blood and ash. It is repulsive. I can smell the decay clinging to me.

"I really need a shower," I mutter, my voice barely a whisper.

"You really do," Rose says, her nose wrinkling slightly as she looks me over. Then, her brow furrows, her eyes travelling over the sleek, unfamiliar material of my gear. "Where did you get that fancy armour?"

"Legba," is all I can say.

The name feels burdensome on my tongue, a reminder of the cost of this protection. Legba gifted me this armour to survive, and in exchange, he was erased from existence. The guilt tastes like copper in my mouth.

I look into Rose's eyes, searching for any sign of the fear she felt earlier. She is the only thing anchoring me to reality, but as much as I want to pull her into my arms and lose myself in her scent, I can still feel that dark, monstrous presence lurking in the shadows of my mind. It isn't gone; it's just sleeping. It is a patient predator, waiting for the next moment of weakness to tear its way out.

"How do you feel?" Rose asks.

In the background, Luca and Freya continue to watch me with a cautious, rigid posture. They aren't convinced I'm safe.

"I am okay. Truly. I just have a massive, world-ending headache."

She reaches up, her soft thumb gently tracing where she struck me. The touch is so tender it almost hurts more than the blow itself. "I had to do it, Ava. You were entirely gone."

"You did exactly what you had to do," I assure her softly, leaning into her warmth for a fleeting second before pulling away.

I can't afford to relax too much. Relying on her or dropping my guard only makes her vulnerable to the darkness inside me. "You saved me. But at this moment, I just need a hot shower and some peace and quiet to clear my mind. Is that okay?"

Rose looks into my eyes, hesitant. She's reluctant to part with me but recognises the importance of space. After a moment, she nods and steps back to give me room. "Don't take too long. We need to talk about our next step before that man makes his move."

I offer a brief, appreciative nod to Freya, deliberately ignoring the wariness still present in her stance, for Luca though I give him a look of disappointment, I thought we had an agreement that if I ever lost it and I put Rose or any of the others at risk, he was to deal with me, to end me, not tie me up with plants and wait for me to come down.

As I walk past, I don't blame them for doubting me. I doubt myself more than they ever could. As I head toward the stairs, I feel a strange, inexplicable pull toward the corner of the room. I hesitate, looking toward an old wooden desk with a heavy iron safe beside it. Something inside is calling to me—a low-frequency hum that vibrates in my teeth, a magnetic attraction that makes the hair on my arms stand up.

Not now, I tell myself, shaking the sensation off. *I don't have the luxury of curiosity.*

The Harper house feels unnervingly silent as I head towards the upper floors. The typical chaos caused by the sisters is missing, replaced by a sombre, heavy silence. The only sounds are the consistent, rhythmic hum of the medical equipment struggling to sustain Devika upstairs and the muffled noise of the Tv that someone must be watching.

As I walk through the kitchen towards the stairs, I glance back quickly. My sword remains strapped to my back, its weight familiar and reassuring. I feel a small sense of relief—either they couldn't detect it or forgot about it, because it is magically concealed; it effectively doesn't appear to them, except that Freya would be able to see it. So I don't understand why they left it strapped to my back.

As I approach the stairs, I spot my go-bag. Someone must have brought it in from our car. Someone says, "Ava, are you okay?" I don't know who it is. I grab my bag from beside the stairs and head straight upstairs to the bathroom, locking the door behind me with a definitive click. The click of the lock is a small victory, a boundary between me and the world.

My head throbs with a dull, rhythmic agony, a lingering

phantom pain from where Rose's fist had forcefully disconnected my consciousness from my body. I groan, a dry, rasping sound, and slowly peel my heavy eyelids open.

The harsh, sterile fluorescent light of the bathroom forcefully stabs at my sensitive pupils, making my eyes water.

My body feels incredibly heavy, drained of that euphoric, crackling energy that had turned me into a god of death in the French Quarter. Now, there is only a hollow, echoing emptiness in my chest, a profound sense of violation.

I grip the edge of the porcelain sink, my knuckles turning white, and I then turn on the hot water tap. I slowly, reluctantly lift my head and fix my gaze on my blood-stained reflection in the rapidly fogging mirror above the sink.

For a terrifying, heart-stopping moment, staring into my own eyes, I do not recognise the woman looking back at me.

My usually warm brown hair, now leached of pigment, turned a stark, icy, translucent white that shimmers with faint blue undertones in the harsh light. It is my face that makes my stomach violently churn. My skin is deathly pale, resembling polished marble, smeared heavily with the thick, dried, and crusted blood of everything I had slaughtered.

And my eyes. The pupils are dilated too wide, the gaze entirely too sharp and predatory. They glow with a faint, residual, icy blue luminescence. There is something profoundly, undeniably hungry lurking in those depths, a lingering, dormant shadow of the beast that completely took over my soul in the ruins of the city.

I part my lips, trembling, and stare at the faint, sharp points of my fangs resting against my lower lip.

I am a monster.

The realisation doesn't hit me with a frantic burst of panic; it settles over me like a heavy, suffocating blanket of freezing lead. I am exactly the kind of horrific, bloodthirsty creature that my team and I have spent our time hunting down and eliminating in the shadows. I had looked at Rose—my mate, my anchor, my entire world—and I had only seen food. I had tried to kill her.

A sudden, violent wave of nausea crashes over me. I grip the edges of the sink and dry heave, my body violently rejecting the horrific reality of what I have become.

I completely ignore the scalding heat of the water as it pours over my trembling hands. I aggressively cup the water and splash it onto my face, scrubbing frantically at my skin to clean it. It does look like someone has started cleaning parts of my face. My heart gives a sudden jolt; it must have been Rose.

This isn't quick enough, so I turn on the shower. I strip off my heavy, gore-soaked armour and the ruined, bloody shirt and pants beneath it, leaving them in a discarded, filthy pile on the tiles. I climb into the shower and start to scrub until the dried blood flakes away and mixes with the water, turning the porcelain base of the shower cubicle a horrifying, diluted pink. I scrub at my neck, my arms, and every part of me that has been soaked in blood, my nails digging into my own flesh until it is raw, red, and stinging. I am desperately, pathetically trying to wash away not just the physical blood of our enemies, but the lingering, disgusting feeling of the hunger itself. The memory of how euphoric it felt to tear a creature's throat out.

When I'm done, I grab a towel and scrub my chest and arms, shivering uncontrollably despite the scalding heat of the water, which has warmed my body and filled the room with steam.

Once I am finally clean—or at least as clean as I can possibly get with the stain of monster lingering in my marrow—I pull on fresh, dry clothes from the small duffel bag I left on the closed toilet lid.

As I pull a clean black T-shirt over my head, the crushing weight of the night finally presses fully in on me.

I press on and clean my armour as that weight tries to suffocate me. While I'm scrubbing, I can't help but notice the house is entirely, suffocatingly silent. It is the kind of quiet that feels fragile, as if the entire house is holding its breath, terrified of waking the monster in the bathroom.

Then, my enhanced hearing picks it up.

Footsteps. Light, cautious, and incredibly hesitant. They pad softly down the corridor, pausing directly outside the thin, hollow wooden door of the bathroom.

I freeze. I can smell her. Vanilla and rain and wildflowers, cutting right through the overwhelming scent of the body wash and soap I used. I can hear the slight hitch in her breathing, the subtle, erratic flutter of her heartbeat.

I close my eyes, a fresh wave of hot, devastating tears pricking the corners of my eyes. I can vividly imagine her standing out there in the dim hallway, leaning her beautiful forehead against the wood, her hands curled into fists at her sides, desperately wondering if I am okay. Wondering if the woman she loves is back, or if the beast is still waiting on the other side of the door, ready to strike.

I am so sorry, Rose, I project into the silence of my own mind, the thought a broken, jagged thing.

If I am ever going to face my friends again—if I am ever going to truly protect Rose without risking becoming the very nightmare we are fighting against—I have to master this darkness. I have to learn how to lock the Destroyer in a cage so deep and so heavily warded that not even the scent of blood can wake her.

I cannot do that here. I cannot learn to control my hunger while surrounded by the people I am most terrified of draining. Every moment I spend near Rose is a moment her pulse taunts the parasite in my blood. Every moment I stay in this house, I am a loaded gun with a faulty safety, pointing directly at my own team and friends.

I cannot risk it. I will not be the reason she dies.

I turn my gaze away from the door and look toward the small, frosted glass window above the bathtub. Thank God I had already cracked it open earlier to let the steam escape.

The cool, crisp, blessedly clean night air of Luna Falls rushes in through the narrow gap, brushing against my damp, pale skin. It smells sharply of damp earth, deep pine needles, and a vast, sprawling sense of nocturnal freedom that feels almost alien to the suffocating confines of my current reality.

I shove the now clean armour into my bag, then I step silently onto the edge of the bathtub, my movements fluid, graceful, and entirely silent—the movements of a predator.

I reach up and push the window open wider, the hinges giving a tiny, almost imperceptible squeak that makes me wince. I pause, listening intently to the hallway. Rose hasn't moved. She is still standing there, standing guard over a monster.

Without looking back at the locked wooden door, without saying a final, spoken goodbye to the woman who just saved my soul by violently knocking me unconscious, I slip my body silently through the narrow frame.

I drop my heavy duffel bag out first, my enhanced hearing catching the soft, muffled thud as it hits the damp grass below. Then, I twist my body, slipping through the gap and dropping gracefully into the heavy, concealing shadows cast by the side of the house. I absorb the impact flawlessly, bending my knees, making absolutely zero noise as my boots connect with the earth.

I am a ghost haunting my own life.

I stand up in the soft, dew-soaked grass. The rhythmic sounds of the lake lapping against the shore drift across the dark yard like a mournful siren song, calling me into the wilderness.

I grab the strap of my bag, hoist it over my shoulder, and begin to run.

I run as fast and as hard as my newly mutated legs can carry me. I do not look back at the house. I do not look back at the window. I let the supernatural speed overtake me, turning the trees and the landscape into a dark, rushing blur.

My lungs burn with the exertion, my muscles screaming as I push them past their limits, desperate to put as much physical distance as possible between me and the people I love. Every step is an agony of separation, a tearing of the prime mate bond that stretches taut across the miles, but I force myself to keep moving.

Hopefully, one day I can return, I tell myself, the thought a fragile, desperate prayer cast out into the uncaring dark. *Hopefully, I can learn to chain this beast. Hopefully, I can still do what Papa Legba asked of me—to keep them safe from the shadows, and to find a way to bring Reya back from the Underworld.*

But for now, I cannot be a Captain. I cannot be a lover. And above all, I cannot be a friend.

I am a profound, lethal threat. I am an apex predator wandering in a fragile world of prey. And for my own sake, and for the absolute safety of the woman I love more than life itself, I must disappear completely into the dark.

OTHER BOOKS BY CATHERINE M. CLARK

The Harper Legacy Series

The Weeping – A Novella - Book 0.5

No Witchin Way – Book 1

Dark Intentions – Book 2

Ava the Destroyer Series

The Mission – Book 1

Bloodlines & Chains Series

I Think I'm A Monster – Book 1

You can contact the author via the following means.

Email. authorcatherinemclark@hotmail.com

TikTok. www.tiktok.com/@catherine.m.clark

https.//www.facebook.com/groups/themoontree/

www.catherinemclark.com

www.ingramcontent.com/pod-product-compliance
Lightning Source LLC
LaVergne TN
LVHW010049110826
845155LV00028B/265

* 9 7 8 1 9 1 9 2 2 7 6 3 4 *